MASTER OF SOULS

PETER TREMAYNE

headline

First published in 2005
by HEADLINE BOOK PUBLISHING

First published in paperback in 2006
by HEADLINE BOOK PUBLISHING

A HEADLINE paperback

6

ISBN 978-0-7553-0228-4

Typeset in Times by Palimpsest Book Production Limited,
Polmont, Stirlingshire

Printed and bound in Great Britain by Clays Ltd, St Ives plc

Headline's policy is to use papers that are natural, renewable and
recyclable products and made from wood grown in sustainable forests.
The logging and manufacturing processes are expected to conform to
the environmental regulations of the country of origin.

HEADLINE BOOK PUBLISHING
A division of Hodder Headline
338 Euston Road
London NW1 3BH

www.headline.co.uk
www.hodderheadline.com

For Seamus J. King of Cashel
to commemorate
the Cashel Arts Festival
of November, 2004,
and
Treasa Ní Fhátharta
for the seanfhocal

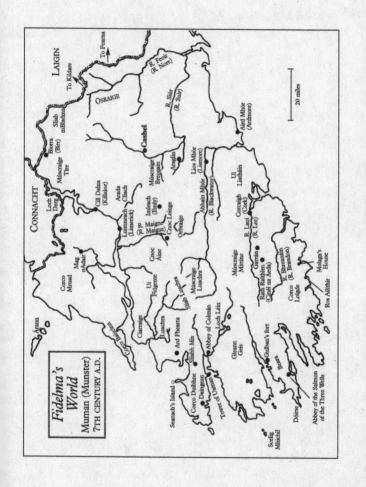

Fídelma's World
Muman (Munster)
7TH CENTURY A.D.

20 miles

To Fearna

LAIGIN

To Kildare

R. Feoir (R. Nore)

OSRAIGE

Sliab mBladma

Biorra (Birr)

Múscraige Tíre

Loch Deirg

CONNACHT

Cashel

R. Siúir (R. Suir)

Araglin

Lios Mhór (Lismore)

Aird Mhór (Ardmore)

Cill Dehin (Killaloe)

Imleach (Emly)

Arda Cliach

Uí Liatháin

Luimneach (Limerick)

R. Maigne (R. Maigue)

Cnoc Loinge

Orbraige

Abhain Mhór (R. Blackwater)

Mag nAdair

Corco Mruad

Uí Fidgenie

Cnoc Áine

Corco Baiscinn

Ciarraige

Sliab Luachra

Múscraige Luachra

Múscraige Mitíne

Corcaigh (Cork)

R. Laoi (R. Lee)

Garrán

R. Bheeanáin (R. Bandon)

Molaga's House

Rath Raithlen (Cipíd na Aeda)

Araim

Luachra

Ard Fhearta

Abbey of Colmán

Loch Léin

Corco Loígde

Ros Ailithir

Sliab Mis

Gleann Geis

Gulban's fort

Seanach's Island

Corco Duibne

Daingean

Tower of Uamain

Béara

Dóirse

Abbey of the Salmon of the Three Wells

Scelig Mhichil

An té a bhfuil drochmeas aige ar a shaol féin, beigh sé ina mháistir ar shaol duine eile – fainic, éireoidh le'n a leithéid máistreacht a fháil ar anamacha.

He who despises his own life is soon master of another's – beware, for such a man can become master of souls.

Brehon Morann

pRINCIPAL ChARACTERS

Sister Fidelma of Cashel, a *dálaigh* or advocate of the law courts of seventh-century Ireland
Brother Eadulf of Seaxmund's Ham in the land of the South Folk, her companion

On the Sumerli

Esumaro, captain
Coros, his first mate

At Inis

Olcán, leader of the wreckers
Abbess Faife of Ard Fhearta
Sister Easdan

At Ard Fhearta

Conrí, warlord of the Uí Fidgente
Socht, one of his warriors

Abbot Erc
Brother Cú Mara, the *rechtaire* or steward
The Venerable Cináed, a scholar
The Venerable Mac Faosma, a scholar
Brother Benen, his student
Sister Sinnchéne
Sister Buan, wife to Cináed
Brother Feólaigid, the butcher
Sister Uallann, the physician
Brother Eolas, the *leabhar coimedach* or librarian
Brother Faolchair, his assistant
Brother Cillín, the *stiúirtheóir canaid*, or master of music

Mugrón, a merchant
Tadcán, lord of Baile Tadc

At Daingean

Slébéne, chief of the Corco Duibhne

At Sliabh Mís

Iobcar, son of Starn the Blacksmith
Ganicca, an old man

At Baile Gabhainn

Gáeth, the smith
Gaimredán, his assistant

Note: Please see the *Pronunciation Guide* on p.422 for an explanation of Irish names and words.

Bréanainn (which means 'prince') was the name
of the sixth-century Irishman who founded the abbey
of Ard Fhearta (Ardfert, Co. Clare). Revered as a saint,
he has become more widely known by the Latinised
forms of Brandanus and Brendanus of which the
English form is Brendan and the modern Irish is
Breandán.

This story takes place in the month of *Dubh-Luacran*,
the darkest days (January) of the year AD 668
following the events narrated in
The Leper's Bell.

CHAPTER ONE

Esumaro turned, frowning slightly. His weather-beaten face was raised towards the dark, lowering clouds. He let out a soft hiss from between crooked, blackened teeth and shifted his balance on the swaying deck before glancing swiftly about him. The seas around the broad-beamed ship were already reflecting the blackness of the clouds and the surface of the water was broken by short, choppy, white-crested waves. The seas were becoming angry and threateningly alive, although partially shrouded by sheets of gusting rain.

Esumaro moved his thoughtful gaze to the straining sails above him. The wind was increasing rapidly from the north-west, causing even the mainmast to groan, protesting against the onslaught.

Beside him, Coros, his mournful-featured first mate, stood uneasily by the tiller, keeping an anxious eye on the captain.

'That's Inis Mhic Aoibhleáin ahead,' he ventured, shouting to make himself heard above the moaning winds and breaking sea. He had stretched out a hand towards the

1

dark outline of an island, almost obscured by the rain but slightly to portside of the vessel's bows. 'The wind is turning us to the east, captain. We won't be able to weather the island in these seas and if we keep it on our larboard we shall be driven on the rocks.'

Esumaro did not reply immediately. Already the motion of the squat timbered vessel had changed and the deck was bucking beneath his feet as if the ship were a horse not yet reconciled to its rider. The *Sumerli* was a sturdy high-bowed Gaulish merchantman, made for use in the heavy seas and violent gales of the ocean. It was a descendant of the ships that the Veneti of Armorica had used against Julius Caesar and his Roman invaders, built in the image of those solid oak, heavy vessels that had caused the lighter Roman war galleys so much hardship.

Esumaro had spent his life in such ships, and he had not been sailing these waters for twenty years without becoming familiar with the coastline and its dangers. He had already seen that they would not be able to beat around the islands of which Inis Mhic Aoibhleáin was the southernmost. The Gaulish captain knew every cross-timber and joint of the *Sumerli*, her iron bolts and chains and her heavy sails. He was sensitive to every protesting creak and groan of her timbers, and knew that this storm, which had suddenly arisen out of the darkening Atlantic with no more than a few minutes' warning, could dash her to pieces on any one of the numerous rocky islets that dotted this particular stretch of the coast of the kingdom of Muman. He had already estimated the dangers and had decided his next course of action. He did not need Coros to advise him. However, the first mate was only doing his duty.

'We'll turn and run before the wind,' Esumaro shouted

back. 'We'll keep south of the islands and turn into the bay for shelter.'

'Those are dangerous waters, captain,' Coros called. 'That's Daingean Bay.'

Esumaro frowned in irritation.

'I know it well enough. I know these waters. I intend to run the *Sumerli* right up to the abbey of Colmán. I've traded there before. They'll take our wine and silver in exchange for wool, salted hogs and otter skins.'

The first mate looked surprised.

'But are we not supposed to be trading with Mugrón of An Bhearbha?' Coros was nothing if not conscientious. 'We can find a sheltered bay and ride out the storm.'

Esumaro grinned in the driving rain.

'We'll lose days if we wait for this blow to end. And we'll be trading with the devil if we try to beat around the islands to the land of the Uí Fidgente before we get a calm sea.' He shook his head in emphasis. 'Believe me, I know these waters. The good merchant Mugrón won't miss one cargo and we can still make a profit from the abbey of Colmán. Swing her on to the starboard tack, Coros. We'll run before the storm into the bay.'

Coros hesitated barely a moment.

'Aye, captain. Starboard it is,' he shouted back as the wind increased its tempo.

He signalled to the two sailors who stood at the tiller, for it needed at least two of them to steer in the heavy seas, and together they pulled the great wooden arm across the deck.

Immediately, as she turned broadside on to the storm, the howling winds crashed against the larboard side of the vessel with terrific force. The sails shuddered and the wind, whipping through the rigging, screamed in protest.

Esumaro seemed to keep his feet on the deck with the same dexterity as if the ship was in still waters. His gaze was fixed on the straining sails. He knew he was going to put the ship into some heavy weather before they reached the safety of the calmer waters of the bay.

'Rig the lifelines fore and aft,' he called, sending Coros running forward to oversee the task.

Now the wind was like a musician in the taut weather rigging, plucking at the tightened strings like a maniacal harpist. Great frothy grey waves began to pound the side of the vessel and the ship heeled a little before coming upright again. Then she heeled again as once more the wind drove into her. In spite of the men at the tiller, the vessel swung awkwardly and the stern rose ponderously while the bow dipped dangerously towards the water. The captain knew that he must reduce the amount of canvas that the ship was carrying or the increasing winds would cause them to capsize.

'We'll take in a reef on the mainsail, Coros. Steady!' This last instruction was to the men on the tiller. 'Keep her stern to the wind.'

Each sail was divided into horizontal portions, called reefs, which could be rolled or folded to reduce the area of the canvas exposed to the wind. Each reef was marked by a reef-band, a strengthened portion of perforated canvas used for securing the sail to the sheets, or stay ropes, by means of reef knots.

Coros was already calling for the hands to shorten sail.

It was not long before the straining of the ship eased, but the wind was still vibrating through the rigging like fingers strumming against harp strings. The *Sumerli* was running quickly now into the broad entrance of the bay. The land on either side would eventually narrow like a funnel. Once they passed beyond the finger of land called simply Inis, 'the island', they would be in the calm sheltered waters of Loch na dTri Caol, approaching the harbour for the abbey of Colmán. Esumaro had entered that harbour many times, though never with a darkening sky and in such a storm.

To larboard, Esumaro could begin to make out the dark jagged shapes of the mountains that, like a lizard's spine, ran along the peninsula there. To starboard, similar dark mountain tops could be seen through the rain. He could sense the bay narrowing from its broad entrance.

As the dusk of the winter's evening settled in, combining with the dark storm to create an impression of night, the wind was unabating. It hummed and groaned through the rigging. The ship still heaved and pitched and the heavy seas continued to batter against the stern timbers. He glanced back and clenched his jaw as he saw a wave rolling towards them like a large black mountain with a combing white top, threatening to overwhelm them. Then it crashed down under the stern, lifting the ship up and sending it speeding forward. Starboard and larboard Esumaro could see the white fringes that edged the breakers, the rocks that marked the shore-line, with the high dark land looming up behind.

Esumaro's eyes rested for a moment on the pale-faced sailors clinging to the tiller and he smiled to hearten them with a reassurance that he did not feel himself.

'We'll soon be sheltered,' he shouted. 'Ahead of us are two points of land which will bring us into a stretch of quiet water where we can make landfall.'

Suddenly there came a roaring gust and the sound of tearing, and for a moment the men on the tiller nearly lost their hold of the beam of wood, which suddenly became alive and threatened to wrench itself out of their grasp. They recovered even as Esumaro sought to regain his footing, for he had stumbled against the rail. It had prevented him from being tossed overboard, but it had winded him for the moment. He stood gasping, having to swallow mouthfuls of salt spray and rain. Then his eyes went searching upwards. The storm staysail had become a series of tattered ribbons fluttering on the yards. He could feel the ship swinging round as if it had a mind of its own and wanted to lay its bow back to the sea.

'Bring her around!' Esumaro did not mean to scream the order but he saw the danger of capsizing before many more moments had passed.

The men on the tiller, already alert to the danger, were throwing their weight against it, defying the rage of wind and sea. The waves were coming higher and were more curling than before, flinging themselves at the ship like anxious, clawing hands, accompanied by a deafening shrieking wind. Esumaro was praying silently, his skin cold and not from the weather conditions. His breath came in quick, short gasps. For a moment or two, the ship seemed to stand still, defying man and weather to move her, and then, reluctantly, slowly, she swung her bow back on course.

Esumaro's jaws clenched tight and he peered anxiously forward. They must be nearing what the locals called Island Point and Black Point. He knew there were shallow banks there but with such a sea running he should be able to negotiate his way through with plenty of water under his keel.

'A light dead ahead, captain!' cried Coros.

Esumaro stared in surprise into the blackness of the sheeting rain.

He thought that he was near the turning point where the land called Inis jutted out into the bay. It was a small islet separated from the northern mainland only during the high tides, and he had to steer south to avoid it. But there was a light to the south and it was bobbing up and down. Only another vessel could cause that motion. What was a ship doing there and in this weather? It must be anchored in the shelter of the southern shore. He decided that he must be too far to the south.

'We'll pass her on our starboard side,' he yelled quickly. 'Give her sea room.'

They pulled the tiller over a little to pass north of the light.

A moment later there came a panic-stricken cry from Coros.

'Oh, God!'

Esumaro heard the cry a split second before he saw the white line in front of the *Sumerli*'s bows. Then there was an awesome crashing sound, the vessel swung round in her own length and rolling waves crashed against her wooden planking, carrying her sideways against a shallow rocky shoreline. Now he could not hear the screams of his men at all but saw several of them simply washed away even as the deck slid from under him and he grabbed out at the ship's rail to prevent himself from following them.

The merchantman heeled over on its port side, broadside on into the shallows with monstrous seas washing over her. There came the sound of cracking as the masts broke with a splintering crash. Then a cataract of solid water was rending the wood of the vessel. Plank after plank was ripped away under this assault of Nature. With the deck at a forty-five-degree angle, clinging with both hands to the taffrail,

Esumaro realised not only that his ship had been driven aground but that he and his crew were lost.

Around him, the sea was like a boiling cauldron. He could hear the fearful roar of the undertow sucking the pebbles from the shore, before another great wave smashed over the vessel.

Esumaro glanced around, trying in vain to look for survivors, but he was alone. He gave a gasping cry, begging God for help, and knowing that there was no reasonable chance of survival. The ship was breaking up, that was for certain. He would not have long to cling to his precarious hold. Indeed, his arms were aching already as he tried to prevent the cascading weight of water from tearing him away. The wrenched muscles in his upper arms and shoulders were making him feel like screaming in pain. There was only one thing to do. As soon as the next wave started to recede he would have to slide down the deck into the shingle and run for the shore before the subsequent wave hit. How long he would have he was not sure. Everything was in darkness. He could not even judge the high water mark.

Esumaro was not one to be sentimental but now the images of his wife and children back in his home port of An Naoned swam before his eyes and he sobbed with a great, choking sound. Yet it was no good feeling sorry for himself. Even a rat fought when it was drowning. Now was the time to fight, whatever the outcome.

Once he heard that grim, sucking undertow passing below, he let go his hold, trying to control his forward motion as best he could as he slithered down the sloping deck. He hit one knee painfully on the far rail and then leapt over it, landing on all fours in the shingle. Fear drove him on. He was up, scrambling through the wet, slippery pebbles which did their best to clutch at his ankles and delay him. Several times he fell, yet terror forced him to pick himself up and move painfully forward. He could hear the roar of the approaching wave, hear it smashing the timbers of the ship behind him.

He restrained himself from looking round but he knew the wave was close. Immediately in front of him a sharp rock rose up, and he flung himself down, clasping his arms round it as one would hug a beloved after a long separation, as the raging, foaming waters hit and flooded over him. For a long, long time, or so it seemed, the waters boiled over him and he became desperate for air. He was tempted to release his clasping hands and try for the surface. Then he felt the powerful tug of the water as it began to recede. It was dragging him, dragging his hands apart. He exerted all the power he could to keep them clasped tight together. Abruptly, the water was gone and he heard the ominous grinding sound of the pebbles as the tide dragged them down in its wake.

Gasping, spluttering, moaning involuntarily in his fear, Esumaro clambered to his knees, peering round to get his bearings and then scrambling forward towards the beach again. He was among rocks, crawling upwards. He could hear the next wave coming in but then he was on sand and then grass. Even then he did not stop but went lumbering forward until a thorny bush prevented his progress by tearing at him and he collapsed face down in its midst and passed out.

It was still dark when he came to but the wind seemed to be dying away. He could hear the rumble of thunder in the distance and lightning silhouetted the tops of nearby mountains. Esumaro raised his head cautiously. He had been lying face down, where he had fallen, in the middle of an area of some undergrowth. He could hear voices in the distance and he blinked once or twice to clear his eyes. Then he made to get up but found he was quite weak with exhaustion.

He levered himself up on his elbows and manoeuvred himself round to face the dark blustery sea. He was on a grassy knoll above a wide stretch of shoreline that faintly gleamed white with sand. Men were walking along with lanterns held high to illuminate the scene. The stretch of sand was littered with wreckage and bodies. To his right, where he had come ashore, the land rose up and was protected by a rocky coastline against which the *Sumerli* had been driven aground.

He shook his head to clear it and was about to call out to the men below to announce his presence. Another second and he would have done so. But then he heard a voice calling out in the language of the Éireannach, which he had learnt well during his years of trading with them.

'This one's alive, Olcán.'

Esumaro actually saw a man begin to raise a heavy wooden cudgel in the lantern light.

'Wait!' Another figure appeared holding a lantern in one hand. 'Stand him up!'

Figures bent down and dragged a man up into the light. From this position Esumaro could not see the features but it was clear that the figure must be one of his crewmen.

'Do you understand my language?' came the voice of the man who had been addressed as Olcán.

The sailor who had survived coughed and tried to find his voice. Obviously he had indicated that he understood for Olcán's voice came again.

'What ship?'

There was a pause and the question was asked again more sharply.

'The *Sumerli*, from Gaul.'

Esumaro, watching the scene with confusion, recognised Coros's voice.

'Gaul? A merchantman?'

'Aye, sailing out of An Naoned.'

'What cargo?'

'Wine, and some gold and silver for the artisans of the abbeys.'

Olcán gave a curious chuckle that sent a shiver through Esumaro's body.

'Excellent. Kill him!'

The heavy cudgel descended and the figure of Coros dropped to the beach without another sound.

'We'll start salvaging at first light and stack the booty in the tower. Gold and silver, eh? We might have struck lucky.'

One of the men called: 'Shall I take the lantern off the horse?'

'That you may. The beast has served us well in luring this ship ashore.'

'How did you learn that trick?' The man who had killed poor Coros seemed to be cleaning the blood off his cudgel by wiping it in the sand.

'Trick? That a lantern fixed to a horse's head, bobbing up and down, can easily be mistaken in darkness for the light of a ship? Indeed, it is a good enough trick. The master taught me that. Make sure the men stack everything they find in the old tower. We have to be ready to leave soon after first light. We can return for the booty later.'

'I don't understand why we cannot stay and make a better job of it, Olcán,' protested one of the men.

'Are you questioning the orders of the master?' snapped the leader.

The man shook his head. 'But why . . . ?'

'Because we have an appointment on the coast road. And the master will be here soon to make sure we keep it. Now let's get this spoil back to the fortress and get some rest. First light is not far off and it will be a long ride over the mountains tomorrow.'

He made to move away but his companion stayed him.

'Shouldn't we make a thorough search for any survivors?'

Olcán gave his humourless chuckle again.

'Anyone who survived would have made for this stretch of friendly sand. It's the only place there's a chance to land. The waves will have dashed most of them to their deaths on the rocks there. There'll be no survivors. If there are, we can make sure of them when it's light.'

Horrified, Esumaro pushed himself back into the undergrowth, not even noticing the pricking of the brambles. He tried to make himself smaller, wishing he could vanish into the ground. Then he glanced at the sky. He would have to get away from this place before dawn when those men, whoever they were, came searching for survivors. They would surely kill him as they had killed poor Coros in cold blood.

It was beginning to get light when Esumaro came to his senses. He had a vague remembrance of walking in the darkness, of hiding behind clumps of reed and bushes, of crossing a stretch of waterlogged sand, of being propelled by fear: fear of those who had killed his first mate Coros and been responsible for the deaths of all his crew. He was trying to come to terms with the realisation that his ship had been purposely wrecked. Wrecked for its cargo. What kind of barbarians dwelt in this godforsaken place? Outrage, but predominantly fear, combined to propel him to place as much distance as he could between him and that awful shore before first light. He had no wish to suffer the same fate as Coros. When the fear had subsided, he told himself, he would find help to seek revenge on the wicked miscreants who had done this terrible deed.

He blinked his eyes in the morning light. It was so bright. He groaned, for he realised he was frozen. It was a moment before he understood what was causing the brightness. He lay in a great expanse of snow. Even the trees bent their branches under its weight. He felt weak and chill and groaned again. He was trying to move when there came the sound of a woman's nervous cry.

'I think he is alive, Reverend Mother.'

Esumaro blinked again and tried to focus his eyes. It was painful.

He realised that a young woman was bending over him. Under a heavy fur cloak, she wore the brown woollen robes of a religieuse with a metal cross hung from a leather thong round her neck.

A few yards away six other women, similarly clad, were standing watching with nervous expressions. They were mostly young.

The one who stood by him turned and called again more cheerfully: 'He is alive.'

Esumaro tried to ease himself up on one elbow. One of the watchers, a tall, handsome woman of middle age, came to her young companion's side and stood looking down. She wore a more ornate cross. She smiled and bent down.

'We thought you were dead,' she said simply. 'Are you ill? What has brought you to lie out here in the open in the middle of a snowstorm? Your clothes are soaked and torn. Have robbers attacked you?'

Esumaro strained as he tried to follow. Her speech was quick and accented.

'I . . . I am cold,' he managed to say.

The woman frowned.

'Your speech is strange. You are not from this land?'

'I am . . . am of Gaul, lady,' he stammered.

'You are far from Gaul. You seem to be wearing the clothing of a seaman.'

'I am . . .' Esumaro clenched his jaw suddenly. He realised that everyone in this land was a potential enemy until they proved otherwise.

'What are you doing here?' continued the woman. 'You could freeze to death in this winter snow.'

'I was walking when I was overcome with fatigue.'

'Walking?' The woman looked at his feet with an inquisitive smile.

Esumaro glanced down and saw that he was wearing only one of his seaman's boots. He had no memory of losing the other. He was unsure whether it was lost during his escape from the wreck or later.

He asked quickly: 'What are you doing here, lady? Who are you?'

'I am the Abbess Faife from the abbey of Ard Fhearta. We are all from Ard Fhearta. We are journeying on the annual pilgrimage to the oratory of the founder of our abbey on Bréanainn's mount.'

Esumaro regarded her with some suspicion.

'But Ard Fhearta is to the north across these mountains.

I have seen Bréanainn's mount from the sea and that also lies on the north side of this peninsula. This is the southern shore.'

Abbess Faife frowned but replied easily: 'You seem well acquainted with this area for a Gaulish sailor, for that is what I presume you are. But you seem distrustful, my friend. We have spent two nights at the abbey of Colmán, where we had business to conduct. Having passed two days there, we are now on our journey westward to Bréanainn's mount. Why are you so suspicious?'

Esumaro felt slightly reassured.

'I am sorry, lady,' he said, deflecting her question. 'I am cold and hungry and very fatigued. I beg your pardon for my churlish questions. Is there some dry shelter nearby where I can rest?'

'There is a shelter a short distance behind us. We can spare some food and a dry cloak – even shoes. The fire will still be warm for we have just paused to break our journey. We left the abbey of Colmán well before dawn. Do you think you can walk?'

The Abbess Faife bent forward to help him as Esumaro rose painfully to his feet. He staggered for a moment and then managed to regain his balance. The young woman who stood by him came forward to help.

'And in what direction is the abbey of Colmán?' he grunted.

'Not far along there to the east, but you have to walk round the bay.' She indicated the direction by inclining her head. 'You cannot walk far in your condition.'

'Thank you. I will rest awhile and then make my way to the abbey.'

'First you must get warm, put on some dry clothes and

have some food. Come, let us get you to the shelter and you may change out of those sodden garments.'

Esumaro looked alarmed and the religieuse smiled.

'Have no fear. We are taking a bundle of clothing and shoes to Brother Maidíu who keeps the oratory on Bréanainn's mount. He is about your size, and if you have no objection to wearing the robes of a religieux for a while, his robes will fit you exactly.'

Abbess Faife turned and together with her younger companion helped Esumaro stumble a short distance across the snow. It was not far before he saw they were leading him to a small, conical, beehive-shaped hut of stone. He remembered that it was what people in these parts called a *coirceogach*, a very ancient stone dwelling. It stood back among the trees, hardly noticeable from the main track on which they had found him. Only the disturbed snow showed that people had used it recently. As they climbed towards it, he saw a wisp of smoke rising from it. Abbess Faife had been right.

There was soon a fire blazing. By its warmth he stripped off his sodden remnants of clothing and was given dry woollen robes from some of the bundles carried by the young Sisters of the Faith. The abbess had been correct when she had judged that the robes would fit him. They were warm enough and he did not complain. By the time he had changed, the young woman who had helped him was pressing on him a drink of some distilled spirit, and there was bread, cheese and cold meat laid out for him. Esumaro received them with expressions of gratitude but his eyelids were dropping and he could not hold back the wave of sleep engulfing him.

It was one of those short sleeps that, as captain, he had grown used to taking on board ship. It was deep but lasted only an hour before he raised his head, blinking and feeling refreshed. To his surprise, the group of religieuse were still seated by the fire.

The young woman who had discovered him was by his side and smiled softly.

'We thought it better to remain until you awoke,' she explained. 'There are wolves in the woods along here.'

The abbess moved over to them as he rubbed his eyes and sat up.

'I am rested,' he assured her before she had a chance to ask the question already forming on her lips.

'Are you sure that you will be all right now?' she asked. 'Rest a while further if you must, but do not fall asleep unless you can be sure of waking immediately. Wolves abide in these forests, as Sister Easdan has explained. But your journey to the abbey will be easy now. As for us, we must press on to the west, otherwise we will not reach our destination before sundown.'

'I am very well now,' Esumaro asserted solemnly. 'I am invigorated already and can never repay you for your kindness. Perhaps I will be able to pick up a Gaulish ship at the abbey of Colmán?'

Abbess Faife shrugged.

'We saw no large ships when we were there and the steward of the abbey told us it has been several weeks since any arrived. It seemed to worry him. The abbey relies on the sea trade,' she added, not realising that Esumaro knew that fact well.

He was about to ask another question when the sound of galloping horses came to his ears. He joined the abbess to peer from the doorway of the stone hut and saw several horsemen riding swiftly along the track just below them.

One of the men gave a sudden cry, pointing up towards them. The company changed direction and within a moment a dozen or so rough-looking warriors had surrounded them, their horses stamping and giving out great smoky wreaths of hot breath. The warriors carried their swords in their hands. Esumaro saw that in their midst was a shorter figure swathed from head to foot in grey robes so that no part of the body was visible. The cowl was drawn well down over the head. The figure was slight and the shoulders were rounded.

The Abbess Faife went forward and stood facing them with a frown.

'What do you seek here?' she demanded authoritatively.

The leading horseman, a coarse-looking man with a rough black beard, and a scar across his forehead, chuckled. It was not a pleasant sound.

'Why, we seek you and your religious brood, woman. Our master has need of you. So you are to come with us.'

Esumaro felt himself go cold. He recognised the voice as that of the leader of the wreckers from whom he had escaped. What was his name? Olcán!

'We serve only one master, that is the Christ, Jesus,' the abbess was replying. 'We are on our way to—'

'I know where you thought you were going, woman,' snapped the man. 'But I know where it is that you are now destined for. You will soon serve another master.' He spoke as if in a dark humour. 'Come, we have no time to waste.'

The abbess stood resolutely.

'I am the Abbess Faife of Ard Fhearta. Put up your swords and depart in peace. For we intend to go on to Bréanainn's mount and—'

Esumaro noticed that the black-bearded leader had

glanced in the direction of the small grey-robed figure. There was an almost imperceptible movement of the cowled head.

But it happened without warning. It happened quickly.

The bearded leader simply leant forward from his saddle and thrust his sword swiftly into Abbess Faife's heart.

She was dead before she began sinking to the ground with an expression akin to surprise. As she fell back, the leader of the warriors turned to the abbess's shocked companions.

'I presume that no one else wants to argue with me? Gather your bundles and walk ahead of us or you will remain here with your abbess . . . and join her in the Otherworld.'

Any cries of distress were silenced by momentary disbelief at what had happened.

Then the young religieuse who had first discovered Esumaro threw herself on her knees by the body of the slain abbess.

'You have killed her!' she sobbed, seeking in vain for a pulse. 'Why did you kill her? What kind of brute are you? Who are you?'

The man raised his sword again in a threatening manner.

'You ask too many questions, woman. Do you wish to remain here with her?'

Esumaro moved quickly forward, holding up a hand as if to ward off the man's blade. At the same time, he bent swiftly and raised the young woman from the ground.

'Now is not the time to protest!' he whispered quickly. 'Not if you want to live.'

She paused for a fraction, glancing at the threatening warrior, turned her eyes to Esumaro and then nodded quickly, regaining her composure with just a tightening of the mouth to show the effort it took. As she rose, she reached out one hand as if to touch the breast of the abbess. Only Esumaro saw her fingers clutch at the thong that held the abbess's cross and wrench at it quickly. It came apart in her hold. She turned as if she was allowing Esumaro to help her away from the body and pressed the cross into his hands.

'You had better become one of us, until we find out what this means,' she muttered under her breath. Esumaro was surprised at the girl's quick thinking.

He took the cross. As his fingers closed over it, the voice of the warrior's leader snapped at him.

'You! That man there!'

Esumaro turned to him with narrowed eyes.

'Who are you?' The leader was looking suspiciously at him. 'You are not of the community of Ard Fhearta. I had not heard that a Brother of the Faith was accompanying this band.'

Esumaro thought rapidly, glancing towards the still silent figure hidden in the grey robes.

'Why . . . I am . . . Brother Maros, accompanying these Sisters in the Faith to Bréanainn's mount for the vigil.'

'Yet you do not wear the symbol of the Faith on your robes?'

Esumaro hesitated a moment. Then he held up the crucifix the quick-thinking young religieuse had passed to him.

'I was adjusting it when you and your men rode down on us. Do I have your permission to finish replacing it round my neck?'

'You are not from these parts?' The warrior's voice was suspicious when he heard Esumaro's accent.

'We of the Faith have to travel far and wide in search of souls to save,' intoned Esumaro with what he hoped was the correct tone of reverence.

The young woman, defiance on her features, came to his help.

'Brother Maros joined us at the abbey of Colmán. He is a noted scholar from Gaul.'

The warrior frowned suspiciously. Again he seemed to glance for instruction to the grey-robed figure.

'From Gaul? How did you get to the abbey of Colmán? There have been no ships reaching there in many months.'

'I came to the port of Ard Mór in the south and have spent some months travelling through your country. How else would I speak your language so well?'

The warrior thought for a moment, glanced again at the small silent figure and shrugged. He seemed to see logic in the reply but was not completely satisfied.

'Yet you do not wear a tonsure. All religious wear tonsures.'

It was the young woman who answered for him.

'Brother Maros is a follower of the Blessed Budoc of Laurea, a learned scholar in his own land. His followers do not wear a tonsure.'

The warrior's eyes narrowed at her intervention.

'Can't he answer for himself?' he snapped.

Esumaro edged forward protectively in front of the young woman.

'I can. It is as my Sister in the Faith, Sister Easdan, says. I follow the Blessed Budoc.' He was glad he remembered the name that Abbess Faife had identified the girl with.

The black-bearded leader grunted, seemed about to say something, and then glanced once more at the robed figure. It was as if some communication passed between them again for he turned away and gestured for the company to move.

'Forward now and in silence,' he called. 'Remember, it

is up to you if you wish to live or die. My men will be watchful.'

Esumaro turned his head to the young Sister Easdan with a look that he hoped conveyed his gratitude. He would have to ask her who this Budoc was. But what situation had he landed himself in? God in heaven! What evil had he been plunged into?

CHAPTER TWO

It was still dark when Abbot Erc left his warm chamber in the great abbey of Ard Fhearta, throwing his woollen cloak around his bent shoulders, to make his way through the *vallium monasterii*. It was still dark although he could see that the clouds were low in the sky and the rain was fine like an icy spray against his face. The winter sun would not rise for several hours yet but the community of the abbey would soon be waking to the tolling of the bell that announced the start of a new day. For the ageing abbot this was a special day, for it was the feast of the Blessed Íte, 'the bright sun of the women of Muman', who had fostered and taught Bréanainn, the founder of Ard Fhearta. Today, special prayers would be offered in the tiny oratory where, it was said, Bréanainn had first read the principal triad of Íte's teachings to those men and women whom he had called together at this place. He had exhorted them, as Íte had, to have a pure heart, live a simple life, and be generous with their love. Since then the community had lived as a *conhospitae*, a mixed community, men and women working together in the service of the New Faith.

Abbot Erc paused for a moment outside the small, stone-built *aireagal* – the house of prayer, as it was called, although many of the brethren preferred to use the Latin term *oraculum*. Then he pushed open the wooden door and stood for a moment in the utter darkness of the interior. He was surprised that there was no light inside and his immediate reaction was irritation. It was the task of the *rechtaire*, the steward of the community, to ensure that a lamp was always lit in the *aireagal*. He had also expected the Venerable Cináed to be waiting for him so that together they could bless the oratory and light the altar candles ready for the morning prayers.

He turned and looked back through the gloom and misty rain towards the darkened buildings of the abbey behind him.

There was no sign indicating that the Venerable Cináed was on his way. That was unlike the abbey's oldest scholar. Cináed was reputed to be so old that many of the younger religious felt he must surely have known Bréanainn himself. The truth was that Cináed had, indeed, known some older members of the abbey who had, in turn, known the blessed founder. He had been at Ard Fhearta longer than anyone else and when Erc had been elected by the community to be abbot here, he had been worried by the thought that it was a position which Cináed should rightfully hold. But Cináed was content to confine himself to his cell with his manuscripts and writing materials and indulge in his scholastic pursuits. He occasionally taught the young ones in the arts of calligraphy and composition. More important, while the Venerable Cináed was a religieux he was not ordained into the priesthood and showed no inclination to be so. However, it was a tradition that as the oldest member of the community he should assist in the ceremony of blessing the oratory on Íte's feast day.

Abbot Erc paused for a moment or two longer and then turned to the shelf by the door on which he knew a tallow candle stood. A tinderbox reposed close by. He reached out, feeling rather than seeing in the gloom, and with a practice born of long years he was able, after a few minutes, to ignite the shavings to produce a flame for the candle.

Feeling a little calmer, he moved forward into the *aireagal* and came to a halt before the altar.

Awkwardly, he lowered himself to his knees, placed the spluttering candle before him, and stretched out his arms to make a symbolic crucifix form with his body in order to intone the *cros-figill*, the Cross prayer before the altar.

He was about to start the ritual when he noticed something on the flagstones just before him. He frowned and reached forward. It was a bronze *crotal*, a closed bell: a pear-shaped metal form in which was a loose metal ball, which created the musical tone. As he picked it up, he realised that its surface was wet . . . sticky wet. He drew his hand away and looked at it in the light of the candle. The sticky substance was blood.

Abbot Erc reached for the candle and clambered to his feet, peering round in the gloom. The *aireagal* was clearly empty, unless . . . He looked at the altar and noticed the dark stains before it.

'Is there anyone there?' Abbot Erc's nervous question came out as a croak. He cleared his throat. 'In the name of God, is there anyone there?' he called in a stronger tone.

There was no reply.

He moved forward. The altar was a solid block of lime-stone, carved with the names of the *Sanctissimus Ordo*, the first holy saints of Éireann. He edged round it, holding the candle high.

The body was stretched on its back with its hands above the head as if someone had dragged it behind the altar by the outstretched arms. There was blood all over the skull, matting the white hair, and it was obvious that someone had used some heavy cudgel to batter the head.

The abbot let out a low moan.

'Oh, my God! Not again! Not again!'

Abbot Erc had recognised the corpse immediately. It was the Venerable Cináed.

The *rechtaire* was so excited that he quite forgot to knock on the door of Abbot Erc's chamber. He burst in, causing the grey-haired abbot to glance up from his chair as he sat before the blazing fire. He frowned with annoyance towards the youthful, fresh-faced steward.

'They have arrived,' cried Brother Cú Mara. Before the abbot could reprimand him, he went on, 'They have been seen approaching the abbey. The lord Conrí rides at their head. I will go and greet them at the gates.'

Before Abbot Erc could say a word in reply, the young steward, seeming to forget all sense of place and protocol in his excitement, turned and hurried off, leaving the chamber door open and a draught whistling through.

The abbot put down the goblet of wine he had been sipping and rose to his feet. He shuffled to the door, paused a moment and then, with a sigh, shrugged and closed it.

Although he kept a passive expression on his features, he had to admit that he shared something of the steward's excitement. It had been ten days since he had asked Conrí, warlord of the Uí Fidgente, for help. Last month, six young female members of the community had left the abbey with Abbess Faife. They had only been gone a few days when Mugrón, a merchant who was well known at Ard Fhearta, had arrived at the abbey with horrifying news. He had found the body of Abbess Faife near the roadside south of the Sliabh Mis mountains. There had been no sign of her six companions. By coincidence, Abbess Faife's nephew, Conrí, the warlord of the Uí Fidgente, was visiting the abbey at the time. Having recovered the body of the abbess and attended the rituals of burial, Conrí had assured Abbot Erc that he knew of only one person, a *dálaigh*, who could solve such a mystery as that now facing them. He had left the abbey with two warriors, promising to find the *dálaigh* and return to the abbey as soon as possible.

And now Conrí was returning. But in the meantime a second tragic mystery had occurred: the murder of the Venerable Cináed.

Abbot Erc shivered slightly as he remembered finding the Venerable Cináed's body in the oratory. God! What evil cursed the great abbey that such things could happen? The abbot stared moodily into the fire and wondered what manner of person it was whom Conrí was bringing to his abbey to resolve these mysteries and in whom he had so much faith.

Conrí, King of Wolves, warlord of the Uí Fidgente, paused on the brow of the hill and patted the neck of his bay stallion. He was tall and well-muscled, with a shock of black hair, grey eyes and the livid white of a scar across his left cheek. In spite of that, he was a handsome young man whose humour was especially marked when he smiled. It was the smile that changed the haughtiness of his expression into a look of boyish mischievous fun. He turned to his companions and pointed north-westward across the plain.

'There is the great abbey of Ard Fhearta, lady.'

His companions were a red-haired religieuse and a stocky man wearing the tonsure of St Peter. Behind them rode two young but dour-looking warriors. The woman and her companion edged their horses close to Conrí and followed the line of his outstretched arm.

'Well, Conrí, our journey has not been long from Cashel,' observed the woman.

'It is as I promised,' agreed the young warrior. 'I am only sorry that I felt no other choice was left to me but to ask you to come here to help us.'

The religieuse's companion grimaced sceptically. 'Since you put your case so well, Conrí, how could we refuse you?'

Conrí glanced suspiciously at him.

'I have no eloquence, Brother Eadulf,' he replied shortly. 'I think the lady Fidelma was persuaded by the strangeness of the facts.'

Brother Eadulf was about to make some rejoinder when Sister Fidelma held up a hand and put her head slightly to one side.

'Listen! What is that noise?'

There came to their ears a faint rhythmic sound like the distant pounding of a drum. It seemed to have a slow but regular beat.

'Have you never been in this corner of Muman, lady?' asked Conrí. He always addressed Fidelma by her rank as sister to Colgú, king of Muman, rather than her religious title.

'I have not crossed beyond the Sliabh Luachra, the mountain barrier that divides us from the heartland of the Uí

Fidgente,' she replied. Then she grinned mischievously, adding, 'For obvious reasons, as you will appreciate, Conrí.'

It was not so long ago that the Uí Fidgente chieftains had led their people into a futile war to overthrow her brother, newly placed upon the throne at Cashel. The Uí Fidgente had been defeated at Cnoc Áine scarcely two years ago. Out of their defeat, young Conrí had been elected as the new warlord, and he had proved his diplomatic skills by forging an alliance with Cashel on behalf of the new chief Donennach.

'I thought these lands belonged to the Ciarraige Luachra, not the Uí Fidgente?' Brother Eadulf was snappish. He had disapproved of this journey from the start. However, he had decided to do some research in the library of Cashel before they had set off.

Conrí did not lose his good humour.

'Two generations ago, our chieftain Oengus mac Nechtain brought the Ciarraige Luachra into our territory. But you are right, Brother Eadulf, the main Uí Fidgente territory is more to the north-east.'

'So what is the sound we hear?' Fidelma demanded, reverting to the unanswered question that she had posed.

'That is the sound of the sea. We are scarcely six kilometres from it.'

'I have been closer to seashores before and not heard such a noise.'

'Before the abbey, beyond those hills, is a wide sandy shore which runs south to north some eleven or twelve kilometres. We call it Banna Strand, the sandy seashore of the peaks. The sea is so very high and tempestuous here, even on the calmest days, and its rollers are so thunderous, that you might feel as if the earth is trembling as you get nearer.

The winds that whip off the sea are fierce at times and produce a good robust air by which the people here prosper in health, or so I have been told by the apothecaries.'

Brother Eadulf viewed the scene before him with critical eyes.

'It does not seem that the trees prosper,' he observed. 'Those that are inclined to grow are bent almost along the ground. They are gnarled and distorted like phantoms from another world.'

Not for the first time, during the two days of their journey from Cashel, Fidelma shot Eadulf a glance of disapproval at his carping tone. Then she turned back to the vista that stretched before them.

The abbey, its buildings enclosed by a circular defensive wall like most of the monastic settlements in these parts, was built on the crown of a hill. Round the bottom of the hill a river meandered its way to the sea. Eadulf could see a number of fortified homesteads and farms dotted here and there across the valley and reminded himself that until recently the Uí Fidgente had been a very martial people. There seemed to be no clusters of buildings immediately outside the walls of the abbey, which unlike some of the great monasteries was clearly not used as a centre of habitation.

Conrí was at pains to point out the number of holy wells in the vicinity, the standing stones and thriving farmsteads. 'Ard Fhearta is over a hundred years old,' he told them, and there was pride in his voice. 'It was built by the great Bréanainn—'

'Of the Ciarraige Luachra,' Brother Eadulf could not help but interpose. 'I have read the story.'

'The name Ard Fhearta means "height of the graveyard",

doesn't it?' Fidelma mused, ignoring him. 'So the abbey is built on the site of an old pagan burial ground?'

'As are many abbey foundations and churches of our new Faith,' agreed Conrí. 'I am told by Abbot Erc that the purpose of doing so is to sanctify the old sites so that all our ancestors may join us in the Christian Otherworld.'

Brother Eadulf frowned. His people, the South Folk, who traced their descent to Casere, son of the great god Woden, had believed that the only way to achieve immortality was to die sword in hand, the name of Woden on their lips. Then and only then would they be allowed into the afterlife, to sit with the gods in the great hall of the heroes. Now and then the indoctrination of his early years rose and fought with his conversion to the New Faith. Eadulf still sought guarantees, and that was why he had rejected the teachings of the Irish who had converted and educated him for the more fundamental absolutes of Rome.

The small band continued on their way towards the grey stone and wooden buildings of the abbey. They rode along a wide avenue between stone hedges, passing a tall standing stone to the west, and across the valley floor where the sound of the sea was not so prominent, being deflected by the hills. A drover moving a small herd of goats hastened to get the animals out of their way, apparently recognising and saluting Conrí, while giving an inquisitive glance at the warlord's companions.

As they made their way up the incline towards the walls of Ard Fhearta, the wooden gates opened and a young man emerged. He stood awaiting their approach with ill-concealed excitement on his features.

'God be with you this day, Brother Cú Mara,' said Conrí, reining his horse to a standstill in front of the open gates.

'God and Mary protect you, Conrí son of Conmáel.' The young man gave the ritual response. Then he turned to greet the others and his eyes suddenly narrowed as they beheld Fidelma.

'Brother Cú Mara is the *rechtaire* of the abbey,' Conrí said.

'Welcome to Ard Fhearta, lady.' The coldness of his tone did not match the words.

Fidelma raised an eyebrow. 'You seem to know who I am?'

The young man inclined his head slightly. 'Who does not know of Fidelma, sister to Colgú, king of Muman? Your reputation as a *dálaigh* has spread in all five kingdoms of Éireann.'

Fidelma glanced accusingly at Conrí. 'I thought you said that you had not warned anyone here that I would be coming?'

Before Conrí could speak, Brother Cú Mara intervened.

'I only knew myself a moment ago when I recognised you.' He spoke in a curiously disapproving tone.

'Then you have seen me before?'

'I studied the art of calligraphy under Abbot Laisran at Durrow, lady. I saw you several times there.'

Fidelma smiled. Durrow – the abbey of the oak plain. It seemed an age since she had last been there. The genial Abbot Laisran had looked upon Fidelma as his protégée, having persuaded her to join the religious after she had won her degrees in law at the great school of the Brehon Morann. Dear, kindly Abbot Laisran, and his infectious humour.

Brother Cú Mara had turned to Eadulf with the same serious scrutiny.

'And you are . . . ?'

'This is my companion, Brother Eadulf,' said Fidelma.

The young monk's expression did not alter.

'Of course,' he said shortly. He turned back to Conrí. 'The abbot will doubtless be eager to speak to you, lord Conrí, especially when he knows the identity of your companions.'

Fidelma could still hear the disapproval in the young man's tone.

'I will see him directly, then,' Conrí assured him. 'I presume there is no word from the missing religieuse?'

The steward's expression turned into an unpleasant grimace.

'No word from them, lord Conrí. However, the abbey has received a further tragic blow.'

'Then do not keep us in suspense, Brother,' Conrí replied shortly.

'Three days ago, the Venerable Cináed was found dead in the oratory.'

'The Venerable Cináed?' It was Fidelma who asked the question. 'Would that be Cináed the scholar?'

'Do you know his work, lady?' The steward seemed surprised.

'Who does not know of his treatises on philosophy and history?' she responded at once. 'His work was renowned throughout the five kingdoms of Éireann. Do I judge that he was elderly? I hope he died a peaceful death?'

Brother Cú Mara shook his head. 'He was elderly, just as you say, lady, but he died violently. A heavy blow apparently crushed the back of his skull.'

Conrí gasped while Fidelma's eyes widened a little.

'I presume, from your choice of words, that this was no accident?' she pressed.

'His body was found behind the altar in the oratory and there was no sign of the implement which caused the death blow.'

'Has the culprit been discovered?' Conrí demanded. He glanced to Fidelma and added: 'This is bad news, indeed. Cináed was a great supporter of our new chief, Donennach, and was one of his advisers.'

The steward did not look unduly grief-stricken.

'There are some here who think that this place has become cursed because of the surrender of Donennach,' he said quietly.

Fidelma's mouth tightened as she identified the hostility in the steward's tone.

'Cursed?' She made the word sound belligerent.

'Perhaps it is the shades of past generations of the Uí Fidgente who lie buried here – perhaps they are released from their Otherworld slumber to come back and wreak havoc upon us for the misfortune brought on them?'

Fidelma stared at the youthful steward in surprise. He seemed so reasonable and so matter of fact with his question. She could not tell whether he was serious or possessed of some perverse sense of humour.

'As a member of the Faith, Brother, you should know better than to voice such superstitious nonsense.'

'I merely articulate what many here are thinking. Indeed, what some have actually voiced already,' the steward said defensively. 'The abbey was built on an ancient pagan cemetery and perhaps we have angered the old spirits of the Uí Fidgente by our defeat?'

'It seems that we have arrived at an opportune time,' said Eadulf seriously. 'We have come to save you Uí Fidgente from slipping back into fearful idolatry.'

Only Fidelma recognised the tone of voice when Eadulf spoke in jest.

Brother Cú Mara was about to respond in anger but then he turned away, speaking over his shoulder.

'I would not keep Abbot Erc waiting, lord Conrí. As for the lady Fidelma and her companion, the abbot will doubtless expect you both to join him after the evening prayers and meal. Come, let me take you to the *hospitium* so that you may refresh yourselves after your travels.'

Eadulf noted the use of the Latin term.

'Do you follow the Roman rule here, Brother?' he asked as they dismounted and followed the steward on foot, leading their horses, into the abbey complex.

Brother Cú Mara shook his head immediately.

'I perceive that you bear the tonsure of Rome, Brother Eadulf, but here we adhere to the teachings of our Church Fathers. Nevertheless, Latin is much in fashion in the abbey. Our scholars pride themselves on translating from the Latin texts. The Venerable Cináed was keeping a great chronicle in Latin wherein he was recording the history of this abbey since its foundation by the Blessed Bréanainn.'

Conrí had handed his horse to one of his companions, a taciturn warrior named Socht, and departed to find the abbot. The young steward fell silent as he guided the rest of the party through the abbey grounds, through buildings of various shapes and sizes that made up the complex, to a large wooden structure they presumed was the *hospitium*. Brother Cú Mara paused.

'There are no other guests at the moment so the guesthouse is all yours. Make yourselves welcome. Sister Sinnchéne is inside. She will attend to your wants. I will come to collect you after evening prayers and take you to Abbot Erc's chamber.'

Without another word, the young steward turned and left.

The warrior Socht and his companion took charge of the horses and led them away to the abbey stables.

Eadulf pulled a face in the direction of the vanishing Brother Cú Mara.

'I get the impression that that young man is not exactly pleased to see us,' he commented.

'Remember that we are in Uí Fidgente territory, Eadulf,' Fidelma replied. 'My brother was victorious in battle over them just over two years ago. Some people do not forgive and forget so easily.'

Eadulf opened the door to the guest-house and ushered Fidelma inside. They entered a large chamber of red yew panels which, it appeared, was a general room where guests could rest before a fire. The sky was already darkening, for dusk came early on these cold winter's days, but there was a cheerful fire crackling in a stone-flagged hearth. A young woman was bending over an oil lamp set on a central table and adjusting its flickering wick. She glanced up, startled by their silent entrance, and Fidelma noticed that her eyes seemed red-rimmed. The light flickered on the tears gathered on her lashes.

She straightened up quickly, raising a hand to wipe her eyes. Fidelma took in the girl's attractive features. She had a fair skin, blue eyes and a shock of golden hair.

'I am Sister Sinnchéne,' she announced with a sniff. 'I presume that you are the guests we have been expecting? How may I be of assistance to you?'

It was clear that they had entered on some private moment of grief that she had no wish to share.

Fidelma introduced herself and Eadulf. It was clear that

the young woman did not know of Fidelma's relationship to the king of Muman.

'Will you be wanting to bathe after your journey, Sister?' she asked. 'I can have hot water ready in the bathhouse shortly. Our facilities are primitive so there are no separate arrangements for men and women. If your companion can wait until you have finished, I will ensure there is hot water for him as well.'

Eadulf had never really understood the Irish passion for such fastidious cleanliness. In the land of the South Folk, bathing had consisted of a dip in the river and that carried out none too often.

'I can wait,' he agreed hurriedly.

'There are separate chambers for your sleeping quarters,' Sister Sinnchéne continued, pointing to a corridor that led off from the room behind her. 'The bathing house and *defectarium* stand beyond.'

'The lord Conrí and two of his warriors accompanied us here. They will be wanting beds,' Fidelma pointed out.

'The warriors will doubtless make do with beds in the dormitory.' Sister Sinnchéne's voice was brisk and business-like. 'If you will choose your chamber, Sister, I shall return and tell you when the water is heated.'

She moved off in a brisk fashion.

Fidelma went into the corridor. There were three or four cell-like rooms leading off it, each only big enough for a cot-like bed and little else. She entered the first room and threw her bag down on the bed with a sigh. Eadulf took the next room and followed Fidelma back to the main chamber, where she sank into the nearest chair.

'While we have this moment alone,' she said abruptly, 'you'd best tell me what troubles you.'

Eadulf raised his eyebrows.

'Should anything trouble me?' he asked in feigned innocence.

Fidelma grimaced with annoyance.

'All through the journey here you have been as querulous as an old woman. It would be better to say what is on
your mind now rather than leave it until later.'

Eadulf hesitated, shrugged and sat down opposite her.

'What troubles me is the same matter that has troubled
me since Conrí came to Cashel,' he said heavily.

'Which is?' prompted Fidelma sharply.

'It is barely a few weeks since our son, Alchú, was
abducted. Thanks be to God that we recovered him safely.
We had scarcely reunited as a family, scarcely made it back
to safety in Cashel. It was clearly time to settle down for a
while. Then along comes Conrí and you decide to go
charging off into dangerous territory. This area may still be
within your brother's kingdom but it is an area that has been
in constant rebellion against him. And all because this Conrí
pleads with you to do so.'

Fidelma returned his gaze with an expression of sadness.
For a moment, Eadulf recognised the hurt in her eyes.

'Eadulf,' her voice was heavy with emphasis, 'I am
Alchú's mother. Do you think I care nothing about my son?
My pain in leaving him in Cashel after so short a time is
as great, if not greater, than your own. However, I am sister
to the king and, as well you know, above all things, I am a
dálaigh. That is my training, that is my skill in life. You
know the problems that my brother has had with the Uí
Fidgente. Now I am presented with an ideal means to build
on the fragile peace between Cashel and this wild people.
Conrí, the warlord of the Uí Fidgente, came to Cashel

seeking my help as a *dálaigh*. By extending that help to him, I will strengthen the move to reunite my brother's kingdom.'

Eadulf saw her argument but his personal feelings did not allow him to be convinced by it.

'I could understand that if all else had been equal for us but it is not so,' he protested. 'It is only a matter of weeks since we settled down at Cashel, united as a family again, and started to plan the ceremony by which we will be permanently bound together, which was supposed to be on the feast of Imbolc, when the ewes come into milk. On that day you were supposed to become my *cétmuintir*.'

For nearly a year now Fidelma and Eadulf had been joined as *ban charrthach* and *fer comtha*, partners for a year and a day, a legal marriage under the law, but a temporary one. After a year and a day, if incompatible, they could go their separate ways without blame and without payment of compensation to one another.

Fidelma examined Eadulf with a sad expression.

'Do you have cause to doubt that it will happen?' she asked softly.

Eadulf raised an arm in a brief gesture almost of helplessness and let it fall.

'Sometimes I am not so sure. We seem to be constantly drifting from one drama to another.'

'Then let me tell you this,' Fidelma said earnestly. 'It was my brother's wish that I should come here, not my response to Conrí, which would have not been enthusiastic in the circumstances. My brother is king. My decision was made in response to the wishes of the king. I tried to explain that to you before we set out.' As Eadulf opened his mouth to reply, she held up her hand, as if to silence him, and went on. 'A resolution of this particular drama, as I said, is important to my brother's kingdom, Eadulf. And since we have arrived here at Ard Fhearta we find the drama has intensified because the Venerable Cináed has been murdered. The Venerable Cináed is known and respected throughout all five kingdoms and is admired by the High King himself. His death will create a greater shock throughout these lands than even that of Conrí's aunt, the Abbess Faife.'

Fidelma's brother, Colgú, had certainly made the political importance of helping Conrí clear enough when they had spoken together. If Cashel could respond to an Uí Fidgente call for help in solving the mystery at the abbey of Ard Fhearta, it would be important in helping to heal the rift that had for so long set the rulers of the Uí Fidgente and the kings of Muman against one another.

'I know what Colgú has argued,' acknowledged Eadulf with asperity. 'He is not the one who has had to enter Uí Fidgente country without escort and chance the dangers . . .'

Fidelma suddenly smiled mischievously.

'Why, Eadulf! Are you saying that you are solely concerned for my safety?'

Eadulf grimaced in irritation at her levity. Then he said: 'I am concerned for the safety of both of us. The warriors of your brother's guard should have escorted us. Men we could trust. Now we have to rely on Conrí and the good-will of the Uí Fidgente.'

Fidelma shook her head in disagreement. 'I put my trust in Conrí.'

'I remember very clearly my time as a prisoner of the Uí Fidgente. You cannot expect me to trust them.'

'Yet you went alone through Uí Fidgente territory in

search of Alchú,' Fidelma reminded him. 'You were not concerned with safety then.'

'I had only myself to worry about. You were safe in Cashel.'

Fidelma shook her head, smiling.

'As it turned out, I was not,' she said. 'I was a prisoner of the rebel Uí Fidgente myself. And it was Conrí who helped me escape.'

'Fidelma, I will never win an argument with you.' Eadulf raised his hands as if fending off some imaginary attacker. 'I should know better than to try. Since we are here, let me be at peace with my concerns.'

'That I will find hard,' Fidelma replied solemnly. 'Anyway, we shall soon be meeting Abbot Erc. I hope you will overcome any antagonism you feel. There appears enough antagonism here as it is. I need your mind and support to help me in this matter. Remember Muirgen and Nessán are nursing little Alchú in the safety of my brother's fortress. The plans that we have set for the feast day of Imbolc remain in place and they will happen. And here we are, together, with a problem to face and to solve. What better situation can there be?'

Eadulf reluctantly smiled at her infectious enthusiasm.

'Very well, Fidelma. I will put a curb on my fears. But I shall look forward to the day when we can return to Cashel.'

There was a movement at the door as Sister Sinnchéne returned.

'The water will be ready when you are, Sister.'

'Excellent.' Fidelma rose immediately, picking up her *ciorbholg*, her comb-bag in which all Irish women carried their toilet articles. 'Show me to this bathhouse, Sister, for I am ready now.'

Sister Sinnchéne led Fidelma along the corridor to a room in which stood a large wooden tub called the *dabach*. It was already steaming. A cauldron of water was simmering on a fire in the far corner. There were shelves on which were displayed bars of *sléic* and linen cloths. Nearby were little jars of oil and extracts of sweet-smelling herbs boiled into a liquid to anoint the body. The place was well equipped with a *scaterc* – a mirror of fine polished metal – and a selection of clean combs.

'I shall attend you, if it is your wish,' said the young sister.

Fidelma nodded absently. It was usual to have an attendant to pour the heated water and pass soap and drying cloths.

She undressed and climbed into the *dabach*. The water was not too hot and she relaxed with a sigh, lying back while Sister Sinnchéne passed her a bar of soap.

'Have you been long in this abbey, Sister?' asked Fidelma as she began to lather herself.

Sister Sinnchéne was checking on the heat of the water.

'I have been here ever since I reached the age of choice,' she replied.

The age of choice, the *aimsir togú*, was the maturity of a girl arrived at her fourteenth birthday.

'I would say you have not yet reached twenty summers?' hazarded Fidelma.

'I am twenty-one,' corrected the girl, turning to pick up a big metal jug and scoop water from the cauldron. She brought it to the tub and poured it in, carefully so as not to scald Fidelma.

'I presume that you knew the Venerable Cináed?'

There seemed some hesitation and Fidelma looked up.

She was surprised to see a red tinge had settled on Sister Sinnchéne's cheek.

'We are a small community, Sister,' the girl returned with an abruptness of tone that caused Fidelma's eyebrow to rise slightly.

'Of course,' Fidelma agreed. 'I am sorry. Naturally you are upset by his loss.'

'He was a kind and generous man,' replied the other with a catch in her throat.

'Do you have any idea how he came by his death?'

The young woman frowned, facing Fidelma as if seeking some other significance to her words.

'Everyone knows his head was smashed in while he was in the oratory.'

'Are there any ideas circulating in the abbey about who could have done such a thing?'

For a moment the young sister looked as if she were about to give vent to the tears that she was trying so desperately to hide. Her face contorted for a moment and then she controlled herself.

'It is not my place to speculate about gossip,' she finally said. 'You must ask the abbot.'

'But you must know . . .' began Fidelma.

'If that will be all, Sister?' Sister Sinnchéne interrupted pointedly. 'I have other duties that I must attend to.'

Fidelma said nothing but inclined her head. She knew when to back away from questions that people did not want to answer. Sister Sinnchéne went quickly out of the bathhouse, leaving Fidelma gazing after her with a thoughtful frown.

ChAPTER ThREE

The evening meal had been eaten and the brethren had departed to their various tasks before retiring for the night. Abbot Erc, who had only formally greeted Fidelma and Eadulf before the meal, which – according to a tradition set by the founder of the abbey – was consumed in total silence, now invited them, together with Conrí, to accompany him to his chamber to discuss matters. Abbot Erc was elderly and grey-haired, with a sharp angular face, thin lips, small dark eyes and a permanent look of disapproval. Conrí had already warned Fidelma that the abbot, who had been a supporter of the old Uí Fidgente regime, did not entirely approve of the presence of Fidelma in the abbey. It seemed that he shared the views of his steward, Brother Cú Mara, who accompanied them to the abbot's chamber.

The steward was coldly polite towards them. As they entered the room, Eadulf asked him why the meal had been eaten in strict silence.

'Our blessed founder believed that food and drink, that which sustains life, is a great gift from the Creator, and should therefore be consumed with meditative thought on the wonders of that creation. To speak is both to insult the cook and to scorn one's own existence, for it is only by food and drink that one exists. Indeed, it is to disdain the Creator Himself who gave us that food and drink so that we may live and glorify Him. So now it is a rule of the abbey.'

Eadulf was thoughtful.

'I have not heard such emphasis placed on the contemplation of food. Our minds should be open to receive the food of knowledge as well as paying silent tribute to what we eat. Isn't there a saying about excusing the ignorant when their feeding is better than their education?'

Abbot Erc, overhearing this, commented irritably: 'Our meditation on food is limited to the space of our meals and these, as you will have remarked . . .' He paused and eyed the Saxon monk with something approaching contempt. 'You will have noticed that we do not believe in over-feeding as is done in some communities. We believe in the saying that when the fruit is scarcest, its taste is sweetest.'

A fire had been prepared in the chamber and Brother Cú Mara brought a tray of mulled wine. Eadulf raised an eyebrow as he took his goblet with its generous measure. Once again the old abbot caught the expression and interpreted it correctly.

'We Uí Fidgente have another saying, Brother Eadulf, that it is not an invitation to hospitality without a drink.' He silently raised his goblet and they responded. 'Now, it is no longer the time to contemplate the fruits of the earth.' He gestured to the chairs that had been set before the fire. 'I have invited you to my chamber to discuss serious matters. Let me say at once, I cannot approve of lord Conrí's wisdom in bringing you here, Fidelma of Cashel. There are many Brehons of repute among the Uí Fidgente who should be able to resolve our problems, without involving Cashel.'

'Cashel is not involved,' Fidelma assured him evenly, as she settled into the wooden chair before the fire. 'I am not confined by territories or kingdoms in the exercise of my duties as a *dálaigh*. So, let us start with an account of the facts as you know them.'

Abbot Erc sat down, took a sip of the wine, and then placed the goblet on the table at his side, leaning back in his chair. He did not look particularly happy and for a moment Eadulf thought he was going to refuse to co-operate with them. But the abbot simply said: 'I believe that there is little to add to that which Conrí has already told you.'

'Pretend that he has told me nothing.' Fidelma smiled but her voice was sharp. 'It is better to seek knowledge first-hand than to hear it from others.'

'We are, as you have seen, a *conhospitae*, a mixed house of males and females,' Abbot Erc began. 'Our children are raised to the service of Christ. I cannot say that I approve of this, as I have come to support those who argue for celibacy among the religious.' He paused and shrugged. 'However, I have served as abbot here for ten years while Abbess Faife had been seven years as head of the female religieuse. Each year for seven years she has taken groups from the community on the annual pilgrimage to Bréanainn's mount, where our blessed founder was called to set forth and establish communities to glorify Christ and the New Faith.'

He paused but no one commented.

'Well, Abbess Faife departed from our gates with her charges. She travelled overland, south to the abbey of Colmán for there was some business to be enacted there between our two abbeys. After that she was to proceed through the territory of the Corco Duibhne to where Bréanainn's mount rises.'

He paused but there was silence again and so he continued.

'The first time I knew that anything was amiss was when the merchant Mugrón appeared at this abbey. Mugrón carries on his trade from our nearest sea harbour, An Bhearbha, which is on the coast some eight kilometres from here.'

'An Bhearbha? A curious name for a port, surely? Doesn't it mean a place where the water boils?' asked Eadulf, anxious to improve his knowledge.

'It is named after a river which enters the sea at that point,' explained the abbot. 'The river is turbulent and its currents are unpredictable. Mugrón had been dealing among the Corco Duibhne. Due to the inclement weather that prevented him sailing back across the bay, he was returning along the coastal road to the abbey of Colmán. It was cold and the snow was starting to drive thickly along the road. Mugrón knew the area and knew there was a small stone cabin by the roadside, and he decided to seek shelter there. That was where he found the body of Abbess Faife. She had been stabbed through the heart. He decided to bury the body in a snowdrift as a means of preserving it and then come here with all speed.'

Fidelma asked: 'What did you do on receipt of the news?'

'As chance would have it, Conrí, who is the Abbess Faife's nephew, was at the abbey. He and his warriors elected to take Mugrón back to the place to recover the body. It was still cold and the snow had preserved . . . er, preserved things. But there was no sign of the missing six religieuse. Conrí and his men returned via Colmán's abbey in order to find out if Abbess Faife and her charges had passed that way before they reached the place where she was discovered.'

'And they had?'

Conrí intervened. 'As I told you, lady, all was normal until after they left the abbey of Colmán. The Abbess Faife and her six charges had conducted their business there and passed on their way.'

'And where is this stone cabin where her body was found in relation to the abbey?'

'As one leaves the abbey and travels on to the peninsula of the land of the Corco Duibhne, along the road that runs south of the mountains by the shore, I would estimate that it was no more than twenty kilometres.'

Eadulf was frowning. 'Isn't that close by a place called the Island where once Uaman, who called himself Lord of the Passes, had his stronghold?'

Abbot Erc's eyes narrowed. 'Do you know of that place?'

'I was once a prisoner of Uaman the Leper. I saw him die and I was not sorry to see his end.'

'You are right, Brother Eadulf,' affirmed Conrí. 'The blackened ruins of his stronghold, Uaman's Tower, stand almost within sight of the place where the abbess's body was found. They say that the local people destroyed it – the tower, that is.'

Eadulf's lips thinned with grim satisfaction.

'I can vouch for that destruction. I saw the people do it after Uaman was drowned, caught by the quicksand that made the journey to his island fortress at low tide so hazardous.'

'People did suffer grievously through his actions,' agreed Abbot Erc quietly. 'Uaman's bands extracted money from all who travelled through his territory. But I will say one word of good. There lingered in him a remembrance that he was once a prince of the Uí Fidgente and he never harmed the passing religious. Abbess Faife passed through his territory several times in safety on her annual pilgrimage to Bréanainn's mount.'

'As Brother Eadulf says, Uaman is dead and his men dispersed,' Conrí pointed out quickly. 'We must concentrate on what explanations now exist.'

Fidelma was sitting with her hands folded in her lap before her.

'You say, then, this spot is near the coast? Is there any chance that some sea raiders could have come to shore there and carried off the six young women? Saxon and Frankish pirates have often attacked parts of our southern coast in search of such plunder.'

Abbot Erc considered this.

'A possibility, perhaps. But the weather was very intemperate at that time, especially along these coasts. It would be a foolhardy captain who would lead a raid across the great oceans in such weather.'

'A possibility not to be discounted, though,' Fidelma said. 'Merchant vessels land at these ports. Which reminds me, I would like to speak to this merchant, Mugrón.'

'He can be sent for,' said Brother Cú Mara. 'He can be here tomorrow, after the morning meal.'

'That will be convenient,' agreed Fidelma. 'I feel that there is no more to be learnt until I see him. We will leave that matter aside. However, there is now the killing of the Venerable Cináed to be discussed.'

Abbot Erc raised his head in surprise.

'Are you claiming authority to conduct an investigation

into Cináed's death as well as the death of Abbess Faife?' he demanded. It was clear from his tone that he objected to the very idea.

'I am a *dálaigh*,' responded Fidelma quietly. 'It is unusual for two prominent members of the same community to be murdered. We must ask if there is some connection between these two events.'

'I don't see how there could be,' the abbot retorted in displeasure. 'Abbess Faife could only have been killed by bandits. I presume that her companions have been abducted as slaves. However, Cináed was bludgeoned to death in the oratory here. That could only be a result of malice. There seems no connection.'

'I will make some inquiries all the same,' Fidelma said firmly.

The old abbot gazed at her thoughtfully for a moment, realising that behind her quiet tone was a strong will. He shrugged as if he were no longer interested in what she did.

'What do you wish to know?'

'Let us begin with the finding of Cináed's body. I understand it was you who discovered it? And this was three days ago?'

'I did. I went to the oratory to prepare for the annual ceremony to commemorate the feast day of Íte, who taught our beloved Brénnain. Usually it was the Venerable Cináed and myself who prepared the chapel for the ceremony. The place was in darkness and, at first, I did not think he was there. Then I found his body, behind the altar, with his skull smashed in.'

'Show me where the wound was,' said Fidelma.

The old abbot touched the back of his skull.

'The corpse was lying face down . . . ?'

Abbot Erc shook his head. 'It was not. He lay upon his back.'

Fidelma pursed her lips but said nothing.

'Was there any sign of a weapon?' asked Eadulf.

'None that we found.'

'Yet it must have been a heavy weapon to deliver such a blow,' Eadulf observed quietly. 'And what of the blood? Surely such a wound would have caused much blood to spray out, staining the clothing of whoever was responsible?'

Fidelma cast an appreciative glance at Eadulf and turned to the abbot.

'Was anyone seen with blood on his or her clothing? Was a search made for any such clothing?'

It was clear that such a thought had not occurred to him. He glanced at his steward.

'Well?' he asked. 'Was such a search made?'

The young steward spread his hands in a helpless gesture.

'I will do so now,' he said defensively.

Fidelma grimaced disapprovingly. 'A little late, perhaps. But it will do no harm. I presume that there is a communal laundry for the brethren?'

'There is, indeed, a *tech-nigid*, a washhouse,' confirmed the steward.

'And when is the washing done?'

'Every week on *Cét-ain*, the day of the first fast.'

Eadulf's face brightened. 'That is tomorrow. So the laundry has not been done since the murder?'

'I suppose not,' replied Brother Cú Mara.

'Who is in charge of the *tech-nigid*?' asked Fidelma.

It was Abbot Erc who responded.

'At the moment it is Sister Sinnchéne. Each month the

task of being in charge of the washing is changed. It is Sinnchéne's turn this month.'

'Sinnchéne the young sister who looks after the *hospitium*?' Fidelma turned to the steward, who nodded confirmation. 'Ensure that nothing is touched. Nothing is to be washed until all the clothes are examined, which we will do tomorrow morning.' She glanced at Eadulf. 'I am afraid that will be your task while I am questioning the merchant Mugrón. Conrí's two warriors will doubtless help you.'

Eadulf accepted the task without enthusiasm.

Fidelma turned back to Abbot Erc.

'So much for the manner of his death. What of the manner of his life? His work was well known. Had he enemies who would want to take such extreme vengeance on him?'

Abbot Erc appeared shocked at the suggestion.

'The Venerable Cináed led a blameless life. Everyone loved him. He had no enemies.'

Fidelma smiled sceptically. 'One thing I have learnt is that you do not achieve fame and wide respect without someone feeling that you have done them a wrong. It may be through jealousy of achievement. It may be some slight had been given without intention.'

Abbot Erc was indignant. 'The Venerable Cináed was a great scholar.'

'The greater the scholar, the more people grow envious,' pointed out Eadulf.

Abbot Erc made a dismissing gesture with a frail hand.

'Scholastic debate is encouraged here but that does not mean that those who disputed with the Venerable Cináed would murder him because they did not like what he said. Even I did not agree with everything he taught.'

Fidelma pursed her lips cynically.

'I have come across many such cases where a dispute of ideas leads to a clash of personalities and the growth of hate. Who disputed with him? Let us start somewhere in unravelling this mystery.'

Abbot Erc was shaking his head.

'Surely you know his scholastic reputation, Sister? No one would . . . I refuse to believe in such a possibility.'

Fidelma spoke with suppressed irritation.

'I am not asking questions to while away the time,' she said pointedly. 'I know very well the reputation of the Venerable Cináed. I have read his discourse on the *Computus Cummianus* and *De Trinitate Interpretatio Perversa*. While the old saying goes that fame is more lasting than life, nevertheless, he is dead. He has been murdered and the culprit must be found to make amends according to our law, of which I am a representative.'

There was a silence. A young Sister of the Faith had not spoken to the old abbot in such a tone before. He flushed in anger.

Brother Cú Mara, the steward, moved forward nervously.

'The Venerable Cináed encouraged lively debate and questioning, lady.' The steward stressed the title in recognition of her secular authority with a glance at the abbot. 'He liked to be questioned sharply and was just as sharp in his replies.'

Abbot Erc, reminded of Fidelma's authority, recovered his equilibrium.

'My *rechtaire* is correct. Some of our most renowned debates have seen many scholars gather here; scholars from many colleges in the land – even from the great college of Mungret.'

Fidelma had always wanted to visit Mungret, which lay

in the heart of Uí Fidgente territory. It had been founded by
Nessan, a disciple of Patrick himself, but was made famous
by the Blessed Mongan the Wise who gathered one thousand five hundred religious to worship at a complex that
boasted six churches. A saying had entered the language: to
be 'as wise as the women of Mungret'. She suddenly smiled
as she remembered the story she had been told in her childhood. The wisdom of the scholars of Mungret had become
so proverbial that the scholars of another college grew
jealous, and challenged the scholars of Mungret to a debate.
On the day of the arrival of the challengers, the scholars of
Mungret decided to play a joke. They set out disguised as
washerwomen, placing themselves at the ford across the
river that bordered their territory, where the challengers
would have to cross.

The challengers came upon the 'washerwomen' at work
by the stream. When the challengers found out that the
'washerwomen' could speak excellent Latin and Greek and
could debate easily with them, they decided they should withdraw. If the washerwomen of Mungret were so learned, what
hope had they of debating with the scholars of Mungret?

'Something amuses you, Sister?' snapped Abbot Erc.

Fidelma drew herself back to the present.

'Just a story I had heard,' she replied.

'These debates provoked no animosity?' queried Eadulf.

'None at all,' said the abbot. 'The Venerable Mac Faosma
attended many. You may ask him.'

Fidelma raised her head sharply.

'The Venerable Mac Faosma of Magh Bhile? What do
you mean? Does he dwell in this abbey?'

'Indeed he does. Do you know him?' replied the abbot
in surprise.

'I know of him. He was spoken of with the same reverence as the Venerable Cináed. It is astonishing that you have . . . had,' she corrected herself, 'two great philosophers at your abbey.'

The old abbot gestured as if dismissing the point.

'Ard Fhearta is the home of many good scholars,' he said shortly.

'Of course,' Fidelma replied with a smile. 'But what is a man of Ulaidh doing here in the country of the Uí Fidgente?'

Once more, to cover the old abbot's ill composure, it was Brother Cú Mara who answered her.

'The Venerable Mac Faosma came here three years ago. This was the country in which he had been born. He trained here and then the *peregrinatio pro Christo* took him to study at Finnian's great school at Magh Bhile. He returned to live out the rest of his days among his own people and to contemplate the mysteries of the Faith.'

'So he is not teaching here?'

'Indeed, he does so now and then. As the abbot says, he took part and even presided in many of our scholastic debates.'

'How was his relationship with the Venerable Cináed?'

Brother Cú Mara suddenly looked uncomfortable and glanced at Abbot Erc.

'He did not agree with everything that the Venerable Cináed taught.'

Fidelma actually smiled mischievously at the formula of the words.

'As, indeed, your abbot confesses was his attitude. Well, I do not doubt it. I cannot see room for agreement here with the Venerable Cináed's argument for monotheism and his dismissal of the triune godship. That would have been anathema to the Venerable Mac Faosma.'

Abbot Erc seemed surprised by her knowledge but allowed his steward to reply.

'There were some lively arguments . . .' the young steward acknowledged. He caught sight of the abbot's frown and added: 'I mean, lively *discussions* between the two of them.'

Eadulf hid a smile. 'So not everyone saw this Venerable Cináed in terms of sweetness and light?'

Abbot Erc cast an irritable look at him. 'What are you implying, Brother? That the Venerable Mac Faosma killed him because of a disagreement on the subject of the Holy Trinity?'

'The choice of the term Holy Trinity implies that you, too, did not favour the Venerable Cináed's argument for monotheism?' Fidelma could not resist the mischievous impulse to tease the stern-faced abbot.

Abbot Erc looked startled. 'What are you saying? The Venerable Cináed was my friend. Surely we can all hold different opinions without resorting to physical anger?'

'That, indeed, is the objective we should strive for,' agreed Fidelma calmly. 'Alas, mankind often finds it easier to settle disagreements by showing who is physically stronger. Do we not have a saying that might will prevail over right?'

Abbot Erc sniffed. 'So you think that the Venerable Cináed was murdered because someone disagreed with his teachings?'

'I did not say that,' Fidelma replied. 'On the other hand, such a theory cannot yet be discounted. Not until we have all the facts gathered in can we begin to speculate. It is the facts that I want.' She paused. 'Now, who were Cináed's friends in the abbey?'

The young *rechtaire* said quickly: 'Everyone was friendly with the Venerable Cináed.'

'He was a very popular man and the sort of man who, in spite of his scholastic status, was humble and approachable to everyone, from the cowherd to his fellow scholars,' affirmed the abbot.

Fidelma sighed with impatience.

'I am, of course, talking about particular friends,' she said pointedly.

The abbot shrugged. 'I was his friend, of course. We two have been longest in this abbey.'

'Anyone else? Particular friends, that is?'

'I knew him well in my capacity as *rechtaire*,' offered Brother Cú Mara, 'but I cannot say I was a close friend. And, of course, Sister Buan. She attended his wants for he was slightly frail. She cleaned and ran messages for him.'

Fidelma nodded. 'Anyone else?'

'I take it the Venerable Mac Faosma was not considered a friend?' observed Eadulf.

Abbot Erc sighed impatiently. 'Let it be said that Cináed and Mac Faosma were like chalk and cheese. Cináed was grounded in his philosophy while Mac Faosma preferred law and history. They both had views on each other's subjects and argued them. They did not mix much within the abbey except at times of discussion and debate.'

'Anyone else?' repeated Fidelma.

'Brother Eolas, naturally.'

'Who is Brother Eolas? And why "naturally"?' Fidelma pressed.

'He is our librarian, the keeper of all the books we hold here.'

'You mentioned a Sister Buan who attended to his wants. Who is she?'

A look of disapproval formed on the face of the abbot and it was the *rechtaire* who replied.

'One of our community.' He seemed to hesitate, unwilling to expand further under the annoyed gaze of his abbot. 'She . . . she is . . . was . . . a companion of the Venerable Cináed,' he ended lamely. 'As well as helping him, she often travels the surrounding countryside to trade the goods made at the abbey.'

'Isn't that your business as steward?'

'My business is to attend to the smooth running of the abbey. We have good craftsmen here, making items from gold and silver and the precious stones, the rocks and crystals, that are found in the surrounding countryside. Sister Buan meets with merchants like Mugrón to purchase the gold and silver for our craftsmen and then to sell the goods they make.'

Abbot Erc continued to look uncomfortable and suddenly rose from his seat.

'Since we have raised the subject, I am reminded that Sister Buan found something in the grate of the Venerable Cináed on the day after the murder. It was a piece of burnt paper and she thought it might be a clue.' He bent to a chest and took something from it. 'I kept it just in case,' he said.

The paper was scorched and torn. He handed it to Fidelma.

The only readable matter she could make out was '. . . midnight. Orat . . . alone . . . Sin . . .'.

Eadulf peered at it over her shoulder and shook his head.

'It makes no sense. It could mean anything. Why would this Sister Buan think it was significant?'

'She said that the Venerable Cináed must have burnt it on the night he went to the oratory.'

'Well, we will doubtless have a word with this Sister Buan,' Fidelma said. 'Have we now identified all Cináed's friends? Is there anyone else . . . any particular friend of Cináed?'

'Not that I know of,' Abbot Erc replied and made to take back the piece of burnt paper, but Fidelma shook her head with a smile.

'We'll hold on to this for the time being,' she said, putting it carefully in her *marsupium*.

Slightly put out, the abbot reseated himself.

Conrí, who had been silent during most of the discussion, coughed slightly to draw attention to himself and said: 'My aunt, the Abbess Faife, was a close friend of the Venerable Cináed. You have forgotten her. She often helped Cináed in the library, for his eyesight was not of the best as he grew older.'

Abbot Erc flushed.

'Of course,' he said stiffly. 'There was the Abbess Faife, but as she is . . . no longer with us, I did not think her name need be mentioned.'

Eadulf's lips twitched in a grimace.

'On the contrary, it is useful to know there was such a link between the two victims of violent death.'

'Do you think that there was some connection between the deaths then, Brother Eadulf?' the steward demanded.

'Perhaps. We need . . .' he avoided Fidelma's eyes, 'we need facts before we can speculate.'

'Your primary task was to find out why the Abbess Faife was killed and where her charges are!' the abbot exclaimed in disapproval. 'This cannot be accomplished in this abbey.

You should go to the lands of the Corco Duibhne and make inquiries there.'

Fidelma rose abruptly from her seat.

'You are quite right, Abbot Erc. I do mean to proceed very shortly. But not until I have made those inquiries here that I think necessary. However, as it grows late, and we have had a long ride today, we shall retire now and continue in the morning.'

The abbot also rose, looking confused. He had apparently expected some argument or some further discussion.

The young *rechtaire*, taking a lantern, conducted them from the abbot's chamber through the grounds of the abbey to the guests' quarters.

'If there is anything you wish, call upon me or Sister Sinnchéne.'

He was turning to go when Fidelma stayed him.

'You will remember that Brother Eadulf will be conducting a search of the clothing in the washroom tomorrow?'

'I have not forgotten.'

'Nor that I shall be expecting the merchant, Mugrón, at the abbey tomorrow in the morning.'

'Neither have I forgotten that, lady.'

'Excellent.' Fidelma smiled. 'Then first thing in the morning, I would like to talk to you while we await Mugrón's arrival.'

Brother Cú Mara looked surprised.

'Me, lady?'

'I need your advice as the *rechtaire*.'

'Of course.' The young man was puzzled but acknowledged her request. 'I shall be at your service.'

* * *

The morning service was over. The bell denoting the end of prayers had scarcely ceased to toll before the community of the entire abbey became a hive of activity as the religious dispersed to their individual tasks. Some had gone to tend the herds of cattle and flocks of sheep, others to the herb gardens or to the fields, although there was little to do in the freezing wasteland at this time of year. Even during the more clement weather the crops were not bountiful in this open stretch of coastland where the winds off the great western sea were so fierce and constant. Other members of the community departed to the libraries – the scriptors, the artists, the researchers and the students.

Brother Eadulf, with the two warriors who had accompanied Conrí, had set off to the *tech-nigid*. Conrí, wanting to be active, had volunteered to ride south along the road to meet Mugrón the merchant and escort him to the abbey.

Seizing the quiet time that ensued, Fidelma accompanied Brother Cú Mara to a corner of the herb garden where they could speak without being overheard.

'Last night you said that you needed my advice, lady,' the young man said, as they seated themselves on a wooden bench in a sheltered corner.

'I did,' agreed Fidelma. She paused to make herself comfortable. 'I think that you wanted to tell me something about Sister Buan but were dissuaded by the presence of the abbot. Is it not so?'

The young steward flushed and seemed to hesitate. 'I suppose I was about to say that Sister Buan was more than the Venerable Cináed's companion.'

Fidelma gazed at him with interest. 'In what sense are you speaking?'

'As in male and female,' he said as if in embarrassment.

'Does that cause some concern? Is that not a normal relationship for men and women to follow?'

'Oh, truly.'

'Is not this abbey a *conhospitae*, a mixed house in which male and female live together working for the glory of God and where their children are raised to that ideal? Mind you, I have not seen many children here.'

'It is so. We are a *conhospitae*. However, children are not encouraged here and there are some who . . .' Brother Cú Mara hesitated.

'Who would welcome these new ideas of celibacy coming from Rome?' ended Fidelma.

'Indeed. The Venerable Mac Faosma, for example, since he arrived here has been a vociferous advocate of the idea of celibacy. He would have all the females expelled from here and the abbey given over to being solely a male house.'

'I see. Does that meet with the approval of the Abbot Erc?'

The *rechtaire* grinned cynically. 'Since the Venerable Mac Faosma came here, things have changed.'

'So the arguments of Mac Faosma are clearly heeded by the abbot?'

'Oh, there are many who support the argument for celibacy within the abbey.'

'But the Venerable Cináed did not?'

'He did not and could quote from the holy writings, chapter and verse, to support his contention that the religious life was never meant to deny people what he described as that basic part of their humanity.'

'That must have brought forth some response from the Venerable Mac Faosma?'

'Indeed, it did. His words were quite violent and . . . oh!'

The young man raised a hand to his mouth and looked shocked at the admission he had made.

Fidelma did not comment. 'I presume that Abbot Erc was well aware of their conflict?'

Brother Cú Mara nodded unhappily.

Fidelma sighed. 'It seems our inquiry begins to show that poor Cináed was not so universally loved as it was first claimed. He had a fierce antagonist and that antagonist had supporters in this abbey.'

'But it was merely a conflict of ideas – celibacy versus non-celibacy. That has been debated within many communities and at many times.'

'True enough,' agreed Fidelma. 'However, to begin to see the garden one must clear away the weeds.'

Brother Cú Mara looked bewildered.

'I don't follow.'

'It is of no consequence. Your information is most useful. Is there anything else that I should have been informed about?'

The young steward continued to look puzzled.

Sister Fidelma unbent.

'Last night we were asking about people who nurtured possible enmity against the Venerable Cináed. We are at first informed that everyone loved him. Little by little we learn that the Venerable Mac Faosma was his scholastic enemy and used violent words against him. Not just that, but that the Venerable Mac Faosma had a following. Were they equally violent towards the Venerable Cináed? Were there others who displayed hostility to him?'

Brother Cú Mara shrugged.

'I do not think that the Venerable Mac Faosma or any of his supporters would go so far as—'

Fidelma made a quick cutting motion with her hand.

'Perhaps that is for me to decide . . . once I am given the relevant information.'

The young steward shook his head.

'I have only heard cross words exchanged between them during their debates. Although I have heard the Venerable Mac Faosma berating Sister Buan in private for her relationship with Cináed.'

Fidelma closed her eyes for a moment.

'You told me last night that you knew Cináed well. How long have you been *rechtaire* of the abbey?'

'Less than a year.' The words seemed to be an admission of some guilty secret.

'That is not long,' Fidelma observed gently. 'And before you became steward?'

'I was a scribe.' Now the words were defensive and the young man had coloured again.

'I see. Did you work for Cináed in the library? Were you his copyist?'

Brother Cú Mara hesitated.

'Brother Faolchair, the assistant librarian, always copied the Venerable Cináed's works. I was only promoted to being a scribe when the Venerable Mac Faosma came to the abbey. I worked under his direction.'

There was a brief silence.

'So? Are you one of the supporters of the Venerable Mac Faosma?'

Brother Cú Mara raised his chin defensively.

'As steward I am above such things . . .'

'But during the time the Venerable Mac Faosma was your superior, you being his scribe, you must have had some sympathy with his ideas?' pressed Fidelma quickly.

The young man raised his hands helplessly.

'I . . . I was impressed by what the Venerable Mac Faosma had to say. I'll not deny that.'

'Did you ever enter the arguments . . . the debates, that is . . . between Mac Faosma and Cináed?'

'I attended them, that is all. And, no, I did not harbour any angry thoughts, towards the Venerable Cináed, that is. We are all entitled to our opinions but in the end truth will always prevail without our help.'

Fidelma smiled quickly.

'So, other than your inwardly held beliefs that Cináed was wrong in his outlook and teachings . . . ?'

'I harboured no ill will towards him.'

'And as *rechtaire* do you declare your stand, that you favour the new ideas of Rome?'

'I do not!' The words came indignantly. 'As steward, holding a high office in the abbey, my beliefs should not be an influence on the others . . .' He paused a moment, his lips pressed tightly together.

'So where do you stand on this matter of celibacy?'

The young man flushed.

'As I said, I am the steward of the abbey. I have to be independent.'

'That is a hard thing to be on such a matter,' Fidelma pointed out. 'Did the Venerable Cináed know your views? Your real views?'

'I told you, I keep my views to myself. They are no concern of others. However, if you must know, I support Abbot Erc. That doesn't mean that I killed Cináed, if that is what you are implying.'

The young man had risen to his feet but Fidelma regarded him with a mild smile.

'You wear your temper on the sleeve of your robe, Brother Cú Mara. I have not imputed anything but have simply asked you some questions. It is my task as a *dálaigh* to ask questions and it is your obligation to answer them. Now, be seated and calm yourself.'

Brother Cú Mara stood undecided for a moment or two and then he shrugged and sat down again.

'Excellent,' she approved. 'Now tell me, when did you first learn of the death of the Venerable Cináed?'

'When?' The young man frowned. 'It is now four days ago. It was before dawn. I had arisen and washed and was about to go to the chapel to attend the service for the Blessed Íte, which we hold on her feast day. She it was who—'

Fidelma interrupted impatiently. 'I know who Íte was. Go on.'

'I was on my way there when one of the community came rushing up saying that he had heard shouting from the oratory.'

'Shouting? As in an argument?'

'Someone crying for help. It turned out to be the abbot, for I went there without delay and found the abbot in great distress. He had discovered the body of the Venerable Cináed lying behind the altar and the rest you know. I helped carry the body to the physician. We then learnt that the old man had been murdered and the method – a blow on the back of the skull. The body was laid out and waked for the required day and night and then at midnight on the next day we buried Cináed in the graveyard behind the abbey.'

'I see. As *rechtaire*, what steps did you undertake to investigate the crime?'

The young man looked uncomfortable.

'I am not a *dálaigh* like you, lady.' The words were uttered as a protest.

'So you did nothing?'

'On the contrary. I asked the members of the community if anyone knew anything.'

'They did not, of course?' Fidelma said cynically.

'They did not. It was generally agreed that some wandering bandit probably entered the abbey grounds and was discovered by Cináed who then paid with his life for attempting to stop the thief.'

'Having obliged his assailant by turning his back to him?'

The young man did not understand Fidelma's sarcasm and said so.

'By whom was it generally agreed?' pressed Fidelma, ignoring his remark.

'By the elders of the community.'

'Being the abbot . . . and who else?'

'The Venerable Mac Faosma, Brother Eolas the librarian, our physician . . .'

'Was anything stolen by these wandering bandits?' interrupted Fidelma.

'Stolen?'

Fidelma felt the young man was being deliberately obtuse.

'Presumably, in your oratory, you would have icons and items worthy of theft? Why else would this hypothetical thief break into the abbey?'

The young steward paused a moment and then shook his head.

'Nothing was taken. The oratory was searched for a weapon. It was not found, showing that the murderer took it away with him.'

'So much for the theory of the thief,' Fidelma observed coldly.

Before Brother Cú Mara could respond, Eadulf emerged at the entrance of the herb garden, hurrying towards them with a triumphant expression. He bore a bundle of clothing in his arms.

'Success!' he cried.

He held out two robes. They both bore the unmistakable dark patches of bloodstains.

CHAPTER FOUR

Fidelma rose from the bench to examine the bloodstained robes that Eadulf held out to her.

'Indeed, it is dried blood and splattered in such quantity that the wearer must have bled profusely or been in contact with someone whose blood has drenched their clothing.' She gave an appreciative look at Eadulf. 'Well done. Now, is there a way of finding out the identity of the wearer?'

Brother Cú Mara was staring at the clothes with a curious frown.

'Did you not ask Sister Sinnchéne?' he inquired. 'She is very particular about the washing and would not mix such stained garments with the other clothing for wash.'

Eadulf looked a little crestfallen.

'I was so agitated by the discovery that I came straightway to inform you, Fidelma. Sister Sinnchéne was not in the *tech-nigid* when I discovered them and so I did not think to ask. They were certainly in a pile set to one side,' he added defensively to the young steward.

Fidelma reached out a hand to touch Eadulf's arm.

'Go now and repair the omission. Seek the identity of

the wearer of these garments but do not approach them until I am ready. I see,' she glanced across the herb garden, 'Conrí has returned and that must be the merchant with him. I will deal with him and then we will pursue the wearer of these clothes.'

A little downcast, for he realised that he should have discovered the information before coming to Fidelma, Eadulf nodded and went back to the *tech-nigid*.

Fidelma turned to watch Conrí approaching with his companion.

Mugrón looked more like a sailor than a merchant. He was a stocky man, barrel-chested and walking, arms akimbo, with the rolling gait of someone more used to being on the swaying deck of a ship than terra firma. He had large hands, sturdy legs, a short neck and a round, florid face set with dark hair that was beginning to streak with silver. His eyes were of a fathomless blue, almost violet.

'Greetings, Fidelma of Cashel. We have met before.' He had a deep, rasping voice.

Fidelma frowned, searching her memory but gave up with a shake of her head.

'I do not recall . . .' she began.

The merchant interrupted with a smile.

'You would not. You were a little girl. I was a young merchant, sailing my ship up the River Siur to the trading post that serves Cashel. Máenach mac Fíngin was king at that time. You and your brother had come down to the quay to see my boat come in.'

Memory came back to her. Her father, King Failbe Flann, had died when she was a baby. She had little memory of her father's successor, King Cuán, who had also died when she was four or five years of age. But Máenach had been king during most of her childhood until she had been sent away to study under the great Brehon Morann at Tara. She and her brother Colgú had looked upon Máenach as a kindly uncle for he was certainly, in their eyes, old enough to be so, although he was actually their first cousin. He had been the son of Fingín, the elder brother of their father Failbe Flann. He had looked after Fidelma and Colgú well, ensuring that they were properly educated. He had died two years before she had set out for the great Synod at Hilda's Abbey in Northumbria, and another cousin, Cathal, had taken the throne until he died of the Yellow Plague. Máenach had been the only relative that she could think of in terms of what it must have been like to have a father. And she did remember playing along the banks of the great Siur with her brother and watching the trading boats coming up and down the river.

'Lady?'

She started and guiltily realised that she had drifted off into the world of her remembrance. She brought herself back to the herb garden and to the gaze of the stocky merchant and Conrí. It was Brother Cú Mara who had spoken.

'I am sorry,' she said. 'I was trying to recall something, but no matter. Come, let us sit awhile, Mugrón. I want you to tell me the story of how you came to find the body of the Abbess Faife.'

She and the merchant seated themselves on the wooden bench while Conrí and the steward took up positions nearby.

'It was purely by accident,' the merchant began and then hesitated. 'I am not sure where to start.'

Fidelma smiled encouragement.

'Let us start with how you came to be on that road in the land of the Corco Duibhne.'

The merchant paused for a moment as if to gather his thoughts.

'As you have probably been told, I am the main merchant in this area and dwell on the coast to the south-west of here.'

'I have been told,' confirmed Fidelma solemnly.

'I have several ships and we do good business along this coast and often have commissions to supply goods to the abbeys.' He paused again. 'Several weeks ago, I set out to trade some goods with the Corco Duibhne. I deal regularly with them.'

'You set out on foot?'

Mugrón shook his head.

'The easiest way to transport goods is a short sail from the port of An Bhearbha across the great inlet to the peninsula, which is their territory. In good weather it is a simple run due west, then around a finger of land that pokes up from the peninsula to a group of islands, through these and round into Bréanainn's Bay. There is a good landing in the bay and that is where many of the merchants of the Corco Duibhne gather. Also it is not a hard climb into the mountains, to Bréanainn's mount where this abbey keeps a small community at the very spot where the founder—'

'I know of Bréanainn's mount,' interrupted Fidelma, suppressing a sigh of restlessness. 'So you went to Bréanainn's Bay on the north side of the peninsula by ship to trade. How was it that you were later on foot on the south side of the peninsula heading eastward away from your ship?' She hesitated as another thought occurred to her. 'How was it that the Abbess Faife did not take her charges by this quicker and easier route to Bréanainn's mount? Why, in the midwinter snows, was she taking her charges on foot on what was surely the longest way to her objective?'

Brother Cú Mara coughed awkwardly.

'If I might remind you, lady? There were two good reasons. One reason being that her first goal was the abbey of Colmán where she had business. It is easier to get there on foot from Ard Fhearta. But she always followed the original route of the Blessed Bréanainn on his journey to the mountain—'

'Of course, of course,' cut in Fidelma sharply. 'I had forgotten that point for a moment. But it still does not explain why you, Mugrón, should have abandoned your ship for such an arduous route home?'

Mugrón was smiling broadly.

'As I said, lady, there is no quicker route with fair weather and a westerly wind to bring you from the great bay back to my safe little harbour here. The journey there was fine enough. We had a good breeze blowing off the coast from the east and there were no problems. But not long after we landed and were exchanging cargoes, the winds rose, the snows came down and we were forced to seek shelter close inshore. I had business that would not wait and so I negotiated for a fine horse from a local trader. I left my ship, telling my crew to wait until the weather improved before setting out to return here.

'I took the route south-west through the mountains to pay my respects to Slébéne, the chieftain of the Corco Duibhne, at his fortress of Daingean. It did not put me out of my way. I could also proceed to the abbey of Colmán and conclude some other business. Then the ride home would be easy.'

'I see. Go on.'

Mugrón massaged his forehead with his fingertips for a moment.

'Perhaps I should tell you that Brother Maidíu, who is

in charge of the community on Bréanainn's mount, had come down to see me at the ship. We carried supplies for him.'

'And?'

'He told me that he was worried as he had been expecting the Abbess Faife and some of her companions. It was the first time that she had not turned up on the day they usually celebrated the enlightenment of the Blessed Bréanainn on the mountain.'

'So she was already overdue?'

'She was.'

Fidelma turned to the young steward.

'How many are there in this community under Brother Maidíu?'

Brother Cú Mara smiled.

'To call it a community is merely to flatter it, lady. He has no more than three or four Brothers of the Faith who reside on the mountain all year round. It is a cold and harsh environment and only suitable for those who have a vocation for the life.'

'I see.' She returned to the merchant. 'I am sorry. Please continue.'

'When I had made my mind up to continue on horseback, I told Brother Maidíu that I would look out for Abbess Faife along the road as I was sure that she was on the way but had probably been caught up and delayed by the snows.'

He paused, as if to gather his thoughts again.

'I left the fortress, An Daingean, and rode along the south coast road eastward towards the abbey of Colmán. It is a long straight track with mountains on one side and the sea's great inlet on the other. On a pleasant, dry day, it is an easy ride. The abbey of Colmán lies about thirty-five or so kilometres from Daingean. I was confident of reaching there before nightfall. The wind was from the south-west, so it was, thanks be, at my back, but the snow was falling thickly and it was causing drifts. I was feeling quite exhausted when I reached the place that is called simply the Island, where, until a short time ago, Uaman, Lord of the Passes, had his fortress. It is in blackened ruins now for the people rose up against him—'

Fidelma nodded quickly.

'We have heard the story,' she said. 'What happened?'

'Near there is a disused *coirceogach*, a round stone hut, where I have sheltered several times. I thought that I would rest again and try to dry my clothes, keeping out of the snow for a while, rather than press on the remaining distance to the abbey. I had no difficulty locating the place despite the drifting snow, for I had the position of Uaman's Island to guide me.'

'The *coirceogach* is easy to find,' added Conrí.

'What was your first impression?' queried Fidelma. 'Were there any signs of disturbance around that you noticed?'

The merchant shook his head.

'Don't forget, lady, the snow was coming thick and fast. I saw nothing but a white blanket across the ground. I tried to pull my horse into the shelter of some trees and made towards the entrance of the *coirceogach*. I was aware that I had trodden on something that did not feel right. I don't know how else to explain it. But it was not hard like ground or rock and when I looked down I saw there was something dark beneath the snow. I scraped away and realised it was a body.'

He paused and passed a hand over his forehead as if to wipe it.

'My first thought was to rebury it but . . . but then I

realised that it was an odd place to bury a body, just under a layer of snow. My curiosity got the better of me and I removed more snow to see if I could discover any reason for this. As I uncovered the features of the corpse I was horrified. I knew the Abbess Faife well. I saw that a terrible blade wound to her breast had killed her. For a while I stood not knowing what to do. Then I made up my mind. I removed the corpse and carried it behind the stone hut and reburied it under the snow, packing the snow tight.'

'Why did you do that?'

'My idea was to preserve the body as best I could. If I left it where it was, someone else might find it. My thought was then to hurry on to Ard Fhearta to report the matter for, as I say, it was clear that she had been murdered.'

'And you saw nothing else which would give any indication as to why she came by her death? No sign of what might have happened to her companions?'

Mugrón shook his head firmly.

'I was halfway to the abbey of Colmán when I realised about her companions,' he confessed. 'But there had been no sign of anyone else. As I have said, the snow lay thick on the ground. It had been snowing on and off for several days.'

'So there were no other bodies?'

'Not where I found that of the abbess.'

Fidelma looked at him sharply. 'Does that imply there were other bodies in the vicinity?'

Mugrón nodded. 'There must have been some wreck along the coast. There was fresh wreckage nearby, floating along the shore, and among it were one or two bodies. There was nothing I could do about them. Remember, I was alone.'

Fidelma sat back and was silent for a few moments. Then she asked: 'Your first intention was to enter the *coirceogach* and get dry. Did you go in at all?'

The merchant hesitated.

'I did, but only for a moment.'

'And there was nothing inside that presented you with any information as to what might have happened?'

'I saw that the fire had recently been used.' He frowned. 'There was some discarded clothing in a corner.'

Conrí nodded in agreement.

'The rags were still there when we returned. There was also a water-soaked boot by them.'

Fidelma raised an inquisitive face to the warlord of the Uí Fidgente.

'A boot?'

Instead of using the word *cuarán* for an ordinary shoe he had used the word *coisbert* for something larger.

'It was the sort of boot that a seaman might wear,' the merchant chimed in. 'But it was of foreign origin.'

Fidelma regarded him with interest.

'How do you know that?'

Mugrón smiled complacently.

'It is my trade, lady. If I did not know a native boot from a foreign one, I would be a poor merchant. This boot was one that I would expect to see in Gaul. In fact, I would say it was a type that many of the seamen of Armorica wear.'

'Are you certain?'

'When I returned with lord Conrí, we examined the clothes and the boot.'

'What did you do with them?'

'We left them in the hut.'

There was a silence as Fidelma considered the

information. After a while, she said: 'There is nothing else that you can tell me?'

'Nothing, lady.'

'Nothing that struck your mind about the scene that caused you any thought? Even if it was unrelated to the death of the abbess?'

The merchant was about to shake his head when he caught himself.

'There *was* something?' Fidelma pressed.

Mugrón shrugged. 'It was absolutely unrelated. I mentioned the wreckage of the ship and the bodies. A lot of ships have foundered around that coast. I just noticed that it looked very recent. The timbers that lay along the shore had not been discoloured. It was just a passing thought, no more. Then I went on.'

'I see,' Fidelma said thoughtfully. 'So it might be that your Gaulish boot might have come from a survivor of that wreck. A ship from Gaul.'

Mugrón responded only with a faint shrug.

'And all this occurred about ten days ago?' she asked.

'More like fifteen days now.'

Fidelma gave a soft sigh and sat back.

'Well, Mugrón, I will not detain you further. If I want to talk to you again how shall I find you? At this harbour of yours? An Bhearbha?'

'Ask anyone and they will direct you to me. But within a day or so, I have a cargo to run to Bréanainn's Bay.'

'Ah, then it may well be that I might need to book a passage on your vessel for my companions and myself.'

'You would be most welcome, lady.'

The burly merchant rose from the seat and bowed stiffly towards her. As he was turning to leave, Fidelma called softly: 'Oh, and Mugrón . . . my thanks for reminding me of a pleasant period in my life. My childhood on the banks of the River Siur. They were good times.'

The merchant answered with a smile and raised a hand in salutation before leaving the herb garden.

For some time Fidelma sat in silence, turning over in her mind the information that she had garnered.

Finally, an anxious clearing of his throat by Brother Cú Mara attracted her attention. She looked up and realised the steward and Conrí were waiting for her to speak.

'What now, lady?' Brother Cú Mara asked.

'What now, Brother?' She stood up. 'Now we shall go in search of Brother Eadulf and discover what he has found out about the bloodstained clothing.'

She quickly explained to Conrí about Eadulf's find in the washing house.

Brother Cú Mara led the way to the *tech-nigid*, a wooden structure conveniently sited next to a stream which gushed from a spring and made its way across the hillside on which the abbey buildings were distributed. As they approached, Eadulf was emerging with the bloodstained clothing in his arms.

'I have the names of the owners,' he said in triumph, as he saw them.

'Then let us have a word with them,' Fidelma replied.

'The first is Brother Feólaigid,' Eadulf said.

Brother Cú Mara guffawed immediately.

They turned on him with some astonishment.

'You seem amused, Brother,' Fidelma observed coldly. 'Is there some joke that can be shared with us?'

The young *rechtaire* did not lose his expression of amusement.

'I will take you to where Brother Feólaigid is working,' he said in a tone that held some inner mirth. Fidelma and Eadulf exchanged a look of mutual bewilderment and followed him, with Conrí bringing up the rear.

Brother Cú Mara led the way to a far corner of the abbey complex, to a building also alongside another of the numerous little streams that were to be found in this countryside. In construction it was rather like the *tech-nigid*. The doors stood wide open and as they approached Eadulf became aware of an odour he could not quite identify. There was a sound, too. It was halfway between someone chopping wood and the smack of something heavy on flesh.

'This is where Brother Feólaigid works,' the young steward said, this time scarcely able to conceal the mirth in his voice.

At the door, peering into the interior of the building, they saw a burly man with an axe, hewing at a carcass. Blood was everywhere. The carcass was that of a pig. The man was expertly reducing it to joints of meat. Around him, hanging on metal hooks, hung large joints and whole carcasses of more pigs and lambs.

'Brother Feólaigid is our butcher.' There was no disguising the amusement in Brother Cú Mara's voice. 'If there was no blood on his robes, it would be more of a mystery than otherwise.'

Fidelma turned with irritation on her face and was about to launch into a homily on the wasting of a *dálaigh*'s time. Then she glanced at Eadulf and the look on his face made her suddenly chuckle.

'Well, Brother,' she turned back to the *rechtaire*, 'you have had your little joke on us. But there is still another bloodstained robe to be accounted for.'

Eadulf was clearly irritated.

'Your brethren would seem to over-indulge in eating the flesh of animals,' he observed testily to the steward. 'Such indulgence in meat eating is frowned upon in Rome.'

The young *rechtaire*'s expression was smug.

'I have heard the Venerable Mac Faosma quote from an ancient book upon which our religion is founded and which the Greeks called "the beginning" – Genesis. In this holy book God tells Noah, "Every creature that lives and moves shall be food for you."'

Conrí, not really understanding the cause of Eadulf's ill-humour and believing him not to know the widespread practice of eating various meats in the country, added: 'The abbey has many people to sustain, Brother Eadulf. It has its own flocks of sheep, even cows to provide milk and occasional meat. The cook in this abbey is renowned throughout the lands of the Uí Fidgente for his *indrechtan* and *maróg*.'

Eadulf, who was just being surly and certainly had no real objection to meat eating, did not understand the words that Conrí used and said so.

It was Fidelma who explained.

'They are meat dishes in which the intestines of a pig, cow or sheep are stuffed with minced meat to which is added grain or diced apple. Then they are boiled and put aside until wanted. They are regarded as great delicacies in many parts of the country. Now let us not waste time. To whom does the other bloodstained robe belong?'

'Sister Uallann,' Eadulf replied.

Brother Cú Mara turned away and coughed several times as if to hide some urge to laugh. Fidelma waited impatiently while he recovered.

'Now take us to where this Sister Uallann works,' she snapped.

It was Conrí who answered.

'There will probably be as good a reason for Sister Uallann's robes to be bloodstained as there was for the robes of Brother Feólaigid,' he said quietly.

'Indeed?' said Fidelma defensively. 'Do you know this Sister Uallann?'

The warlord of the Uí Fidgente nodded.

'She is the physician of the abbey, lady. It was she who examined and prepared the corpse of my aunt, the Abbess Faife, when we brought it here for burial.'

Fidelma let out a long, low exasperated sigh.

'And doubtless did the same for the Venerable Cináed?'

Brother Cú Mara had regained his composure.

'Indeed, she did, lady. I am afraid the bloodstained clothing that Brother Eadulf has found will lead you nowhere.'

Eadulf was trying to hide his embarrassment.

'Does this abbey have a woman physician?'

'Do you not have women physicians among your own people?' demanded Conrí in amusement at the other's discomfiture. 'In ancient times, there was a cult of women who followed the teachings of Airmed, daughter of the old god of healing. She was said to be the first to identify all the healing herbs. We have always had female physicians.'

Eadulf, who had studied the apothecary's art for a time at Tuam Brecain, knew the fact well enough. His cheeks were crimson with mortification and he was merely doing his best to avoid Fidelma's censure. He should have inquired not only about the names of the owners of the garments but about their tasks in the abbey.

'You had better return the clothing to Sister Sinnchéne,' she told him. 'But I want to see this physician anyway, so we will speak to her now.'

Eadulf's mouth became a thin slit of anger as he departed back along the path to the *tech-nigid*.

Sober-faced now, Brother Cú Mara led the way along the path towards the main abbey buildings.

'Those are the quarters for the bachelors.' The *rechtaire* indicated one building with a gesture of his head. 'The married rooms are behind there and beyond are the quarters for the unmarried sisters.'

'Are there many people in this abbey?' inquired Fidelma.

'Scarcely more than five hundred souls,' Brother Cú Mara replied.

'It is surely enough,' Fidelma observed with surprise.

'We have heard that the great abbey at Ard Macha boasts the attendance of seven thousand students and then there are the members of the Faith who instruct them.'

Fidelma had passed through Ard Macha, which lay in the northern kingdom of the Uí Néill. She had been sent there to get instructions from Bishop Ultan on her way to the great council in Northumbria, and had found Ard Macha too crowded, too city-like and ostentatious for her. And, she had to confess, she was not impressed with Ultan, who seemed the product of his environment for he, too, was ostentatious and full of his own importance. As his abbey had been founded by the Blessed Patrick, who was now being claimed as the first preacher of the word of Christ in the five kingdoms, Ultan was seeking recognition as the Primate, the head of all the churches in the kingdoms. Violent arguments were springing up, especially from Imleach which the bishop and abbot pointed out had been founded by Ailbe, who had preached Christianity in the five kingdoms before Patrick, as had many others.

'Ard Macha should not be judged by the numbers of people who live there but by what it achieves in the manner of the lives of those it influences,' Fidelma said now.

Brother Cú Mara had paused before a stone building set slightly apart from the main structures of the abbey and indicated a door.

'This is the apothecary of Sister Uallann, lady.'

He tapped gently at the door.

A voice curtly bade them enter.

Inside the large room, the pungent scents of a hundred hanging herbs and plants was overwhelming, mixed as they were with an odour rising from a cauldron in which a strange-looking liquid was bubbling over a fire. Benches filled with amphorae, jugs and pots stretched round the room. Above one bench was a shelf containing several ageing manuscript books. At one end was a table made of a thick block of wood that was almost large enough for two people to lie down upon. Its stained and grooved surface showed to what use an apothecary could put it.

Nearby, at a smaller table, sat a woman with mortar and pestle, pounding something in the bowl.

She was almost masculine in facial appearance, with wispy dark hair, piercing blue eyes and ruddy skin. She had a large nose and a hint of moustache-like dark downy hair over her upper lip. It was hard to guess her age.

'Well?' she cried, her voice shrill, as she glanced up at them. 'I am busy. State your illness. I have little time.'

The young steward glanced apologetically at Fidelma.

'This is Sister Uallann, lady.' He turned to the physician. 'Sister Uallann, this is Fidelma of Cashel. She is the *dálaigh* come to investigate the deaths of the Abbess Faife and of the Venerable Cináed.'

Sister Uallann remained seated.

'Of Cashel? *Of* Cashel? Does she not know that the Uí Fidgente have no business with Cashel? We owe allegiance to Eoganán. We have no need for a Cashel *dálaigh*.'

Conrí coughed with embarrassment and moved forward.

'Sister Uallann, do you remember me? I am Conrí—'

The woman sighed pointedly and laid aside her mortar and pestle with a resounding thump on the table.

'Of course I know you, lord Conrí. Do you consider that I am senile?'

Conrí was embarrassed.

'Eoganán was killed at Cnoc Áine two years ago. The Uí Fidgente have pledged allegiance to Cashel now. Sister Fidelma is blood sister to Colgú, legitimate king of all Muman. She is the *dálaigh* we have asked to come to investigate the violent deaths of the Abbess Faife and the Venerable Cináed.'

Sister Uallann frowned and sat for a moment as if considering this.

'My husband is also dead. Dead by the design of Cashel. The Uí Fidgente are now at peace. Yet still there are violent deaths in the land.'

Fidelma moved forward and as she did so her feet crunched on something on the floor. She looked down to see several granular crystals.

'You seem to have spilt something, Sister Uallann.'

The physician glanced down and appeared embarrassed for a moment.

'It is nothing. I spilt a preparation.'

Fidelma noticed the crystals clung to the woollen arm of

Sister Uallan's robe and reached out to pluck off a few. She kept them in her hand, wondering what they were.

'I hope that whoever uses the preparation does not have to ingest it. These are as hard as little rocks.'

'What exactly is it that you want?' snapped Sister Uallann impatiently.

Fidelma sat down directly opposite the physician, dropping the granules on the floor.

'There are a few questions that I must ask you, Sister Uallann.'

The physician blinked and focused her pale eyes on Fidelma.

'I understand that you examined the body of Abbess Faife when it was returned here to Ard Fhearta.'

'That is so, that is so.'

'And then you prepared her body for burial?'

'Of course, of course.'

'Can you tell me anything about the manner of her death?'

The physician sniffed irritably.

'A wound made by a blade. Simple. Sharp. I would say such a wound would cause death instantaneously. Instantaneously.'

'You cannot say what caused the wound other than a blade?'

'I will say that it was either a sword or a broad dagger. It would be the weapon of a warrior.'

Fidelma raised her eyebrows slightly.

'Why do you specify a warrior?'

'Because of the sharpness of the blade and its cleanness. Only a warrior tends to keep his blade sharp and clean. That it was sharp and clean is certain from the nature of the wound it inflicted.'

'It is a logical conclusion,' agreed Fidelma.

'The body had begun to decay but not much because of the cold. It had been lying in snow and ice, I think, and that had slowed the decaying process. So the marks of the wound were clear and the thrust was delivered downwards. Yes, downwards.'

Again, Fidelma was amazed at this senescent physician's ability to be certain.

'How do you deduce that?'

'The nature of the wound, the angle of its entry into the breast. I have been treating battle wounds for many years. I know about sword and dagger wounds. I would say that Abbess Faife must have been kneeling on the ground or her assailant was on horseback and she afoot.'

Fidelma paused for a moment digesting the information.

'Very well. Did you notice anything else which might give a clue as to the assailant?'

Sister Uallann shook her head.

'Now let us come to the death of the Venerable Cináed,' Fidelma went on. 'You examined his body and prepared it for burial.'

'That was only a few days ago,' said the physician petulantly.

'But the cause of his death was . . . ?'

Sister Uallann glanced at her in surprise.

'I would have thought that you would already be aware of that?'

'I need to hear it officially from the physician who examined him.'

'He died instantly from a heavy blow on the back of his skull which smashed the bone and shattered it so that fragments pierced the brain.'

'Just one wound?'

'One blow. There was no need for more.'

'After that blow, are you saying that he could not have moved?'

Sister Uallann stared at her as if in pity.

'If you believe a dead man can move, then he was capable of movement,' she snapped sarcastically.

'I am trying to clarify the facts,' replied Fidelma evenly. 'The blow was struck from behind with such a force that it shattered his skull, is that right?'

'I have said so.'

'But the body was found lying on its back.'

Sister Uallann was not perturbed.

'Then it is surely logical that, after the blow was struck, the killer turned it over on its back.'

'Clearly logical,' Fidelma smiled thinly, 'but it would be a poor *dálaigh* who does not consult the physician to seek verification of the medical logic. I presume that you knew the Venerable Cináed well?'

'Well enough.' It was said in a truculent manner.

'Would you say that you were a close friend of his?'

'Not close. I respected some of his arguments. He was, after all, a careful scholar. Yet I did not agree with his fundamental attitudes.'

'About the Faith?'

To her surprise Sister Uallann shook her head.

'I did not like his essay *Scripta quae ad remplicum geredam pertinent* – his writings on how the Uí Fidgente should govern their temporal lives. Cináed had views on everything. Those views angered many people. Eoganán, when he was king of the Uí Fidgente, sent his warriors to seize Cináed but Abbess Faife, who was in control of the abbey in Abbot Erc's temporary absence, refused to hand him over.'

Brother Cú Mara intervened.

'I have heard the story. It happened just before the defeat at Cnoc Áine where Eoganán was killed. Had Eoganán been victorious, I don't doubt that he would have sent his warriors back to the abbey to seize Cináed whether the abbess protested or not.'

'Did Abbot Erc support the abbess in her refusal to hand the Venerable Cináed over?' asked Fidelma.

The physician sniffed. 'By the time he returned, there was no need to make a decision one way or another. Eoganán was defeated at Cnoc Áine. That was where my husband was slain, too,' Sister Uallann added pointedly. 'There are many here whose husbands were slaughtered by the Eoghanacht.'

Fidelma turned to Brother Cú Mara and spoke in a slightly sarcastic tone.

'So, far from the Venerable Cináed being a scholar beloved by everyone, we now find out that he had many enemies. Not least, the supporters of the late Eoganán!'

'Ah, poor Eoganán!' Sister Uallann exclaimed in a whisper.

Fidelma turned quickly back to her.

'You have made clear your views, Sister. You believe that your people should not have made peace with Cashel?'

To her surprise, the physician shook her head.

'I am of the Corco Duibhne but my husband was Uí Fidgente.'

'And you are saying that the Venerable Cináed made enemies among the Uí Fidgente because of his political writings?'

'We dwell in the territory of the Uí Fidgente but Cináed believed, even before the disaster at Cnoc Áine, that we should owe allegiance to the Eoghanacht of Cashel and not to our own rulers.' She stopped, eyes narrowing suddenly. 'I have said enough.'

Fidelma sat for a few moments staring at the grim-faced physician and then she stood up.

'I am grateful for what you have said, Sister Uallann,' she said quietly.

Outside they found Eadulf, having returned from the *technigid*, looking for them. Eadulf was about to ask how Fidelma had fared when he caught the warning look on her face. She turned to Brother Cú Mara.

'All I need ask you is to guide us to your *tech-screptra*, then we shan't need your assistance until after the *etar-suth*.' She used the term 'middle fruits' which was the more popular name in monastic foundations for the *etar-shod* or 'middle meal' of the day.

'The library?' queried the *rechtaire* with a frown.

'That is what I said. I need a word with Brother Eolas, your librarian.' Fidelma added to Eadulf, 'I think there may be some important information that we could find there.'

CHAPTER FIVE

Even Eadulf was impressed by the size of the *tech-screptra*, the great library of Ard Fhearta. He knew of the fame of the Irish ecclesiastical colleges for learning. That meant that each one had need for books for students and therefore they had good general libraries. He had seen that these libraries contained not only works in the native language but books in Latin, Greek and Hebrew. As he followed Fidelma into the room he paused in astonishment at the rows and rows of racks with their pegs from which hung leather book satchels, the *tiaga liubhair* which not only were employed to carry books from place to place, being slung from the shoulder by one or more straps, but provided an excellent means of keeping the books in good condition in the libraries. Eadulf estimated that there were many hundreds, hanging along the racks.

There were also shelves on which stood many obviously valued volumes in elaborately wrought and beautifully orna-mented leather covers, some of which were kept in *lebor chomet* or book holders made partly or wholly of metals. Eadulf had noticed that special books were kept in very ornate and valuable metal and wood boxes, which were piously called book shrines. The *tech-screptra* had several of these set to one side.

In the centre of the library was a row of desks occupied by the copyists and scribes. Each had a wooden chair and a desk of yew wood, a plinth topped by a frame on which the book or manuscript page rested. A maulstick was used to steady the hand of the copyist. Half a dozen men now bent to their task using quills from geese or swans and writing on vellum or parchment. Other scholars, simply researching from the books, were using the standard writing tablets, wooden frames in which melted wax had been allowed to set. These could then be a temporary means of making notes with a *raibh*, a sharp-pointed stylus of metal. After the notes had been used, or transcribed into the vellum books, the wax could be melted again and remoulded into the tablet to be used again.

A round-shouldered man, his arms folded before him in the sleeves of his robe, came shuffling forward as they entered. He seemed smaller than he actually was because of his hunched appearance. It was obviously the product of many years bent to his literary endeavours. He peered from one to another.

'I am the *leabhar coimedach*,' he intoned in a whisper. 'How can I be of service?'

'I am Fidelma of—'

'The *dálaigh* from Cashel?' interrupted the librarian, still whispering. 'You are most welcome, lady. I saw you and your companion, Brother Eadulf, at the evening prayers yesterday. I know why you are here. The *tech-screptra* is at your disposal.'

'Thank you. I take it that you are Brother Eolas?' When

the man bowed his head in acknowledgement of the fact, she went on, 'I am interested in the works of the Venerable Cináed.'

'The Venerable Cináed? Come this way.' He led them to a corner of the library. 'This is the section of original books and writings made by our brethren. We have had many scholars who have contributed to our library during the many decades of our history. See, there, that book contains the hymns of Colmán moccu Clusaig who stayed here during the year of the Yellow Plague. He wrote many of his hymns here, including *Sén Dé*, the Blessing of God. Our master of song, Brother Cillín, became a great friend of Colmán. If you have an interest in music, you must speak to Brother Cillín about his own songs before you leave. And in that volume,' pointing, 'we have some letters which the abbot of Iona, Cuimine Ailbhe, wrote to the Venerable Cináed arguing about the dating of the Cásc.' He glanced at Eadulf. 'You Saxons call it Easter. I believe you insist on retaining the feast of your goddess of fertility?' There was disapproval in his voice. 'Abbot Cuimine has accepted the new dating that Rome has adopted. However, like many of our great scholars, the Venerable Cináed disagreed with him and believed that Rome was wrong in its calculations. But Abbot Cuimine Ailbhe remained a friend of the Venerable Cináed and sent him his own work *De Poententiarum Mensura* as a gift which is now in the book shrine there' – he gestured to it – 'as one of the great works we hold and—'

'But the works of the Venerable Cináed themselves . . .' Fidelma interrupted, trying not to show her impatience. After all, librarians always tended to be boastful of the works they held in their libraries.

'Of course,' Brother Eolas replied, a little crestfallen.

'Here they are.' He indicated a shelf and picked up a writing tablet. 'In fact, I have been making a catalogue of his works here.'

Eadulf glanced at the tablet. 'It seems a rather long list.'

Brother Eolas smiled in satisfaction. 'The Venerable Cináed was one of our best scholars. He had many interests. I think that you would call him eclectic. He even wrote a discourse entitled *De ars sordida gemmae*, denouncing the local trade in precious stones, which he handed to Brother Faolchair to copy just a short time before his death. But his *Disputatius Computus Cummianus* is a classic and—'

'And *De Trinitate Interpretatio Perversa*?' Eadulf asked.

The librarian looked a little shocked. 'You have read that?'

'I know people who have,' admitted Eadulf truthfully, trying not to look at Fidelma.

'It is not well liked in some quarters of this abbey,' the librarian said shortly. 'He wrote far better things. His poems in our native tongue, for example, and his setting down of some of our old tales and historic traditions are regarded as excellent and—'

'What of his *Scripta quae ad rempublicum geredam pertinent*?' Fidelma asked sharply.

Brother Eolas gave a shake of his head.

'You appear to be interested in his most controversial works. Ah well, we have them all here but, while the Venerable Cináed had his followers, he also had his enemies as well.'

'So we have now begun to learn,' Fidelma agreed. 'Do you have any thoughts as to why he should have been murdered?'

The librarian looked shocked.

'Are you implying that . . . that he was killed by someone who did not like what he wrote? That is ridiculous. In this land scholars are treated with respect even when they are in dispute with others. Each has the right to speak their mind freely, to write their thoughts and discuss ideas without rancour, as have others to disagree whether in private or in public. Learning is not a matter to kill over.'

'There is nothing that instils deep rage so much as a scholar's views,' pointed out Fidelma. It was something her mentor, Brehon Morann, used to say.

'I refuse to believe that,' replied Brother Eolas.

'Never mind. Let us get down to the task in hand. I would like to read this work on government by the Venerable Cináed. Where is it?'

Brother Eolas consulted his wax tablet and turned to the shelf.

'It should be along here . . .'

He paused and frowned. Then he checked again.

'It seems to be missing. And another of his works is not here.'

'Missing?' Fidelma used the word so sharply that several of the scholars in the library looked up to see what was amiss.

Brother Eolas frowned in admonition at her and raised a finger to his lips. Then he turned and waved to a youth who was carrying a pile of vellum to a scribe on the far side of the library. He caught the boy's attention. The boy deposited his burden with the scribe before turning to join them. He was young and eager, no more than fifteen or sixteen years old.

'Brother Faolchair, two of our books are missing.' He

pointed to the spaces. 'They should be on the shelf there but they are not. Who has taken them?'

The boy looked at the titles that his superior indicated.

'The one on trading precious stones is the one I have for copying. The other has been taken from the library, Brother Eolas.'

The librarian's eyebrows shot up.

'Taken from . . .' he began. 'How can this be? Only the abbot and . . . Who has taken it?'

'The Venerable Mac Faosma sent Brother Benen for it yesterday morning. He has the authority to do so, Brother Eolas.'

The librarian paused and then shrugged.

'Very well. Be about your duties.' The boy hesitated, looking anxious. The librarian relented. 'You are right, Brother Faolchair. He does have the authority to take the book out of the *tech-screptra*.' He waved the youth back to his work before turning to Fidelma to explain. 'In normal circumstances, no one is allowed to borrow books from the library. They are only allowed to sit here and read them. There were three exceptions . . . well, three until the death of the Venerable Cináed . . .'

'So the abbot and the Venerable Mac Faosma can remove books from the library?'

'Just so.'

'So if we want to see this book we should go to the chamber of the Venerable Mac Faosma?'

The librarian looked a little awkward. 'He is reclusive and does not receive visitors.'

Eadulf chuckled. 'From what I hear, the man is not reclusive enough to refuse to take part in scholastic debates in front of hundreds of students.'

'Taking part in a debate on a platform is not the same thing as receiving people in intimate surroundings,' stated the librarian.

'It is a fine point that you are making. Is the behaviour of this man so strange?' Eadulf smiled.

The librarian shrugged. 'Let me say that all great men are entitled to peculiarities.'

'And the Venerable Mac Faosma is, in your estimation, a great man?' Eadulf asked pointedly.

Fidelma gave a warning glance at him before smiling at the librarian.

'We are grateful for your help and may seek it again. You have a great library here, Brother Eolas, and I hope that we may have time to spend a while viewing your magnificent treasures.'

Brother Eolas gave a half-bow, trying to appear dignified, but it was clear that her words gave him pleasure.

Outside, she turned to Eadulf.

'No need to annoy the librarian, Eadulf. But I have been thinking that we should call on the Venerable Mac Faosma. We will wait until this afternoon.'

'What of the business of the Abbess Faife?' inquired Eadulf. 'After all, that is what has brought us here.'

'I am not neglecting that,' she assured him. 'But the trail that led to her death is a fortnight old while the death of the Venerable Cináed is still fairly fresh. I thought we could spend another day here and then set out to see what leads we could pick up in the land of the Corco Duibhne.'

'But surely there are no obvious connections between the two deaths?'

Fidelma grimaced. 'There is the connection that Abbess Faife and the Venerable Cináed were both well-respected and important members of the same religious house. And it seems they shared a similar political outlook about the future of the Uí Fidgente. Coincidences happen, but not often.'

Eadulf shrugged as if dismissing the point.

'That does not mean a connection between their deaths. The abbess was travelling outside the abbey while Cináed was an elderly scholar still within its walls. One was slain by a sword stroke and the other was hit over the head. Now what connection can there be?'

'As you say, there are no obvious connections.' Fidelma put a slight emphasis on the word 'obvious'.

'You sound as though you think there is a connection?' Eadulf pressed.

'I have told you before, you cannot make suppositions without facts. For the moment, I want to see what it was that Cináed wrote to upset people in this abbey and which may . . . I say, *may* . . . have led to his death.'

Eadulf slowly shook his head.

'Every time I come to this western part of your brother's kingdom, it is always the Uí Fidgente behind all the mischief.'

'But with Conrí as their warlord, they have become calmer. The defeat of Eoganán at Cnoc Áine has caused them to settle down. It is only the people who have been marked by the conflict who yearn for the past.'

'Remind me again, what is the basis of the quarrel between the Uí Fidgente and your family, the Eoghanacht?'

Fidelma took him by the arm, for they had been standing outside the door of the *tech-screptra*, and led him towards the *hospitium*. She explained as they walked.

'It goes back some generations. The Uí Fidgente claimed admittance to the councils of Cashel and claimed the kingship. Needles to say, they were rejected, and since then until the time of Eoganán they have intrigued and plotted and several times risen up against the Eoghanacht of Cashel.'

'I understand that,' agreed Eadulf. 'But from what I know of your laws of inheritance, I cannot understand how they can claim the kingship, which descends only through the Eoghanacht. I am aware of this business about the council, or what you call the *derbhfine*, having to elect the best man out of the extended family to the kingship. I know that there is no such thing as automatic inheritance by the eldest son as is our system in the Saxon lands. But I still cannot see the basis of their claim.'

'Simple enough,' replied Fidelma. 'All the branches of the Eoghanacht trace their descent back to Eoghan Mór, the greatest king of Cashel, son of Ailill Olum, son of Mug Nuadat. That is why we are called Eoghanacht. However, the Uí Fidgente, when they sought entry to the council, made the claim that they had a better right to the throne at Cashel than the descendants of Eoghan Mór. The Uí Fidgente claimed that they were descended from the elder brother of Eoghan Mór, who was called Cormac Cas. Some had taken to calling themselves the Dál gCais, the descendants of Cas. This argument and the spurious genealogies that they have persuaded their bards to construct were discussed many years ago by the council at Cashel and dismissed for what they were – fakes. It was agreed by the most learned in the kingdom, with the High King and the Chief Brehon of the five kingdoms acting as unbiased arbiters, that the Uí Fidgente were descendants of the Dáirine, a southern tribe not related to the Eoghanacht at all.'

'I see. But if all this was agreed generations ago, why is there such conflict between your peoples?'

'Because the Uí Fidgente have never accepted the judgement that was given against them. Not even those who have made peace with Cashel have accepted that ruling. They mean to topple the Eoghanacht from power. Until now the Uí Fidgente have not submitted to paying tax without threat of force. They have not allowed any representative of the Eoghanacht into their lands. That is why I have tried to convince you that it was so important to come here when Conrí actually came to Cashel to ask for our help. This could break through the antagonisms, as we have wanted. It could be the first real step to uniting the kingdom under Cashel.'

Eadulf sighed softly.

'I think I begin to understand. It is hard for me, however, to appreciate all the nuances of the intrigues that go on here.'

Fidelma looked sympathetically at him.

'Well,' she said, as a bell began to toll, 'that is something that it is not hard to understand. The bell for the *etar-suth* – the midday meal. Come, we can leave this talk of intrigue until later.'

CHAPTER SIX

The sturdy young brother stood with his arms folded outside the chamber of the Venerable Mac Faosma, his back against the door, barring their progress.

'He has given instructions that he will not see you, Sister,' the young man said stubbornly. He had identified himself as Brother Benen, the student and servant of the ageing scholar.

Fidelma began to tap her foot impatiently.

'I am not here to argue, Brother Benen. Tell the Venerable Mac Faosma that he has no choice under law for I am not here as a religieuse but as a *dálaigh* investigating the crime of murder. I should not have to remind him that he is compelled to obey the law.'

The young man spread his arms helplessly.

'I have already taken your message to my master, Sister Fidelma. He is adamant. He will see no woman of the Eoghanacht, especially one who seeks to assert authority in the lands of the Uí Fidgente. Nor one who is accompanied by a foreigner from beyond the seas.'

Fidelma glanced at Eadulf whose face was beginning to redden in ill-concealed anger.

'Eadulf,' she said quietly to him, 'will you go to Conrí and tell him that the Venerable Mac Faosma is refusing to see me and suggest that he report this blatant disregard for law to the abbot?'

Eadulf hesitated, looking from Fidelma to the implacable young religieux, and then inclined his head and hurried away.

When he was gone, Fidelma suddenly sat down cross-legged in front of Brother Benen. The young man frowned down at her.

'What are you doing, Sister?' he asked in an embarrassed tone. 'You cannot sit in this corridor outside the door of these chambers.'

'You will perceive, Brother Benen,' she replied evenly, 'that is precisely what I am doing. I have informed you that I am a *dálaigh* whose power is bestowed by the laws of the five kingdoms. The Venerable Mac Faosma is compelled by law to see me and answer my questions truthfully.'

'He will not,' replied the other. 'There is no physical force that can compel him to do so.'

Fidelma smiled thinly.

'Physical force defeats the purpose. I shall not speak of that. However, I am asserting the only force that he has left to me. I am declaring that I shall sit here in *troscud* until the Venerable Mac Faosma decides to redeem his honour and speak to me as a *dálaigh* as he is legally and now morally obliged to do.'

The young monk frowned.

'I do not understand, Sister.'

'Then take my words to the Venerable Mac Faosma and ask your master to instruct you in law. He has time to make his response before the abbot and my witnesses arrive and my *apad*, my declaration, becomes known to everyone.'

Brother Benen hesitated and then turned into the chamber and closed the door behind him.

As it shut, Fidelma wondered, with a sinking feeling, if she was being too dramatic. But she was so frustrated by the arrogance of the Venerable Mac Faosma that she felt she had no other choice than to resort to the ancient ritual. The *troscud* was a means of fasting to assert one's rights when faced with no other means of obtaining redress. It was made clear in the law tract *De Chetharslicht Athgabála* that, having given notice, she could sit outside the door of the recalcitrant philosopher. If he did not come to arbitration, if he allowed the protester to die on hunger strike, then the moral judgement went against him. Shame and contempt would be his lot until he made recompense. If he failed in this he was not only damned by society but damned in the next world. He would be held to be without honour and without morality.

It was an ancient Irish law that stretched back into antiquity and not even the coming of the New Faith had eliminated it. Even Patrick himself had used the ritual fast, or hunger strike, to assert his rights and the Blessed Cairmmin of Inis Celtra had declared a *troscud* when King Guaire Aidne of Connacht infringed his rights. Within the memory of some, the population of the kingdom of Laghin had declared a *troscud* against Colmcille when he rode roughshod over their rights. Even kings were known to resort to the *troscud* when their rights were challenged.

She had barely settled herself into her position when the door opened and the young Brother Benen re-emerged. He was red-faced and embarrassed, his eyes not focusing on her.

'He will see you, Sister. He will see you under protest.

But he will not see the Saxon brother. On that he is adamant.'

Fidelma slowly rose to her feet.

'In that case, you may tell Brother Eadulf to wait here for me.' She knew when to compromise. It was information that she was after and not dominance over the reluctant old man.

The Venerable Mac Faosma was, indeed, elderly but certainly not frail. He was a robust man with a shock of snow-white hair and a fleshy, red face. Had he been given to smiling, he could have been described as cherubic, but his features were sternly drawn with deep frown lines. The lips, though also fleshy, were petulant, with the lower lip stuck out aggressively. The eyes were a strange pale colour that seemed to change like the sea, one moment green, the next blue, the next no colour at all. His large frame reclined in a carved oak chair to one side of a smouldering turf fire set in a large hearth.

He watched Fidelma from under shaggy white eyebrows as she crossed the room towards him. He made no attempt to rise in deference to her status.

Fidelma did not register her feelings but went to a chair on the opposite side of the hearth and sat down.

A low, long whistling sound escaped from the old man.

'You forget yourself, Sister.'

The voice was deep, used to commanding or questioning students; a voice that boomed throughout the room, resonating in the corners.

Fidelma was not cowed.

'I am Fidelma of Cashel, sister to Colgú, *dálaigh* qualified to the level of *anruth*. What have I forgotten?'

She kept her voice mild but the challenge was unmistakable.

She had reminded the Venerable Mac Faosma that she was not merely a religieuse, but sister to his king, and holder of a position that allowed her to sit even in the presence of provincial kings without asking permission first. In this way, she also reminded the Venerable Mac Faosma that it was his place to rise when she entered a room.

The Venerable Mac Faosma cleared his throat to disguise either his annoyance or his embarrassment.

'I have nothing to discuss with you, Fidelma of Cashel,' he finally said.

'But I have something to discuss with you, Venerable Mac Faosma,' she responded evenly.

'Nothing is so powerful in drawing the spirit of a man downwards as the caresses of a woman,' snapped the old man.

For a moment Fidelma was nonplussed and then her lips began forming angry words but the Venerable Mac Faosma raised his hand, palm outward as if to placate her.

'I quote the wise words of the Blessed Augustine of Hippo who argues that to administer the Faith we cannot and should not have intimacy with women.'

'I am aware of those who preach this idea,' replied Fidelma, controlling her irritation. 'Nevertheless, it is a fact that the majority of priests here and even in Gaul and Frankia are married. Was it not Pelagius, the second of his name to be called the Holy Father, who decided less than a century ago that there was no harm in the religious being married so long as they did not hand over church property to their wives or children? In the inheritance of property lies the real reason for this idea that men and women who take to the religious life should not naturally join with one another and have children.'

Venerable Mac Faosma returned her bold gaze from beneath a lowering brow.

'Nevertheless, there is a growing number of us who believe that light and spirit are good, and darkness and material things are evil, and that a person cannot be married and be perfect. Was it not the Holy Father Gregory the Great who pronounced that all sexual desire is sinful in itself?'

Fidelma snorted in disgust.

'You mean that such a natural desire is therefore evil? Is it then suggested that the God we worship created such an evil?'

Mac Faosma made to speak but Fidelma interrupted him with a gesture of her hand.

'While such theological discourse is entertaining, Venerable Mac Faosma, this has little to do with the reason I am here.'

'I wish to make it clear that I am of the body that believes that we of the religious should live in celibacy,' replied the old man stubbornly. 'I adhere to the ruling of the Council of Laodicea that women should not be ordained and that women presiding at the Eucharistic meals is something that should not be tolerated.'

'You have made your views known,' replied Fidelma patiently. 'But now let us speak of the matter which has brought me here.'

'And that is?'

'I believe that you are interested in the work of the Venerable Cináed who was murdered in this abbey a few days ago?'

'Interested?' The word was a sneer. 'The man was a charlatan and, moreover, a traitor!'

'I believe that you often debated your views in public.'

'If his ramblings could be held worthy of debate. I merely put the correct view lest he corrupted the minds of the youthful students at this place.'

'In what way do you claim that he led his students into error?'

'In what way . . . ? In ways that you would not be able to comprehend because it requires someone who has studied philosophy to come near to such an understanding.'

Fidelma kept her features immobile as she sought to control her own temper at the arrogance of the old man.

'Someone qualified to the level of *anruth* is not entirely devoid of intelligence, Venerable Mac Faosma,' she said quietly.

'Someone qualified as an *ollamh* might think differently.' The old man sneered but scored a point, for an *ollamh* was the highest degree available in the secular and ecclesiastical colleges of the five kingdoms. 'What would you know of the argument of the concept of the Holy Trinity?'

Fidelma's eyes narrowed at the challenge.

'I know that the term denotes the doctrine that God is a unity of three persons – the Father, Son and the Holy Spirit – and that Tertullian coined the term three centuries ago. I know that it has become an official doctrine in the Creed . . .'

'*Quicunque vult salvus esse* . . .' The Venerable Mac Faosma made the opening words into a question, challenging Fidelma to continue. 'Whosoever will be saved . . . What is the prime article of the Faith?'

' . . . *ut unum Deum in Trinitate, et Trinitatem in unitate veneremur* . . .' continued Fidelma in Latin. 'That we worship one God in Trinity, and Trinity in Unity, neither confounding the Persons nor dividing the substance.'

The Venerable Mac Faosma regarded her carefully for a moment or two.

'So you possess some basic intelligence?' he said sourly. 'Very well. Cináed was a monotheist. Do you know what that is?'

'That he believed in one God and not in the three. As I understand it, he would argue that Holy Scripture makes no explicit statement of the trinity. It was the acceptance of Christ as a divinity, at the Council of Nicaea – and not just a divinity that was created but a deity of himself – that caused some of the early philosophers to conceive the idea of the triune God. As I understood it, the creed that was adopted at Nicaea simply accepted the idea of Blessed Gregory the wonder-worker from Neocaesarea.'

The Venerable Mac Faosma was nodding.

'Challenging those learned Fathers of the Faith is to imperil the soul. Cináed wrote blasphemous rubbish!' he snapped. '*Qui vult ergo salvus esse, ita de Trinitate sentiat.* He, therefore, that will be saved must thus think of the Trinity. Cináed was wrong. Utterly wrong. Rome has declared that there are neither three gods nor three modes of God but that they are co-equally and co-eternally God.'

Fidelma bowed her head.

'Of course, that must be the logical outcome otherwise the concept of trinity would deviate from the uncompromising monotheism of the religion of Abraham which Christ gave us a new interpretation of.'

The Venerable Mac Faosma stared at her in irritation.

'We must accept the Creed that the Blessed Bishop Athanasius of Alexandria has given us, for it is specifically stated that except one believe faithfully, they cannot be saved. And will go down into everlasting fire . . . *qui vero mala, in ignem aeternum*!'

Fidelma smiled softly.

'I would like to think that such a supreme deity would look more kindly on the beings he created with minds to question. I remember that the Venerable Cináed also questioned the belief that this Creed was even penned by Bishop Athanasius three centuries ago. He claimed that the Creed is Latin in its symbolism and had Athanasius really been the author he would have written it in Greek. He argued that we have enough of Athanasius's work to see the absence of the phrases that were dear to him. Athanasius would have used words like *homoousion* for essence or substance and not *substantiam*, which is a Latin usage.'

The Venerable Mac Faosma gave a sneering laugh.

'So, Sister, you claim to be a scholar of language as well as philosophy?'

'I claim nothing of the sort. I have simply read the Venerable Cináed's discourse on the Trinity. All I claim to be is a *dálaigh* investigating his murder.'

'And what has his death to do with me?'

'When did you last see him?'

The question was suddenly sharp and caused the old man to blink rapidly.

'The day before his body was discovered. I passed him in the *tech-screptra*. We did not speak. I have no reason to speak to a person whose views are beyond the orthodoxy of the Faith unless in public debate.'

'You never saw him again?'

'I have said as much. My servant, Brother Benen, came

to me on the following day to say that Cináed's body had been discovered. That is all I know about the matter.'

'So you last saw him in the library.'

'I have said so.'

'Speaking of the library, I believe that you borrowed one of Cináed's discourses.'

The Venerable Mac Faosma sucked in his breath, a soft sound, between his teeth.

'You have been busy, Sister. Have you been asking questions about me?'

'I was searching for that particular book,' Fidelma replied. 'Since you did borrow the book, you might be able to tell me why you did so?'

'We speak of an evil text,' replied the old man venomously. 'More insidious than Cináed's usual prattling on religion.'

Fidelma folded her hands in front of her and leant back.

'An evil text?' she prompted. 'I am told that this was a discourse on politics.'

'Cináed was an Uí Fidgente. This land gave him birth and its colleges gave him education and opportunity. Like a cur, he turned on that birthright.'

'I think that you must explain what you mean.'

'You are an Eoghanacht and therefore you will have no understanding.'

'I am a *dálaigh* before I am an Eoghanacht just as you should be a scholar before you are an Uí Fidgente. We both owe allegiance to the truth,' replied Fidelma softly.

The Venerable Mac Faosma sat silently watching her, his expression fixed. Then he made a gesture with his shoulders. It was as if he had been struggling to respond and then decided he would let the matter pass.

'Very well. Cináed wrote an argument denouncing the chiefs of the Uí Fidgente, as he claimed, for betraying their true ancestry as Dáirine by claiming to be Dál gCais, descendants of Cormac Cas, brother of Eoghan Mór . . . I am sure that you, as an Eoghanacht, will know the genealogy of the family? Cináed argued that it was the duty of the chiefs to pay fealty to Cashel and honour the Eoghanacht kings and not try to overthrow them.'

There was humour in Fidelma's smile. 'To an Eoghanacht, it sounds a reasonable judgement.'

The Venerable Mac Faosma scowled angrily. 'To an Uí Fidgente, it is treason.'

'Not so. Times have moved on since Eoganán raised his clans in rebellion and marched on Cashel.'

'Our king,' he emphasised the word, 'our king Eoganán raised his clans to throw off the curse of Cashel.'

'And met his end in rebellion on Cnoc Áine. As I said, times move on. The current chieftain has made peace with Cashel and his choice of warlord, Conrí, is proof that we can build a new life together and in peace.'

The old man snorted in disgust. 'That remains to be seen.'

'So you have borrowed Cináed's book which would welcome in this new era of peace. Why?' Fidelma went on. 'It was written some time ago and you must have read it before.'

'Why would any scholar seek to obtain the book of another scholar?'

'Perhaps you will tell me?'

'I am currently writing a corrective to his arguments by showing that the Uí Fidgente are truly descendants of Cas, brother of Eoghan Mór, and of the bloodline of the true kings of Cashel.'

'So you still support the rebellion of the Uí Fidgente?' Fidelma's eyes narrowed slightly.

'Rebellion is your word, not mine. As you said earlier, Fidelma of Cashel, my duty is merely to the truth. I am not concerned to what use the truth is put.'

'The truth *as you see it*,' muttered Fidelma with emphasis. Then she added: 'I would like to see this book. The book of Cináed which you have borrowed.'

The old man sat silent for several moments, for so long that Fidelma wondered whether he was simply making a silent defiance. Then he raised his head.

'Brother Benen!' he called.

The door opened and the young muscular religieux entered.

'Go to my study and fetch the book of Cináed that you will find there on my reading table. Bring it to me here.'

'At once, Venerable Mac Faosma.'

The old man turned back to Fidelma as the young monk hurried away on his errand.

'After this, I trust I will be left in peace?'

'Nothing is guaranteed in this life, Venerable Mac Faosma,' she replied quietly. 'I have to continue along the path towards the solution of this mystery no matter where it leads and whom I have to meet along it.'

The old man snorted again.

'I will be honest with you . . .' he began.

'I trust that you have been honest with me from the start,' she riposted.

'I will tell you frankly that I have no sorrow in me that Cináed is dead. Either he was a fool or, as I believe, he was recreant – a renegade and a scoundrel. The world is better off without such mischief-makers.'

Fidelma examined the old man carefully.

'Such views can rebound on those who utter them,' she said softly.

'I thought you wanted honesty,' replied the old man sarcastically.

'Very well. You have been honest. Continue to be so and answer me this . . . did you personally encompass, or did you cause to be encompassed – by word or deed – the death of Cináed?'

For the first time, the old man chuckled. It was a dry, rasping sound.

'Now if I had done so, would I tell you? There is a limit to virtuousness, Sister Fidelma. If everyone were so honest, what need would we have of the likes of a *dálaigh* and from where would you get your stimulation and satisfaction in solving such conundrums as this murder?'

Fidelma let the corner of her mouth twitch in humour.

'That, at least, is said in honesty, Venerable Mac Faosma.'

There was a knock at the door and Brother Benen returned. He looked nervous, uncomfortable.

'Master . . .' he began and then paused, looking from the Venerable Mac Faosma to Fidelma and back again.

The old man waited impatiently and when the young man did not speak he heaved a sigh of exasperation.

'Come, come. Where is the book I sent you for? I do not have all day and have wasted enough time on this matter already.'

Brother Benen licked his lips and then tried to form the words.

'The book . . . the book of Cináed . . . it is . . . it is . . .'

The Venerable Mac Faosma frowned.

'What? Can't you find it? Where is it? Mislaid?'

Brother Benen shook his head.

'I think perhaps it would be easier if you came to your study, Venerable Mac Faosma.'

'Come to my study?' The old man was indignant. 'Can I not rely on anyone to carry out a simple errand that I have to go myself?'

'If you please . . .' begged the young man.

Fidelma rose.

'Obviously something is worrying this young man, Venerable Mac Faosma. Perhaps we should all go . . . ?'

The Venerable Mac Faosma rose abruptly, showing himself to be as agile on his feet as his physique indicated.

'There is a way to my study through here,' he said, not going the way that Brother Benen had gone but moving through his living chamber to where a tapestry hung. He drew it aside to reveal a wooden door, which he unbolted. Then he led the way down a narrow stone passageway and through another wooden door into a chamber that resembled a library, with many manuscript books, and a scribe's tripod book stand. Tables, stools and writing materials littered the room. There were three doors, one opening, Fidelma estimated, on to the passageway in which she had declared her *troscud*, while the third was on the opposite wall. The remains of a fire smouldered in the hearth.

The Venerable Mac Faosma began to move to the wooden tripod book stand.

'I left the book here this morning,' he said with a frown. 'It is no longer here.' He turned to the nervous brother. 'What does this mean?'

'Master . . .' Brother Benen pointed towards the fire.

The old man followed the line of his finger.

'God look down upon us!' he whispered, moving with

surprising rapidity across to the hearth and then bending down to pick something up. Fidelma could see that it was scorched and burnt pieces of parchment. She breathed deeply.

'I presume that was Cináed's book?' she asked softly.

'I do not know how it came there, Sister.' Brother Benen was almost in tears. 'At noon, the book was on the stand. I saw it there myself after the Venerable Mac Faosma retired for the midday meal. After that he always has a nap before resuming his labours. I touched nothing. I swear it.'

The Venerable Mac Faosma was standing looking down at the burnt papers in his hand with an expression of irritation.

'Well, someone touched it and destroyed it.'

'Is it the only copy?' asked Fidelma.

'No one has copied it or ever will,' snapped the old man. 'It was waiting for young Brother Faolchair to make a copy but now . . . now there will be no need for me to write a response.'

Fidelma smiled sceptically. 'That is certainly true.'

The old man scowled and turned to her. 'What are you implying?'

'I never imply,' Fidelma responded quickly. 'If there is an accusation to be made, I will make it. What is being asserted here is that, between noonday and now, someone entered your study and burnt the Venerable Cináed's book. Why would they do that?'

The Venerable Mac Faosma raised his chin sharply.

'There are plenty in this abbey who would be happy to see this work of treachery destroyed. I am not the only one.'

'Those same people might go so far as to burn it?'

'It would seem so.'

Fidelma looked round the room slowly, then went to the hearth and confirmed that the book had been well and truly destroyed. Only a few scorched pages remained, and they were beyond reading except for a few words here and there.

'There are three doors here. Are they all locked?'

'My assistant has a spare key to that door, the one that leads into the corridor. The door between my chamber and this room bolts on the inside of my chamber and I always keep my chamber locked so there can be no access from there. That door there,' he pointed to the third door, 'leads into the courtyard where I sometimes sit on summer days. A key on the inside always locks it. There is no access from there.'

'You have the only key to that outside door?'

'I believe so.' The Venerable Mac Faosma frowned. 'Anyway, there is no need to make a fuss on my behalf. It is best that the book should be destroyed with its vile insinuations and prejudice. I have no complaint to make.'

Fidelma was about to respond but then thought better of it. She merely commented: 'I lament every time I see a book destroyed, as it means the loss of human thought if not of knowledge.'

The Venerable Mac Faosma assumed his sneering look again.

'Then I presume you would be critical of our beloved Patrick to whom we owe so much?'

'In what respect?'

'I would have thought that a person with the knowledge you aspire to would have already read the life of Patrick as written by his disciple the Blessed Benignus, who was his successor.'

Fidelma smiled wearily.

'I suppose you mean the passage in which Benignus admits that Patrick burnt one hundred and eighty books of the Druids because they were not Christian. Indeed, I deplore that destruction, for who knows what knowledge – Christian or not – they would have imparted to us? There has been too much destruction of knowledge simply because someone else disagrees with it. In a civilised world, there is room for all knowledge and the truth will eventually emerge triumphant over prejudice. If we do not believe that, then there is no hope for us. We might as well resort to living as wild animals.'

The Venerable Mac Faosma raised his eyebrows in surprise as her words ended on a note of vehemence.

'Well, well, you do have a pretension to be a philosopher.'

Fidelma made a cutting motion with her hand to dismiss his words.

'I have no pretensions to be anything other than what I am and I am content with being what I am. Even if you are not concerned with the destruction of what your own *leabhar coimedach*, Brother Eolas, believes is a valuable book, I am sure Abbot Erc will consider that a crime has been committed with its burning.'

'And you, of course, will demand to interrupt my solitude and study by conducting an inquiry into that crime?' jeered the old scholar. 'I shall complain to the abbot and I shall protect my right to respect.'

'Nothing I have done or said has been disrespectful to you, Venerable Mac Faosma, even though there has been disrespect shown to me both as a *dálaigh* and as sister to King Colgú in whose lands you dwell. I will not seek redress for that out of deference to your age, as you may have forgotten the rights and duties that you owe to the law.'

The Venerable Mac Faosma's jaw slackened in surprise at her directness and the sharpness of her tone. Before he could frame a response, she had turned and sought the exit through the door into the corridor, which Brother Benen had left unlocked in his haste.

As she closed it behind her, she found Eadulf and Conrí accompanied by a harassed-looking Abbot Erc hurrying along the corridor.

'I am told that you are complaining because the Venerable Mac Faosma does not wish to see you, Sister,' the abbot said immediately. 'That is his right, you know, and—'

Fidelma halted as they came up.

'I have seen and questioned the Venerable Mac Faosma,' she said shortly. 'Moreover, it seems that after the *etar-suth*, the book that he took from the *tech-screptra*, Cináed's political discourse, was deliberately burnt in his study.'

Eadulf's eyes widened.

'You mean that he burnt it?'

'I simply state the fact. I do not accuse anyone – yet.'

Abbot Erc's harassed expression grew more intent.

'The Venerable Mac Faosma is a scholar. Why would he want to burn a book?'

Fidelma glanced at the abbot pityingly.

'Mac Faosma was not exactly an admirer of Cináed,' she said with a touch of derision. 'This work, especially, seems to have upset the old man.'

'What do you want me to do?' The abbot was tight-mouthed.

'Nothing, as yet. The Venerable Mac Faosma has adopted an attitude that is totally hostile to my inquiries. But, for

the time being, I shall keep an open mind on what has
happened here. Anyway, tomorrow we shall be leaving Ard
Fhearta to pursue the matter of the missing members of this
community.'

The abbot looked almost relieved for a moment and then
his expression grew serious.

'Do you mean that you have given up trying to find the
person who killed the Venerable Cináed?'

Fidelma immediately shook her head.

'I do not mean that. I mean that I shall seek some other
line of investigation to achieve that end. I shall come to
your chamber before the evening meal and bring you up to
date with our inquiry before we leave.'

Abbot Erc hesitated and then realised that he had been
dismissed. He inclined his head briefly and turned and shuffled away.

Fidelma saw that Eadulf was about to open his mouth
and raised a finger to her lips with a frown, indicating with
her head towards the closed door of the Venerable Mac
Faosma's study. She glanced at Conrí.

'Let us find a more comfortable place to talk,' she
suggested.

Conrí pointed along the corridor and led them down it,
through a side door and on to the path to the chapel. The
chapel was deserted but its gloom was relieved with candles.
They seated themselves in a corner on a bench.

'Well?' demanded Eadulf.

Fidelma sketched out her interview with the Venerable
Mac Faosma.

There was a brief silence before Eadulf said: 'So you
think that this Mac Faosma took Cináed's book and burnt
it because he disagreed with it?'

'It is possible.'

'And if he is capable of that he might also be capable of killing Cináed?'

Fidelma grimaced in agreement.

'It is possible again, but we need more than suspicion to proceed. What I do know is that he is an unrepentant supporter of the Uí Fidgente chief Eoganán.' She turned to Conrí. 'I know that you are desirous of peace between the Uí Fidgente and the rest of Muman. Let me speak, however, as a *dálaigh* rather than as an Eoghanacht. Even since Eoganán's death at Cnoc Áine, I presume that many of the Uí Fidgente are still opposed to my brother's rule?'

Conrí looked slightly embarrassed.

'There are many, lady. All it needs is a strong leader and the people could easily rise up and be led again down the wrong path into more violence and bloodshed.'

'The Venerable Mac Faosma might be such a leader?' queried Eadulf.

Conrí shook his head.

'Such a leader would have to be more of a warrior than a scholar. And one born from the line of Bríon, one of our great chieftains. Mac Faosma, as his name suggests, is not of any noble line. Since Eoganán was slain, his line has more or less ceased to be. Our current chieftain, Donennach, is as committed to the peace with Cashel as I am.'

'I do not understand.' Eadulf frowned. 'I mean, your reference to Mac Faosma's name?'

It was Fidelma who explained.

'It means "son of protection", which implies that he was someone who was adopted because there was no one left in his blood family to raise him.'

'Exactly. For someone to gain enough authority with the

Uí Fidgente to become leader, they have to have a direct
bloodline connection with our chief family. Eoganán's line,
as I say, was virtually wiped out.'

'Then how was this Donennach accepted as your ruler?'
demanded Eadulf.

'Because the genealogists could trace Donennach's
descent nine generations back to Bríon. Eoganán descended
from another son of Bríon.'

'So such a leader might exist, someone else descended
from this Bríon?' Eadulf pointed out. 'And Mac Faosma
could be the catalyst trying to stir things?'

'Both are possible,' admitted Conrí. 'But I fail to see
anyone who is popular enough to attempt to overthrow
Donennach.'

Eadulf grinned sourly.

'A few months ago Uaman might have been that man,'
he pointed out.

Conrí sniffed.

'Uaman the Leper, even living, would not have been
accepted under our law,' he reminded him. 'A chieftain must
be a man without blemish, physical or mental.'

'Anyway, we might be travelling down a wrong road in
considering this,' Fidelma suddenly intervened. 'Perhaps the
argument over the Uí Fidgente between Mac Faosma and
Cináed has nothing to do with Cináed's murder. All I have
put forward is that some strong emotions existed between
Mac Faosma and Cináed. We should not discount them.'

Eadulf sighed. 'So where do we turn now in this matter?
You told the abbot that we shall be leaving Ard Fhearta. To
go where? Where do we start searching for the missing
members of this community?'

'At the place where they disappeared, in the lands of the

Corco Duibhne,' Fidelma replied. 'I propose to ask Mugrón to take us there when he sails. He told me he was due to go there within the next day or so.'

'Have you given up on the murder of Cináed?'

Fidelma frowned in annoyance. Abbot Erc had made a similar suggestion and she had wondered, for a moment, whether it had been made with desire.

'I never give up on a task half finished. You know that, Eadulf. We can leave Ard Fhearta as soon as the weather is good and Mugrón is prepared to sail. Meanwhile, I have not, as yet, questioned Sister Sinnchéne or Sister Buan.'

CHAPTER SEVEN

Fidelma sent Conrí to see Mugrón, the merchant, in order to make arrangements for the voyage to the land of the Corco Duibhne when he was ready. After he had departed on his errand, she and Eadulf went in search of Sister Buan. They found her in the chambers where the Venerable Cináed had lived and worked. It was soon obvious that these were Sister Buan's living quarters as well.

Sister Buan was a fairly plain-looking woman, of an indiscernible age, although Eadulf judged her to be about forty years. She was a slight but sharp-faced woman with somewhat rounded shoulders, corn-coloured hair and bright blue eyes. Her features could have been pleasant had she allowed a smile to sit upon them. Now those features were moulded into an expression of sorrow, the eyes red-rimmed. She bore her grief in every line of her face and movement of her body.

When she opened the door to admit Fidelma and Eadulf she showed no surprise and did not question why they had come.

'I have been expecting you,' she said simply, as she stood

aside to admit them into the chambers. 'You are the *dálaigh* from Cashel and you are her Saxon companion. You were pointed out to me last night in the refectory. I will do my best to answer your questions.'

'Thank you, Sister Buan,' said Fidelma as they seated themselves in the cold chamber. The turf fire had been allowed to blacken and die. 'We have been told that you were the companion of the Venerable Cináed?'

'I was his *cétmuintir*,' she replied.

Fidelma glanced quickly at Eadulf.

'You were his legally married wife?' he asked in surprise.

Sister Buan raised her chin defiantly.

'Does that astonish you?' she demanded. 'I would not take you for one of those who followed the ideas emerging from Rome that we should all follow the rule of celibacy.'

'Of course not,' Eadulf responded. 'It's just that—'

'Then you must disapprove because Cináed was a generation or so older than I was.' The woman made it into a challenge.

'I was going to say, it is just that no one mentioned your exact legal position,' Eadulf continued evenly.

'We are certainly not here to pass any moral judgements, Sister Buan,' Fidelma added.

'Buan – that is a martial name, is it not?' Eadulf went on, trying to persuade the woman of his good intentions. 'Doesn't it mean "the victorious one"?'

'No, Brother Saxon. It is a name which means "lasting" or, rather, "enduring".' She became suddenly sad again.

'How long were you the wife of Cináed?' Fidelma asked.

'Five years.'

Fidelma was wondering why no one at the abbey had bothered to tell her that Cináed had died leaving a widow.

'I presume there are no children of this union?' Eadulf asked.

Sister Buan turned an almost pitying look on him.

'We have not been blessed with children. Poor Cináed was not capable of becoming a father when we joined our lives together. It was for companionship that we made the *lánamnus*, our marriage contract. Even if it were possible, children are frowned on among the community.'

'How long had you known Cináed?'

'Seven years. Cináed was here when I came to the community, but I did not really know him until I came to work for him.'

'And you have been in this community for – how long?'

'I was in this abbey for over twenty years.'

'What brought you together?'

The slightly built woman shrugged.

'He wanted someone to keep his chambers tidy. He was given special privileges because of his scholarship. He did not have to participate in physical work because of his age and learning and so he was allowed someone to assist him. He was one of only two scholars here who had that privilege.'

Eadulf grimaced sourly.

'I suppose the other was the Venerable Mac Faosma?'

'Just so. And he has Brother Benen to help him.'

There was a tone of censure in the woman's voice. Fidelma looked at her keenly.

'You disapprove of that?'

'What a man does in his private life is no concern of mine,' she replied, as if uninterested.

Once again Fidelma caught Eadulf's eye and this time shook her head slightly. It was obvious what the woman meant.

'So you began to clean for Cináed and that led to your relationship?'

'I did and it did.'

'And you became interested in his work?' Eadulf asked.

For the first time the woman actually smiled.

'His work? I had no understanding of it. I am no scholar.' She held out her hands. 'These are not the hands of a Latin scholar, Brother Saxon.'

Eadulf glanced at them. They were rough and callused.

'What would a scholar want with someone like me?' There was no bitterness in her voice. Neither of them responded to her question. She went on: 'Human beings want companionship at times and not simply for intellectual discourse. In Cináed's case he wanted someone to nurse him and fetch and carry for him.'

Eadulf looked uncomfortable but she went on without seeming to notice.

'I knew there was no meeting of minds with Cináed but he was a wonderful man. I came here to escape poverty.' Sister Buan now sounded slightly bitter. 'I was disowned by my father after he divorced my mother, who was his second wife.'

Fidelma was interested.

'For what reason did he divorce her?'

'Because she fled her marriage contract on becoming enamoured of a young man, so I was told. From fear of my father, she became a fugitive in the mountains. I was told that she perished there.'

'So she did not take you with her into the mountains?'

Sister Buan shook her head.

'I was sent to be fostered among the Corco Duibhne, by their chief, and told never to return to my father's rath again nor seek help from my half-brothers. Nor did I. Thus when I left my foster parents, I decided to seek security in the religious life. Eventually, I came to the abbey and for two years I did all the chores that no one else wanted to do. Then the abbot found I had a talent for bargaining with merchants. So he allowed me to sell the work of our artisans to local traders. I began to travel to the abbey of Colmán and even north to Loch Derg to trade. The trips were neither many nor frequent and I continued to do other chores.

'So I also went to work for Cináed. I enjoyed working for him, nursing him in sickness, helping him in health, and when he offered to legalise our relationship I could ask for no greater happiness.'

'You knew that he was regarded as a great scholar?' Fidelma asked.

'I knew that he regarded himself as a tired and frail old man who sometimes needed his chest rubbed with oils to keep out the cold vapours of the night.'

'But you know how highly his work was thought of?' pressed Fidelma.

'I know some in this abbey did not think so highly of it,' she corrected.

'You mean the Venerable Mac Faosma?'

'And his followers.'

'You felt their antagonism?'

'Isn't there an old saying – three things that come unbidden – love, jealousy and fear? All three have visited these chambers.'

'Fear?'

'The day before he died, poor Cináed expressed his fear to me.'

Fidelma's eyes widened.

'He was fearful? Fearful of whom?'

Sister Buan sighed and shook her head.

'That, alas, I do not know for sure.'

'Can you recall what he said? How did he express this fear?'

Sister Buan spread her hands in a negative gesture.

'He came back here in a state of anxiety after the evening meal in the refectory . . . It was one of the special feasts that he was obliged to attend. More often he would eat simply in these chambers with me, having dispensation to do so because of his age.'

'But you imply that you did not attend that particular evening meal? Why?'

'I was not well. A stomach sickness.'

'I see. Go on.'

'I remember that I went to get water for myself and passed that window . . .' She pointed across the room to where a window opened on to a small quadrangle. Fidelma suddenly realised it was the same quadrangle that gave access to the Venerable Mac Faosma's chambers through the door into his study. She rose quickly.

'Your pardon, Sister Buan. Which is the door to the Venerable Mac Faosma's chambers?'

'It is that door directly across the quadrangle from us.'

'Thank you. Continue. You passed by this window and . . . ?'

'It was dark, of course, but the quadrangle is lit with torches at night. I saw Cináed enter the quadrangle from the archway entrance to the right . . . that leads to the refectory. He was walking slowly with someone and engaged in animated conversation.'

'Did you recognise who it was?' queried Eadulf.

'Sister Uallann.'

'The physician?'

'The same,' she confirmed. 'They appeared to be arguing but in low tones and Sister Uallann was throwing her hands in the air as if to make her points. She can be very dramatic at times. A strange woman, given to outbursts of temper. It seemed to me that Cináed broke off the conversation for he turned and came to our door.'

'What did he say?' demanded Fidelma.

Sister Buan shrugged.

'Nothing.'

Fidelma looked taken aback for a moment.

'Nothing? You had just seen him in argument. You said he came back here fearful . . . of what? Of whom? Sister Uallann?'

'I saw he was agitated. Naturally, I asked him what was amiss and told him what I had seen outside. He said that it was just a silly quarrel, that was all. Something about his work. But I knew Cináed. Behind his light dismissal of the event, I knew that he was afraid.'

'How was that fear expressed?'

Sister Buan shrugged again.

'It is hard to explain. I grew up on the western peninsula. I was fostered by a chieftain there who believed that his fosterlings should learn animal husbandry. I came to know when the animals were fretting. Sheep would know when a wolf was near and you did not have to ask for an explanation. You could see it in their bodies, the movement of their heads. It is the same if you know someone intimately. You become used to their habits, their ways. It was like that with Cináed. He did not have to say when he was thirsty or when he was tired. I knew. I knew from the way he behaved that evening that there was something on his mind and he was fearful of it.'

'Did you ask him to tell you what was wrong?'

'I did. He told me not to worry. He said, and these were his very words, that he would sort things out the next day. He would be going to see the abbot and resolve matters.'

Fidelma and Eadulf sat back for a moment.

'Resolve matters? With the abbot? That is an interesting choice of words. And he made no further explanation?'

'None. He said that he would see the abbot after the service – the service for the feast day of the Blessed Íte. He and the abbot usually went to the oratory to prepare it for the service together. I remember hearing him leave and thinking it was very early for him to do so. It was still very dark. I am not sure when it was but I thought it was not long after midnight. All I recall is that it was light when Brother Cú Mara came to me with the news that . . . that . . .'

Her features began to crumple and Fidelma reached forward to lay a hand on her arm.

'And you know nothing more of the matter that he had promised to resolve with Abbot Erc?' pressed Eadulf gently.

She shook her head, recovering her poise.

'Have you told anyone else about this?'

'I told the abbot, of course.'

'You did? And what did he say?'

'He said that he had no idea of any matter that needed resolution. He said that Cináed was probably worried about some detail of his work. Oh, and, of course, I handed a piece of paper I found in the hearth to the abbot. It was not there when I went to bed but I saw it there the next day. Obviously, Cináed must have burnt it during the night.'

Fidelma drew the paper carefully from her marsupium.

'And this was the paper?'

Sister Buan looked at it with some surprise and then nodded.

'The abbot passed it to me,' explained Fidelma. 'And what do you make of it?'

'I think it is the note that enticed poor Cináed to the chapel that night. See, the words are clear: "midnight" and "Orat . . ." burnt away could mean "oratory", and "alone" could be an invitation to go there alone. The next word is part of a name – "Sin".'

Fidelma pursed her lips thoughtfully as she studied the woman's face.

'You appear to have an astute eye, Sister Buan.'

'It is that I am suspicious. Cináed loved his work and even when that arrogant man Mac Faosma challenged him to public debate, he was not disturbed by it. He was not concerned by the views of others because he had the strength of his convictions. But he was disturbed that night. I do not think it was a matter of a problem with his work. I believe that he was enticed to the oratory by his killer.'

Eadulf examined her keenly.

'You talk of the debates. Did you attend Cináed's debates and could you understand the arguments? Could you understand them enough to realise whether Cináed's views were right or that Mac Faosma was simply arrogant?'

Sister Buan shook her head.

'Of course I did not. I have told you, I could not understand any of the arguments,' she said in reproof. 'But I do understand when a man is arrogant in his behaviour. Cináed treated Mac Faosma with humour. The worst I have ever heard him say of him is that he was trying to be a "master of souls". That is a derogatory term among our people.'

'And you say that Cináed did not mind Mac Faosma's criticisms?'

'Whenever Cináed returned from those debates he was in a good humour,' replied Sister Buan. 'They did not worry him – Mac Faosma's sneering comments and the baying of his students. Truly, I have never seen Cináed worried until that night, the night before . . .'

She paused, hesitated a moment and gave way to a quiet sob.

'Did you ask Sister Uallann what the argument was about?' asked Fidelma softly.

Sister Buan recovered herself with a sniff.

'She thinks it beneath her dignity to speak to me as an equal. She is like Mac Faosma in her arrogance.'

'But you did ask her?' pressed Eadulf.

'Of course I asked, but she told me it was on a matter I would not understand and brushed me aside.'

'So, apart from the abbot and Sister Uallann, we are the only people you have told about this argument?' Fidelma asked.

'That is so. I knew someone was coming to investigate the death of Abbess Faife and would naturally seek to understand the events behind Cináed's murder. So I have said nothing about this to anyone else.'

Fidelma exchanged a glance with Eadulf.

'You assumed whoever came here would investigate Cináed's death as well as Faife's. It is an interesting assumption. Do you think they are connected?'

Sister Buan suddenly glanced about in an almost conspiratorial manner.

'I believe so. I overheard something someone said.'

'What did they say and who was it that said it?' demanded Fidelma curiously.

Sister Buan looked about her again as if deciding whether some unseen eavesdropper could overhear her.

'It was the *rechtaire*.'

Fidelma frowned. 'Brother Cú Mara?'

She nodded quickly.

'And what did he say and in what circumstances?'

Sister Buan licked her lips.

'I was taking the washing to the *tech-nigid*. It was the day after the burial of Cináed. I had cleared out his clothes. Those that needed washing I took there so that they could be distributed later to the needy. Brother Cú Mara was in the *tech-nigid* speaking to Sister Sinnchéne. Neither of them saw me because the door was only partially open and as I came up I heard Cináed's name spoken by Sister Sinnchéne and so I halted and did not go inside.'

'Why did that make you halt?' Fidelma queried.

'Because I knew that Sister Sinnchéne had an unhealthy passion for Cináed and that fact stopped me.'

Yet again Fidelma and Eadulf could not help but exchange a surprised glance.

'But she is very young,' pointed out Eadulf.

Sister Buan's gaze rested on him for a moment.

'What has that to do with it? I am not that aged. Old men have passions for young women, old women for young men, and so the reverse is possible. That young woman was always simpering after Cináed.'

'Simpering is an interesting term,' Eadulf observed. 'Was Sister Sinnchéne's passion, as you call it, reciprocated?'

Sister Buan flushed.

'No,' she said firmly. 'There was no foundation to it. But the girl seemed jealous of me. But, as the saying goes, all cows do not come equally well into the field. She did everything she could to lure Cináed from me. She was a little vixen by nature as well as by name.'

Fidelma was reminded that 'little vixen' was the meaning of the name Sinnchéne.

'Why should she want to do so? To lure Cináed away from you, I mean?'

'She must answer that question.'

'What did your husband say?'

'He said he thought she was a silly child enamoured only of his reputation and prestige. He thought that she wanted to use his position to make a place for herself.'

'But you and Cináed were married,' Eadulf pointed out.

'In some places second marriages are not proscribed,' Sister Buan replied. 'A man or woman can marry a second spouse while still married to the first.'

Fidelma knew that some of the old laws of polygamy had survived from the time before the New Faith. But the New Faith frowned on having more than one wife or husband.

'Do you mean that she attempted to get Cináed to take her as a *dormun*?' she asked. The term was the old one for other female marital partners or concubines.

'I believe so.'

'Did you ever challenge Sister Sinnchéne about it?' queried Eadulf.

'I once told her to leave him alone. But she was insulting and openly defiant. She replied with the old saying that the man with one cow will sometimes want milk.'

'Were you angry at that?'

'I knew Cináed,' she said emphatically. 'He had no interest in her. Besides, do not the country folk have another saying – an old bird is not caught with chaff?'

'Did you ask anyone to advise Sister Sinnchéne that the practice is frowned upon by the New Faith?'

'As a matter of fact, I did. Brother Eolas has some knowledge of the law but when I went to see him he seemed to support the old ways. He quoted some book to me that said there was a dispute in the law on the matter, and concluded that as the Chosen People of God lived in polygamy, so it was much easier to praise the custom than to condemn it.'

Fidelma sighed. She knew the passage from the *Bretha Crólige* in which the Brehon showed from the ancient texts that the Hebrews dwelt in a plurality of unions. She tried to return to the immediate matter.

'So you heard Sister Sinnchéne and Brother Cú Mara speaking together?' she said. 'You did not make your presence known because you thought you might hear what Sister Sinnchéne had to say about your husband? Something important?'

'Once I heard Cináed's name spoken, I paused outside the door. Sinnchéne had said something about Cináed and then the *rechtaire* said, "We cannot be over cautious." Sinnchéne replied, "Surely there is no way that Cináed would have revealed that secret to the Abbess Faife?" The *rechtaire* responded, "Yet the abbess's body was found near that very spot. That must mean there was some connection." There was a pause and, thinking that I had been discovered, I fell to making a noise as I came in with the clothing for the wash.'

'You have a good memory, Sister,' observed Fidelma. 'Was anything said to you?'

Sister Buan shook her head.

'Brother Cú Mara pretended that he, too, had brought washing in and made a point of thanking Sister Sinnchéne for taking it as he left.'

'Did Sister Sinnchéne say anything else to you?'

'She scowled at me, which is her usual way, and took the clothing from me in an ungracious manner, so I left.'

'Did you deduce anything from this exchange?'

Sister Buan shrugged.

'That this secret, this fear, that Cináed had on the night before his death, might have been a fear that he had shared with the Abbess Faife.'

'But how?'

Sister Buan looked puzzled at Fidelma's question. It was Eadulf who interpreted it for her.

'Abbess Faife must have been dead over ten days when Cináed was killed, and she was found a long way away from the abbey. How then could he have shared this secret, or fear, as you put it?'

She appeared not to have considered the point before.

'I have no way of knowing. The day before Abbess Faife and her followers left for the abbey of Colmán, I set out to trade for silver on behalf of our craftsmen. When I returned to the abbey, Cináed told me the news that Mugrón had arrived with word of Abbess Faife's death. Apparently her companions had disappeared. Cináed did not tell me of any secret he shared with her but sometimes they would work together in his study, and they combined on writing one or two of his works.'

'Indeed?' Fidelma raised an eyebrow.

'She was a kind woman. Abbess Faife had known Cináed for many years. She was one of the *aire* – the nobles of the

Uí Fidgente. She was aunt to Conrí the warlord who brought you hither.'

'And you did not mind her working with Cináed?' Eadulf suddenly asked.

She looked at him in bewilderment.

'Why should I do so?'

'Well, I presume that you would object to Sister Sinnchéne working in his study?' replied Eadulf. 'Don't you have a saying here that it is easy to knead when meal is at hand?'

Sister Buan looked as if she was about to smile, then she shook her head.

'You have a wicked sense of humour, Brother. And I will confess this: Cináed was not capable of rising to such an occasion.'

'So Cináed's relationship with the abbess was purely to work with her, or she with him, on some of the scholastic projects?' clarified Eadulf. 'Do you know which works she co-operated on?'

Sister Buan raised a shoulder and let it fall.

'I know there was a recent one that had just been completed before the abbess left for Bréanainn's mount. Cináed had passed it to Brother Eolas the librarian who, having read it, came to see Cináed in a state of great excitement.'

'What did he say?'

'I do not know. Cináed took him into his study but I heard their voices raised.'

'Do you know why? Didn't Cináed make any comment?' asked Fidelma.

Sister Buan simply made another negative gesture.

'All I know is that, as he was leaving, I heard Brother

Eolas say that the Venerable Mac Faosma would fall in such a rage when he read this work. Ah, yes, I recall . . . He said that "even with Eoganán two years dead, this will cause division and anger". Even as he left, I think he was trying to persuade Cináed not to insist on placing it in the library.'

'Do you recognise the title *Scripta quae ad rempublicum geredam pertinet*?' asked Fidelma.

The woman gestured helplessly. 'I have told you that I have no knowledge of any other language saving my everyday speech.'

Fidelma sighed. 'I will ask Brother Eolas about this. I suspect, however, that it is the political tract that he wrote supporting the new ruler of the Uí Fidgente and decrying the old philosophies of conflict.'

'It may be so,' agreed Sister Buan. 'He was a great one for preaching how this or that ruler should behave towards their neighbours.'

'Did Cináed do all his own calligraphy?'

Sister Buan looked bewildered.

Sister Fidelma was patient. 'When he wrote his work and made the final draft, did he write it all himself?'

The slight woman brightened. 'Oh yes. He was proud of his hand. But he did use Brother Faolchair as a copyist. Faolchair made copies of most of Cináed's works.'

'Of course,' Eadulf said in an aside, 'Brother Eolas told us that Faolchair was copying that book on precious stones, what was it – *De ars sordida gemmae*?'

'A last question,' Fidelma said, after a moment or two's thought. 'How did Cináed and you get along with Abbot Erc?'

'Abbot Erc?' Sister Buan pursed her lips thoughtfully. 'He left us alone. To me he was always remote.'

'Remote?'

'I came to this abbey because I had no family to support me. No status except that I was young, strong and ready to work. So I came here and joined the brethren.' She sniffed. 'And for the first years I found that life was just as hard. The abbot gave me the chance to trade for the abbey but he disapproved of my marriage to Cináed.'

'But when you married, when you became Cináed's *cétmuintir*, the abbot must have acknowledged you as such?' Fidelma said, making it into a question.

Sister Buan made a sound that seemed to indicate derision.

'Abbot Erc was so against our union that he refused to perform the ceremony. In fact, no one here would do it for fear of the abbot's displeasure.'

Fidelma's brows came together.

'So Abbot Erc was not such a friend to Cináed or you?'

'No friend at all. Had it not been for the visit of an old acquaintance of Cináed's from the abbey of Colmán, one who was ordained to confirm the marriage contract, we would have had no one to bless our union, for Cináed was not able, in his frail years, to travel far.'

Fidelma rose slowly from her seat, followed by Eadulf.

'Thank you, Sister Buan, you have been most helpful. What is your intention now? I presume that you will remain in the abbey?'

The woman looked almost helpless.

'That I don't know. No one has advised me on my position. I was *cétmuintir* to Cináed. Am I allowed to stay in his chambers? Am I allowed to pursue compensation for his murder? Can I keep his possessions? I do not know my rights in this matter.'

'No one has spoken to you?'

'No one. There is no trained Brehon in the community. Only Brother Eolas has some knowledge of the law and he is hardly sympathetic to me.'

'Then leave it to me, Sister Buan. I will see what the books of law have to say on this matter. But I am sure you have certain rights as his widow.'

Fidelma knew that all religious communities were still subject to the law of the Fenechus. Each abbey was part of the territory of the ruling clan and the clan assembly allotted the use of the lands on which the abbeys and churches stood to the clergy for their support on the condition that it was not regarded as private property. One of the assembly members, a lay person, acted as the liaison between the abbot and bishop and the local ruler who ensured the law was carried out. In this instance, Fidelma had already learnt that Conrí was that person.

However, Sister Buan's case lay in an area of law that Fidelma had not considered before and had little knowledge of. The relationship of individuals and their own property within the abbey needed to be checked. She would have to look up the exact position of Sister Buan within those laws. Was she considered to have the same rights as the wife of a layman? If so those rights were considerable. She was sure the abbey library, the *tech-screptra*, would have the necessary law books.

Sister Buan rose with a brightness in her eyes.

'How can I thank you, Sister? You have been most kind to me . . .'

Fidelma felt a little uncomfortable as the woman grabbed her hands with enthusiasm.

'No thanks are necessary for I have not yet done anything.

But I will do so. I may be away from Ard Fhearta for a short time but have no fear. I shall return and resolve this matter of your status as well as that of the murder of your husband.'

Outside the chamber, Fidelma paused and looked at Eadulf who had grown fairly quiet towards the end of their interview.

'You seem distracted.'

Eadulf, still deep in thought, raised his head.

'Distracted? Oh, it's just that I had a curious feeling of having met Sister Buan somewhere before. But I can't recall where. It's irritating, like an itch you want to scratch but can't find the location of.'

Fidelma smiled indulgently.

'Well, I find Sister Buan most interesting,' she said.

Eadulf raised an eyebrow in query.

'In what way "interesting"?' he asked.

'The amount of information that tripped from her lips compared to the stone wall that has been erected by everyone else, from the abbot to the physician, from the steward to the Venerable Mac Faosma. None of them have been as forthcoming as Sister Buan. And her reports of conversations, her interpretations of the burnt note . . . so exact. The question is "why?". Why has everyone else sought to give us as little information as possible?'

'Because they all have something to hide?' hazarded Eadulf.

'Or is it that Sister Buan is misdirecting us?' suggested Fidelma pointedly.

'I don't think that she is intelligent enough to play such a deep game.'

'Never underestimate a woman's intelligence, Eadulf,' Fidelma admonished.

Eadulf glanced slyly at her.

'That is the last thing I would do. If I have learnt nothing else in my life these last few years, I have learnt that simple philosophy. On the other hand,' Eadulf went on, 'maybe there is some strange conspiracy here? What was it that Cináed was fearful of?'

'And if there was a conspiracy, why would the abbot, if he is part of it, allow Conrí to ride to Cashel to bring us here to investigate the matter?'

'You forget that he did not know who Conrí would be bringing to the abbey,' Eadulf pointed out. 'But I'll agree that Abbot Erc did not really want us to investigate Cináed's death.'

'It is bewildering,' agreed Fidelma. 'One thing is certain, we will have to question everyone again in the light of what Sister Buan has told us.'

'Might that not endanger her?'

She ignored his question. 'The person I am now looking forward to speaking to is Sister Sinnchéne. If Sister Buan is at all right in her accusations, then, indeed, she is the one on whom suspicion must fall.'

'Well, from what you have told me about the attitude of the Venerable Mac Faosma, he is certainly responsible for the burning of Cináed's book. Therefore, he could well have been responsible for his death. Even if he did not do it physically, he might well have ordered another to do it – that Brother Benen, for example. My suspect is the Venerable Mac Faosma.'

Fidelma smiled without humour.

'You may well be right. There is a tangled skein here

that needs to be unravelled. At least, thanks to Sister Buan, we have some ends of the skein to begin to pick at and hopefully disentangle.'

CHAPTER EIGHT

Conrí had returned to inform Fidelma and Eadulf that Mugrón, the merchant, was prepared to take them across the sound to the land of the Corco Duibhne in the morning providing the weather was reasonable. The dangers of the waters round the coast meant that he would not attempt the crossing if there was bad weather. However, the prospects were favourable, for the storms and high winds they had been experiencing should, by tradition, lead to dull, wet weather with softer winds and a warmer temperature.

'It should be a fine morning,' conceded Conrí, 'but I would not count on it.'

Eadulf frowned.

'Why not?' he demanded.

Conrí indicated the sky with a gesture of his hand. The clouds that afternoon were very high and wispy in appearance. Fidelma explained their significance to Eadulf.

'We sometimes call those clouds mares' tails. They can foretell that bad weather is on the way. Never mind. We still have plenty of tasks to keep us occupied here.'

When Conrí expressed surprise, Fidelma briefly recounted some of the information that Sister Buan had given them.

Conrí made a soft whistling sound.

'I cannot see what link there could be between my aunt's murder and the killing of the Venerable Cináed,' he said. 'Do you really think there is one?'

'We cannot reject the idea,' Fidelma replied. 'All we can say is that while people are not exactly lying to us, they are not telling us the complete truth. We have to ask the question – why?'

Conrí nodded agreement. 'So what do you mean to do now?'

'I mean to question Sister Sinnchéne next.'

'Should I accompany you?'

Fidelma hesitated, then shook her head firmly.

'Perhaps it would be better if you and Eadulf did not come with me. This questioning may touch on matters that are delicate for her, which she may better deal with woman to woman than with a male present.'

'That is no problem,' Eadulf agreed. 'If there is nothing specific that you want me to do, I heard from one of the brothers that there was to be some chant practice in the abbey church. I would be very interested to hear it.'

'Then I will accompany you, Brother Eadulf,' Conrí volunteered. 'I know something of the singers.'

They left Fidelma heading for the *tech-nigid* and made their way to the main church building of the abbey complex. They could hear the voices of the abbey's *clais*, or choir, already raised in what sounded to a surprised Eadulf like some martial war chant. They entered the high-roofed chamber and took their place at the rear of the building. The *clais* were all males and before them the songmaster stood intently, his very body trembling, as he imparted the tones and rhythms of the music to the singers.

Their voices rose intensely.

> *Regis regum rectissimi*
> *prope est dies Domini*
> *dies irae et vindictae*
> *tenebrarum et nebulae.*

Eadulf listened to the unusual rhythms of what he recognised as a Gallican chant. The melismatic flourishes, the long series of notes on a single syllable that characterised the chant were utterly unlike the Latin or the wailing chants from Iberia. The melodies of the Gallican chants had arisen among the Gauls, whose language was close to that of their neighbours the Britons. When Christianity had spread to Ireland it was from the Gauls that the early Irish Church had taken their religious music form, mixed a little with their own traditions. At least Eadulf could understand and feel the Latin words. Their spirit was not so different from his own Saxon war chants.

> Day of the King most righteous,
> The day is close at hand,
> The day of wrath and vengeance,
> And darkness on the land.

The *clais* sang several more chants in similar tone and metre before returning to the first martial song. When the rehearsal was over the choristers received a blessing from their master, rose and departed. Conrí moved to catch the attention of the choirmaster. He was a tall, thin-faced individual. His dark eyes, sleek hair and swarthy features made him look furtive, as if he had a secret to hide. Eadulf noticed that he wore a silver crucifix round his neck, which was notable because it hung from a string of alternately yellow and green coloured stones. He thought they were garnets.

'This is Brother Cillín, the *stiúirtheóir canaid*,' Conrí said, as he led the man back to where Eadulf waited. 'Brother Cillín, this is Eadulf from Seaxmund's Ham.'

The songmaster bowed his head and, on raising it, examined Brother Eadulf with a wary eye.

'I have heard of your coming, Brother Eadulf, and wonder what the companion of the sister of the king of Muman seeks in our poor songs.'

'Music is a food for the emotions and a feast that everyone enjoys,' returned Eadulf.

The master of music sniffed disdainfully.

'Not everyone,' he corrected. 'Some may listen to the tune but they do not hear the music.'

'I have heard that this abbey is renowned for its music,' Eadulf pressed on.

The choirmaster pulled a face as if to deny it.

'There are many abbeys that produce better music than we – however, we are progressing.'

'Progressing?'

'We are going to perform at the great gathering of Aenach Urmhuman next spring,' Brother Cillín said with some pride.

'The Assembly of East Muman? I have heard of it.'

Brother Cillín smiled thinly.

'It is a famous gathering. Each year there is a singing contest at the great stronghold of the kings . . . er, the chieftains of the Uí Fidgente by Loch Derg. I am hoping that we will win the contest next year.'

'Well, the last piece you sang was an excellent hymn,' observed Eadulf. 'I do not think I have heard it before. It seems so full of battle imagery that it is hard to reconcile it with the peace of the Faith.'

The choirmaster shrugged.

'Yet it was written by Colmcille – the blessed dove of the church. It is called the *Altus Prosator*. It is a good work but not a great work.'

'It does not sound like a work of peace,' Eadulf repeated.

'Perhaps Colmcille saw that war was often the only way forward to assert one's rights, Brother Eadulf,' remarked the songmaster wryly. 'The Uí Fidgente learnt that lesson struggling against the Eoghanacht of Cashel.'

Conrí frowned in annoyance.

'And learnt another lesson when they were defeated,' he pointed out sharply.

Brother Cillín was about to reply when one of the choristers approached them and coughed meaningfully to attract the attention of the master of song.

Brother Cillín looked irritably at him. 'Speak, Brother,' he instructed.

'Your pardon, master, we need to consult you on the unending circle.'

Brother Cillín's features became uneasy as he glanced at Eadulf and Conrí. With a muttered apology, he turned and stalked off, followed by the abashed-looking chorister.

'A strange, almost surly character,' observed Eadulf.

Conrí grinned.

'There is no harm in Brother Cillín. He has a good reputation as a teacher of music, especially in the *clais-cheól*.'

'Choir-singing? I wish that I had heard more of it. I'd like to know these musical terms – "unending circle", the chorister said. I've not heard of that.' Eadulf sighed. He paused and then said suddenly: 'Why is it that the Uí Fidgente resent the Eoghanacht at Cashel so much?'

Conrí stuck out his lower lip in a thoughtful expression before answering.

'The lady Fidelma has never spoken to you of this matter?'

Eadulf smiled softly.

'She has given me the Eoghanacht side of the story. That is natural. I would hear the Uí Fidgente viewpoint.'

Conrí gave a quick laugh.

'A great diplomat was lost in you, Brother Eadulf. Well, we have been taught over many generations that the Eoghanacht have denied the rights of the Uí Fidgente.'

'How so?'

'As you know, Brother, in this land our peoples are bound by genealogists who set forth each family's line, generation by generation. Our ancestors are important to us, my friend. Those who have gone before often continue to govern us who live now.'

'That is often the natural order of things,' confirmed Eadulf. 'I was an hereditary *gerefa* – a magistrate – in my own land. I held that position because of my ancestors and not from my choice.'

'The Eoghanacht dynasties of Muman take their name from Eoghan Mór,' went on Conrí. 'Eoghan's grandson was a great king of Cashel called Ailill Fland Bec. He had three sons. The eldest of these was Maine Mucháin whose son was Fiachu Fidgennid from whom we take our name the Uí Fidgente, the descendants of Fidgennid.'

Eadulf was frowning.

'Is that relevant? I have been here long enough to understand that your laws of succession are not governed by eldest male inheritance. At least three generations of the extended family have to meet together to elect the man best fitted for the task of kingship. That is usually done in the lifetime of the ruling prince, and the man chosen as his successor is called the *tánaiste*, or tanist. Is that not so?'

'You understand the system perfectly, Brother Eadulf. But the point I am making is that we are true descendants of Eoghan, just as much as the Eoghanacht of Cashel, the Eoghanacht of Áine, the Eoghanacht of Glendamnach and of Chliach and of Raithlind and of Locha Léin. We should be part of the great assembly of Muman. Yet we are excluded. We are told that we are not Eoghanacht and that our genealogists have forged our genealogies.'

'You obviously believe that your genealogists are right?'

Conrí thrust out his chin aggressively.

'I am an Uí Fidgente,' he replied simply.

'But the Eoghanacht believe that your genealogists are wrong.'

'That is the frustration,' admitted Conrí. 'That is what led to the conflict even during the time of Erc, who was our chieftain five generations ago. That is why Eoganán, who believed the genealogists and called himself king, led our people to overthrow the Eoghanacht. He was wrong to squander the lives of his people in such a hopeless manner and his defeat and death at Cnoc Áine and our resulting shame have shown that he was wrong.'

He paused for a moment and when Eadulf did not comment he went on.

'Now that Eoganán is dead and Donennach is our ruler – indeed, many still call him king – we have accepted the rule of Cashel but that does not mean we have accepted the cause of our grievance was mistaken. We still believe that we are the descendants of Eoghan Mór, as our genealogists show. Donennach is fourteen generations in descent from Eoghan Mór in spite of what is claimed at Cashel. We hope one day to persuade Cashel – I would argue that this should be done by peaceful means – to accept us as a voice in the great assembly.'

Eadulf was quite impressed by both the length of the speech and its intensity from the usually quietly spoken and taciturn warlord of the Uí Fidgente.

'Surely you can appeal to the law courts of the five kingdoms and bring your case before them.'

Conrí grimaced ruefully.

'After our defeat at Cnoc Áine, the High King and his Chief Brehon would hear none of our arguments. We had to pay compensation and tribute. It will be many years, or a new High King at Tara, before we can make such an appeal. That is why, Brother Eadulf, you will find among the Uí Fidgente many who will not yet accept the uneasy peace that has fallen between us and Cashel. The Uí Fidgente will continue to be suspicious of everything Cashel does.'

'Then why are we here? Here in the lands of the Uí Fidgente? Why did you invite Fidelma to come here?'

'Has she told you why she accepted my request?'

Eadulf reluctantly confirmed that she had. Conrí smiled knowingly.

'Then that is why I invited her. Anything that can contribute to mending the schism between us.'

Eadulf rubbed his chin thoughtfully.

'But what if the reverse happens?' he asked.

It was Conrí's turn to look puzzled.

'I do not think that I am following you.'

'Simple enough. What if Fidelma finds out that there are some internal politics at play here?'

'Be more explicit.'

'Take the death of the Venerable Cináed. From what Fidelma tells me, Cináed was of the opinion that the Uí Fidgente genealogies were forged and that the people should accept the rule of Cashel without complaint. What if that belief led to his death?'

Conrí was quiet for a moment or two as he thought over the question.

'Truth and its discovery are the principal intent, Brother Eadulf,' he said drily. Then, abruptly, he moved off, saying quickly over his shoulder: 'Now, let us see if the lady Fidelma has finished her questioning of Sister Sinnchéne.'

Fidelma had made her way to the *tech-nigid*, where she found Sister Sinnchéne sweeping the main room with a broom of twigs.

Sister Sinnchéne looked up and a suspicious look entered her eyes.

'I would like a word with you, Sister,' Fidelma said brightly.

Sister Sinnchéne's suspicious look deepened.

'About what?' she responded curtly, almost rudely.

'About the Venerable Cináed.'

The young woman carefully put aside her broom and stood tensely before Fidelma.

'I suppose you have been talking to Sister Buan?' she asked in a matter-of-fact tone.

'What makes you say that?'

Sister Sinnchéne shrugged. It was a defiant gesture.

'I know that you are a *dálaigh*. The gossip among the community is that you are now investigating the death of the Venerable Cináed as well as that of Abbess Faife and the disappearance of the members of our community.'

'Let us not stand in the cold,' Fidelma said, motioning towards the cauldron simmering on the fire. Sister Sinnchéne followed her towards it, collecting a couple of stools from nearby. They seated themselves by its warmth opposite one another.

'When did you last see the Venerable Cináed?' Fidelma opened the questioning.

'You mean before his death?'

Fidelma was patient. 'You saw his body afterwards?'

'Of course. After the physician conducted her examination and the body was placed in the *fuat*, the funeral bier. It was when we all paid our last respects to him.'

'I see. So when, exactly, before he died, did you last see him?'

Sister Sinnchéne paused, head to one side, considering the question.

'It was on the evening before his death. He came here to the *tech-nigid*. It was after the evening meal. I was working late.'

Fidelma tried not to show surprise.

'Here to the washhouse? Did he say why he came?'

The girl thrust out her chin.

'He often came here.'

'As Sister Buan does his washing, I presume that it was not to bring his laundry?'

The girl laughed sardonically.

'That is so. He came here to see me.'

'I see. Was there a specific purpose to these meetings?'

'You are naïve, Sister,' replied Sister Sinnchéne as if amused by the question.

'If the Venerable Cináed was twenty years younger, then I might well be accused of naïveté with good reason. But, bearing in mind his age, and the fact that he was married to Sister Buan, and as she attests that he was impotent in his advancing years, I have to put the question to you – was there a specific purpose to these meetings?'

The girl's expression was not nice.

'I advise you to question Sister Buan a little more closely about her relationship with Cináed.'

'Are you suggesting that Sister Buan has lied to me?'

The girl shrugged indifferently.

'That is no answer,' Fidelma said sharply.

'The Venerable Cináed and I were lovers.'

'Lovers?' Fidelma looked keenly at the girl. 'And is this a claim that you can substantiate?'

Sister Sinnchéne's eyes burnt with anger for a moment.

'You do not believe such a relationship could exist?'

'I am not saying that. I do say that given the sixty years that separate your age from Cináed's, it needs support. What I question is this – you are young, Sinnchéne. An attractive young girl in the full bloom of youth. What would attract you to such a frail, ageing person as the Venerable Cináed, who I gather was not in the best of health?'

The young woman sniffed disdainfully and was silent.

'Love?' pressed Fidelma and when the girl refused to respond she continued: 'So what is this chemistry called love? Can it overreach the natural barriers that separate youth from age?'

'Why not?' snapped the girl. 'Why is it so hard to believe?'

It was Fidelma's turn to reflect for a moment or two.

'Very well. What you are saying is that the Venerable Cináed and you were having an illicit affair.'

'Illicit?'

Fidelma had used the old law term *aindligthech*.

'Improper. Not sanctioned by law, rule or custom.'

A colour came to the girl's cheeks.

'It was not an improper relationship!'

'You knew that Sister Buan was his legal wife and that he was living with her?'

'Of course. And we both told her of the situation.'

'Both?' queried Fidelma in surprise.

'We had nothing to hide. If it was unlawful, then it could have been corrected if Buan had accepted me as a *dormun*, which is provided for in law. Cináed told me.'

'It is a law still practised,' Fidelma admitted, 'although it is frowned upon by the New Faith and the term *ben adaltrach* has been introduced to replace the earlier title for such a concubine. It is a law that will doubtless be abolished at the next council called by the High King.'

Every three years there was an assembly at which the High King and the provincial kings gathered with the leading churchmen and Brehons from all five kingdoms of Éireann to discuss and revise the laws.

'But it is still the law now,' the girl said stubbornly.

'And this is what Cináed wanted as well as you?'

'Of course.'

'And he said as much to Sister Buan?'

'He did.'

Fidelma exhaled softly.

'And what if Sister Buan denied that he said this?'

'Then she would be lying.'

'Could you prove that this happened? Were there any witnesses?'

Sister Sinnchéne hesitated a moment and then shook her head.

'Nevertheless, it does not alter the fact that it is the truth,' she said defiantly.

Fidelma noticed that the girl's robe had loosened around her neck and caught a glimpse of a necklet of semi-precious stones.

'That is hardly the jewellery one expects a member of this community to wear,' she observed drily.

Sister Sinnchéne's hand went to her neck and then she shrugged. She lowered it to reveal a glittering necklet of silver set with amethysts and topaz.

'Cináed gave it me,' she said quietly. 'He told me to keep it safe, to let no one here see it.'

'Why?'

'It will not hurt to tell now, I suppose. He said that it was evidence.'

'Evidence of what?'

'He did not explain. Perhaps evidence of his love for me.'

'Well, let us accept what you say,' Fidelma finally said. 'The evening before his death, the Venerable Cináed came to this washing room and you were here?'

'That is correct,' confirmed the girl.

'And accepting that you were lovers, what other than the obvious transpired? Did you talk?'

The girl looked irritated.

'We were not animals,' she replied angrily. 'Of course we talked.'

'What was the subject of conversation? Did you speak of philosophy, theology, history . . . what?'

Fidelma knew she was being a little sarcastic with the girl for it was obvious that she was no more of a scholar than Sister Buan. In fact, the *dálaigh* was beginning to wonder what sort of person the Venerable Cináed really was behind his great reputation as a scholar.

Sister Sinnchéne was looking sourly at her.

'You seem to think that our relationship was based on lust,' she said.

'I am trying to understand it,' Fidelma confessed.

'We spoke of life, not dead, musty books; not of the past, or the future, nor of things unseen that had no immediate concern for us.'

'Life?'

'Cináed had a great lust for life. He observed everything. The seasons, the weather, the plants growing. He was a very active man. Had he not spent most of his life in the shadow of dark libraries, he would have been a gardener.'

'And this was the subject of the conversation that evening?'

'We talked about the herb garden and ways to improve it but we also talked about Sister Buan.'

'Ah. What about Sister Buan?'

'Don't get me wrong. Cináed had a very generous spirit and felt deeply for Buan. She was fostered in the land of the Corco Duibhne. I presume she was an orphan and later came to the abbey when she was still young to escape poverty. She fulfilled a part of Cináed's life. She mothered him, did his cleaning, prepared food for him – for he liked to eat separately from the community most times. She was not his lover but a . . . a . . .' The girl struggled to find the right word.

'Housekeeper?' suggested Fidelma.

The girl nodded. 'Exactly so. But she filled no other need. He was no longer intimate with her.'

'So, if Sister Buan believed that he was impotent, you would argue that it was because of his rejection of her in bed?'

Sister Sinnchéne gestured disdainfully. 'I don't think they even slept in the same bed.'

'But he had no such inhibition with you?' Fidelma asked softly.

'We enjoyed our physical beings. That is no sin.'

Fidelma shook her head. 'The old laws make allowance for human nature provided it offers no harm to others. But you should know, Sister Sinnchéne, that the New Faith preaches a different attitude. Sexual intercourse with someone other than one's spouse or indulging in general sexual infidelity, even in thought and word as well as deed, is considered a sin. Holy Scripture says the Christ put an emphasis on such infidelity as a sin *against* someone as well as *with* someone. Such sexual activity is considered a rejection of the divine intention.'

Sister Sinnchéne stared at Fidelma. 'That which gives pleasure cannot be sinful otherwise God would not have created it.'

Fidelma had to admit that she could accept that Sister Sinnchéne was probably right.

'We have to accept the guidelines given by Paul in his letter to the Corinthians when he called on Christians to deal decisively with sexual immorality in the communities.'

Sister Sinnchéne sniffed deprecatingly.

'You sound like the Venerable Mac Faosma,' she muttered.

'In what way?' demanded Fidelma.

'He preached such a sermon to me as you do. Yet I feel that your heart is not in it as was his.'

Fidelma's brows came together in a defensive look, angered that this girl could see the doubts in her own mind.

'Are you saying that the Venerable Mac Faosma knew about your relationship with Cináed?' she asked.

'He did. Some weeks ago, he came unexpectedly into the *tech-nigid* and . . . well.' She shrugged. 'He saw us.'

'What happened? What did he say?' Fidelma asked curiously.

'Nothing.'

'Nothing?' repeated Fidelma.

'He simply turned and walked out. Then a few days later he met me outside the oratory and started to give me this homily about the new sexual morality. He was more scholarly than you are, Sister,' she added with a grin. 'He quoted so many sources, gospels and epistles that I thought I would go mad.'

'Did he raise the matter with the Venerable Cináed?'

'He never did.'

'How do you know?'

'Because I told Cináed and asked him if the old . . . if the Venerable Mac Faosma had approached him. He told me that he had not mentioned it.'

'I see.'

Fidelma was silent for a while and then shook her head.

'Let us return to that evening – the evening before Cináed's death. You say that you were in the washing room? You have . . . you had intercourse and then talked about the herb garden and then the problem with Cináed's wife, Buan. Is that correct?'

'Not necessarily in that order,' interposed Sister Sinnchéne.

'In whatever order,' agreed Fidelma. 'Then what? Did he simply leave?'

'Not exactly.'

'Then what exactly?'

'The time was passing and it was dark and Cináed began to worry that Buan would get suspicious that he was with me . . .'

'Suspicious? I thought she knew what was going on from your own lips . . . from both Cináed and yourself?'

'That is true but we did not want her making a fuss, raising a search among the brethren and having a public confrontation. Abbot Erc is of the same mentality as the Venerable Mac Faosma. I think he would entertain the idea of throwing out the old laws and putting in their place the laws of the New Faith, as I have heard some have.'

'Do you mean the Penitentials?'

The girl nodded.

'And so what happened then?'

'It grew late and Cináed rose and said he would see me at the feast of the Blessed Íte, which fell on the next day. It is held every year in the little oratory.'

'And he seemed all right?'

'I am not sure what you mean? He was in good health, yes.'

'And in good spirits?'

'He was in excellent spirits and was talking about some new work that he had written in Latin which he said would annoy Mac Faosma. They were enemies, you know. Enemies fighting with their pens. He would argue and Mac Faosma would respond and so back and forth. I never understood much of it. But that was only one part of his life. However, this was something that especially seemed to put him in a good humour and he went away chuckling and . . . and . . .'

Suddenly, the girl gave a sob. For some time her shoulders heaved and Fidelma felt a little awkward until the girl seemed to catch herself and wiped her eyes quickly.

'Forgive me. I thought I had overcome that. Now and then it creeps up on me unaware. I miss Cináed deeply.'

'You were crying when we arrived yesterday. For his memory?'

She nodded nervously.

'That is all I can tell you,' she said. 'He went off in a good humour. I watched him from the door of the washing room as he vanished into the darkness.'

Fidelma examined her sternly. 'And are you sure that you did not see him again . . . before his death?'

The girl shook her head.

'You did not meet him later in the oratory?'

Sister Sinnchéne flushed and started to protest. Fidelma once more took out the burnt paper and laid it before her.

'You did not write this?'

The girl grimaced.

'I cannot write,' she answered simply. 'You can ask anyone. I was never taught. So whoever wrote this note was not I.'

Fidelma asked: 'Was there anyone in the abbey who did not know you could not write?'

The girl thought for a moment.

'Perhaps,' she said vaguely. 'Mac Faosma knew I couldn't write and so did Brother Cú Mara. Anyway, I did not see Cináed after he left the washing room . . .'

She paused and then her eyes widened a little. Fidelma noticed the reaction immediately.

'You have remembered something else?'

'He was nearly out of sight in the darkness when he was joined by another figure. Then they vanished together. It's just . . . just that I thought I heard a raised voice. A voice raised in anger.'

'Did you recognise who it was who had joined him?'

She shook her head.

'And the next day . . . how did you learn of his death?'

'I awoke late, when it was getting light. There was no one in the *hospitium* to make me rise early. No cleaning to be done, or preparations to be made. But I became aware of activity outside and loud voices. I put on my robe, neglecting to wash, and went immediately to see what the excitement was. At first I thought it was the return of Conrí who had gone to Cashel about the matter of Abbess Faife. We had been expecting his return.'

She took a deep breath.

'But you found out that it was not the arrival of Conrí. What then?'

The young woman pulled a face.

'People had gathered round the chapel. I saw the Abbot Erc there with Brother Cú Mara and some others. Sister Buan was also there, with tears flooding down her cheeks . . . I went towards them and as I approached Sister Buan swung round, saw me, and raised a finger towards me. She cried out something like, "There she is! There is the bitch that did it!" Or words to that effect. The word "bitch" was frequently used as she cried out in some incoherent ramble. Sister Uallann managed to restrain her and she and another sister calmed her and led her away.

'I asked Abbot Erc what had happened. He looked at me and asked whether I really did not know. Whereupon I was indignant. Why would I ask, if I knew? He told me that that morning he had found Cináed with his head smashed in, lying behind the altar in the oratory. I was stunned. I could not move. I think I went rigid, as if I was in a dream. I think I asked if I could see the body there and then but they refused. It was only later after the body had been prepared for burial that I was allowed to see it, to pay my last respects along with all the others of the community, as it lay in the main chapel.'

Fidelma folded her hands together and examined Sister Sinnchéne's features carefully. She realised that it was a beautiful and expressive face. No wonder Cináed could lust – she hastily corrected her thought – could fall in love with the young girl. There seemed no guile in those features. The eyes were wide and clear although they were now lined with red where tears gave an appearance of frailty and vulnerability.

'So, was anything else said to you after that outburst by Sister Buan?'

'Brother Cú Mara came to see me. He was nice. He asked me what Sister Buan had meant by her claim.'

'And you replied?'

'I told him that such a question was best answered by Sister Buan. So far as I was concerned, my conscience was clear.'

Fidelma rose slowly to her feet.

'One other matter before I leave. Did you have much to do with Abbess Faife?'

The girl suddenly smiled warmly.

'Of course. She brought me into this community and was my mentor.'

'How did you come to meet her?'

'She was passing through the village where I lived. It was a week after my mother died of the Yellow Plague. There was no one left to care for me. Many of my family had died in the Yellow Plague, you understand.'

'Including your father?'

The girl hesitated, then shook her head.

'He had left our home some years before. He was a warrior who followed Eoganán. My father was probably killed in some battle or other. We never heard from him after he left. I was on my own when Abbess Faife invited me to join her in this abbey.'

'I understand that the abbess worked very closely with the Venerable Cináed?'

'She did,' agreed Sister Sinnchéne. 'She helped him with some researches he was doing and in the preparation of his work.'

'Do you think there might be a connection between Abbess Faife's death and that of the Venerable Cináed?'

Sister Sinnchéne looked astounded at the question.

'Do you think there is?' she countered.

'I merely ask the question. For example,' Fidelma went on, looking keenly at the girl, 'why would someone wonder whether Cináed had revealed a certain secret to Abbess Faife? Why would someone else think that the discovery of Abbess Faife's body at the spot where it was found indicated that there must be a connection?'

Fidelma knew that her repetition of the words that Sister Buan claimed to have overheard was a gamble. The expression on Sister Sinnchéne's face showed that they meant something. She looked confused and did not appear to know how to answer.

'They are the words that you exchanged with Brother Cú Mara, aren't they?' Fidelma pressed.

Once again the girl's chin came up defiantly.

'I will not confirm or deny them until I have spoken to Brother Cú Mara,' she said sullenly.

'So I can deduce from that that the words spoken are reported accurately?' Fidelma asked confidently.

'I do not believe that they have any relevance to Cináed's death,' Sister Sinnchéne responded determinedly.

'But you do believe that something Cináed might have told Faife was connected with her death. Why?'

'I have told you as much as I can, Sister. I must speak to Brother Cú Mara.'

Fidelma sighed impatiently.

'You realise that, as a *dálaigh*, I can impose a heavy penalty on you for not answering my questions when you have been told to?'

The girl was still defiant.

'I cannot help you and your stupid rules. I will not answer until I have spoken to—'

Fidelma raised her hand to silence her.

'I have heard you. Very well. We shall send for Brother Cú Mara. But perhaps you could tell me why you are so adamant that these words have no relevance to Cináed's murder?'

Sister Sinnchéne raised her eyes to Fidelma and gazed into them for some seconds before she replied in a tight voice.

'It is because I know who killed Cináed.'

This time Fidelma could not disguise her surprise.

'And will you name that person?'

The girl was emphatic.

'Of course. It was Sister Buan.'

CHAPTER NINE

Eadulf and Conrí arrived in search of Fidelma just as Sister Sinnchéne had made her accusation. They stood hesitantly at the door. Eadulf knew better than to react at the words and he caught the warlord's eye and shook his head to indicate that he should not enter the conversation either.

Fidelma was examining the girl thoughtfully and ignored their entry.

'And what is the basis of your claim?' she asked quietly.

Sister Sinnchéne sniffed. It seemed that this was her habit in times of stress.

'I do not know what you mean,' she replied.

'What evidence do you have?'

'What need of evidence? It is obvious.'

Fidelma was patient. 'Perhaps it is not so obvious to me. Let us go through your reasoning behind this accusation. Is it because of your relationship with Cináed? The fact that Sister Buan disliked you and you disliked Sister Buan.'

'Sister Buan knew of our relationship. Cináed and I told her. We told her what we wanted. She refused us and was angry. She hated me and she must have hated Cináed. She killed Cináed in her jealousy.'

'Jealousy? Surely the most likely victim of her jealousy would be you, if Cináed were rejecting her for you?'

'The woman is spiteful; spiteful enough to vent her feelings on Cináed.'

'She must have been a powerful woman to deliver such a stroke as crushed his skull, as the physician has reported.'

Sister Sinnchéne laughed shortly.

'She is strong, that one. And Cináed was elderly and frail.'

Fidelma shook her head sadly.

'Accusations without evidence are not valid. What you are telling me is that you suspect Sister Buan's involvement but have no proof. In which case, Sister, I should remind you to watch how you express that suspicion. The *Din Techtugad* warns that spreading false stories, satirising a person unjustly and giving false testimony is an offence that results in the loss of one's honour-price.'

Sister Sinnchéne scowled.

'Law!' She made it sound like a dirty word.

'The law is there for the protection of everyone,' replied Fidelma. 'I simply warn you to be careful with the words you choose.'

She turned and seemed to notice Eadulf and Conrí at the half-open door for the first time.

'Conrí, could you or one of your men find Brother Cú Mara and ask him to come here?'

The warlord nodded without speaking and left.

Fidelma smiled at Eadulf.

'We will catch up on matters shortly,' she said, but before she could elaborate further Conrí re-entered with the *rechtaire*.

'He was just passing outside,' the warlord explained, 'so I did not have to search far.'

'You wanted to see me, lady?' asked Brother Cú Mara, glancing with a frown from Sister Fidelma to Sister Sinnchéne and back again.

Fidelma nodded and gestured for the steward to seat himself on a stool, which she placed beside Sister Sinnchéne's. She reseated herself facing them. There was strategy in Fidelma's indicating where he should sit. Seated alongside one another, the two would find eye contact difficult and so it would be impossible to pick up any warning expression from the other.

'I need to ask you for your comments on a conversation that has been reported to me,' she began, looking at the *rechtaire*. 'A conversation between you and Sister Sinnchéne.'

The steward frowned.

'And this conversation?'

'It took place before the death of the Venerable Cináed.'

'And?'

'Sister Sinnchéne wondered whether a certain secret had been revealed by Cináed to Abbess Faife. You responded that it could not be a coincidence that the body of the abbess was found at a certain spot. What was the meaning behind those words . . . do not look at Sister Sinnchéne,' she suddenly said sharply as he began to turn.

Brother Cú Mara's face reddened as he turned back to her.

'I was trying to recall . . .'

'You don't recall that conversation?' Fidelma smiled. 'Sister Sinnchéne does.'

'I do recall it,' he finally admitted. 'But it was some time ago.'

'It was after Abbess Faife was found and before Cináed was killed. Not that long ago.'

Brother Cú Mara's features relaxed in a smile.

'Ah,' he said, 'I remember now. You may have learnt that the Venerable Cináed and Abbess Faife sometimes worked together?'

Fidelma waited silently.

'I think that Sister Sinnchéne had discovered that Cináed was working on a denouncement of the claims of Eoganán who led the Uí Fidgente against—'

Fidelma interrupted him with a motion of her hand.

'This work was completed and placed in the *tech-screptra* some time ago. What of it?'

'Did you know that Eoganán had two sons?'

'We did.'

'One of the sons, Torcán, was killed at the time that Eoganán led the Uí Fidgente in battle against Cashel. But he had another son—'

Eadulf broke in impatiently.

'Uaman the Leper who called himself Lord of the Passes around Sliabh Mis.'

Brother Cú Mara glanced at him in surprise.

'Go on,' snapped Fidelma with an irritated glance at Eadulf. 'What of Uaman?'

'Cináed heard word that a month or so ago Uaman was reported killed, his fortress burnt and his followers dispersed.'

Fidelma shot Eadulf a warning glance in case he interrupted again.

'What has this to do with my question?' she demanded.

'Cináed had heard rumours that Uaman's followers were still active, trying to raise support for a new movement against Cashel. As Sister Sinnchéne would have told you, Cináed confided this to Sister Sinnchéne and said he was keeping this a secret until he could discover more.'

'And so what was the meaning of the conversation?' prompted Fidelma.

'Simple,' answered the *rechtaire*. 'When we had news of the Abbess Faife's death and where her body had been found, Sister Sinnchéne wondered if the Venerable Cináed had told her that Uaman's followers might have continued their activities before she left for the land of the Corco Duibhne. Had he asked her to make inquiries? That is what was meant.'

'And your reply?'

'I thought he must have told her for I did not think it coincidence that her body had been found almost opposite the island where the ruins of Uaman's fortress stood.'

Fidelma turned to Sister Sinnchéne.

'And you agree with this account?'

The young girl nodded quickly.

Fidelma thrust out her lower lip slightly in thought.

'There are a couple of things that worry me, though . . .' she said slowly. 'A question for you, Brother Cú Mara: why did you think that the Venerable Cináed would confide such secret information in Sister Sinnchéne?'

The *rechtaire* stirred uncomfortably.

'Why, because of her . . . her . . .'

'Her relationship with the Venerable Cináed?' supplied Fidelma.

Brother Cú Mara nodded quickly.

'A relationship that you neglected to inform me of when I spoke to you earlier,' observed Fidelma heavily.

The young man's face reddened.

'I did not think it my place to tell you . . .'

'Whose place did you think it was?' snapped Fidelma. 'When a *dálaigh* conducts an inquiry no relevant information should be withheld from her.' She turned quickly to the young girl. 'And then I am worried by the fact that you say Cináed told you this secret. As soon as you heard of the abbess's death, why did you not ask him, in view of your special relationship, whether he had confided also in the Abbess Faife and whether he thought the death relevant?'

The girl seemed at a loss for words and floundered helplessly in an attempt to articulate some form of reply.

'It . . . it did not occur to me until I was speaking to Brother Cú Mara.'

'And why did it come up then?' went on Fidelma relentlessly. 'It seems strange that you did not discuss this with your lover, of whom it was an intimate concern, but you could discuss this with the *rechtaire* of the abbey? Indeed, Cináed told you this as a secret and yet you confided in Brother Cú Mara. Why?'

Sister Sinnchéne loosed a quiet sob and her hand reached out to find that of an embarrassed Brother Cú Mara.

Fidelma noticed the movement and suddenly relaxed with a grim smile.

'I understand,' she said quietly.

There was an uncomfortable silence for a moment and then, to Eadulf's surprise and Conrí's bewilderment, she said to the *rechtaire* and the young girl: 'That will be all for now. You may go.'

As bewildered as Conrí they rose hesitantly. As they did so the light from the candles that had now been lit flickered on the sleeve and front of the robe that Brother Cú Mara was wearing. Little pinpricks of light danced on it. Fidelma frowned and reached out to touch the robe. She felt the hard granular objects between her fingertips.

She glanced inquisitively.

'I deduce that you have been leaning on Sister Uallann's workbench recently.'

Brother Cú Mara frowned.

'I have not been in her apothecary since I took you there,' he replied firmly.

Fidelma's eyes widened a fraction before she motioned them to leave. Brother Cú Mara and Sister Sinnchéne made their way out of the *tech-nigid* without another word.

Eadulf turned to Fidelma as the door closed but even as he began to open his mouth she shook her head, knowing what was in his mind.

'The art of a good interrogation is to know when to stop pushing,' she told him. 'When to know the moment to allow a space of uncertainty to occur. Often people continue to ask questions when it merely strengthens the suspect. Uncertainty can often work more upon the fears of the suspect than bludgeoning them into forming replies that strengthen their position. But tell me what you make of this?'

She sprinkled half a dozen minuscule grains into the palm of his hand. He went to hold it by the light of the candle.

'Just ground stone,' he said after a while. 'You might pick this up on a beach where the seas grind the stones down into such fine specks. I think it is called corundum.'

Fidelma brushed the rest of the grains from her hands. 'It is probably of no importance.'

Eadulf walked to the stool that the *rechtaire* had vacated and slumped down.

'I think that you had best bring us up to date on your interrogation of Sister Sinnchéne,' he suggested quietly.

Briefly, but without leaving out any of the relevant points, Fidelma gave them an account of her exchange with Sister Sinnchéne.

'If they were lovers, I think we can rule out Sinnchéne as a killer,' Eadulf finally commented.

Fidelma immediately shook her head.

'There is much power in that word "if", Eadulf. Certainly one of the two is not being entirely truthful.'

'But which one? Sister Buan or Sister Sinnchéne?'

'There are inconsistencies in both their accounts,' agreed Fidelma. 'But I am more suspicious of Sinnchéne at the moment. Did you see the way she reached out for Brother Cú Mara in a moment of stress?'

Eadulf shook his head.

'I was too busy watching Cú Mara's face to see if he was lying. I do not think he was being honest.'

'Those two have something to hide. I think that the good Sister Sinnchéne has found another lover with status in this abbey.'

Conrí looked shocked.

'You mean that while she was supposed to be having some affair with the Venerable Cináed, she was also having an affair with the *rechtaire*?'

Fidelma smiled cynically.

'Such liaisons are not entirely unknown. However, this relationship with Brother Cú Mara may have started after Cináed's death. Remember the girl is young, emotional and probably needs someone for support.'

'But—'

'We have to move on. If the weather is fair tomorrow we sail for the land of the Corco Duibhne. I would like some resolution to this matter before that time. However,

I suspect that we will not get it. I have a strange feeling that it is all connected. To disentangle such a mystery, you have to find a path to follow. It is like unravelling a ball of string. You take a piece and pull and hopefully you are able to follow it to the end so that the ball falls apart. I don't think that we have found the right piece of string to unwind yet. Perhaps we should visit this fortress of Uaman the Leper?'

Conrí was shaking his head. 'We have only the girl's word for these rumours Cináed is said to have heard about Uaman the Leper and his followers.'

Eadulf was in agreement. 'As I recall, Uaman had only a few men with him and they were slain by Gormán. We let one of Uaman's warriors go free for he surrendered and could do no harm to us. I saw the local people rise up and torch Uaman's fortress. So Abbess Faife died within sight of that ruined pile. What does that prove? Certainly Uaman had followers but not many. None of them could be intent on leading a new plot to destroy Cashel.'

'I think Brother Eadulf and I speak as one here, lady,' Conrí agreed. 'There can be no more Uí Fidgente plots. We will argue our case against Cashel under law but not by force of arms. You have our chieftain's word on that.'

'Because you and I agree, Conrí,' she replied, 'because your leader Donennach and Colgú my brother have agreed a treaty, it does not mean to say that others agree. Peace is kept by vigilance. Do you know the aphorism of Vegetius – *si vis pacem para bellum*?'

'If you want peace, prepare for war,' muttered Eadulf. 'It sometimes can be misinterpreted to justify a kingdom's making itself powerful and then asserting its own terms of peace over its neighbours. The *Pax Romana*, for example, was nothing but the peace dictated by the strength of the Roman army.'

Fidelma was impatient. 'Anyway, it is scarcely the time for philosophy and semantics. I merely say that one should not blind oneself to possibilities just because one wants to believe in the good of others. We must be watchful.'

'Very well, but does that help us now? Remember it is my aunt of whom we speak. Abbess Faife was of the nobility of the Uí Fidgente opposed to the continuation of the conflict with Cashel.'

'I am not forgetting that fact, Conrí.'

Conrí blinked at her sharp tone.

'I have other business to conduct with the abbot so I will meet you at the evening meal,' he said shortly and left.

After the door had closed on him, Eadulf glanced at Fidelma.

'I think he is irritated,' he ventured.

'I don't doubt it,' replied Fidelma gravely but a smile played at the corners of her mouth.

Eadulf was puzzled for a moment.

'You wanted him to leave?' he said accusingly.

She leant forward. 'Eadulf, I need to speak to certain people and I do not want Conrí in attendance, especially if it turns out that there is some Uí Fidgente plot brewing again.'

'But you have often pointed out that Conrí is on our side,' protested Eadulf.

'And if that is true, don't you think that he would be putting himself in danger if what I suspect is correct? Better that he keep out of the affair until I get more information.'

She rose and went to the door.

'Where now?' asked Eadulf wearily, as he joined her.

'We shall have another word with the physician, Sister Uallann.'

They were passing the *tech-screptra* when a young religieux came running from it, his hair dishevelled, his breath coming in sobs. He nearly ran into them but Eadulf grasped him by the arm.

'You are in a terrible hurry, Brother . . .' he began.

The young man, who had his head down as he was hurrying, looked up. It was the young library assistant, Brother Faolchair. He was clearly upset.

'Sorry. I . . . I . . .' he began to stammer, not able to form words.

Fidelma gave the boy a look of encouragement.

'What is it that makes you upset?'

He focused wide eyes on her with an expression of distress.

'My work, Sister. My work – ruined.'

'Your work?'

'I have just returned to the library and found all my copying work ruined, the book I was copying from . . .'

Fidelma was suddenly very still.

'You were copying a book by the Venerable Cináed, weren't you?' she said sharply.

The boy nodded.

'I was. The book has vanished. I went to the shelves to see if someone had replaced it. All the books of the Venerable Cináed had been swept off the shelves. Sister, they have been burnt.'

Fidelma glanced at Eadulf and turned back to the boy.

'All the books? Burnt? How do you know that?'

'I saw that the fire was black and smoking and something drew me to it. I saw that books had been piled on the fire and had been destroyed but for a few pages.'

'All the books of the Venerable Cináed?' repeated Eadulf. 'No other books?'

'All those of the Venerable Cináed only, the ones that we had in our library,' confirmed the boy. 'I am just going in search of Brother Eolas to tell him.'

'Then there was no one else in the library?'

'The library was closed for an afternoon service in the oratory. Brother Eolas and I had to attend. I did not return to the library until a short time ago.'

'You are certain that no other works were destroyed apart from those of the Venerable Cináed?'

The boy looked woeful.

'None, Sister. Now there is no work of the Venerable Cináed surviving in our library. It is disaster. Nothing left. We will have to seek copies from other libraries and then we cannot replace them all, for some were unique to this place.' He hesitated.

'Except?' prompted Fidelma instinctively.

'Nothing important. Just some notes he made which he inadvertently inserted in a copy of the *Uraicecht Bec* and left in it when he returned the text to the library. I only discovered them the other morning.'

Fidelma was thoughtful. The *Uraicecht Bec* was a law text said to have been written by the famous female judge Bríg Briugaid on the rights of women. It reminded her of her promise to look up Sister Buan's rights as a widow.

'I would like to look at these notes later,' she said, then seeing the boy was still distressed gave him a quick smile of encouragement. 'Very well. You may find Brother Eolas later but let us examine the library first. Don't worry. You shall not get into trouble.'

Led by the boy, Fidelma, followed by Eadulf, entered the still deserted library. There was certainly a smoky odour in the air and in the fireplace that heated the hall they found the evidence which Brother Faolchair had seen. Fidelma glanced at the shelves where the proud Brother Eolas had displayed the books of the Venerable Cináed.

Eadulf rubbed the back of his neck as he stared at the empty shelves.

'Does this have something to do with his murder?' he asked.

'It probably has everything to do with it,' Fidelma replied with a soft, thoughtful smile. 'But there is nothing we can do here except make sure that Brother Eolas does not blame the poor boy. We have to continue our investigation. Let us see the physician again.'

Sister Uallann was clearly unhappy at being disturbed. She frowned as they entered the apothecary. She sat on a stool before her work bench mixing two curious-looking liquids in a bowl from bottles she held in her hands.

'I am busy,' she snapped as they entered.

'So are we,' Fidelma replied complacently. 'As you may recall, we are here to investigate murder. I must ask you more questions.'

Sister Uallann put down the bottles and wiped her hands, staring at Fidelma with eyes that seemed menacing.

'And if I do not you will remind me that you are a *dálaigh* and I am liable to penalty if I refuse?' Her tone was sarcastic.

Fidelma smiled brightly.

'Something like that, Sister Uallann,' she agreed evenly.

'Then ask away and then be gone. I have my work to do.'

Fidelma glanced at the mixture in the bowl. Sister Uallann followed her gaze.

'It is a drink that I am preparing for someone who has a disorder of the bladder. The main ingredient is barley, to which I am adding some seaweed that I have gathered along the coast here. I have boiled them separately in water and am now mixing them together, making sure that there is more barley than seaweed in the mix. It should ease the disorder.'

Sister Uallann sounded patronising as she described her cure.

'Tell me, Sister Uallann,' Fidelma said without responding, 'what was the cause of your argument with the Venerable Cináed on the night before he died?'

For a moment the physician looked confused.

'Did I have an argument?' she countered, trying to recover from her surprise.

'Do you deny it?'

For a moment both Fidelma and Eadulf thought that she might well be on the verge of denying it. Then she shrugged.

'It was a personal matter.'

'Personal? A man has been murdered. Any information about why he was murdered cannot be classed as personal.'

Sister Uallann looked stubborn.

'It is a matter that I have no wish to discuss.'

'It is a matter that I intend you should discuss,' snapped Fidelma.

For a moment Sister Uallann stared belligerently at her. Her chin came up in defiance.

'Very well.' Fidelma shrugged. 'It is your choice. Do you wish to tell us what the cause of your altercation with the Venerable Cináed was on that night? Or must I use the authority of the law?'

Sister Uallann pursed her lips for a moment. It made her face look ugly. Then, abruptly, she seemed to relent.

'Venerable Cináed was a sinner.'

Fidelma could not hide an amused look.

'A sinner? We are all transgressors against someone or something.'

Sister Uallann was incensed.

'As well as being a traitor to his people, he was also guilty of the sin of fornication. Of carnal lust.'

'And therefore . . . ?'

'You do not appear to be shocked?'

Fidelma's gesture was dismissive.

'I cannot afford to be shocked. Administration of the law allows for no emotions.'

'The Venerable Cináed was having an affair with one of the young religieuse of the Abbess Faife.' Sister Uallann uttered the statement as if revealing some horrifying secret.

'I am presuming that you are referring to Sister Sinnchéne?'

The physician's expression changed rapidly from astonished to crestfallen.

'You knew?' She was disappointed at Fidelma's reaction.

'I knew.'

Sister Uallann's mouth twisted in an ugly grimace.

'Then you will know what my argument was about. I saw Cináed coming from the *tech-nigid*. I knew whom he had been meeting there and why.'

'And so you remonstrated with him?'

'It was dark and well after the evening meal. As he came down the path, heading towards his own chambers, I accosted him. I pleaded with him to give up the affair otherwise I said I would be forced to inform the abbot.'

'What did he say to that?'

'He laughed at me . . . laughed!'

'What did you expect Abbot Erc to do?' asked Eadulf. 'The Venerable Cináed was not a child to be disciplined for what he did in his private life.'

'But Sister Sinnchéne is. I could have had her removed from this community.'

'Ah, so you would have her expelled?' Eadulf observed. 'Isn't that rather narrow-minded? Two people were involved in this affair. But because one is vulnerable you would place all the blame on her.'

Sister Uallann flashed him a look of anger.

'I believe that this relationship brings down shame on the abbey.' She turned to Fidelma. 'Are you saying that you, a *dálaigh*, condone it? It is illicit in the eyes of the law as well as of God.'

Fidelma inclined her head in agreement.

'It was not lawful,' she agreed, correcting the tense of the physician's comment. 'Although I have to admit some grey areas in the law. But by and large, there were grounds enough to disapprove of the Venerable Cináed's behaviour. So, as I said, you remonstrated with him?'

'I did.'

'And this was the sole cause of your argument that night?'

'It was.'

'And how did you and he leave one another?'

Sister Uallann frowned slightly. 'How?'

'Did you part in anger?'

'We did. I accompanied him as far as his living quarters. He told me to attend to my apothecary and leave morals and philosophy to those better able to interpret them. Those were his words.'

'When we first spoke, you made it clear that you were not exactly a friend of the Venerable Cináed. But I did ask you specifically if you disagreed with him on matters of the Faith. I thought that you said you did not, only on his politics.'

Sister Uallann shrugged.

'His dalliance was a matter of discipline not of faith. At the time I answered truthfully and was more concerned with his secular writings. His attack on my husband's people, the Uí Fidgente.'

'You are proud of the Uí Fidgente, aren't you?' Eadulf put in.

Sister Uallann cast him a patronising glance.

'As you are doubtless proud of being a Saxon,' she retorted.

'If you need to be accurate, I am an Angle from the land of the South Folk,' he corrected mildly.

Sister Uallann's smile broadened.

'Exactly so,' she said softly as if her point had been proved.

'But you are not an Uí Fidgente,' Fidelma pointed out sharply. 'You told us before that you were raised among the Corco Duibhne.'

Sister Uallann coloured.

'When I married my husband, God rest his soul, I became Uí Fidgente and since he was butchered at Cnoc Áine I shall remain Uí Fidgente until I join him in the Otherworld.'

'So you were displeased with the Venerable Cináed's work? You saw him as a traitor.'

'Is that wrong?'

'Not unless the displeasure led you to a more violent form of protest.'

Sister Uallann's mouth thinned.

'It is no crime to be proud of one's people nor is it a crime to disagree with scholars. Many people here disagreed with Cináed . . . the Venerable Mac Faosma, for example.'

'When you left him that night, was that the last time you saw him?' asked Fidelma.

'The last time until I was asked to examine his body, about which you have already questioned me.'

The physician appeared to be growing impatient. Just then a bell began to sound from the abbey's refectory.

'That is the announcement of the evening meal,' Sister Uallann said with an expression of relief.

Fidelma smiled without warmth.

'You have been most co-operative, Sister,' she replied with a touch of sarcasm. 'We thank you for your time.'

Followed by Eadulf, she left the apothecary leaving Sister Uallann staring moodily after them.

Outside, Fidelma gave a deep sigh as she realised it was getting late.

'One more task, I'm afraid, Eadulf,' she said. 'But not one you can help me with. I have some research to do in the library.'

She left Eadulf to return to the *hospitium* and made her way back to the library. There was no sign of Brother Eolas but young Brother Faolchair was sweeping the ashes from the hearth, the remains of the destroyed books of Cináed.

Fidelma smiled encouragingly in greeting.

'Brother Eolas is in a great rage,' moaned the youth.

'You told him that we would take charge of the investigation?'

Brother Faolchair put his brush aside.

'That seemed to make him even more furious and he said

he would do his own investigation. He's taken himself to bed and left me to clean the library and get rid of the soot that clings to the books after such a fire.'

'Well, I'll keep you company for a while. I want to look up a law book – the *Cáin Lánamna*, if you have it.'

'Indeed we do.' The boy paused. 'Oh, and didn't you want to see Cináed's notes? They were just a few sentences about law.'

'I'd nearly forgotten,' Fidelma agreed. 'The notes were brought back with another text, weren't they? The *Uraicecht Bec*?'

Within moments the boy had brought her both the books and the single page of notes. Fidelma looked at the scrawl. She was slightly bewildered to see that Cináed had been copying notes about the position of a woman known in law as the *banchormarbae* – the female heir. There was a reference from the *Uraicecht Bec* pointing out that it was permissible under law that, if there was no eligible and suitable male inheritor of a chiefship, a woman could claim the position. Fidelma knew that in the history of the five kingdoms only one woman had successfully claimed the High Kingship and that was many centuries ago when Macha of the Red Tresses had become, according to the bards, the seventy-sixth monarch to rule at Tara. Of course, there had been some provincial rulers who were female and several rulers of clans, but usually a *derbhfine*, the electoral college, preferred a male and it was a poor family where, out of the living generation of males, there was no suitable candidate. Only a strong-minded woman could succeed to such a position. She wondered why Cináed would be interested in the subject. But then he was a scholar and why not?

She turned to the *Cáin Lánamna* which was one of the major texts on marriage and the rights of women under the laws of marriage and swiftly found what she was looking for.

She made some mental notes and went to return the books to Brother Faolchair. She found the young assistant librarian exhausted in a chair in the corner. His eyes were closed, but on feeling her presence he started awake, looking guilty.

'If I were you, I'd close up the library for tonight and return to finish in the morning when you have had some rest,' she advised.

The boy nodded slowly.

'I am exhausted, Sister Fidelma,' he confessed.

She was about to leave when, on an impulse, she said: 'I believe there are many in this *conhospitae* who really would prefer to segregate the sexes.'

The young man nodded moodily.

'There are some who preach against mixed houses and would prefer to see Ard Fhearta as a place of male religious only, Sister,' he admitted.

Sister Fidelma was thoughtful.

'And the Venerable Cináed was not one of them?'

Brother Faolchair grinned and shook his head quickly.

'I once heard him denounce the Edicts of the Council of Nicaea in very eloquent terms,' he replied. 'He believed that companionship was the natural condition for men and women.'

'The Edicts of the Council of Nicaea were not binding on all the churches of Christendom,' pointed out Fidelma. 'But as I recall, the Council was specific in that one of the rules it issued was that a priest could not marry after ordination. And that, of course, raises a question – I have not heard that the Venerable Cináed was ordained as a priest. Do you know if he was so ordained?'

Brother Faolchair shook his head at once.

'The Venerable Mac Faosma was always making sneering references to the fact,' he said. 'Mac Faosma was ordained to conduct the sacrament.'

'So, the rule that the Council of Nicaea wanted to impose on the priests did not apply to Cináed,' Fidelma said thoughtfully. 'Tell me, Brother Faolchair, do you know how many in Ard Fhearta are ordained as opposed to merely entering the religious life – as Cináed did in his role as a scholar?'

The assistant librarian thought for a moment.

'Abbot Erc is ordained, of course. And, as I said, the Venerable Mac Faosma is also ordained priest as well as a scholar. Then Brother Eolas and Brother Cillín are ordained to take the Eucharist . . .'

'And I presume that Abbess Faife was also ordained.'

'And against the rule of the Council of Laodicea, so Abbot Erc argued in my hearing,' replied the youth. 'In honesty, Sister, I do not think he liked Abbess Faife much. He was always fond of quoting the decisions of these councils from the remote parts of Christendom.'

Sister Fidelma patted the boy on the shoulder.

'You have been very helpful, Brother Faolchair.' She smiled, realising that the hour was growing late and she was suddenly very tired. She would explain to Sister Buan about her marriage rights when she could. There was certainly no problem about Sister Buan's claiming any personal inheritance from Cináed if she could show that she was a legal wife of the old scholar. It would also be a good opportunity to press her about Sister Sinnchéne's claims. She handed Brother Faolchair back the books.

'I should keep the Venerable Cináed's note somewhere safe. It might be valuable one day,' she advised, wishing him good night.

Brother Faolchair inclined his head and tried to stifle a yawn.

'I will, Sister. Good night.'

CHAPTER TEN

It was one of those crystal clear winter days. The sea was flat and still. Its soft whispering was only perceptible round the coastline. The sun was pallid, almost unnoticeable in the pastel blue wash of the sky. Only a few white fluffs of cloud drifted high up, wispy like odd clumps of sheep's wool caught on a bush. There was a soft but cold breeze blowing from the north.

Fidelma, Eadulf and Conrí, with his two stolid and silent warriors, had boarded Mugrón's sturdy coastal vessel, a tough oak-built *serrcenn* which was fine for navigating round the coastal waters but not for long voyages on the oceans. Half a dozen men manned its two broad sails and Mugrón himself preferred to handle the heavy carved oak tiller. The ship was stacked with merchandise for trading among the Corco Duibhne. It consisted mainly of metalwork from the silver mines in the north of the Uí Fidgente country and religious items made at Ard Fhearta itself.

Mugrón had smiled warmly as he welcomed them aboard.

'We are lucky today. The breeze promises us a fair sail across to the peninsula,' he said, gesturing to where the mountains of the land of the Corco Duibhne rose to the south, standing out dark and sharp on the horizon. It was an indication of how cold and clear the air was to see their outlines delineated thus, for in warm weather their contours seemed to soften and a mist would hang over them.

'Are those the Sliabh Mis mountains?' asked Eadulf, remembering the last time he had seen them.

'That they are,' affirmed Mugrón. 'We'll pick up the breeze as it swings offshore and it should bring us due west through the Machaire Islands. Then we can head south into Bréanainn's Bay. That is where I land my cargo and where you may acquire horses to journey on to An Daingean, the capital of the Corco Duibhne.'

With the crewmen working the sails to make sure they picked up as much of the wind as possible, and Mugrón using the tiller to keep the stern to it so that the forward momentum was maintained, the coastal vessel pushed out from the sheltered harbour, passing a little rock which Mugrón pointed out as 'the island of beautiful cabbage' which puzzled Eadulf until Fidelma explained that it was an edible seaweed usually called *lus na gcarrac*.

'Ah, samphire,' Eadulf interpreted. 'St Peter's herb.'

It also grew off the coast of the land of the South Folk and he knew it was exquisite to the taste when eaten with an oily fish like a mackerel. He glanced with a longing expression at the little rocky island as they were passing. He could see the squat plants growing in abundance, their ridged skins protecting them from the drying salt winds that whispered about them. But he could see no umbrella head of pale, greenish yellow flowers, and reminded himself that it was not summer.

'Do you truly land there and harvest the samphire?'

'The place provides a bountiful harvest,' Mugrón affirmed. 'Samphire is also to be found on the larger island back there, beyond our stern. You would see a different picture if you were here in the summer's months. That's when the plants display themselves at their best.'

They were now moving slowly across the broad expanse of water towards the distant flat outline of land which Conrí informed them was called the Machaire promontory, a narrow low-lying finger of land pointing due north. At the northern tip was a cluster of islets through which they had to sail to bring the vessel into the broad bay named after Bréanainn.

'I thought Machaire meant a plain?' queried Eadulf, always willing to extend his knowledge of the language.

'So it does,' confirmed Conrí, 'but it also means land that is low lying. The islands to the north are also called the Machaire Islands because they, too, lie low in the sea. There are about eight of them, some no more than rocks jutting out of the sea. I have only twice journeyed in these parts. These are dangerous waters, I have heard.'

Mugrón laughed disarmingly.

'Have no fear, lord Conrí, for I know the waters well enough.'

'Does anyone live on those islands?' Eadulf asked Mugrón, peering forward towards the dark specks.

'Some religious hermits still live on the largest of them, which is known as Seanach's Island. A strange band, they are. Now and then I have brought supplies to them but they do not welcome visitors. One wonders why they have chosen such an inhospitable place. There are no natural wells there and often they have to exist on rainwater, and if it doesn't rain . . .' The merchant shrugged.

'Seanach's Island?' queried Eadulf.

'After the holy man who established their community a century or more ago.'

'I know of two Seanachs,' Fidelma intervened. 'One was abbot of Ard Macha and the other abbot of Clonard. Both of them lived and died nearly a century ago.'

'Ah, but this Seanach was an Uí Fidgente,' Conrí said, almost with a touch of pride. 'He was brother of the Blessed Sennin of Inish Carthaigh. He became famous as the tutor of Aidan who was once abbot of Lindisfarne in the land of the Angles.'

'And you say the community that Seanach set up still lives on this island?'

'Apart from the lack of fresh water it has good anchorage in summer, but it and the other islands are low and flat and the winds can strike them cruelly,' Mugrón said. 'It is more the haunt of seabirds than of men. The oystercatchers are particularly numerous there.'

Eadulf never ceased to wonder at the amazing number of small islands around the land of the five kingdoms. And being reminded of seabirds he became aware of the number of them that had been noisily following them. Squabbling gannets hanging motionless on strong updraughts, warning each other off before diving down into the sea in search of their prey; a small flock of strident kittiwakes with black wingtips flying elegantly northward in search of cliff ledges on which to form their colonies, their cries coming back like the souls of those lost in the sea. Mugrón suddenly shielded his eyes before pointing to some small black specks pattering on the surface of the sea, as if walking on it.

'Storm petrels,' he grunted. 'Probably a storm coming

soon,' he added, echoing the old sailor's belief that they represented such a portent.

No one responded and for a while there was comparative quiet as they glided through the calm seas.

It was still very cold in spite of the brightness of the day. The brightness gave an illusion of good weather but there was no heat and the seaweed that Mugrón had hanging from the mainmast was limp with the moisture that it had absorbed through the atmosphere, which was a sure sign of wet weather on the way. Fidelma and Eadulf were glad of their sheepskin cloaks which they wore over their woollen garments.

Mugrón said something to Conrí who went to a wooden box fixed to the side of the ship near him and extracted a pitcher.

While Conrí took the alcohol to his men further down in the well of the boat, Mugrón spoke to Fidelma.

'How goes your investigation at the abbey? I heard that you were also trying to resolve the death of the Venerable Cináed? Some said that you felt it was linked with the death of Abbess Faífe.'

Fidelma swung round in her seat so that she could face the weather-beaten merchant, who was standing with his feet apart, hand resting lightly on the tiller of the ship.

'I am proceeding apace,' she replied. 'I suppose you knew the Venerable Cináed well?'

Mugrón gave a disarming shrug.

'Not well. Not really well. Occasionally, I have conducted business with his companion, Sister Buan. I have tracked down good quality vellum, some coloured inks that she has bought for him. Of course, he was a respected scholar and I just a merchant. But Sister Buan, well – I knew her better.'

'How so?'

'She sold the gold and silverwork that the abbey smiths produce. Some of it she offered to me and she would always drive a hard bargain too. She was a good trader and went far and wide to get the best deals for the abbey.'

'You know these lands and people well, Mugrón. Do you have any thoughts about these murders?'

Mugrón's face was expressionless.

'All one hears is gossip, lady. Gossip is of no importance.'

'There is a time for rebuke and a time for gossiping,' replied Fidelma, resorting to an old proverb.

Mugrón grinned.

'It is a saying that may well be right. So far as the Venerable Cináed was concerned, saying for saying – be the spring never so clean, some dirt will stick to it.'

'And what dirt stuck to Cináed?' asked Fidelma innocently.

'There was talk about the old man and one of the young girls at the abbey.'

Fidelma was disappointed. She was hoping that Mugrón had some other story to tell.

'Do you know any of the details?'

'Just that the old man was having an affair with Sister Sinnchéne. Well, who can blame him? She is attractive enough, although I would have thought she was the last person to form an attachment to him. But, as the saying goes, do not take as gold everything that shines like gold. It was Sister Buan I felt sorry for.'

'You know Sister Sinnchéne, then?' Fidelma was interested.

'Oh, yes. She is a local girl. I knew her mother slightly.'

'I understand that after the father left, her mother died

during the Yellow Plague. That is why she went into the abbey. Is that so?'

'A sad tale. The mother was carried off by the pestilence but, luckily for the girl, Abbess Faife decided to look after her and took her to the abbey. It changed her life. The father had left them some years before that.'

'I wonder she did not change her name. Was it a nick-name she was given?'

Mugrón frowned for a moment and then his features light-ened in a smile.

'Ah, you mean the name Sinnchéne – little vixen? Oh no, that was no nickname. It was the only thing that ever linked her with her father.'

'I don't understand.'

'Her father's name, that is. He was a wandering warrior in the service of Eoganán of the Uí Fidgente. His name was Wolf, or a name like wolf, I can't remember which . . .'

Eadulf sniffed in disapproval.

'Surely there is only one word meaning a wolf.'

Mugrón smiled wryly.

'You speak our language almost fluently, Brother. However, we have many names that imply a wolf. Names such as Conán, Cuán, Congal, Cú Chaille . . . why, you even travel with Conrí there, whose name is "king of the wolves". I cannot remember which name Sinnchéne's father carried. I recall that her mother called him *ceann an chineóil shionnchamhail* – which is "chief of the wolf clan". Sinnchéne's mother named her daughter to remember him.'

'You were saying that you were sympathetic to Sister Buan and not Sinnchéne,' Fidelma pointed out.

'The gossip was that the girl pursued the old man.'

'Which then might mean that she was attempting to replace her lost father?' suggested Fidelma.

'Perhaps. She always struck me as someone who knows what she wants and goes after it and never mind the feelings of others. Perhaps there was some jealousy, some conflict among the women . . .'

'Are you suggesting that had something to do with Cináed's violent death?'

'Who knows?' The merchant shrugged. 'Where there is conflict among women, jealousy and hatred simmer and such hatred can often lead to violence.'

'But that is merely some gossip that you have heard.'

'Gossip spreads faster than fire. There was much talk about the conflicts at the abbey before I left on my last trip.'

Fidelma frowned. 'You mean that there was gossip about Cináed before the body of the Abbess Faife was discovered by you?'

He nodded. 'Before I left I had heard that Abbot Erc was upset and Abbess Faife had cause to defend the girl before him about this very affair. I think Sister Uallann had told Abbot Erc that she knew about it.'

Fidelma's jaw firmed. So the physician had not told her the complete truth. She had reported the matter.

'So Abbess Faife defended Sinnchéne?'

Mugrón thought for a moment and then shook his head.

'I have misled you. I should say that she defended old Cináed rather than the girl.'

'So did the abbess disapprove of the affair?'

'She did. Or so I am told. So much so that she refused to take Sister Sinnchéne with the rest of her religieuse on that pilgrimage. The girl asked her, apparently. In a way, that turned out well for otherwise Sinnchéne would be missing now along with the others . . . missing or dead.'

Fidelma glanced across to Eadulf and was about to say something, but he seemed to be concentrating on the horizon, his cheeks pale. She had forgotten that he was not a good sailor. She turned back to Mugrón.

'Are you sure that you heard that Abbess Faife was angry about the affair? Why would she defend Cináed but condemn Sinnchéne?'

'Perhaps she knew where blame lay?' the merchant hazarded.

'It seems,' Eadulf suddenly said, shifting his gaze from the horizon for a moment, 'we are concentrating a lot on this domestic strife between Sinnchéne and Buan. Yet if, as is claimed, they were both enamoured of the Venerable Cináed, both in love with him, why would they kill him? Surely in that situation they would be more inclined to kill one another?'

'There speaks the pragmatist in you, Eadulf. But you are right. That would be the logical outcome of such a situation. Yet when have killers ever sat down and worked things out logically? Even in the most cold-blooded killing, there must be a little of illogic for the culprit to ever think that killing someone was the solution to any problem. It merely adds to the problem and ends any hope of resolution.'

Eadulf was now fixing his gaze on the nearing islands.

Mugrón took a hand from the tiller to indicate the approaching land.

'That's Rough Point . . . that headland there. We'll take a wide sweep around it. The tides can be fierce even on a day like this.'

Eadulf could clearly see a number of islands to the north and some ahead of them. He was aware of a subtle change in the rocking motion of the boat and glanced curiously at Mugrón standing feet apart, his stocky frame confident, hands firmly back on the tiller. The merchant caught his glance and gave him a reassuring smile.

'This is why it is called Rough Point. But do not be alarmed, the tide is running smoothly. It only becomes very rough with a westerly wind or big swells against the ebb tide. Then the tide sweeps strongly through the north of those islands.' He jerked his head towards the distant mounds. 'I'll bring the boat well north of that headland there and into calm waters.'

Conrí had made his way back to the stern where they were sitting and was returning the pitcher to the wooden box. As he stood up, he paused and his eyes narrowed.

'There's a sail bearing down on us, Mugrón,' he called quietly.

Fidelma and Eadulf glanced round in the direction he was looking.

'Where away?' asked the merchant, his eyes not moving from the bow as he was engaged in swinging the ship on to a new course.

'Due north of us. It's bearing down from Seanach's Island.'

'Ah, it is probably a Corco Duibhne trading vessel from the religious community going back to the mainland.'

Conrí was shading his eyes.

'I think not. The cut of that vessel is more of a *laech-lestar* than a merchant vessel . . .'

Fidelma had scrambled to her feet to get a better look.

Mugrón, too, having completed his manoeuvre, was peering northward to the oncoming sail.

'A *laech-lestar*? What is that?' demanded Eadulf.

'It's a warship,' Fidelma said shortly.

'She has the wind full behind her, whoever she is, and will be on us shortly.'

Fidelma was concerned.

'Uí Néill?' she asked. There had been several wars with the expansionist northern Uí Néill of Ulaidh.

Mugrón shook his head in disagreement.

'We are too far south. The Uí Néill don't raid these waters in midwinter.'

'She's really straining under full sail,' observed Conrí. 'Her captain means to cross our bow or . . .'

He fell silent.

'What is it?' demanded Fidelma.

'Can you see her *méirge* – her war banner?'

Fidelma glanced to the topmast from which a long banner was streaming. It looked like white satin, blown forward of the mast because the wind was behind the ship. It snapped and fluttered.

'I can't quite see the design,' she called. 'It looks like a tree . . .'

Her gaze had fallen to the deck of the ship. She could see men lined along the rails behind round shields. She could also see the glint of polished metal.

'It is a tree,' confirmed Conrí. There was a strange catch to his voice. 'It's an oak tree being defended by a champion.'

'Do you recognise it, then?' asked Eadulf.

Conrí laughed harshly.

'I do. It's the battle flag of Eoganán of the Uí Fidgente.'

Fidelma was staring at the banner in disbelief.

It was now apparent that the warship was racing down to intercept them. It was also apparent that her crew did not have any good intentions. The distance between the vessels was being closed at an alarming rate. The aim of the captain of the warship was suddenly clear. To the south they were crossing the mouth of a moderately sized bay.

'Should we not run for cover and put in there?' called Fidelma.

No one answered her because a couple of ranging arrows soared from the bow of the oncoming vessel and came curving through the sky, only to fall well short of Mugrón's ship, slapping harmlessly on the sea.

'It won't be long before they have our range,' muttered Conrí. He turned and called to his two warriors. 'Break out your bows and show them we will not be taken without a fight.'

Mugrón was disapproving.

'You and two warriors mean to hold back the thirty or forty men that must be in that ship? Do you want us all killed because you will not be taken without a fight?'

'Rather be killed fighting than killed after we surrender,' snapped Conrí.

'Surrender to whom?' demanded a bewildered Eadulf. 'I thought Eoganán was dead?'

'So he is,' replied Conrí, his voice angry. 'And that means those flying his flag are rebels, outlaws, men without honour who have rejected the peace between the Uí Fidgente and Cashel. They will not spare our lives.'

Mugrón was looking undecided.

'This has never happened before,' he began. 'There have been no raids along this coast since—'

Suddenly there was a soft thud. An arrow embedded itself in the bow rail of the boat.

'They've found our range,' exclaimed Conrí unnecessarily.

He had barely let out the words, when three or four arrows were shot from the nearing vessel. This time they carried a thin trail of smoke behind them.

'Fire arrows!' Mugrón shouted.

The arrows fell near but extinguished themselves in the sea.

'What about running for shelter in that bay?' demanded Fidelma again, pointing to the bay to the south.

'A trap,' snapped Mugrón. 'Once in that bay there is no room to come out. We would be caught like rats in a trap.'

'But we must do something,' Conrí said.

Half a dozen more fire arrows were loosed from the warship. Two hit on the foredeck and two of Mugrón's crew ran forward to tear them loose and throw them overboard. The ships were very close now. They could hear the warriors banging their swords against their shields in exultation. The streaming silk banner was clearly visible now. Conrí was right. It depicted an oak tree and before it a warrior with sword and shield. Eadulf knew the oak tree was one of the trees that were considered sacred among the people of the five kingdoms.

Mugrón was yelling to his crew to take cover behind the bales of trade goods.

'There is an island coming up ahead,' warned Fidelma but Mugrón had seen it and seemed to be steering straight for it. She stood calmly by the merchant as he bent over the tiller. 'Mugrón, the island!' she snapped again.

'I know it,' he muttered.

There came another hissing flight of arrows.

'Take cover, Fidelma!' Eadulf groaned, crouching by the side of the vessel, not feeling his sea legs strong enough to stand upright to protect her.

'He's right, lady,' cried Conrí. 'Best get down into the well of the ship.'

There was a sudden squeal of pain as one of Mugrón's crew was hit by an arrow. Someone rushed to help him.

Reluctantly Fidelma crouched to sit by Eadulf.

They could all see the island approaching dead ahead and Mugrón was swinging the tiller so that it seemed he intended to pass along its northern coast. It was a tiny island, no more than a grassy knoll with rocks along its northern side. Even Fidelma could see that if Mugrón took that course, the warship would be upon them and intercept them in no time.

The captain of the warship realised this as did his men because they heard a wild cheer go up from them.

'Do your warriors have the means to make fire arrows?' snapped Murgrón to Conrí, eyes on the strange vessel.

'What do you mean to do?' demanded the warlord as he confirmed they had. 'Ram her? We are no match for such a vessel.'

'Get them to do so now and wait until I give the word.'

Conrí ran forward to where his two warriors had already used some of their arrows in a futile attempt to hit the steersman on the warship.

Mugrón was now yelling at his crew to prepare to take in sail.

Eadulf exchanged a bewildered glance with Fidelma.

The warship was now turning to bring it in broadside to the point where it would intercept Mugrón's vessel at the north side of the islet. The islet was approaching rapidly. On this course, Fidelma could only presume, as Conrí had, that Mugrón was going to ram into the side of the warship and then try to fight his way out.

It would be a futile gesture.

Then, with a sudden harsh cry, Mugrón pushed his tiller sharply over so that the vessel almost went over on its side. It sheered away from its course and shot suddenly along the sandy south side of the islet.

Mugrón's cry had sent his men pulling on the ropes and taking the wind out of the sails.

Abruptly, they were in slack water.

Eadulf could scarcely believe what had happened.

They were now on the southern side of the islet, alongside a sandy stretch of shore, while the warship had raced down on the northern side, thinking to catch the merchant ship hemmed in against that rocky shore.

For the moment the barrier of the islet protected them.

Mugrón's crew were well trained for they had oars out and were pushing back so that the vessel did not continue its forward momentum, allowing it to remain in the shelter of the southern shore.

Conrí and his two warriors had prepared their arrows.

Mugrón was already untying the small hide-covered dinghy, a *currach*, which trailed behind the vessel.

'The archers will come with me!' he cried, motioning them aft.

Conrí's two warriors, with their blazing fire pot, did not question him but went aft and clambered into the smaller vessel. It seemed only a moment or two later that they landed on the sandy stretch. Mugrón led them in crouching fashion up to the point where they apparently had a view of the war vessel on the other side of the islet.

From the ship Fidelma and the others watched as the two warriors, under Mugrón's direction, loosed off three fire-tipped arrows apiece. No one could see what they were shooting at. Then the three men turned and came scuttling back to the *currach*, launching it swiftly towards the merchant vessel.

They had hardly reached the side when a long thin column of smoke was seen rising from the far side of the islet.

Mugrón climbed aboard with a broad grin.

'Your men can shoot well, Conrí.'

The warlord was looking bewildered.

'You set fire to the warship?'

Mugrón shook his head.

'We merely singed their sails a little. They'll have difficulty following us now.'

'What's to prevent them clambering on the islet on their side and shooting at us?' demanded Eadulf.

The merchant was still grinning.

'It's rocky that side. You can't land. However, I do not intend to wait while they attempt such an experiment.'

He turned and gave rapid orders to his crew who hoisted their own sails. In a moment or two they were moving south-south-west away from the islet.

As they cleared it, they could see that the flames had caught the sails of the warship, which would soon burn away to nothing. The members of the crew were still scurrying here and there hauling leather buckets of seawater up the sides on ropes as they attempted to douse the flames. Even if the vessel carried spare sail, it would take them some time before they could get under way again.

The wind was behind them now and with Mugrón back at the tiller the vessel was already putting distance between it and the strange warship.

With things calmer, Eadulf went forward to attend to the crewman who had been wounded by the arrow. Since his training at Tuam Brecain, the great medical school of Breifne,

Eadulf always carried a small supply of medicines with him. He found that the crewman had, luckily, sustained no more than a flesh wound through the upper arm. The arrow had torn the flesh but not touched a muscle. He would be sore for some days but would recover. Eadulf treated the cut with some dried woundwort which he mixed with some water into a poultice and applied to the wound. It would help in the healing process.

There was an uneasy quiet when he returned to the stern, where Mugrón was still standing rock-like at the tiller. Conrí was staring moodily back towards the vanishing warship, now apparently becalmed against the islet, while Fidelma was sitting in a silent meditative pose.

There was another islet approaching and this time Mugrón was steering to pass it on the north side. Eadulf saw that it was more of a reef for he could see the rocks just under the water as the ship sped by at a reasonable distance from the hidden menace. Then they finally appeared to be free of the islands and into open sea, with a great broad bay extending south of them. It was large and sand-edged, with mountains rising behind the shoreline.

'Bréanainn's bay,' Mugrón announced, breaking the silence. He pointed to the far western side of the great expanse. 'That's Bréanainn's mount, the high peak, straight ahead. We'll land in a small inlet where there is a trading settlement. It's the settlement of Duinn. He will provide you with horses to cross south to An Daingean.'

Fidelma shook her head. 'Do you mean to say that you intend to go back the way we have come?'

Mugrón was equally serious. 'I am a trader, lady. So long as the weather holds, what other way is there than to transport my goods back to An Bhearbha?'

Conrí was worried, knowing what Fidelma meant.

'That warship still presents a menace, Mugrón. We must find out who it is threatening this coast. You cannot chance the journey back before it is dealt with.'

The merchant shrugged.

'True enough. But whose jurisdiction is it to tackle it? It flies Eoganán's battle flag. That's defiance to Donennach, chief of the Uí Fidgente. You are warlord under Donennach, Conrí. What do you intend to do?'

Conrí looked embarrassed.

'I can do little enough with only two warriors at the moment. We encountered the warship in the waters of the Corco Duibhne. Perhaps the responsibility should lie with Slébéne the chief?'

Fidelma interrupted irritably.

'Whether or not it is the immediate responsibility of whatever territorial chieftain, it concerns Cashel and the peace of the kingdom. We will have to find someone who is prepared to send warships to meet this vessel and secure the peace in these waters.'

'There is something else, of course.'

It was Eadulf who interposed. They all looked expectantly at him.

'The warship attacked us sailing from the place you called Seanach's Island. Is that not so?' he asked.

Mugrón gave an affirmative of his head.

'You told us that the only people inhabiting Seanach's Island were a group of religious hermits who have had their hermitage there for a century or more?'

'I did. I fail to see—'

'If the warship is using their island, what has happened to the religious? Someone should go there to ensure that they are safe from this marauder.'

'Eadulf is right,' Fidelma said thoughtfully. 'It may be that whoever this outlaw vessel belongs to, they are now using the island as a base, knowing that no one will land out of respect for the hermits who inhabit it. If so, why are they using it as a base? To ambush unsuspecting merchants such as they thought we were? Somehow I doubt that.'

Conrí was in agreement.

'Those islands would not be ideal for a base. Mugrón has already mentioned the lack of a natural water supply. There must be something else that makes them attack from there. Whatever it is, it must be dealt with.'

'If the hermits can live there,' Eadulf contradicted, 'then a warship can use it as a port.'

'I think our Saxon friend is right,' Mugrón agreed. 'Someone needs to go with warriors to Seanach's Island, make sure the hermits are safe and find out what is happening.'

'But that someone needs to be wary,' Fidelma added. 'If these bandits are prepared to kill unsuspecting merchants, then it is no use sailing to the island in the hours of daylight and simply demanding to see whether the religious community are well. One needs to go with stealth and at night when they cannot be seen.'

Mugrón sniffed deprecatingly.

'I understand your caution, lady, but you do not know these waters. It needs someone who knows them well enough to sail in daytime, but at night . . . ? At night the currents run strong and there are reefs and rocks to consider.'

'So whoever goes must be someone who knows the waters intimately,' interrupted Fidelma. 'It must surely not be beyond the realms of possibility to use a *currach* to reach the island, land at night and check whether the community still dwell there in safety or if indeed they have been overtaken by these outlaws.'

'True enough, lady,' agreed Mugrón. 'We must speak of this to Duinn when we get ashore.'

'Is this Duinn a trader?' asked Fidelma.

'Not a trader although he runs the trading post where we will land. He is also the petty chieftain of the area. He controls the area in which Bréanainn's mountain rises and then his territory stretches west of this great bay and almost south to An Daingean. He is subordinate to Slébéne, chief of all the Corco Duibhne.'

'Whoever he is, I hope he understands the seriousness of this matter,' Eadulf said, 'and realises the need to take immediate action.'

'If there is a warship interrupting his trade,' Mugrón observed with a grim smile, 'then I am sure that he will take the matter extremely seriously.'

chapter eleven

By late afternoon that day they had reached Daingean Uí Cúis, the fortress of the descendants of Cúis, the capital of the Corco Duibhne from which Slébéne ruled the entire peninsula. The great fortress overlooked an excellent harbour on the south side of the peninsula. The harbour had a narrow entrance to the sea. Mugrón's coastal vessel could easily have navigated around the end of the peninsula to it but it was faster to land at the northern harbour of Duinn's settlement and come through the mountain valleys by horse, a distance of some twenty kilometres.

Mugrón had reported the matter of the strange warship to Duinn, who was a rough, almost uncommunicative man, more fitted to be a warrior than a minor chieftain. He did not seem perturbed by their report and felt that the responsibility of sending men to Seanach's Island was not his immediate concern. Even when Fidelma rebuked his lack of enterprise, he was stubborn.

'It is up to Slébéne, Sister,' he said. 'He will make the decision. My task is to make sure that goods are landed safely here, not to go chasing after raiders unless they come into the waters of my territory.'

Finally, Fidelma gave up trying to persuade him. Mugrón had purchased some horses and it was arranged that they could be used by Fidelma and her party, who would eventually ride them back to Ard Fhearta by the land route. Their own mounts were, of course, still stabled at Ard Fhearta. While Conrí was sorting out the details with Mugrón, a monk arrived who identified himself as Brother Maidíu, the keeper of the oratory on Bréanainn's mount. He had come to the harbour to trade with Mugrón and was able to confirm that there was still no sign of the missing members of Abbess Faife's party. Fidelma had expected no less.

They finally left Mugrón and his ship at Duinn's harbour settlement and rode south; Fidelma, Eadulf and Conrí with his two taciturn warriors bringing up the rear. Along the shores of the great muddy inlet that left the stretches of white sand behind, they took the track that led them inland through wooded slopes to the wide waterlogged valley. As they rode along the banks of a broad twisting river, the Abhainn Mhór, Fidelma could not help but gaze up to the great peaks above them to their right. These were the peaks of Bréanainn's mount where the Blessed Bréanainn had formed his first isolated settlement. It was impressive, with its steep sides laced with gushing waterfalls, and deep little lochs nestled in small, balanced plains. The peaks were snow-capped and the weather still chill and not warm enough to melt the frosts from the shady areas. There was no one else on the roadway, which pilgrims often traversed to begin their climb to the little oratory that Bréanainn had built high above.

The party spoke little as they rode along. But soon enough

they reached the end of the long valley, passing by a series of lochs, and then climbing through a short mountain pass before descending almost immediately into the plain that led to Daingean. While Slébéne's fortress of grey stones was eye-catching, what was more striking was the settlement that spread around the harbour before it. Even Eadulf was impressed by the populace and by the vessels clustered in the sheltered harbour. There were even two churches within the settlement, set apart from the other buildings by their small wooden bell towers.

There was no difficulty in finding their way through the streets of the settlement to the great wooden gates of Slébéne's fortress from which the settlement took its name – An Daingean.

Heavily armed warriors barred their way at the gates, demanding to know their business. Fidelma requested to see their chieftain. On being asked who it was who wished to see Slébéne, Fidelma felt the need to impress by announcing herself as Fidelma of Cashel, sister to Colgú, king of Muman. That certainly had the desired effect and they were quickly admitted to the fortress. One of the warriors hurried off to announce their presence to Slébéne. They had barely time to dismount before the warrior came hurrying back to announce that Slébéne would see them immediately. Conrí told his men to stay with the horses and arrange for their feeding. Then the three of them followed the warrior to the great hall of the fortress where Slébéne waited to receive them.

Slébéne, chief of the Corco Duibhne, was a large man with a loud voice who used a great bellow of laughter as a means of punctuation. He was tall but also broad, with a barrel chest, but every inch was muscular. His favourite trick, so they were told later, seemed to be seizing two of his largest warriors by their leather belts and lifting them with arms extended above his head. He had a mane of long silver-grey hair, which flowed into an equally long greying beard that came down to his chest. It was impossible to gauge his age.

He came forward to greet his visitors with a bear hug to each one, even Fidelma, leaving them all breathless in his overwhelming presence.

'Welcome, you are welcome!' he thundered. 'Let me offer you corma – or there is mead if you prefer it?' He waved to an attendant and would hear no refusal on their part.

He bade them all be seated before the fire that crackled in a circular hearth in the middle of his great hall.

'I am honoured to give hospitality to the daughter of Failbe Flann. There is something in your manner, Fidelma of Cashel, that reminds me of him,' he told her with a toss of his silver-grey mane.

Fidelma's eyes widened slightly in surprise.

'You knew my father?'

'Did I know Failbe Flann?' There came the great bellow of laughter. 'Did I not fight at his right hand at the battle of Áth Goan when we overthrew the king of Laigin's men? I fought with him at Carn Feradaig when we put to flight that pretentious whelp Guaire Aidne and his Uí Fidgente allies and sent them with their tails between their legs scampering back to their mothers in Connacht. Those were the days when the Eoghanacht were in danger from the pretensions of their neighbours. Indeed, those were great days when we exerted our authority with swords and axes.'

Fidelma glanced anxiously at Conrí but the Uí Fidgente's face was impassive.

'Carn Feradaig was fought forty years ago,' she pointed out, examining Slébéne curiously and wondering how old he could be.

'I was a young man then,' smiled the chief. 'Young and ready for battle. But age and chieftainship create wisdom and the hardest thing in age is that you have to send the keen young innocents off into battle on your behalf. It is a strange thing, life. Youth will not believe that age will come, or age believe that death will come. I believe I shall live for ever.'

Eadulf smiled thinly.

'*Grave senectus est hominibus pondus,*' he proclaimed.

To his surprise Slébéne slapped his thigh in good humour, understanding the Latin aphorism.

'Age, indeed, is a heavy load, Brother Saxon. But the groans of the aged are often heavier than the load.'

'I would like to speak more of my father, but on another occasion,' Fidelma said, 'for we have little time to spare at present . . .'

'Ah, patience was not a virtue of Failbe Flann either. Never mind. We shall speak more of him at the feasting this night. Look, the day is growing dark already. Such is the curse of a winter's day. Whatever business you have with me will not interfere with the meal, for you will stay overnight at least.'

Thanking him for the hospitality, Fidelma told him about the encounter with the warship on their journey.

The chief listened to the story of the attack with an incredulous expression, and when she had finished Slébéne threw back his great mane of hair and let forth a resounding hoot of laughter.

'A pirate, no less, and in my domain! Well, we've dealt

with them before, by the fires of Bel! Soon there will be one less pirate to trouble the merchants.'

Eadulf winced a little at the pagan oath, glancing at Fidelma. She was not perturbed. She knew that the territory of the Corco Duibhne was still not entirely converted to the New Faith in spite of the prominent churches in the settlement outside the fortress.

'We are concerned, Slébéne,' Fidelma leant forward earnestly, 'for the members of the hermit community of Seanach's Island. Your man Duinn, when we told him, did not share that concern. He said that only you were able to make the decision as to whether a ship should be sent to find out whether the religious on the island are safe.'

Slébéne stroked his beard, still smiling at her.

'Duinn is a cautious man. But have no fear. No one would ever harm a hermit group, especially those of the Faith. Duinn is a good man, when acting under orders. He has little imagination himself.' He glanced at Conrí. 'Fidelma says this warship flew the war banner of Eoganán of the Uí Fidgente.'

'It did.'

'And you, warlord of the Uí Fidgente, reject all knowledge of Uí Fidgente warships in my territory?'

'We are at peace now,' replied Conrí. 'If this is a ship manned by Uí Fidgente, then they are rebels and outcasts.'

The chief chuckled and shook his head.

'Rebels? A difficult word to define. Who is a rebel and who is not? They vary from day to day. Yesterday, Eoganán was a legitimate ruler. Today, those who supported him are rebels. Well, without wishing to cast insult, peace means nothing. For years I have had Eoganán's whelp, Uaman, controlling the passes on my eastern borders. He even dared to call himself Lord of the Passes. Every time I took my warriors against him, he would either shut himself up in that impregnable fortress on that island of his or disappear up into the mountains where it was impossible to find him and come to blows.'

'Uaman is dead,' Eadulf said firmly, trying to bring the conversation to the immediate point. 'The task is to find out who these raiders are.'

Slébéne glanced at him with interest.

'How do you know that Uaman is dead, my Saxon friend?'

'Because I saw him die. I was a prisoner in his fortress but escaped and watched him perish in the quicksand and the tides that separated his island from the mainland.'

The chieftain regarded him in some astonishment.

'I had heard rumours that he died screaming. I did not know there was a witness to his end. But you claim to be that witness, Saxon?'

'I do.'

'Are you sure he died?'

Eadulf coloured a little.

'Do you doubt my word?' he said testily.

'If you say that you saw him die then I accept it. However . . .' Slébéne paused. 'I have reports from the eastern border of my lands that say he is still seen among the mountain passes, still raiding and demanding tribute from my people.'

'That cannot be. He was caught in the quicksand.'

Eadulf grew impatient.

'It is not Uaman that concerns us but—'

The chief held up a giant paw of a hand to still him.

'I am sure that there is no need for you to worry. We've

always had raiders in these waters. Pirates in search of a cargo. Seanach's community has never been harmed before, why would they be now?'

Fidelma was piqued.

'Are you saying that you will not send a vessel and men to investigate?'

Slébéne shrugged.

'I see no great need for it . . .' He paused, catching the dangerous glint in her eye. Then he chuckled. 'But if you feel that I should . . . then of course I'll send a vessel. And if they encounter these pirates,' he chuckled again, 'then we will see how they fight when they have real champions to contend with.'

Conrí pushed out his lower lip. He was angry at the implied insult to him and his warriors.

'There is an old saying, Slébéne,' his voice was dangerous, 'that any man may laugh on a hillside.'

The chief's eyes narrowed and for the first time there was a look of hostility in his eyes. The meaning of the saying was that it was all very well to ridicule one's foes from a safe position. He was about to reply when Fidelma intervened.

'At least we had good Uí Fidgente warriors with us who managed to halt their attack, whoever the raiders were,' she said quietly.

The big man blinked, hesitated and then roared with laughter again, clapping his hand to his knee.

'A dog knows his own faults, Fidelma,' he replied with a smile and using another old saying to counter Conrí's. 'I am sure the warlord of the Uí Fidgente will understand that no slight against him or his men was intended.'

'Therefore no slight is taken,' confirmed Conrí tightly.

'That is well said,' Fidelma added smoothly. 'Yet let me point out that there is a contradiction when you assume that the religious hermits on the island stand in no danger.'

'A contradiction?' demanded Slébéne with interest. 'What contradiction?'

'The very thing that has brought us here. The slaughter of the Abbess Faife and the disappearance of her religieuse who were on their way to Bréanainn's mountain.'

The chief became serious.

'Ah, Abbess Faife. I grieved when I heard the news. She had passed through Daingean many times with pilgrims on the road to the mountain. A sadness has been on me since I heard of her death. But it happened in the eastern passes where we have reports of these marauders. When Uaman the Leper used to control—'

'Did you send warriors to investigate?'

Slébéne shook his head, unabashed at her tone.

'There was no need. Travellers told me that the body of the abbess was recovered and taken back to Ard Fhearta. Is it about this matter that you have come here, Fidelma of Cashel?'

'I am here to find the missing members of the community of Ard Fhearta as well as to find out who was responsible for the abbess's death.'

The chief did not appear particularly concerned.

'Then this evening you will be my guests and we will feast. I will send my steward to fetch you when all is ready. Tomorrow you may travel where you will with my blessing and authority to conduct your inquiries in my territory.'

His tone clearly dismissed them from his presence. Slébéne's good humour seemed to have evaporated. His mood was sullen. Fidelma rose with the others.

'Thank you,' she said, with dignity. 'In that case we shall withdraw and bathe before the feasting starts.'

Slébéne of the Corco Duibhne knew how to arrange a good feast, of that there was no doubt. The meal had been organised in the great hall and there were some forty guests. Fidelma, Eadulf and Conrí were apparently not the only visitors to Daingean that day. There were some merchants and local chieftains who had come to pay their respects and tributes to Slébéne. An officer known as a *bollscari* was employed to instruct guests where they should be seated at the lines of willow tables. Fidelma and her companions found themselves placed at the top table facing the lines of guests of lesser rank. When all the guests were seated, two seats remained empty at the table at which Fidelma and the others sat. Behind one of these empty chairs a broad, muscular man, with bushy red curly hair and beard, whose attire and accoutrements proclaimed him to be a warrior, had taken his stand with folded arms. Fidelma noticed a tattoo on his right arm, a curious image of a serpent wrapped round a sword. This was against all convention, for the young men of Éireann did not usually adorn themselves in such a fashion. But this unusual body decoration was not the cause of Fidelma's disapproving frown. It was unusual for warriors entering feasting halls to carry weapons. This man was well armed with sword and daggers. She presumed that the man was Slébéne's *trén-fher*, his personal champion and bodyguard. But it was a sign of bad taste to invite guests for a feast and parade an armed warrior to protect the chief in the feasting hall.

As soon as all the guests were seated, the *fear-stuic*, the trumpeter, at a signal from the *bollscari*, gave a single blast on his instrument. The company rose and then Slébéne and a young woman entered. She had a hard-faced beauty and arrogant poise. It was not until after the meal that Fidelma heard that this was the chief's latest mistress. Whether Slébéne was out to impress them or the other guests, Fidelma was not sure. The chief of the Corco Duibhne entered the great hall clad in fine regalia; in satins and silks and wearing a silver circlet on his head in which were embedded clear purple amethysts and bright green emeralds. Fidelma had only seen such ostentation at the ceremonial feasts of the High King himself. Of all the company, only Fidelma remained seated as he entered, not as an insult, but as she was entitled to do by her rank as sister to the king of Muman.

Another blast of the trumpet and the formalities were almost complete.

In came the *deoghbhaire*, the cupbearers, with wines, ale and mead, to be followed by attendants carrying bowls of steaming *beochaill*, a broth of meats and herbs, a favourite dish at this time of year for the winter was chill. Attendants came forward to place basins of water by the plate of each diner and a *lámhbrat*, or handcloth, for them to cleanse and dry their hands after the meal. With the empty bowls of broth removed, there came another trumpet blast and three attendants came to present large dishes of uncarved meat for Slébéne's inspection. One dish was of roasted pig, another, Eadulf could tell, was venison while the third he was not sure of.

The chief, who seemed to have recovered from his sullen mood, glanced at the dishes and then pointed to the pork with a grin. The other dishes were removed to the side and the chosen meat was placed on the table before Slébéne. One of the attendants came forward with sharpened knives.

He was known as the *dáilemain*, the attendant responsible for carving the meal and distributing it to the guests. A choice joint was expertly carved from it, placed on a platter and handed to Slébéne, who stood up, took it in both hands and held it up at eye level.

'This is the *curath-mir*,' he intoned loudly. 'It is the hero's portion. To whom does the hero's portion belong?'

One of the guests immediately shouted: 'To you, lord Slébéne! You are the greatest champion of them all.'

Slébéne chuckled in appreciation.

'Yet I am not the only hero who dines here tonight.'

The company continued shouting approval for Slébéne. But the chief turned slightly towards Conrí and suddenly the guests fell silent.

'There sits the warlord of the Uí Fidgente, Conrí son of Conmáel. We of the Corco Duibhne have often tasted the steel of his people. Is he not worthy of the hero's portion? We have met his people in battle several times. Can we not acknowledge the bravery of their warlord?'

An angry muttering started to ripple through the hall.

'Come, do not be shy. Rise up, Conrí son of Conmáel, if you would claim the hero's portion for yourself.' Slébéne gave a bellow of laughter and held out the plate of meat.

Conrí had started to stiffen. Fidelma put a restraining hand on his arm.

Eadulf looked quickly at the chief, realising that Slébéne was deliberately trying to provoke the Uí Fidgente warlord. Behind the chief, his champion stood with a soft smile on his lips. It was clearly an insult, just as it was clear from the eager expressions on the faces of the guests that they realised that Slébéne was challenging Conrí to fight. Such things happened in ancient times at feastings. Although the

New Faith frowned on it, challenges as to who was the better champion still occurred. In the old days, such challenges and their outcome made exciting stories for the bards to relate to their enthralled audiences.

Conrí now shook off Fidelma's restraining hand and rose slowly in his place.

'I . . .' he began.

'I would claim the hero's portion!'

Everyone looked round in surprise.

Fidelma was suddenly on her feet and had issued the challenge quietly but clearly.

There was an awkward silence. Then someone began to laugh but was quickly hushed by their neighbour.

Slébéne stood stock still in wide-eyed astonishment.

Conrí was frowning in annoyance at her. Eadulf was shocked at this turn of events.

'You cannot—' Conrí began.

She turned angrily to him, eyes burning him back into his seat.

'I have issued my claim first. Those who deny it must prove themselves against me.'

'But you are a religieuse, one of the Faith . . .' protested Conrí weakly.

Fidelma threw back her red hair and thrust out her chin slightly.

'I am Fidelma, daughter of Failbe Flann, king of Muman, sister of Colgú, king of Muman, descendant of generations of kings from the time of Eibhear the Fair, son of Míle. In the name of those generations, do you deny me, Slébéne of the Corco Duibhne? Let your bards recite your lineage and if it is greater than mine, then deny me my right to the *curath-mir*!'

She stared defiantly into his black narrowing eyes. For a while there was silence. Then Slébéne swallowed noisily. He shook back his mane of hair and roared with laughter. This time the laughter conveyed good humour and not insult.

'Was there any doubt to whom the portion should go?' He thrust the plate of meat at the attendant. 'To the daughter of Cashel's greatest king, Failbe Flann, goes the hero's portion!' He turned and clapped his hands to bring the other attendants forward. 'Come, quickly now, distribute the meat before it grows cold upon the plates.'

The attendant placed the dish of pork before Fidelma and she slowly sat down. Conrí was still staring at her in bewilderment.

Eadulf, at her other side, was looking relieved.

'Are you trying to get yourself killed?' he whispered harshly to Fidelma.

She smiled quickly at him.

'I was counting on the fact that he would not dare accept my challenge because he knows what would happen if Colgú decided that he had to avenge me.' She bent nearer his ear. 'For some reason Slébéne was trying to provoke Conrí into a fight. The only way to stop him was if I stepped in first to claim the hero's portion. It worked. But Slébéne is a wily one. Keep a careful watch on him, Eadulf.'

The *dáilemain* came forward with a platter offering venison or pork or the other meat that he did not recognise.

Eadulf asked what it was and was told it was *rón*. He was still none the wiser until Fidelma explained in Latin that it was *vitulus marinus*.

'Seal!' Eadulf screwed up his face with a shudder and chose the venison. There was *foltchep*, or leeks, and *mecan*, parsnip, to have as side dishes.

Wheaten cakes and sweet meats, honey kneaded with salmon's roe into little cakes, provided the last course.

At the centre of the table, Slébéne seemed oblivious of the glances that he had received, and was tucking into his meal with relish. His regular roar of laughter even drowned out the playing of the *cruit*, a lute-like instrument, which had accompanied the meal from the start.

It was as the meal came to a close and the *braccat* – a liquor distilled from malt and mixed with honey and spices – was handed round that Slébéne called for his bard to come forward. A handsome young man came to the table and asked, in a soft tenor voice, what the chief's pleasure might be.

Slébéne rapped on the table with the butt of his knife for silence.

'In honour of our guest, Fidelma of Cashel, we shall hear the *forsundud*, the praise song of the race of Eibhear, her own ancestors.'

The *forsundud* was the most ancient form of song in the land, in which the generations of kings and princes were listed and praised.

The young man bowed and stood for a moment until the noise of the feasting hall had died away and then he began softly.

> *Ceatharchad do Chormaic Cas*
> *Ar lath mhór mhumhan mionn-ghlar . . .*

> Cormac Cas reigned over Muman
> For forty years unvanquished
> But by the River Siur his great ambitions
> By Death were basely thwarted . . .

Eadulf listened to the chanting, wild rhythms but, as he had heard it before, after a while he became bored.

He was almost nodding off and had not realised that he had closed his eyes. The volume of sound suddenly shocked him awake.

Six religious had taken the place of the young bard. They were roaring out one of the new chants of the Faith but in a strange mixture of the tongue of the Éireannach and Latin. It was a musical sound that he had recently heard before.

Regem regum rogamus – in nostris sermonibus
who protected Noah with his crew – *diluui temporibus.*
Melchisedech rex Salem – incerto de semine,
May his prayers deliver us – *ab omni formidine.*
Soter who delivered Lot from fire, *qui per saecia habetur,*
Ut nos omnes precamur – liberare digneteur.

It was a joyous chant and Eadulf wondered where he had heard it before.

He had the opportunity of speaking to one of the singers as the feasting drew to a close. He was a barrel-chested man who sung baritone.

'That song is a new one, Brother.' He smiled at Eadulf's question. 'It was composed by Colmán mac Uí Clusaim, who took his people from their abbey at the town on the marshland, and went to the islands when the place was threatened by the Yellow Plague. He and his followers sang it to keep them healthy.'

'So it is only a few years old in its composition?'

The singer agreed. 'It is a beautiful song, Brother.'

'And sung to a Gallican chant,' observed Eadulf thoughtfully.

The singer looked at him with a new respect.

'You know about such things, Brother?'

Eadulf shrugged.

'Only a little,' he confessed. 'I heard something of these chants from Brother Cillín at Ard Fhearta.'

The man was suddenly very interested.

'Brother Cillín? Are you then one of the Unending Circle?'

Eadulf tried to hide his frown of surprise. Obviously this meant something significant. He had heard the term before. But where, and what did it mean?

He smiled and lowered his voice confidentially.

'Are not the enlightened all one with the Unending Circle?' he said, trying to sound more confident than he felt.

To his surprise the singer held out his hand.

'Indeed. And the day will surely come soon, Brother. Brother Cillín has promised us that. We shall all be prepared. Perhaps I shall see you soon in Ard Fhearta when we meet again with Brother Cillín?'

'You know him well?' asked Eadulf. 'Brother Cillín, that is?'

'He was here two moons ago to help us train our little band of singers.'

'He was here in Daingean?'

'Indeed, he was.'

The singer was suddenly distracted by one of his companions and he smiled apologetically at Eadulf.

'*Sic itur ad astra!*' he said softly and was gone before Eadulf could respond. Eadulf was still frowning when Fidelma came up.

'Why so pensive, Eadulf?' she asked.

'*Sic itur ad astra,*' he said quietly.

'Thus one goes to the stars?' repeated Fidelma. 'What are you trying to say?'

'I am not sure. It was said to me. What does it mean?'

'Your Latin is as good as mine. If you want a non-literal meaning, it is something like – this is the path to immortality. So what have you been up to?'

Briefly Eadulf told her.

'Maybe it is some secret society that Brother Cillín has formed, something connected with choristers perhaps? There are several movements among the churches, but mainly among the Franks and Romans, to set up little groups who fondly imagine themselves to be the élite of their professions. They are little groups of artisans and the like, a bit like boys at play with their secret societies.'

The hour grew late and as Slébéne and his lady had already disappeared, Fidelma suggested that the party withdraw to the guests' chambers, leaving everyone else to the continued intoxication of the night's merrymaking.

The next morning the sky was blue and cloudless but this also meant it was cold and a frost lay on the ground, hardening the snow where it lay outside the fortress and its surrounding settlement. Winter harshness covered the landscape.

To their surprise Slébéne was up and greeted them all with a broad smile when they went in to break their fast in the *tech-nóiged*, the meal room. When Conrí returned his greeting without enthusiasm, the chief clapped him on the shoulder with a great roar of laughter.

'You must have humour, warlord of the Uí Fidgente. Do not take our little ways too seriously. It was but a jest.'

Fidelma glanced uneasily at Slébéne.

'It was a jest in poor taste,' she said quietly.

Her rebuke did not dent Slébéne's good humour.

'We are simple folk here, Fidelma of Cashel. We believe in old ways, old customs, and cannot change.'

'Is there not an old saying that change is refreshing?' replied Fidelma in admonishment.

Slébéne bellowed with laughter again.

'I presume,' he said after a pause, 'that you will set off on your quest as soon as you have eaten?'

'That is our intention,' Eadulf confirmed between mouthfuls of wheaten bread and honey.

'You have heard no word of the missing women of Ard Fhearta?' Fidelma asked.

Slébéne shook his mane of hair.

'No word has come to me.'

'I was not clear from our conversation yesterday how far you had looked for them.'

'I have asked my people to spread the word among the eastern settlements.' Apparently Slébéne did not notice her disapproving look.

'When you heard word of Abbess Faife's death and the disappearance of her company, I might have expected you to send your warriors in search of them.'

Slébéne looked genuinely surprised.

'If the marauders along the border have abducted them, it would serve little purpose to send my warriors up into the mountains to be cut down.'

Conrí sniffed in his displeasure.

'Yet you do not mind if we set out alone?'

The chief smiled a little viciously.

'You are warlord of the Uí Fidgente and have two of your warriors with you. Those who once marauded my eastern borders were supposedly of the Uí Fidgente. I am reminded that Uaman was a prince of your people. I presume then that you would surely be safe enough.'

Conrí was on his feet, a hand clapped to his side, before Fidelma could stay him. Had it not been a rule that no warrior could sit at meals without leaving his weapons outside, a blade might have been drawn and worse.

Slébéne was sitting back chuckling cynically at his reaction.

Fidelma stood up and caught Conrí's arm.

'I think we have had enough of your humour, Slébéne. The Abbess Faife was of the Uí Fidgente. Moreover, she was aunt to Conrí. The fact did not protect her.'

It was obvious that the look of remorse that Slébéne assumed was false.

'Then I am contrite indeed. I never thought of her as Uí Fidgente. She was so devoted to Cashel. Yet the abbess was possessed of a great soul.'

Fidelma moved quickly before Conrí took this as a new insult.

'A bad excuse is better than none,' she whispered quickly, looking meaningfully at the warlord.

Conrí hesitated and then nodded.

'We should be on our way, lady, and make the best of the day for travelling,' he said heavily.

'You are right, Conrí,' she said.

Conrí was immediately out of the door pretending to see to his men and organise their horses to avoid the farewell.

Eadulf was embarrassed by the exchange of hostility and he also rose, brushing the crumbs from his clothes.

'You are welcome to return any time, Fidelma of Cashel.' Slébéne smiled, emphasising the word 'you'. 'Then we shall feast and speak of great battles and worthy enterprises. My bard will sing again the great *forsundud* of the kings of the race of Eibhear and this time add a verse praising your adventures.'

'Let us pray that the verse will speak of the success of the current adventure, Slébéne,' Fidelma replied solemnly.

'May success be at the end of your road, Fidelma of Cashel,' the chief intoned equally solemnly.

A little while later, with Conrí's two warriors bringing up the rear, Fidelma, Eadulf and Conrí left the fortress of Daingean and took the road that ran eastward along the peninsula with the mountains rising to their left and the sea at some little distance to their right. They rode in a brooding silence for a long while before Conrí burst out in anger.

'That man! He has been provoking me ever since we arrived.'

Fidelma agreed.

'Mugrón told me of his perverse humour,' she said. 'Maybe you cannot teach an old dog new tricks or an old man the etiquette of a new age.'

'I think this Slébéne is a man of anger and arrogance. There is something about him I distrust,' Conrí said.

'I agree with Conrí,' Eadulf added.

Fidelma smiled and shook her head.

'Perhaps you are both taking his sense of humour too seriously. Perhaps he is a straight and honest man.'

'Is it not said that a straight sapling may have a crooked root?' pointed out Eadulf.

It was not often that Eadulf made up his mind so quickly to dislike someone.

'You must have something on your mind, Eadulf,' Conrí observed.

'I noticed that he was not perturbed by our report of the warship in his waters and the possible fate of the hermits on that island. I will wager that when we ask, we shall discover that no vessel will have been sent by him to inquire as to the safety of the community,' he said.

They received this in thoughtful silence.

'There is another thing,' added Eadulf, 'and I think you both noticed it.'

'Which is?' pressed Fidelma.

'How he was not really concerned about the murder of Abbess Faife or the disappearance of her companions. He made no search for the missing religieuse. Further, he is prepared to let us ride eastward alone, not even offering warriors to escort us; ride east into an area that he claims is still subject to raids.'

Conrí was grim-faced.

'Once more, I agree with Brother Eadulf. For a chieftain of this land, his behaviour is less than gracious. Courtesy never undermined a chieftain's power but he has none. I think we should keep a careful watch.'

Fidelma was reflective for a moment.

'These observations are true,' she finally said. 'But having made them, is there something we can deduce from them?'

Eadulf and Conrí exchanged a glance.

'I am not sure that I understand,' Eadulf ventured.

'Why would Slébéne behave in such a manner?'

'Because he knows more than we think he does.'

'Knows more about what?'

'About whatever it was that happened during the abduction of the women,' suggested Conrí. 'Perhaps there is more in the murder of my aunt and the disappearance of her companions than we can guess at.'

Fidelma grimaced ruefully.

'Suspicion is one thing. But we know nothing and so can guess at nothing. The intention of this journey is to find facts so that we may discover the truth. To speculate on the motives of another, even when one is witness to bizarre behaviour, is not profitable, as I am always telling Eadulf.'

'Well, I am happy that we have put Daingean behind us,' Conrí said firmly. 'I shall instruct my men to keep a careful watch on our backs.' He hesitated. 'I have not thanked you, lady, for what you did at the feasting last night.'

Fidelma smiled.

'I did nothing but demand the *curath-mir* by right of lineage.'

'I realise that Slébéne was deliberately challenging me. He wanted to pick a fight with me. I cannot believe that it was simply because he hates all Uí Fidgente. There was some other reason, of that I am sure, but what it was . . .' He ended with a shrug.

They fell silent again as they rode on.

The whisper of the sea nearby was practically the only sound that broke the white snowscape through which they journeyed. Now and then came the harsh cry of birds and then the howl of a lonely wolf, causing cold fingers to touch at their backbones. But there was no sign of anyone following from Daingean or, indeed, anyone else on the road.

They journeyed leisurely, stopping at midday to prepare a hot broth, and they eventually halted just before nightfall at a *coirceogach*, one of the ancient deserted stone cabins that littered the mountainsides in this part of the world. With a fire lit, it was warm in these small dwellings. One of the two warriors took charge of the horses to ensure they were fed and watered, and made as warm and comfortable as possible. Everyone took turns in keeping watch through the night, but nothing untoward happened. There were no surprises and no signs of anyone with aggressive intent.

ChAPTER TWELVE

It was nearly noon on the next day when they came within
sight of the place that Eadulf had thought he would never
see again, nor wished to. It was a spot that he remembered
too well. For some time, as they had journeyed along the
coastal road heading eastwards, the low-lying island of
Uaman had been resolving from a dim outline to become
sharp and distinct. So clear was it now that Eadulf could
see the blackened walls of what had been the circular fortress
where a few months ago he had been imprisoned. It was
low tide when they approached the deceptive-looking stretch
of sand dunes that linked the island to the mainland. The
solid-looking sand did not deceive Eadulf. He knew that not
only did it contain dangerous quicksand, but when the tide
came in it would often bring a destructive wave two metres
high that would catch the unwary and wash them to destruction. He had seen Uaman the Leper die that way, sucked
into the quicksand and struggling as the wave engulfed him.
Even now Eadulf shivered at the memory.

It was the warrior, Socht, who suddenly called out.

'Look, lord Conrí, down at the shoreline!'

They all followed the line of his extended hand.

There seemed to be a large amount of flotsam and jetsam along the shoreline, and pieces of timber, the unmistakable wreckage of a broken ship.

'It is as Mugrón told us!' exclaimed Eadulf.

'This is the wreckage we saw when we came to collect the body of Abbess Faife,' Conrí confirmed.

'But, lord,' interrupted Socht, 'there are still bodies there. No one has been here to give them proper burial.'

It was true. Several decomposing bodies seemed caught up in the wreckage that lined the sandbank near the shore.

'Should we recover them, lord?' demanded the warrior.

'Do not!' snapped Eadulf harshly as the man began to urge his horse towards the shoreline and the treacherous sands.

They turned to look at him in curiosity.

'I know this place,' Eadulf said simply. 'It is unsafe. There are quicksands there. Apart from that, even in these cold winter months, the rotting corpses will carry disease. Let us keep a reasonable distance.'

They sat on their horses viewing the scene.

'We agreed before that a ship was driven on to the rocky shore further out on the island,' Conrí observed. 'Those poor men must be part of the unfortunate crew who were drowned.'

Fidelma was peering round.

'And where was Abbess Faife's body found in relationship to this place?'

Conrí pointed immediately.

'See there! A short distance along the road and slightly up the mountainside.'

She could see the dim outline of the stone *coirceogach*.

'I wonder whether there was any connection between the two events – the shipwreck and the abduction?' she mused almost to herself.

'What connection could there be, lady?'

'I am wondering why no one has cleared the wreckage and the bodies. Eadulf reported a village nearby and the wreck must have been noticed.' She frowned. 'Eadulf, do you think you can remember your way across the sands to this island? I think we should make an attempt to search it, especially those blackened ruins.'

Eadulf was reluctant.

'That was Uaman's Tower. He is dead. What are you hoping to find there?' he demanded.

She smiled patiently.

'It would be good if we found the missing companions of Abbess Faife for a start,' she said with soft irony.

Eadulf coloured a little.

'It's best if we leave our horses among those trees there.' He had spotted the very place where Basil Nestorios and Gormán had camped on the night of the escape from Uaman's fortress. 'It will keep them out of the wind.'

They tethered their mounts where Eadulf suggested so that the horses had movement and were within reach of fodder. Then Eadulf led the way down to the bank, searching his memory for the path across the shifting sands to the island. They could see that the gates of the grim round fortress still hung open and were blackened where they had been burnt. Even though he knew that Uaman the Leper was dead, and the fortress deserted, Eadulf found the grey stone tower with its circular walls as dark and menacing as ever. Everywhere were traces of the conflagration that had enveloped it, yet the walls were still high, encompassing the central tower itself. It still exuded that atmosphere of threatening evil.

The tide would not be at its flood until early evening. The sandbanks looked firm enough but he knew their treachery. Crabs scuttled about, following the waters, taking refuge in little pools, and here and there a sea bass or pollock had been caught unawares in these pools, splashing in search of its vanishing environment.

'Follow me,' he instructed the others, adding, 'and when I say "follow" I mean follow closely in my footsteps.'

He climbed down from the bank on to the sand, which sank a little under his weight, water running over his feet. Then he began to move forward, traversing the sandy link to the rocky edge of the island proper and making his way up some stone-flagged steps to the grassy knoll on which the Tower of Uaman rose.

As they had seen, the great oak gates, reinforced by iron, hung open, one at an odd angle. There were some skeletons at the gate. They had been Uaman's warriors, cut down by Gormán, their flesh picked clean by the scavenging birds that circled this shoreline. Eadulf had a curious feeling of satisfaction when he saw Conrí and his two warriors loose and remove their swords from their sheaths and peer nervously around. At least he was not the only one who nursed a strange fear of this place.

They passed through the gates into the main courtyard.

'Let us search quickly and depart,' muttered Conrí, glancing uneasily about him.

Fidelma smiled softly, understanding his feelings but not, apparently, sharing them.

'Eadulf, where is the best place to start looking?' she asked.

Eadulf cleared his throat nervously.

'There is a door through there that leads to the cells where Basil Nestorios and I were held. It also gives access to Uaman's chambers.'

'Take me there. Conrí, you and your men can search these outbuildings.'

She turned and made for the door that Eadulf had indicated without waiting for an acknowledgement.

The living chambers of the fortress were certainly deserted and had been ransacked of furniture. They must have been picked bare of goods when the local villagers, long dominated by Uaman, had attacked the place. It was not long before they all met up again in the courtyard, certain now there was no one else in the ruined fortress. However, Conrí was standing with some excitement showing on his face.

'Come and look at this, lady,' he invited, waving his sword towards the doors of what appeared to be storerooms. 'What do you make of this?'

The storerooms seemed full of cases and barrels.

Fidelma went to them and examined them quickly.

'These cases have been immersed in the sea,' she observed. 'It looks as though someone has rescued them from the remains of the shipwreck.' Fidelma noticed the watermarks on the boxes and barrels. 'Mostly oil and wine from Gaul, but look at these.'

They came forward and peered over her shoulder. One of the boxes had been prised open.

'Gold!' exclaimed Eadulf.

'Gold, indeed, and not our native gold because it is too pale,' added Conrí. 'Our gold has a reddish tinge to it.'

Fidelma stood up and regarded the stored goods, head on one side.

'Come,' she finally said. 'Let us go outside and see if there is anything else this island can reveal.'

They left the circular fortress, walking along the grassy knoll. The low tide revealed long stretches of sandy pebbled beaches but at the southern end there were rocks that stretched out under the water. They had no difficulty in spotting the rotting timbers of the main bulk of a wreck still protruding from the water. It was clearly a merchantman but it had been dashed so hard against the rocks that its masts were broken and timbers smashed. Only its stern seemed intact, and even that was fast decaying in the rough winter seas.

Then the smell caught at their nostrils. Among the prickly bushes that lined the beaches lay more decomposing bodies. They had been there for some time and the carrion had been feasting. Trying to control her look of distaste, Fidelma approached one of them. Her eyes took in the remnants of clothing.

'Seamen, foreign seamen,' she muttered. 'I have seen that style of clothing somewhere.'

It was Eadulf who supplied the answer.

'When I was returning from Rome, I took passage on a Gaulish merchant ship, and they wore a similar style of clothing.'

'Gaulish? Mugrón identified the boot that was found as that of a Gaulish seaman. That makes sense.'

'Those poor wretches, drowning so near to land,' muttered Conrí.

'Look at this.' Fidelma pointed to one of the corpses.

Holding a hand over his mouth to avoid the stench, Conrí, with Eadulf at his shoulder, did so.

'This man did not drown. He has a broken sword blade snapped off between his ribs.'

Eadulf was aghast.

'You mean these men made it ashore and were cut down?'

'The man who killed this sailor thrust his sword in but it must have been ill tempered, for when he tried to withdraw the blade it broke,' Fidelma explained. 'Thus the tip of the blade remains in the rotting flesh as a mute testimony to the crime.'

Eadulf pointed to another corpse which lay on its back.

'The skull of this one seems smashed. It might have been done in the wreck or against the rocks . . .'

'Then how did the man manage to crawl up here so far above the waterline?' queried Fidelma. She slowly shook her head. 'We are seeing nothing but plain and gruesome murder. Either that ship was deliberately wrecked or people stood on this shore waiting for the survivors and killed them.'

The usually silent warrior, Socht, had been looking at the channel between the tip of the island and the southern shore.

'It would take a bad seaman and bad luck to run ashore here even in darkness, lady,' he muttered.

'Could it be that the Abbess Faife and her companions were passing here when this deed occurred? They saw this crime and had to be silenced?' Conrí speculated.

'If so, then there are matters that puzzle me,' said Eadulf.

They turned to him with expressions of curiosity.

'Well, if it was the intention to keep this matter a secret, why leave Abbess Faife so close to the scene, along the roadside where Mugrón found her a short time later? Why have these bodies been left strewn on this island and floating in the waters around it? Why leave the booty in the fortress with gates and doors wide open so that anyone could – even as we did – enter and discover it?'

'The questions are pertinent,' agreed Fidelma.

'But are there answers to them?' demanded Conrí.

'It shows that whoever did this thing is supremely confident,' Eadulf concluded. 'That they fear no one in this area.'

No one commented and so Eadulf continued.

'There was only one person who had such power and overweening belief in himself . . .' Eadulf paused and then shrugged. 'But I saw him die. Now there is only one undisputed chief of this land.'

'Slébéne!' muttered Conrí.

'Is there any other?' Eadulf challenged.

'Well,' agreed Conrí, 'only the wronged dead are allowed to come back from the Otherworld on the night of the feast of Samhain to wreak vengeance on the living of this world. As Uaman was not wronged when he perished here, though he wronged many himself, he does not qualify to return on the feast of Samhain. So I agree with Eadulf, we must beware of Slébéne.'

Fidelma peered around the deserted island and a cold wind caught at her, causing her to shiver slightly.

'There seems much wrong in this land of the Corco Duibhne. Yet before we can accuse Slébéne we must gather proof against him.'

Eadulf was unhappy that Fidelma did not support his view that it was more than apparent that Slébéne was to blame.

'There can be no other explanation,' he said determinedly.

'Perhaps not, but I am only interested in what can be argued before the Brehons.' Conrí was about to speak when Fidelma held up her hand. 'We will speak of this no more until we can argue fact and not speculation.'

Another gust of cold air hit them and Eadulf glanced at the darkening, grey sea with its choppy waves. The hour was growing late.

'The tide is on the turn,' he said. 'I think we should go back across the sands to the mainland before we are cut off for the night.'

'What of the goods in the storeroom? What of the gold?' demanded Conrí.

'We must leave it. Our first consideration is to find the missing women,' snapped Fidelma. 'We can deal with that matter later.'

The journey back was an easier one as they had their own footsteps in the sand to guide them safely over the sand dunes to the firm shore. The sky was darkening when they left the island and they could hear the sibilant whispering of the sea as the oncoming tide gathered for its onslaught across the sand.

'We have a short time before darkness. Let me see where the body of the abbess was found.'

They collected their horses and Conrí led them a short distance along the road and then up through some trees towards the dark shape of a conical stone hut.

'Mugrón found her outside the *coirceogach* and then dragged the body behind it, packing it with snow to preserve it until he reached Ard Fhearta to alert us.'

Fidelma dismounted and looked about. She realised there would be little to find. Too long had passed and too many people had been here. Also, there had been several falls of snow since the incident, obscuring everything. But the hope of discovering some significant clue was not the reason for her coming. She merely needed to see and feel the atmosphere of the place where the deed was done as it helped her to recreate it in her mind. She looked around. They were out of sight of the island, being round a bend in the road, and the road itself was a short distance away below them.

Fidelma bent down and entered the stone hut. There were traces of a travellers' fire, some discarded pottery items and a few pieces of rag . . . no, not rags, but clothing. She looked carefully at one of them. It turned out to be a leather jerkin, a seaman's jerkin, of the style she had seen on the decomposing corpses on the island. Nearby was the boot – a *coisbert*.

She emerged from the *coirceogach* and held out the items to Conrí.

'I presume that this is the boot and clothing that Mugrón showed you?'

Conrí gave an affirmative gesture.

'They may mean nothing,' she said, replacing them in the hut. 'There are many ways that the clothing could have come here. There is also a chance someone took it from one of the corpses and brought it here. Perhaps one of the people who killed Faife could have been carrying it or even wearing it. There are lots of possibilities.'

Conrí was looking at the sky with impatience.

'I do not think that we should spend any more time here. We need to find a place to pass the night,' he said. 'It is going to be a cold one and I do not fancy the idea of sleeping out under the trees.'

'I told you that there was a village up the mountainside just here. We should have no trouble in finding a sheltered place. It was people from it who destroyed Uaman's fortress once they learnt they were free from his thrall.'

'Let us hope that they are more hospitable these days,' the warlord muttered.

'People's actions in normal circumstances cannot be judged by their actions in extreme conditions,' replied Eadulf. 'I am sure we will find hospitality there.'

'Then lead on, Eadulf,' Fidelma instructed. 'It has been a tiring day.'

They remounted and Eadulf led the way up the track in the direction he knew the village lay. It was not far up the hillside, on the easy slopes just before the trees stopped and the great bald, rocky hills began to climb into the towering Sliabh Mis mountains. Eadulf swung round a bend on the track and came abruptly into what was the centre of the village. There was a blacksmith's workshop in its usual position at the end of the settlement and a series of buildings, both stone and wooden structures, spread either side of the track. It was not quite dark yet and Eadulf was surprised by the utter stillness of the place. It seemed deserted.

'Are you sure this is the place, Eadulf?' Fidelma found herself whispering as they halted.

'I am sure.'

He leant forward in his saddle and gave forth a loud shout.

'*Hóigh! Hóigh!*'

There was a sudden fluttering of alarmed birds rising into the air but when their angry squawks died away no one had appeared or answered the call.

As an automatic reaction, Conrí's two warriors had their swords unsheathed and ready as they examined their surroundings.

'Your villagers seem to have deserted this place,' commented Conrí unnecessarily.

Eadulf rode forward between the houses, peering in at half-open doorways. It was true. It seemed that the entire village had been deserted, and certainly fairly recently judging by the condition of the buildings and what he could see of their interiors.

Fidelma was resigned.

'Well, if we cannot find hospitality we can, at least, have a roof over our heads this night,' she said philosophically.

Eadulf pointed to a building.

'That looks suitable for accommodation. There is even a well beside it.'

They dismounted and Socht and his companion took charge of the horses and went to find them a suitable shelter. Conrí himself managed to get a fire going in the hearth of the building while Eadulf explored its two rooms. There was a wooden bed frame in one of the rooms, and cupboards which the previous occupants had been rather hurried in clearing out, for a few items had been left inside them.

'From the dust, this place cannot have been deserted for more than a week or two,' Fidelma commented. 'I wonder why the people decided to leave?'

A moment later the second warrior returned. He wore a grin on his face. He said nothing but had his bow in one hand and held up two rabbits in the other.

Conrí smiled appreciatively.

'Well, we won't starve tonight. And we have water at hand and there is still corma in my saddle bag to keep out the winter's chill.'

At a nod from Conrí, the warrior went outside to skin and gut the animals ready for cooking while the warlord constructed a spit that could be turned over the fire he had made.

It was while they were seated in the main room of the deserted building in front of the fire, watching the sizzling carcasses of the rabbits being turned over it, that they all heard a slight, muffled sound.

It was a soft thump. The noise seemed to come from

under the very floor on which they sat. Yet the floor appeared to be a hardened earth surface.

Conrí glanced at the others and placed a finger to his lips. His brows were drawn together. He began to examine the floor without moving from his seat. Then he silently pointed. There was a spot where dried rushes had been strewn and they saw a metal ring almost buried in the straw.

Quietly, quickly, Conrí rose and moved to it. His two warrior companions had drawn their swords ready. The warlord bent down, gripped the metal ring quietly, paused only a moment and then pulled it abruptly upwards. A small trapdoor came away and Conrí peered down.

'Come out of that!' he shouted in a thunderous bellow.

A moment later a small head and shoulders emerged.

A frightened fair-haired boy, freckle-faced, terror in the blue eyes that peered round at the company. His hair was matted and his face smudged with dirt.

'It's a boy!' cried Conrí in surprise, then he bent with one hand and hauled the child bodily up into the room. The lad could have been no more than twelve years old. He stood looking from one to another of them in a fearful fashion. Conrí, meanwhile, took a flaming piece of wood from the fire and peered into the hole from which the boy had emerged. He turned back with a shake of his head. 'Nothing there. It is only an *uaimh talún*, an underground chamber for storing food.'

It was clear that the boy was still very frightened.

Fidelma smiled encouragingly at him.

'Come here, child,' she instructed. 'Come, tell me your name.'

The boy shuffled forward a step.

'I am Iobcar, son of Starn the blacksmith,' he said hesitantly yet with a curious dignity.

'Well,' Fidelma's smile widened at the child's tone, 'well,
Iobcar son of Starn the blacksmith, I am Fidelma of Cashel.
Tell me what you were doing in that souterrain?'

'Hiding,' the boy said simply.

'From whom?'

'From you,' the boy replied without guile, causing some
merriment from the two warriors.

'Tell us, Iobcar son of Starn the blacksmith,' invited
Fidelma, 'why would you be hiding from us?'

'I thought you were the bad people.'

'The bad people?'

'The people of Uaman the Leper.'

Eadulf frowned in irritation.

'Uaman the Leper is long dead, boy,' he snapped and
received a look of rebuke from Fidelma for his manner.

'My father said that he was so bad that the Otherworld
would not have him and he had to return to this one.'

Fidelma tried to hide her chuckle of amusement.

'So your father Starn is a philosopher?' observed Eadulf
sarcastically.

The boy shook his head, taking the question seriously.

'He is a blacksmith,' he protested. 'I have told you as
much.'

'Very well, Iobcar,' intervened Fidelma. 'But tell us where
the people of this village have gone and why.'

The boy examined her thoughtfully.

'I cannot tell you where they have gone, for that is a
secret,' he said after some hesitation. 'But the reason why
is because they were fearful that Uaman would punish them
now that he has returned from the Otherworld.'

Eadulf was about to interrupt to correct the boy again but Fidelma gave him a warning glance. He held his peace.

'So when was this? When did they leave?'

'Last week.'

'And why were you left here?'

'I was not. I returned here to find something that I had left behind.' He glanced nervously over his shoulder at the underground storage space. Seeing the movement, Conrí bent down again and with a grunt of triumph he came up with a small bow, not large but fit enough for use by the boy. The boy's face was immediately troubled but Fidelma again smiled encouragement.

'We do not want your bow, Iobcar,' she said, motioning Conrí to give it to the boy. 'Nor do we want you to betray the secret of where your people have gone. We would like to know more details about why they felt forced to evacuate this place.'

The boy took his bow and stood for a moment staring at Fidelma as if trying to read her mind.

'My father used to say that Uaman was the great curse of our people when he dwelt below on the island. His men would often raid our village for sheep and goats and . . . well, other things. Then perhaps two moons ago it was reported that he was dead and the villagers went down to the island and burnt his fortress and took back what was theirs.'

They waited patiently while the boy paused again, as if to gather his thoughts.

'Not long ago Uaman's men appeared in our village again. They demanded tribute on behalf of the master. The village elders gave them what they could. One day soon afterwards my father went to the island and came back and said these men had wrecked a ship there. The elders met and decided the village must move beyond the mountains. We all left about seven days ago to find a new village. Yesterday I found I had forgotten my bow and so today I came in search of it. I had just found it when I heard you calling and thinking you to be Uaman's people I hid myself in the *uaimh talún*. But you found me.'

'I see,' Fidelma said. 'Well, we mean you no harm, nor harm to your people. We are not Uaman's men. Anyway, it is late now, so eat with us and stay so that you are refreshed to return to your people in the morning.'

The boy was hesitant.

'They will be worried.'

'But more worried if you set out to traverse these mountains in the blackness of the night, Iobcar son of Starn the blacksmith,' she replied solemnly.

Iobcar considered the matter and then, sniffing at the odour of roasted rabbit, nodded slowly.

Conrí began to slice the meat from the carcasses that he had been cooking on his skewer. Eadulf had not finished questioning the boy but he waited until the lad was settled and munching on the roasted meat.

'Tell me, Iobcar,' he asked, 'do you know anything about those you call Uaman's people?'

'Only that my father says they are bad people,' the boy said between mouthfuls of meat.

'Have you heard of any religious being killed near here by them?'

Again the boy shook his head.

'But when my father came back from the island, he said that he saw some warriors taking some women prisoners along the road.'

Eadulf exchanged a quick glance with Fidelma.

'Women prisoners? And that was when he reported to the village that a ship had been wrecked there?'

'The same time,' agreed the boy.

Eadulf looked triumphantly at Fidelma.

'And in which direction were Uaman's men taking these prisoners? Towards the east to the Abbey of Colmán or west to Daingean, the fortress of the chieftain of the Corco Duibhne?'

The boy paused, thinking for a moment.

'Neither. My father said they were going north.'

'North into the mountains?' Conrí frowned in surprise. He and Eadulf had expected that the raiders would be returning to Slébéne's fortress.

'Along the track that leads up the mountain valley, where the River Imligh flows,' agreed the boy. 'They were heading north.'

Eadulf turned to Fidelma.

'I know part of that way, for that is the path we travelled in search of little Alchú.' There was a tense quality in his voice as he spoke which only Fidelma picked up, realising he was remembering his frantic search for their abducted son.

'Then that is the road we must take tomorrow,' Fidelma decided with a firmness that admitted no dissension. She waited until she and Eadulf were alone and then she reached out and laid her hand on Eadulf's arm. 'Memories are hard, I know,' she said softly. 'But our baby is now safe in Cashel. Muirgen and Nessan are protecting him as fiercely as if he were their own child. Once this matter is over, we will soon be back with him.'

Eadulf sighed sadly and patted her hand.

'Yet the memories come, especially in this place. It is such a short time that has passed since last I was here. The memories of what happened here are sharp and I am still anxious.'

Fidelma grimaced and Eadulf realised that her eyes were unnaturally bright.

'Forgive me,' he suddenly said in a soft tone.

She passed a hand over her eyes quickly, as if to disguise the act of wiping them, and frowned questioningly.

'I am being too selfish about my feelings.' Eadulf raised a shoulder and let it fall expressively. 'It is a great fault.' He took her hands in his and squeezed them.

Fidelma forced a smile.

'Brehon Morann used to say, they are truly good who are faultless. I am very aware of my own faults. But I share your anxieties. It is a heavy duty, being sister of the king as well as a *dálaigh*. It often leaves no room for the woman nor for the mother. Yet the woman and the mother are here in this same body. You, above all people, should know that.'

Eadulf bowed his head for a moment. Then he cleared his throat.

'We'd best get some rest for we must start early in the morning,' he said shortly.

Fidelma was the first to wake the next morning. Iobcar son of Starn the blacksmith was gone, along with his bow. She went outside to the well, drew some water, and washed quickly. When she had done, Eadulf and the others were stirring. They decided not to waste time in hunting more game to break their fast, for there was no other food to hand, no fruits nor berries. The midwinter days limited their diet.

They decided to press on immediately and pause at lunchtime for food. Eadulf assured them that by that time they would have reached a hamlet where he knew hospitality would be accorded them. So, slaking their thirst with fresh water from the well, they saddled their horses and set off along the track across the shoulder of the mountain which Eadulf indicated was to be their path.

The patient horses climbed for a while, bringing them to a spectacular view of the inlet below them when they emerged above the treeline.

'Look!' It was Conrí who brought them to a halt. He was pointing down to the island below.

A large vessel had sailed up the narrow waters and was riding at anchor a short distance off the island. Some of the crew were taking down its sails while others launched a skiff from the side of the ship. The vessel looked vaguely familiar to Fidelma and Eadulf, but it was only when the breeze caught at the banner snaking from the mainmast that they realised why. Fidelma turned to Conrí in surprise.

'That is the warship that attacked us off the Machaire Islands.'

Conrí had already realised that fact.

'It must have put on new sail and then passed round the end of the peninsula and sailed up the inlet. Why would they be following us?'

'They cannot be following us,' replied Fidelma with a shake of her head. 'They would not know that we were crossing the peninsula and passing this spot.'

'Then what are they doing?' demanded Conrí.

'Well, the best thing is to dismount lest they see that they are being observed,' Eadulf advised. 'Then we may be able to find out what they are doing on the island.'

Socht took their horses further along the track to a spot behind a group of rocks where they were hidden from prying eyes.

They perched themselves in a clump of boulders from where they could look down into the inlet without being seen. It was not very long before they discovered what the crew of the strange ship was about.

'Why,' Conrí observed in wonder, 'they are loading up with the stores from the shipwreck.'

'Do you think they had any part in wrecking the ship?' Eadulf asked.

'Perhaps they are the wreckers, and hoarded the goods so that they could return for them later,' Fidelma hazarded.

'Then they must be the same men who killed Faife and abducted her companions. They moved north and picked up their vessel on the north side of the peninsula,' Conrí said. 'The prisoners must be on board the ship.'

Eadulf shook his head. 'Why march north if they merely meant to sail back here again? And the wreck and capture of the women was nearly three weeks ago now.'

'That island would be ideal as a spot to lure unsuspecting ships on to its rocks,' mused Socht.

'How so?' demanded Eadulf.

'The passage to the south of the island is narrow, but you can see from the colour of the waters that it is deep water,' Socht observed. 'Ships from as far as Gaul run up here to the safe anchorage at the abbey of Colmán to the east. Once past this island, the ships are protected from the rough ocean waters and find safe harbour there. Can you imagine what would befall a ship running to the north of the island straight on to the sands or, indeed, running into the rocks around that southern extremity?'

'It is more apparent from this vantage point,' Eadulf agreed. 'How do you know such things, Socht?'

Conrí replied for him. 'Socht is one of our best seafaring warriors and knows the coastline around our waters.'

'Terrible crimes have been committed here,' Fidelma commented. 'I think we have seen enough. It is obvious that the ship knew that the stores were there and went straight to them. I think we can assume that the crew are the wreckers. They are responsible for killing the hapless sailors as they came ashore. And we know that this ship lurks around these waters and bears the war banner of Eoganán of the Uí Fidgente.'

'If they are Uí Fidgente, then they are rebels and traitors. We are at peace,' asserted Conrí, feeling the need to defend his people once again.

'I accept that,' replied Fidelma. 'Certainly a flag does not always guarantee the identity of the person who flies it. But our main task is to press on after the abductors. I'd like to reach this little hamlet that Eadulf told us about before we die of hunger.'

'You don't think we will find Abbess Faife's missing companions on that vessel down there?' Conrí was disappointed.

'We can't be sure that the wreckers and abductors are one and the same,' Fidelma replied firmly. She made no further comment as they remounted and rode on.

Although it was still fairly cold, it was pleasant riding through the mountains. The sky was pale blue and the sun, though weak, reflected on the snow and the crystal waters of mountain springs, giving an impression of intense brightness. Eadulf remembered the path and so they rode confidently through the rocky terraces that inclined steeply to a large rushing river as it tumbled down from the far peaks. They passed several old grey standing stones from a bygone age. As the path dipped below the treeline once more Eadulf realised that they must have started their descent to the ford where the hamlet stood. He was about to say as much when there was a curious whistling sound and a thud.

The arrow embedded itself in a tree about an arm's distance from Conrí's right shoulder. His horse shied nervously, causing the mounts of his companions to move skittishly, heads tugging sharply at their reins, whites of their eyes showing in terror.

As Conrí and his men reached automatically for their weapons a harsh voice called out: 'Don't move. That was a warning shot. If we had wanted to hit you, we would have done so. Get down off your horses.'

Conrí was hesitant.

They heard the hum of another arrow. This time it seemed to come from another direction and hit a tree behind them.

'In case you think there is only one archer, let me tell you that you are surrounded. That is enough of warnings. You will get down off your horses and lay your arms on the path before you.'

Conrí glanced at Fidelma and gestured helplessly.

'There is no choice,' she said in resignation as she made to obey.

'Wait!' called the voice. 'You will dismount one at a time. Each walk forward five paces and lay down your arms, leaving your horse where it is.'

Even Eadulf had to admire the technique of the ambush. There would now be no chance of their dismounting and taking cover behind their horses.

'The warriors will dismount first – one by one.'

Conrí, his face red with mortification, went forward first and laid down his weapons. His two men followed individually.

Then Eadulf went forward, dismounting awkwardly, and striding forward to the pile of weapons. He stood feet apart and spread out his arms.

'I carry no weapons,' he called to the invisible bowmen. 'I am a Brother in Christ.'

'You are a man and men often have weapons no matter what clothes they wear,' came back the uncompromising tone. 'Stand aside but keep your arms out, hands well away from your body.'

Fidelma was called forward next.

'I have no weapons either,' she called.

There was no answer and then half a dozen men, all with drawn bows, each aimed at Fidelma and her companions, emerged from behind trees and rocks. The leading man, who had the look of a burly smith about him, suddenly whistled. Three or four young boys, emerging from hiding places among the trees and undergrowth, came forward. Without being asked, some took hold of the horses' reins while others gathered the discarded weapons.

'Who are you?' snapped Conrí.

The burly man, who was obviously the leader, smiled beneath his beard showing blackened teeth.

'You will know soon enough. Now, all of you will turn and march before us down this path. Try no tricks and no one will come to harm. And no talking . . . you'll be given an opportunity to sing your hearts out soon enough.'

Eadulf had time to give their captors a quick scrutiny. He had an idea that he had seen the burly man before but could not place him. The others appeared an ill-assorted group; he would not really equate them with well-muscled warriors like Conrí and his men. They seemed ill fed and more like field hands than military men.

They all moved on in silence, swinging along the path that ran along the hillside through the valley until it came round into an open area with the river flowing along it. Eadulf suddenly knew where he was. There was the standing stone with the ancient writing on it, the ford across the rushing river and the buildings making up the small hamlet. This was the little settlement where he, with Basil Nestorios and the warrior Gormán, had come after the destruction of the fortress of Uaman the Leper.

For a moment his heart leapt and then it plummeted as he realised the buildings were blackened, their stones knocked askew and some pulled down. Many of the wooden buildings no longer existed except for the remains of burnt timbers. It looked as if the place had been overwhelmed by some catastrophe. Were these men responsible? Were they responsible for the death of Abbess Faife?

They were being marched through the buildings from which people were emerging, quiet but angry, some staring at them with hatred. Yet no one made any sound but stared tight-mouthed as they went by.

They were halted before a half-burnt barn, which it was apparent someone had been trying to repair by putting a new roof on it.

Out of the building came an elderly man with parchment-coloured skin and a shock of white hair. His bright eyes were of indeterminate colour as he surveyed the group.

Eadulf recognised him immediately.

'Ganicca!' he called.

The old man frowned. 'Who speaks my name?'

Eadulf moved a step forward. 'It is I. Don't you recognise me?'

The old man stared and then his thin features broke into a slow smile of recognition.

'Why, it is the Saxon Brother. How come you here again?'

'A story that is long in the telling, Ganicca. But this is Fidelma.'

Ganicca's eyes widened and he asked quickly. 'Fidelma of Cashel?'

Fidelma was looking puzzled.

'Ganicca was the man who helped us when we fled from Uaman's fortress,' explained Eadulf. 'It was he who pointed us to the home of Nessán and Muirgen and so was responsible for the eventual recovery of our child.'

Fidelma moved forward with both hands outstretched to the old man in greeting. 'Then this is a blessed meeting, Ganicca. You have my unending gratitude.'

The old man waved his hand in deprecation.

'You are welcome here, lady, but I wish I could greet you in happier circumstances.'

'What has happened here?' she demanded, encompassing the ruined village with a gesture.

'And who are these men who threaten us with their arrows?' added Eadulf.

Ganicca held up a hand, palm outward, to stay further questions and then turned to the burly man.

'No harm will come from these travellers. I know them. Release them.'

Their captors seemed a little reluctant but they put down their weapons and slowly dispersed. Ganicca pointed at the barn behind him.

'It is a harsh winter, so come in. I fear the best we can

offer is some corma and a rude shelter from the mountain winds. Enter and I will tell you what has befallen my people and why you have been treated with such scant hospitality.'

The young boys handed Conrí and his men back their weapons. Others led their horses to a paddock out of the wind.

'Seat yourselves.' The old man pointed to sacking on the floor. 'I regret that we have been left with no luxuries.'

One of the young boys had followed them inside and now poured corma for everyone as Ganicca was introduced to each member of the party.

'Now first,' began Ganicca, 'I heard that Nessán and Muirgen had decided to stay in Cashel after you left here, Brother Saxon. Are they well? And what news of your child, Fidelma of Cashel, does he prosper?'

Fidelma smiled and nodded.

'He does, thanks be to God. Muirgen continues as nurse to him. Nessán tends the flocks of sheep on the hills south of Cashel. They are both well and happy.'

'And how is the stranger from the East called Basil Nestorios? Do the Fates deal well with him?'

'When we last saw him he was well and continuing in his travels, collecting knowledge of this land, Ganicca,' Eadulf replied solemnly.

'And the young warrior, what was his name?'

'Gormán.'

'Gormán, indeed. How fares it with him?'

'He is now deputy commander of my brother's body-guard,' Fidelma replied.

'And your brother, the noble Colgú, is all well with him?'

'My brother is, as ever, concerned for the peoples of his kingdom and worries when ill befalls them.' Fidelma paused and then added: 'He will be concerned at the ill that has befallen you in this place.'

'What has happened since I was here?' Eadulf joined in. 'Why were we ambushed and brought here in such a fashion?'

Ganicca sighed deeply.

'It happened some weeks ago. Until then, we had long dwelt here in an open community without fear. Even in the bad days, so long as we paid tribute to the Lord of the Passes, Uaman, we were never harmed.'

He paused, as if gathering his thoughts.

'It was one afternoon when a band of warriors came along the track just as you have done. They were on horseback. Between them, marching on foot and at swordpoint, was a band of religious . . . they were prisoners.'

Conrí leant forward excitedly.

'Six young females?' he demanded.

'And a foreign Brother of the Faith.'

Fidelma frowned. 'I had no information about a foreign brother.'

'He was a rough-looking young man,' continued Ganicca. 'He appeared more suited to a life spent outdoors than among the pale creatures that are cloistered in the dim recesses of a monastery . . . saving your presence, Brother Saxon.'

'But he was a prisoner and a religieux as well?' queried Eadulf.

'He was.'

'What happened when these warriors and their prisoners came to your village?' pressed Fidelma.

'We offered hospitality, as is the custom. The warriors took corma and demanded food. They dismayed us by ill treating their prisoners, allowing them only water and some bread.'

'Did anyone question the religious as to why they were

prisoners or what manner of warriors their captors were?' asked Fidelma.

Ganicca made a negative gesture.

'The warriors discouraged contact with the prisoners and when our smith, the man who captured you, asked what was happening, he received a slap across the face. The lesson was reinforced by the tip of a sword to deter him from pressing further.'

'And then?'

Ganicca raised his arms as if encompassing the whole settlement.

'Then, my friends, two more warriors came riding up with a third person. That person ordered the warriors to burn the village . . . they burnt and looted it. We had no weapons to hand. They attacked our blacksmith's forge and then started to fire our houses. Most of us managed to escape up the mountains to the shelter of the caves there. Seven of our people were slain, too young or too old to escape the onslaught. Many more were wounded. It is as you see . . . we are a destroyed community.'

Fidelma frowned. 'Have you reported this matter to your chief, to Slébéne?'

The old man shrugged. 'We sent him word. But he has never protected us in the past so why would he protect us now?'

'Slébéne's duty is to protect his people. He is also answerable to my brother, the king.'

'Slébéne is his own man and is answerable only to himself. We selected one of our number to go to Daingean and speak to him. He has not returned.'

Eadulf bent close to Fidelma and whispered, 'See, we were right about Slébéne!'

Fidelma was grim-faced. 'Then I swear, Ganicca, that he shall answer for any transgression. A chief has responsibilities as well as rights.'

Ganicca regarded her calmly. 'You are truly a descendant of Eoghan Mór, lady. However, I knew that Slébéne would not come to our aid.'

'Why so?'

'Because I know that evil figure who ordered his warriors to turn on our village and destroy it.'

'Slébéne himself?' asked Eadulf eagerly. He found the old man's eyes looking sorrowfully at him. 'Well, out with it,' he demanded. 'Who was it?'

'Saxon brother, you told us two months ago that you saw Uaman the Leper die before your eyes. You were wrong. The person who gave the order for this destruction,' he raised his hand to embrace the scene, 'was Uaman. Uaman the Leper. The Lord of the Passes.'

CHAPTER THIRTEEN

'Impossible!' Eadulf exploded after the brief silence that followed Ganicca's announcement. The old man sadly shook his head.

'I wish it was impossible, Brother Saxon. I would know that slight figure of Uaman the Leper anywhere.'

'You actually saw the face?' Eadulf pressed.

Ganicca smiled in reprimand.

'No one looks on the face of Uaman the Leper and lives.'

'I did,' retorted Eadulf.

'You were lucky, my friend. He was not called Master of Souls for nothing.'

Eadulf frowned at the familiar expression.

'Master of Souls?'

'He who despises his own life is soon master of another's – beware for such a man can become master of souls,' Fidelma quoted quietly.

Ganicca glanced at her with interest.

'You know the old saying then, lady?'

'It was a saying of my mentor, the Brehon Morann.'

Eadulf was now frowning in annoyance.

'I have said before that I saw him in the quicksand as it pulled him down. Then a great wave descended and he was gone. No one could have survived that.'

'Then it is a wraith who rides out from the Otherworld and instructs his warriors to destroy my people,' replied Ganicca calmly.

Eadulf made to say something but then remembered the words of the boy Iobcar. He had said something similar.

'So this attack happened some weeks ago?' interposed Conrí. When Ganicca nodded emphatically, he turned to Fidelma. 'Then it is easy to see the train of events. Uaman and his war band wrecked the ship. Then they came on Abbess Faife and her companions. They killed her and took them as prisoners, moving northwards up through the mountains. That's where they picked up the warship. That's why it flies the banner of Eoganán of the Uí Fidgente, Uaman's father.'

Fidelma was thoughtful.

'I am trying to understand what purpose all this would serve. Why wreck the merchant ship? Why kill the abbess but then take her companions prisoner? Who is the male religieux who is with them? A foreigner? Perhaps a Gaul, perhaps a survivor from the wreck?'

Conrí, however, was excited as he interpreted the events. He turned to Ganicca.

'Tell my companions where this road leads.'

The old man looked puzzled.

'Why, it leads northwards out of this valley.'

'But tell them where.'

'Well, if you cross out of the valley by the eastern route over the mountains you can join the road that leads along the coast to the lands of the Uí Fidgente and north again to

Ard Fhearta. But if you cross to the west then you will come to the seashore and the road takes you across a low-lying thrust of land called the Machaire peninsula with the great bay of Bréanainn to the west and the Machaire Islands to the northern tip.'

Conrí was nodding eagerly.

'The Machaire Islands,' he said meaningfully.

Ganicca was perplexed.

'They are nothing except a group of small uninhabited islands . . . well, apart for one that is occupied by hermits. Seanach's Island.'

Conrí turned to face Fidelma with a smile of satisfaction.

'The Machaire Islands,' he said again with emphasis.

Eadulf, recovering from Ganicca's claim that he was mistaken in his belief that Uaman was dead, was regarding the warlord seriously.

'Are you claiming that the wreckage on Uaman's island, the killing of the Abbess Faife and the disappearance of the religieuse and the attack by the mysterious warship are now all connected?'

'I say that they must be. And if Uaman is involved, it makes perfect sense.'

Eadulf pursed his lips sceptically.

'Ganicca is the only one who has positively identified Uaman as part of this affair,' he pointed out.

'The boy also did so,' replied Conrí softly.

'But the boy didn't know Uaman. He was repeating something he had heard adults say.'

'And I know who I saw, Brother Saxon,' Ganicca intervened sharply.

'We must follow the path these people took,' Fidelma interrupted to silence them. She recognised that this exchange might soon lead to an argument. 'I think the answer will be found on those islands that you called the Machaire.'

'It is nearly noon, lady, and we have little hospitality to offer now,' Ganicca said as he realised why Fidelma had stopped the conversation. 'What we have, you are most welcome to.'

Fidelma shook her head and thanked the old man.

'We will move on immediately, my friend.'

'Yet there is no hurry,' the old man pointed out. 'It is now three weeks since this happened and the chances of catching up with these men . . .' He shook his head.

'Nevertheless, we will ride on,' Fidelma insisted firmly. 'Whether the leader is Uaman or not, we must find those who have been abducted.'

'Then may God be on all the paths you travel, lady. It is a dangerous game that you hunt.'

'Thank you, Ganicca. I promise in my brother's name to ensure that your village is compensated for the outrage you have suffered.'

The old man smiled sadly.

'The Brehons have a list of honour-prices for each one of us. But how do you really judge the value of lives, lady? It is not easy. But we will survive, some of us at least. And while the names of our dead are still spoken, then their lives will have meant something in this sad world in which we live.'

A short time later they were climbing their horses along the mountain track and keeping on the west side of the river which ran rapidly through the valley below them. They were almost turning east, paralleling the course of the river, when Conrí pointed to a narrow pass through the hills by a number of ancient stones that had apparently been set up by their ancestors in the dim distant past.

Taking the pass, they found they were now following a smaller stream that rose on the mountain behind them, tumbling northwards. They descended towards a valley and could see a broad plain with the misty sea in the distance.

'We'll have to think about stopping soon, lady,' Conrí suggested, 'otherwise it will be dark before we know it and we haven't eaten since last night.'

'I thought I glimpsed a farmstead on the plain ahead of us,' Fidelma replied. 'We'll seek hospitality there.'

Indeed, when they approached the series of wooden buildings, half hidden in the shelter of a copse of some sturdy oaks, a farmer and his son appeared to be waiting for them. They looked nervous and held some farming implements defensively in their hands.

Fidelma called out a friendly greeting and the two men began to look slightly relieved.

'We saw you coming down the hill road, Sister,' said the elder man, recognising her robes. 'We saw some strange riders only and wondered who you were.'

'No one who means harm to you and yours, my friend. We are just weary travellers who need a shelter for the night,' replied Fidelma, dismounting.

'My wife would be pleased to offer you a bed, Sister,' replied the farmer, rubbing his jaw and seeming to mentally count them. 'But your companions will have to shelter in the barn. We have little room in the house.'

'That will suit us fine, farmer,' Conrí assured him. 'A place out of the wind and warm straw will suit us well.'

'There is the spring in which to wash but plenty of venison to eat and bread to take away your hunger.'

'Your hospitality is generous,' Fidelma replied warmly.

'Yet you still seem nervous. Have there been other travellers on this road?'

The farmer exchanged a brief glance with his son. Fidelma was right. They were nervous.

'In truth, there have, Sister. Travellers that I would not like to play host to. It was several weeks ago but, thanks be to God, they passed on without stopping. They went across the top meadow in the direction of the sea.'

'You appear fearful of them. Why so?'

'They were warriors on horseback but we saw them herding a group of prisoners. They were religieuse, poor young women, with a male prisoner.'

'Herding is an odd choice of word,' Conrí pointed out.

'Herding is the only word that comes to mind, my friend,' the farmer replied almost defensively. 'They passed by and we prayed for their souls.'

'You were looking to the north-west,' Fidelma observed. 'Is that the direction in which they went?'

'Indeed they did. Towards the Machaire peninsula.'

Fidelma's expression was one of satisfaction.

'If you can tell us where we might tether our horses . . . ?'

The farmer glanced round and pointed.

'You can put them in the enclosure at the back. We have some sheep there but I doubt whether they will be bothered. It will keep them out of the cold winds. The spring is over there, and the barn where you may sleep. Sister, come to the house. The food will be ready after you have washed.'

The food was good and the hay was warm and, for the first time in several days, Eadulf slept a deep comfortable sleep without waking once during the night. He did not begrudge Fidelma her more civilised abode. By the time he woke and washed, everyone else was sitting down to a break-fast. Gifts were given by Conrí, who had the foresight to travel with such items, to the farmer, his wife and their son in exchange for their hospitality. Socht and his companion had saddled their horses and after an exchange of farewells they rode on again.

The salty smell of the sea was never far away on the peninsula of the Corco Duibhne but now it was really strong. The air was filled with the crying of gulls, and these were joined by some lost-looking greenshanks, wading along the few freshwater pools and lakes that they passed. But it was the noisy gulls that dominated, especially the great black-backed gull with its fierce, heavy, hooked bill. It was a fearsome butcher of a bird, eating refuse and carrion and preying on the chicks of other species like puffins, shearwaters and kittiwakes. In fact, just as the thought entered Eadulf's mind, there came the strident call of 'kitti-wa-a-k!' like the eerie cry of a lost soul. Two adult kittiwakes swooped along the coastline ahead of them, with their soft grey plumage, white heads and yellow bills.

Conrí was riding in front with Fidelma and Eadulf and the two warriors behind them.

'Well,' Eadulf said, wishing to break the silence that had lasted since they left the hospitality of the farm, 'we have criss-crossed this peninsula twice now. I should know the place by now.'

Conrí glanced across his shoulder.

'No one can ever really know a country like this.' He waved a hand across the mountains behind him. 'I have been through this country before. They call those valleys Gleannta an Easig, the valleys of the waterfall.'

Eadulf could see why. It was a curious land, he thought,

where cliffs rose, overshadowing lakes, and rivers meandered through valleys that were green and tree-covered before changing in turn into bleak and rocky areas and then back again into verdant swaths. The land seemed barely populated but as they passed along the white sandy shore leading to the small finger of what they now knew was the Machaire peninsula, Eadulf could see a few isolated farmsteads and buildings almost hidden here and there among trees and rocks.

They passed within sight of a broad lake to their left, a bright loch which seemed swarming with wildfowl. Smoke rose from a point on its shore.

'It looks like a smith's forge,' Conrí commented as he followed the direction in which Eadulf was staring. The faint clang of metal on metal came to their ears as if in confirmation of the fact.

They rode on down the narrow green spit of land with the white sands on either side until they reached the end bay with low headlands either side like the claws of a crab, edging in and narrowing at the mouth. It was a rock-clustered, inhospitable shore, not like the broad sandy slopes that had stretched either side of the main strip of land that thrust out into the sea. The only sign that man had been here at all was a tall *gallán* or standing stone that rose erect at least five metres above the ground.

Beyond the entrance of the bay they could see some of the distant islands of Machaire. But it was the keen-sighted Conrí who became aware of something else.

'Look there!' he shouted abruptly, causing them to start.

He pointed beyond the rocky eastern headland.

At first, seen against the choppy grey sea, it looked like a dark plank of wood being tossed and thrown about over the waves. Then as it came closer into the bay, heading for the rocky shore, Eadulf realised it was one of the light canoes they used in this part of the world, a wickerwork frame covered with hides stitched together with thongs. There seemed to be only one figure bent to the oars although the light craft must have been eight metres long and a metre or more wide.

'It's a *naomhóg*,' muttered Fidelma, supplying him with the name of the vessel. 'See, the man has just lost an oar. He is in trouble.'

Already Conrí and his two warrior companions were racing their horses on the ground high above the shore, for in this part of the bay the rocks met the waters.

'He'll smash the vessel on the rocks,' Eadulf called unnecessarily, as he and Fidelma followed the others.

'The man is hurt, I think,' replied Fidelma. 'Look, he's slipped to the bottom of the boat. It's out of control.'

The long canoe had swung broadside on to the rocks and was suddenly lifted up by one of the racing breakers and thrown on to them. As the sea receded, Conrí's men, jumping from their horses, raced forward, scrambling and slipping over the wet outcrop. One of them, they thought it was the man called Socht, reached the broken vessel while his companion steadied the smashed remains. Apparently the unconscious man was a lightweight for the warrior threw him across his shoulder and, with a shout to his companion, turned and started for the firm earth just as another breaker smashed against the rocks. The force of the water caused Socht to slip and almost lose his balance, but his companion was there and steadied him with his unconscious burden. Then they scrambled ashore and were above the watermark where Conrí was waiting to help lay the man on the ground.

A moment later Fidelma and Eadulf joined them.

At once they could see that the unconscious man was elderly and deathly pale, with white straggling hair cut into the tonsure of St John. His robes were dirty and torn and there were bloodstains on them. His hands were raw, the flesh torn.

Conrí was shaking his head sadly.

'If he came from the islands, it's a wonder that he made it this far.'

Eadulf, who knew something of the healing arts, bent down by the man and examined him. As he moved him a little, the man gave forth a groan and his eyes fluttered. Eadulf had seen something in the man's side.

'He has been badly wounded by an arrow, I think,' he muttered. 'The life is ebbing out of him.'

Conrí's eyes narrowed. 'Do you think that he was the religieux who was taken prisoner with Faife's companions?'

'This man is no foreigner and he is elderly, unlike Ganicca's description,' Fidelma pointed out. 'But it looks as if he did come from one of the islands.'

'It's a long way for an old man to come alone,' Eadulf remarked.

'We must speak to him,' said Fidelma.

Conrí passed her the container of corma he carried. Fidelma took it and eased the old man's head up, allowing a few drops to trickle into his mouth.

There was a paroxysm of coughing and the old man's eyes opened blearily. They grew wide and fearful as he focused on them.

'You have no need to kill me. I am dying already,' he gasped.

Fidelma bent over him and tried to give him a reassuring

look. Eadulf had continued his brief examination. The old man was beyond hope. It had not been a sword or spear thrust. Eadulf found the head of an arrow still embedded in the man's side. It had gone deep and the victim had apparently tried to break off the shaft. The wound was already festering. Fidelma caught Eadulf's eye and silently asked a question. Eadulf shook his head quickly.

'Have no fear, my friend. We are not your enemies,' Fidelma assured him. 'Who did this to you?'

The old man blinked; already his eyes were glazing.

'They have destroyed us all . . .' He paused, his chest heaving for breath. 'They came . . . those they did not kill . . . they rounded up . . .'

'Who are you, who are they?' pressed Fidelma as gently as she could.

'I am . . . Martan . . . a brother of Seanach's Island.' He gave a sudden gasp of pain.

'Seanach's Island. So we were right,' Conrí muttered.

At the sound, the old man's eyes opened wide.

'Do not go there!' His voice was suddenly strong. 'Do not go there, if you value your life.'

'What has happened to the brethren there?' Fidelma asked. 'What of the women from Ard Fhearta?'

'Dead, dying . . . I escaped . . . but . . . I am dying.'

Fidelma knew the man had not long to live. Part of her wanted to let him die in peace but she had questions that had to be answered.

'Who was it who attacked the brethren?' she demanded again.

The old man was racked by a fit of coughing.

'Who?' she pressed.

'Warriors . . . their leader, they called him the Master.

The Master of Souls! I knew him . . . knew him of old
. . . He . . .'

There was a sudden deep exhalation of breath and the
old man fell back.

Eadulf looked up at Conrí and shook his head.

'It looks as though you were right. There is a link between
all these events. But I cannot accept that Uaman is still alive
and directing them.'

'Let us bury this poor soul,' Fidelma instructed quietly,
'and then we can decide on what we must do. It is clear
that Slébéne has not sent a ship to investigate the islands.'
She glanced at the smashed *naomhóg*, the hide canoe, and
then shook her head. 'A pity! That's beyond repair.'

Eadulf stared at her aghast as he guessed what was
passing through her mind.

'You don't mean . . . you weren't even thinking about
going out to the island?'

Fidelma gestured indifferently.

'There is no other way of ascertaining the situation,'
she said simply. 'But, as I say, let us bury this poor soul
first.'

The two warriors dug a grave for the old man as best
they could with their bladed swords. It was shallow but func-
tional, and Fidelma said a prayer over it and marked it with
a makeshift cross of sticks.

'I swear that Brother Martan will have a proper memorial. We will return and place a slab of stone over the grave
and get a good artist to inscribe a cross upon it.' Then she
turned to Conrí. 'You said that you had passed this way
before. Do you know of any settlements along the way,
places where we might get a boat?'

Eadulf groaned slightly.

'I think that it is folly,' he protested. 'To go out to the islands—'

'We would need to find a man who knows this coast,' Conrí pointed out, ignoring his protest. 'A man who could run us to the island under cover of darkness. These can be dangerous waters, lady. I know of no such place.'

'We must know what is happening out there,' Fidelma insisted.

It was Socht who cleared his throat and ventured to make a suggestion.

'If it please you, lady, you will remember that we did pass a smith's forge by the lakeside. Perhaps the smith might know of some local fishermen who would take us out?'

'I remember the spot. Then that is what we will do.' Fidelma's tone admitted no questioning and they took to their horses once more. The flat land presented them with an easy ride and soon they came to a little wooded area where a cluster of buildings stood. It was easy to recognise the forge in which a couple of men, stripped to the waist, in spite of the chilly day, were working on dousing a fire from which steam was rising into the air.

One of them heard their approach and shouted something to his companion. It sounded like a warning. Then the man grabbed a large hammer in one muscular hand while his companion reached for a sword lying on a nearby bench.

Fidelma drew rein immediately, holding up her hand to halt her companions.

'What hospitality is this?' she called, frowning at the aggressive stance of the two smiths.

The one with the hammer, still holding it menacingly ready, examined her carefully. Then his gaze encompassed her companions. He was of middle age, bearded and powerfully built. His comrade was of slighter stature, with the bleak-looking expression of someone who cannot envisage that any human has the right to be happy.

'No hospitality at all,' snapped the man with the hammer. 'What do you want here, strangers?'

'What most travellers want – hospitality and information.'

'Most travellers seem to want more than that, especially when they travel with warriors,' was the roughly spoken response.

'It is all we want,' replied Fidelma firmly.

'Then why have you three warriors behind you with sharp-ened weapons? Last time we gave hospitality to religious with warriors guarding them, they stole our food and threatened our lives.'

Fidelma leant forward a little at the news.

'When was this?' she demanded.

'A few weeks ago.'

'And in what manner did this party come?'

'Half a dozen religieuse and a foreign monk, guarded by a dozen warriors. The person who seemed in charge was a strange figure clad in robes from poll to feet so that none could look on him.'

Fidelma expected as much.

'We seek these people, for the warriors have taken the religious captive,' she explained.

'The strange monk, the one whose face we could not see, was no captive,' replied the smith.

'Even so, the others were. They had been abducted and their abbess had been murdered.'

'And you seek them? Why?'

'I am Fidelma of Cashel. I am a *dálaigh*. Let us dismount,

my friend, and I will speak further. You may well be able to help us in our quest.'

The smith with the hammer looked at his companion. They still hesitated.

'I am intent on bringing these killers and abductors to justice,' Fidelma added with emphasis. 'These are my companions, Brother Eadulf, Conrí, warlord of the Uí Fidgente, whose relative was the abbess who was slain, and his warriors. Now tell us to whom we speak?'

The smith hesitated a moment and then he lowered the hammer with a shrug but did not release his hold.

'My name is Gáeth and this is my assistant, Gaimredán.'

Fidelma looked at the bleak features of his companion and suddenly smiled broadly.

'You are well named, my friend.'

Gáeth could not help but chuckle at her jest on the meaning of his assistant's name.

'Indeed he is, lady, for never was there a person of more wintry countenance and lack of humour.'

'May we dismount now?' asked Fidelma.

The smith gestured his assent and turned to lay aside his hammer.

'I accept that you mean us no harm, but after the visit of the others . . .'

Fidelma and her companions dismounted and Socht collected their horses and tethered them.

She glanced around the collection of smithy buildings that stood alongside a gushing stream that emptied into the waters of the lake.

'You are isolated here, Gáeth.'

'Yet not too isolated to have unwelcome visitors,' replied the other philosophically. He indicated one of the buildings that appeared to be the dwelling house. 'Come inside. We have been left with enough corma to make you welcome on this cold winter's day.'

The smith's house was an old-style one-roomed circular house, whose floor was merely the earth made hard over centuries of use. The central hearth gave out a comfortable heat and rush matting on the floor provided their seats.

'We live a frugal life here, lady,' Gáeth announced. It became obvious that his comrade Gaimredán never spoke unless he had something important to contribute. 'I suspect it is unlike the rich palace in which you must dwell at Cashel.' He smiled. 'I'll wager it is even more opulent than Slébéne's hall. Ah well, my companion and I like to dwell in isolation. We are self-sufficient here, for the earth provides us with vegetables, the mountains behind us with game, the air with birds and the sea with fish. What more could we want?'

Eadulf had been examining the room and had noticed the lack of any Christian icons. But he saw some items that he had seen now and again in his travels and knew the meaning of them.

'Do I understand that you are not of the Faith?' he asked brusquely.

Gáeth seemed amused.

'It all depends what you mean by Faith, Saxon brother. You imply there is one Faith. Well, we are not Christians, if that is what you mean. That is why we dwell apart in order that those who would proselytise us do not bother us. Argument is a tedious thing. We each come to the Dagda, the Good God, along our own path.'

'It seems that you are also well named, Gáeth,' Fidelma said, for the name meant clever and wise. 'But we did not come to discuss the Faith. I presume that you both dwell here as hermits?'

'It is true that we prefer to dwell in isolation from others. But many know our work and come to us.'

Gaimredán was handing round pottery cups filled with corma. The raw spirit made Eadulf gasp.

'So you know many people in these parts?'

Gáeth inclined his head in acknowledgement.

'Well, the strangers who came here were indeed strangers. They were not of these parts. We heard from our neighbours that after they ransacked our storehouse for food they went on to the coast. There is a sandy shore not far from here to the north-west and we heard from a shepherd that these strangers were met there by a warship and taken out to sea. Who knows where they went?'

Fidelma smiled grimly.

'We think we know where,' she replied. 'To those islands you call the Machaire Islands, where they have taken the hermits of Seanach's Island prisoners or worse.'

'Are you saying that they have harmed the group of Christian hermits that dwell there?' The smith frowned.

'Mortal harm has come to at least one of them,' Fidelma replied. 'We found one who had escaped from the island and rowed to this mainland, but he died of a wound they had inflicted on him. He barely made it ashore and died in our presence. He told us his name was Brother Martan.'

Gáeth whistled softly under his breath.

'Brother Martan was a good man. We differed in our beliefs but he was a holy man and the leader of the hermits there. Who are these people? The warriors, I mean? What do they want?'

'Have you heard stories of Uaman the Leper?' Conrí asked.

The smith's eyes flickered, indicating that he had.

'By the fires of Bel,' he said softly. 'Many stories are connected with that one. Thankfully, his raids never reached here for he was content to demand tribute from those who came through the eastern passes into this peninsula. He never ventured further west than the Emlagh and Finglas valleys. But we heard plenty of stories about him.'

'For hermits, shunning other folk—' began Eadulf.

'We prefer to live alone, but we do not shun other folk, as you put it,' snapped Gáeth. 'Only you Christians run away and hide from life in your communities. We live here and welcome the visitor as a natural event.'

Eadulf swallowed hard. Fidelma caught his eye and shook her head.

'It may be,' she said hurriedly, 'that it was Uaman and his men who visited you.'

Gáeth's eyes widened.

'So far to the west? And what would he be doing with religious prisoners?'

'That is why we are following them . . . to find out,' Conrí explained.

'There was a rumour that Uaman was dead. I wonder if Slébéne will finally be forced to do something now.'

Fidelma stared at him for a moment.

'You speak as if Slébéne never did anything to counter Uaman's activities in his territory. After all, all this land from the abbey of Colmán westward is the land of the Corco Duibhne and he is responsible for its protection and well-being.'

'That may be so, but Slébéne believes in Slébéne. He was content to leave Uaman to his own devices.'

'Do you mean that Slébéne never made any effort to capture or destroy Uaman?' asked Eadulf.

Gáeth nodded.

'But that is not what Slébéne told us.'

Gáeth looked pityingly at him.

'What would you expect the man to say? That he is a gutless warrior? That he is great on talking, on blustering, on threatening, but a coward when it comes down to lifting a sword against equals? I even believe that he left Uaman alone because he received gold from him.'

Conrí was staring at the smith. He was thinking about the challenge that Slébéne had issued to him over the 'hero's portion'.

'If he is a gutless warrior, what if someone challenged him to a combat? How would he avoid it?'

'He does not have to avoid it. He is the chief. I have never known him to fight an equal combat in years.'

'Then how . . . ?'

'Slébéne keeps a *trén-fher*, a strong man, a champion, to answer all challenges to single combat. You must know the system, Conrí, for are you not an *aire-echta* yourself? Even the Blessed Patrick, your so-called Christian man of peace, kept a *trén-fher* in his household; an attendant to protect him. That was Mac Carthen, whom he made first bishop of Clochar, the stony place.'

'I know the system,' Conrí said tightly. 'I did not think a man such as Slébéne purports to be would stoop to getting others to fight his battles. How could he last as a chief without being challenged?'

Gáeth chuckled in amusement.

'That is precisely the sort of blustering man Slébéne is, my friend. He does not move without his champion.'

Conrí remembered the tall, broad-chested and shaggy-haired man who stood armed behind the chief during the meal.

Eadulf was also looking thoughtful.

'But can that be legal?' he asked Fidelma.

She nodded.

'The laws allow it,' she replied shortly. She turned to Gáeth. 'If, as you say, Slébéne is all bluster and has not been fulfilling his duties as chief and protecting his people, why has no complaint been sent about him to the king in Cashel? For it is the ultimate duty of the king to ensure that his nobles obey the law.'

Gáeth smiled condescendingly.

'Cashel is a long way away. And would Cashel really be interested in what happens in a remote corner of the kingdom? So long as a chief does service to Cashel and pays tribute, what more is Cashel interested in?'

'I will answer for my brother, Colgú, and say that Cashel will be interested and more than interested. I have come here for that very purpose, to ensure that justice prevails in this part of the kingdom.'

Gáeth looked impressed in spite his obvious scepticism.

'It would certainly help all the people of the Corco Duibhne if there was a new chief,' Gaimredán said abruptly, to the surprise of those who had presumed he never spoke at all.

'That would surely be up to the *derbhfine*, the living generations of Slébéne's family meeting to elect a new chief?' Eadulf pointed out, comfortably aware that he had mastered the successional laws of the country. 'They can surely throw out a bad chief?'

'There will be no help there.' Gáeth smiled grimly. 'Slébéne made sure that any who might challenge him was either killed or chased out of the territory.'

Fidelma could not disguise her astonishment.

'You seem to know a lot about Slébéne,' she remarked thoughtfully, '. . . for a hermit, that is.'

Gáeth hesitated a moment and then shrugged.

'I know him better than anyone,' he announced simply.

They waited for a moment and then Fidelma prompted him.

'How so?'

'Because he is my *aite*, my foster father.'

Eadulf knew that at the age of seven most children were sent away to be educated or instructed by a system of fosterage called *altrram*. In this way a child was educated and the foster child, the *dalta*, remained with the foster parents until, in the case of a boy, he was seventeen years old. Fosterage was either for payment or for affection. When a chief was the *aite*, the child had to be of equivalent rank. Eadulf knew that the laws on fosterage were numerous and intricate. The practice brought about close ties between families and usually such relationships were regarded as something sacred. Fidelma had told him that there were many cases where a man had voluntarily laid down his life for his foster father or foster brother. Had not the great Uí Néill King Domnall, fighting against his rebellious foster son, Congal Claen of Dál Riada, at the battle of Magh Roth, a generation ago, showed anxiety that Congal, although a mortal enemy, was not to be hurt?

'Were you fostered for affection or for payment?' Fidelma asked.

'I was supposed to be fostered for affection for my family was descended from the line of Duibhne. But fosterage never brought the branches of our families closer. Slébéne was not a man to be close even to his own natural sons or any of his fosterlings.'

'Did he have many?'

'None of his natural sons survived. Need I say more? As for those in fosterage – there was another chief's son from his eastern border as well as myself. Then there was a girl from some eastern noble's family. Her name suited her – it was Uallach.'

When Eadulf looked puzzled, the smith unbent and explained.

'It is a name that means proud and arrogant. I think Uallach had a better relationship with Slébéne than his male fosterlings. But, as far as I know, they all left him as soon as they were legally entitled to.'

'Was Slébéne ever a great warrior in his youth, as he claims?' Conrí asked, with a swift glance at Fidelma.

'None of his contemporaries in battle, those fighting on the same side, have lived to tell the tale. Only the bards that he pays sing songs about his fame as a youthful warrior.'

'I was told that he fought at the right side of my father Failbe Flann.'

'If he ever did so, lady, then your father was lucky to survive.'

'There is bitterness in your voice, Gáeth.'

'A bitterness that was put into my mouth by my foster father,' replied the smith shortly.

There was an uncomfortable silence.

'When did you take up the art you now follow?' asked Fidelma.

'I suppose I used to watch Slébéne's smith when I was a child. I spent more time with him than with Slébéne. Having to listen to the chief's boastful tales of his prowess in battle was bad enough, but to have to put up with being instructed in the use of weapons when a mouse might challenge and defeat him was worse. As soon as I was able, I shook the mud of his fortress from my feet. I prayed to Brigit—'

'I thought you were a pagan?' interrupted Eadulf.

'I do not talk of the Christian Brigit of Kildare,' responded Gáeth patronisingly. 'I speak of Brigit the triune daughter of the Dagda, the Good God, Brigit goddess of wisdom and poetry, Brigit goddess of medicine and Brigit goddess of smiths and smithwork. She led my footsteps through hidden passes under An Cnapán Mór and up to the black lake, high up in the mountains, beside whose shores I found my master, Cosrach the Triumphant. Ten years I spent at his anvil until he pronounced me a *flaith-goba* – the highest rank of all the smiths. I gave thanks to Brigit and promised that I would never heed the New Faith but keep to the old ways.'

'Each man must find God in his own way,' asserted Fidelma quietly.

Eadulf glanced at her in surprise. He had grown up in the pagan religion of his people and had been converted to Christianity by a wandering Irish missionary when he was in his early manhood. He still had the fervour of the converted and felt uncomfortable when confronted by those who held to their old religious beliefs. Nevertheless, Fidelma ignored his disapproving look.

'So you have been here ever since?' she went on.

'I built this forge as soon as I left the forge of Cosrach. Within a week, Gaimredán joined me.'

'And the old saying is that there are three places where one can gather news – the priest's house, the tavern and the smith's forge,' Conrí observed, reminding them of why they had come there.

Gáeth chuckled softly.

'I thought that you were garnering a lot of information.'
Fidelma responded with a smile.

'We were talking of what has befallen those on Seanach's Island.'

'We were,' agreed Gáeth.

'We, my companions and myself, have decided that we should try to reach Seanach's Island, preferably under cover of darkness to avoid the attentions of the warship that guards the waters. We have to discover what has happened to those prisoners and the hermits who live on the island.'

Gáeth regarded her with a look of admiration.

'It is an admirable enterprise, lady. One that requires courage.'

'It merely requires determination,' Fidelma replied. 'Moreover, it requires a vessel and a guide.'

Gáeth's eyes lit with understanding.

'And that is what you are in search of? A vessel and a guide to take you to the islands?'

Fidelma nodded.

'It needs to be a swift *naomhóg*.'

Gáeth examined them and his look became doubtful.

'I presume that your companions have handled a *naomhóg* before? You would be facing the turbulent seas that separate these shores from that island.'

'My warriors and I can row,' Conrí asserted.

'Row? But can you row a *naomhóg*? Can you guide it through tempestuous waters to reach the island? And you say that you intend to do this in the hours of darkness?' He smiled sadly. 'Give up the idea, lady.'

'Leave the question of our skills to us,' replied Fidelma firmly. 'If you can just tell us where we may find such a vessel, that will be sufficient.'

Gáeth gazed thoughtfully at her and then turned to his silent companion.

'Well, Gaimredán, what do you think?'

The man had been watching Fidelma with his woeful expression. He suddenly leant forward as if peering into her mind.

'Insight, reason and intellect. Impulsive, hot-tempered but sincere and unbegrudging. Positive, active and dominant, withal almost masculine but a mutable quality. This one is full of fire, searching restlessly for new fields to conquer.'

Gáeth was chuckling at Fidelma's surprised expression.

'Do not mind my friend, lady. He has a gift. I presume that you have recently celebrated a birthday?'

Eadulf was staring at the smith and his comrade in astonishment.

The smith glanced at him and his smile broadened.

'It is no trick, Brother Saxon, merely the ancient knowledge.' He turned back to Fidelma. 'You were born when Danu, our mother goddess, was rising in the sky – the constellation of Eridanus. We are forgetting Eridanus, preferring to call it Toxetes as the Greeks do or Sagittarius as do the Latins. Both represent the fiery archer, but did not Danu also have a bow of victory, the *fidbac bua*?'

Fidelma, who knew something of the astrologer's art from old Brother Conchobhar, the apothecary at Cashel, was following what he was saying. It did not surprise her that Gaimredán had fathomed such matters. She had seen it done often. But, interested as she was in the old knowledge, she was growing a little impatient.

'What has this to do with my question?' she snapped.

Gáeth and Gaimredán exchanged a look and both burst out laughing.

'Impulsive, hot-tempered and brusque!' chortled Gaimredán.

Gáeth controlled his mirth, seeing Fidelma's brows drawing together, and held up a hand, palm outward.

'Hold, lady, and we will tell you. You are setting out on an honourable course. My partner and I have such a *naomhóg* as you seek. We use it for fishing. Mostly we fish in the lake here, Loch Gile, the bright lake. Sometimes we will take ourselves out into the seas. And we have fished in the deep waters around the islands where we can lift crayfish, lobster, flatbacks and pollack.'

She was still frowning so he continued.

'What I am saying is that we will take you out to the islands in our *naomhóg*.'

Fidelma's frown dissolved into a look of bewilderment.

'You will do this simply because of the constellation under which I was born?'

Gáeth shook his head.

'Because of the character that you have revealed to us,' he replied firmly.

'And what do you ask in return?' Eadulf demanded, distrusting the smith and his companion.

'What are you asking as payment for going to the islands to find out if the hermits are alive and well?' Gáeth replied quietly.

'Nothing, of course. We do not do this for payment.'

Gáeth smiled thinly.

'Then that is what we ask for in return. Nothing.'

For a moment there was silence.

'It is a very dangerous course that we embark on,' Fidelma said slowly.

'Did we not tell you so?' replied Gáeth. 'Let us simply

say that in doing this we can repay those who have tried to despoil the tranquillity of this land. Now, we have a *naomhóg* that can be rowed by six oarsmen, so it is big enough to accommodate us all. We can use your two warriors there to row with us to compensate for the extra weight in the boat. We can, at least, give them some instruction in the art of *naomhóg* rowing. Is it agreed?'

Fidelma glanced at the warriors for affirmation.

'Agreed,' she said.

'Then I suggest you leave your horses here, in our pen. Our vessel is beached on the shore of Loch Gile, so we will carry it overland from there to the beach in Bréanainn's bay.'

Eadulf stirred uneasily.

'Carry it? Surely it is a long way?'

Gáeth shook his head.

'Even the two of us have been known to carry it. It is very light. It is the oars that are heavy and so we keep spare oars in a hiding spot on the beach itself, as well as at the lake. It will take us but a little while.' He glanced up at the sky. 'We have time for a cold meal and to prepare ourselves for the journey. Then, by the time we have reached the headland and stand out to the islands, it will be growing dark.'

For the first time, Eadulf realised the enormity of what they were doing.

'Are you sure that you know the waters well enough? When we sailed through those islands a few days ago, I saw so many rocks and tidal currents that I would be unsure of navigating the passage in broad daylight, let alone at night.'

'My friend,' Gáeth said reassuringly, 'all you have to do is be a quiet passenger in the vessel. Leave the navigation to us. But if it reassures you, Gaimredán was born here on this shore and knows these waters so well that he can name each individual rock. The tide and the gods will be with us.'

Gaimredán was already preparing dishes of cold meats, cheeses and bread. A jug of cider was produced.

'The wind is coming up from the south-east,' Gáeth was saying, 'so it will be at our backs and in our favour. It is when there is a westerly blow that we can expect a very rough sea and big swells.'

'How can we approach Seanach's Island without being seen?'

Gáeth rubbed his chin.

'Dark will cover us all the way but there is only one sure place to land in safety. That place is the steep sandy beach on the east side. The landing is easy there and the community have their buildings just south of the landing place.'

'Is there any other anchorage?' Conrí asked.

Gáeth shook his head.

'Then that might be a problem,' went on the warlord. 'If the warship were already anchored at the island, that would be its natural harbour. It would dominate the landing place.'

'I understand what you mean,' agreed the smith. 'However, it will be dark when we come round the headland and stand into the sandy beach. Unless a watch is being kept on ship and shore we have a good chance of not being seen.'

'Are you sure that there is no other place to land?' pressed Fidelma.

'The rest of the island is protected by fairly steep rocks and to attempt to scramble up them in the darkness is simply to court disaster.'

Fidelma pursed her lips thoughtfully.

'I wonder how the old man managed to flee in his little boat without being pursued across the sea?'

Conrí shrugged.

'Whoever shot him with that arrow probably thought that he was already dead. He was as good as dead anyway.'

'We will have to keep our wits about us,' Gáeth advised. 'It will be no journey for the faint-hearted.'

Conrí smiled and glanced knowingly at Eadulf, who had seemed oblivious of the conversation. His features were drawn into deep contemplation.

Fidelma followed Conrí's meaningful gaze.

'Eadulf has been in more dangerous situations than this one,' she said stoutly in his defence.

Eadulf glanced up at his name and frowned.

'Sorry, I was thinking of something else. What is it?'

Conrí grimaced with amusement.

'I think that Gáeth may be concerned in case you are over-anxious about the forthcoming trip.'

Realising Conrí was doubting his courage, Eadulf's brows came together in an annoyed expression.

'It is said that there are only two sorts of people who are fearless – the drunkard and the fool. I am neither.'

'Fear is worse than fighting,' replied Conrí in a mocking tone.

'Knowledge is better than ignorance,' replied Eadulf spiritedly. 'Ignorance is the real cause of fear. It is better to think out the possibilities before running into a dangerous situation when knowledge might save a life.'

Conrí made a barking noise as if containing a laugh.

'That is the timidity of a mouse.'

Eadulf kept his temper.

'*Mus uni non fidit antro*,' he said softly.

'And what is that supposed to mean?'

'A wise person named Plautius pointed out that even a mouse does not rely on one hole.'

Gáeth slapped his knee appreciatively at the intensity of the argument.

Even Gaimredán nodded in approval. He peered closely at Eadulf and smiled.

'This one is silent, almost passive but receptive. Intuitive, just and kind. Reliable but worrying, at one with the spirit of the two natures of man.'

Gáeth looked directly at Conrí.

'Do not concern yourself, warrior. A man who goes into danger without fearing it is a man who is himself to be feared. A man who knows fear and still confronts it is a man to be relied upon who will stand steady.'

Conrí flushed in irritation.

'I have no time for homespun philosophy. Is it not time to set out on this venture?' he said sharply.

Gáeth's glance encompassed them all.

'If you are all ready . . . ? Then we will collect our *naomhóg* and commence this undertaking. May all our gods go with us.'

chapter fourteen

Eadulf was doing his best to prevent himself from giving way to seasickness. While he had an horizon to look at he could control it, but as dusk gave way to darkness there was little to focus on. The up and down motion of the *naomhóg* was difficult to gauge. He found himself desperately clinging to the side of the vessel for support as the frail craft began the slow climb up the waves before falling with a suddenness that left his stomach in the air behind him.

In front of him, backs to the bow, sat Socht and his companion, each with the curious bladeless oar which was traditionally used with these vessels. Behind them were Gáeth and Gaimredán, also with an oar apiece. The four men bent their backs, using great reaching strokes to send the craft through the dark waters. Fidelma and Eadulf sat facing the bows, directly in front of the two warriors, while Conrí sat behind in the stern, ready to grasp a fifth oar to use it as a tiller if it was needed.

Gáeth had told Eadulf to place his feet carefully in case he inadvertently stuck his foot through the hide covering of the canoe. Eadulf had to place them on the wooden framework to which the hide was tightly sewn. He hoped those in front of him were unable to see his white face, his panic-stricken features, as the boat heaved in the waves, and, now and again, when the sea threw its salt waters over him.

He shivered slightly and hoped no one could see him in the darkness. Then he hoped, if his companions had seen him, that they might take it as a reaction to the penetrating cold of the winter's evening. Even though everyone had furs and sheepskins wrapped round them, the icy winter fingers permeated their clothing.

Since the boat had been launched from the broad sandy beach of Bréanainn's bay no one had been able to speak. The noise of the waters around them, at the low level they were in the boat, drowned out any sound except the strongest of shouts. Eadulf was glad of that. It stopped him having to engage in conversation and thereby betray his fear. The vessel had moved rapidly, helped by the receding tides, northward out of the bay. They reached the northern headland and turned towards Machaire Islands although no one could see them, relying on the expertise of Gáeth and his companion to navigate in the darkness.

Once or twice, through the darkness, Eadulf saw the white of pounding surf and realised that they must be passing some rocks or small islets. It only increased his fear, not knowing whether they might strike a rock any moment and be precipitated into the waters. In the darkness, so far from land, it would be an agonising death. He tried to concentrate his mind on the prayers that he had been taught and realised that the words that came into his mind were not the prayers of the New Faith but the prayers of his childhood to the ancient sea gods and goddesses of the Saxons.

He glanced at the shadows of the oarsmen before him. In spite of the gyrations of the craft, their dark figures seemed to sit relaxed, moving back and forth in unison, all swaying in an easy, flowing motion, as if they were part of one another, the oars slipping easily into the sea in spite of the waves. Down went the four oars together, never missing a stroke. Eadulf envied them. Envied their ability at the oars; envied their apparent calm.

He glanced to his side. Fidelma was a still shadow in the darkness. He wondered what she was thinking as she sat there so relaxed. Did she share any of his fears? No, not Fidelma. She seemed fearless. Fearless as usual. Quiet, determined and logical.

He became aware of a slightly different sound above the noise of the wind and waves and glanced up, narrowing his eyes and trying to focus in the gloom. Ahead of them was a line of white water showing in the darkness. They seemed to be rowing straight forward. A panic seized him. He was about to shout a warning when Gáeth gave a bellow and the oars ceased their stroke. The craft was left bobbing up and down on the waters.

Eadulf peered round. The turbulent seas had stilled a little and he realised, to his amazement, that they were standing near the shore of a large island, almost sheltered from the wind and the brisk larger waves.

Fidelma leant close to his ear and shouted, pointing to the white breakers.

'This is Seanach's Island!'

Eadulf realised he had been so buried in his thoughts that

the time had passed quickly and he had almost forgotten his nausea.

It seemed that Gáeth had given an order and the two warriors had shipped their oars, leaving it to the smith and his companion to guide the boat along the rocky shoreline. Eadulf could make out nothing on the island. It was just a dark mass rising a little way above them. The craft moved quickly along. Judging by the blackness of the shape, he guessed they had come to a headland of sorts where the south-east corner of the island met its eastern shore. This was where Gáeth claimed that there was a sandy beach where a safe landing might be made.

The sound of the heavy seas and wind had died away now as they reached the shelter of the island and Eadulf heaved a sigh of relief.

As they swung round the rocky outcrop, Conrí gave a sharp warning cry.

They had almost collided with the dark outline of a large ship at anchor. Eadulf recognised its lines. It was the warship that had chased them. It appeared to be in darkness except for one lantern bobbing at its stern.

Gáeth and his companion brought their craft almost under the bows of the vessel. Luckily the craft was so light that it made not a sound as it came into the shadow of the warship. Gáeth and one of the warriors put out their hands to minimise the impact of the craft against the wooden timbers of the larger vessel.

They heard a harsh voice calling from the stern.

'Did you hear something?'

A sleepy voice replied from nearby.

'Are you joking? Oystercatchers, terns and gulls – isn't that enough noise for you?'

'I thought I heard a cry.'

'You are lucky to hear anything after a few weeks on this bird-infested island.'

'We are supposed to be on watch,' snapped the other voice.

'Watch for what? The old man was killed, wasn't he? Didn't Olcán say as much?'

'He was, but no one has recovered the body.'

'We saw the *naomhóg* floating away with the old man slumped in it. You could see the arrow sticking out of his back. Do you think he was going to recover, spring up and row that craft all the way to the mainland? You have a great sense of humour.'

'Well, what of the woman and her companion? I suppose we don't have to worry about them?'

'We'll collect them tomorrow morning. If they made it to that other island safely, that is. They took the last of the hermits' canoes and it was a leaky one at that. That's why Olcán didn't bother to destroy it. No sane person would have attempted to put to sea in that. They are probably drowned anyway. I don't think we have to bother looking for them.'

There was silence for a moment.

'Well, Olcán wants us to look over the island anyway.'

'Why does Olcán think that they have gone there? There are plenty of nearer islands to the north and east.'

The other voice laughed harshly.

'When it was found they had escaped, a search was made, and Olcán spotted their canoe heading to the north-west. It's the only island of any size in that direction.'

'They will have probably missed the island altogether in the darkness . . . if they didn't sink first,' the other responded.

'When Olcán comes aboard at first light we'll go and have a look. He doesn't want to fall into disfavour with the Master.'

'Who would?' said the other one and the words were uttered with a note of fear in them.

In the darkness, Gáeth was indicating towards the headland around which they had come. He and Gaimredán laid into their oars, quietly sculling the boat back around the rocky outcrop and finding a stretch of quiet water. Then they shipped their oars.

'Did you hear that, lady?' Gáeth called in a low voice.

Fidelma leant forward. 'I did.'

'It seems as if someone called Olcán is in charge,' Eadulf observed, feeling he should contribute something.

'The point is, lady,' the smith continued, ignoring him, 'that the religious are prisoners here and well guarded. From what was said, when the old man tried to escape, these people had no scruples but simply shot him. That was the old hermit you found dying, wasn't it?'

'It was.'

'It sounded as if someone else has escaped from these people and fled to one of the other islands,' Eadulf pointed out.

'Well, no use worrying about them.' From behind them, Conrí entered the council. 'They said their boat was leaking. They would not last long on these seas.'

Gáeth was rubbing his chin.

'From what they said, they were heading to the large island to the north-west. I know it. But that's uninhabited. If they made it, then our friends in the warship will doubtless recapture them tomorrow.'

Fidelma looked at him with interest.

'What are you suggesting?'

The smith was reflective for a moment or two.

'That it is pointless landing on this island. It is well guarded and we know now that the religious are prisoners there. It needs more men than we have to effect any rescue. We might also put ourselves in danger of capture and then we would be unable to summon help.' He paused.

'Go on,' Fidelma urged. 'Your arguments are logical so far.'

'If the two who escaped have made it to the other island, we might be able to rescue them and find out from them what is happening and who is behind it.'

Conrí was sceptical.

'You heard what the two men said. The boat probably sank and they are drowned.'

'On the other hand, the boat might just have made it to the island,' replied Gáeth. 'The choice is yours, lady.'

Fidelma hesitated, then asked: 'Do you think you can navigate to this other island?'

'It is a place where Gaimredán and I have often lifted crayfish. I know it well.'

'Then the sooner that we start out, the sooner we shall arrive.'

Without a further word, Gáeth and his company pushed out and manoeuvred the craft back to the open seas. At once the winds rose and the waters became choppy.

Eadulf's fears came back again as he clung to the side of the pitching boat and once more all four oars were used to propel it across the black sea. Eadulf hoped there were no hidden rocks in the black waters. To his eyes, the seas appeared petulant and heavy, although a seasoned sailor would have observed that the waters were fairly calm.

He eventually became aware of a dark shape looming, just discernible against the western horizon where the sky touched the sea. He was surprised by the height of the cliffs that rose up before them, but then realised it was simply an optical illusion. From sea level the rocks appeared enormous even though they were only four or five metres high. He wanted to ask Gáeth whether it was feasible that they could ever land in such a place but it was impossible to ask questions. He merely hung on and hoped for the best.

Gáeth and his companion began to manoeuvre the boat towards the north end of the island. Sheltered from the south-westerly winds, the water grew calmer but was black and fearsome. Eadulf could see the white edges of rocks here and there. Suddenly he saw that they were heading for a black hole in the cliffs, and as it grew closer realised that they were approaching a small cave entrance. He thought a landing impossible. But there were large boulders forming a storm beach at the cave and Gáeth guided the boat up into a small natural harbour. He was out first, taking the bow rope and holding it while gesturing for the others to climb carefully for'ard and out of the vessel. Once everyone was out, the smith and his companion heaved the boat upwards and on to the smooth boulders above the sea so that it would not be harmed by any rebellious waves.

The air was more peaceful now. While the whispering of the sea continued, a soft breath of a night breeze filled the air. Eadulf realised that he could hear a curious croaking sound. Gáeth, when asked, told him it was merely the male natterjack toads that made the island their home. Now and then came the angry sound of a disturbed tern or gull. He followed the example of the others by stamping his feet to restore the circulation, having been so long in the boat in one position and chilled by the cold of the winter night.

It was then that Eadulf realised just how resourceful Gáeth was, for the smith had removed a leather bag from the boat. From this he took an object which a few moments later revealed itself to be a storm lantern, which the smith lit with the expert deployment of flint and tinder.

He held it up and the others gathered by its light.

'It looks a large island,' Fidelma commented, peering into the darkness around them.

'Not very large. There are only two places where a landing could be effected,' Gáeth replied. 'You have seen one. The other is midway down the eastern side where there is another cave. There is no sign of a boat here so if they have managed to make it ashore, the only place they will be is in the other cave.'

'Do you have another lantern?' asked Fidelma. 'It would save time if we split into two parties. One group to search here and the second to look at this cave you mention.'

Gáeth had, indeed, foreseen the need for a second storm lantern. They were of a type Eadulf knew was called *lespaire*, made from bronze, and probably the smith had fashioned them himself. They were filled with oil but what type Eadulf could only guess.

'I will go with one party and Gaimredán will lead the other,' Gáeth announced. 'We both know the island and it will be best if both groups have a guide.'

Fidelma and Eadulf chose to go with Gáeth to the second cave while Conrí and his men went with Gaimredán to make sure of the cave at the spot where they had landed.

Eadulf was still a little dizzy from the trip and found he had difficulty keeping his balance on the rocky earth. But the others did not notice in the darkness.

They moved south, passing the rising hill that marked the centre of the island. Eadulf noticed that there seemed to be some shadows on it, just visible against the night sky. They looked like buildings and he remarked upon this.

'Ancient stones put up when our gods and goddesses were young,' Gáeth replied shortly.

It was not long before they came to the second cave.

'If they made it, then that would be the landing place, down there on those stones. Then they would shelter in the cave.'

'Can we get down there?' asked Fidelma dubiously.

'There is a path here, cut by the ancients who built that.' He jerked his thumb towards the solitary dark hill. 'Follow me carefully and step where I do. It's only a three-metre drop but the stones below are sharp.'

He began to descend to sea level by a series of ledges, to where a shelf of stones separated the cliff from the sea and led along to the cave entrance.

They had all reached this level in safety when Gáeth suddenly surprised them by letting out a soft oath and raised his lantern higher.

'What is it?' Fidelma whispered, trying to see what he was looking at.

The smith pointed ahead.

'Just there, see it?'

They moved forward. Eadulf could see the broken pieces of wood and torn strips of hide lying in the surf.

'Do you think it is their canoe?' Fidelma asked. 'Could they have made it ashore?'

'We will soon find out,' said Gáeth, turning for the cave.

He led the way in, holding the lantern up before him. The cave was not large and it did not take long to discover that it was empty.

Gáeth sighed deeply.

'Well, unless Gaimredán had better luck, there is nowhere else on this island that they could be.'

Fidelma pulled a face in the gloom.

'So if that was the remains of the *naomhóg* they did not make it ashore.'

'If,' pointed out Eadulf logically. 'We don't know that for certain.'

'Let's go back,' Gáeth said abruptly. 'There is nothing here.'

They scrambled up to the top of the short cliff and began to move back across the island. They were skirting round the base of the small hill when Eadulf stared up towards the black shadows of the rocks on top. Something caught his eye and he came to a halt.

'What is it?' asked Fidelma as she nearly collided with him. Gáeth turned and paused.

'Are there any animals on this island?' asked Eadulf in a low voice.

'None that I know of,' Gáeth replied.

Suddenly, Eadulf was running up the slope in the darkness. It was only a short one, an incline rising three metres above where they had been standing. On top were several stone slabs. As he reached the top something launched itself at him. Hands grabbed him round the waist and he was knocked to the ground, falling so hard that his breath left him. A muscular body was on him, grasping at him, trying to pin him down. He was hard pressed to prevent himself being injured by the strong arms that searched for a hold round his neck.

He managed to cry out and the next thing he heard was Gáeth struggling with his assailant. Then Fidelma's voice cried out.

Eadulf felt himself drifting into unconsciousness but then, mercifully, the pressure on his neck was released. He was coughing, gasping for breath, and the nausea came back with a vengeance. The weight of the person who had attacked him was gone. He sat up cautiously.

Gáeth was holding the lantern up and Fidelma was by his side.

Before them stood a tough-looking man, clad in the torn remnants of a religious robe, fists balled in a defensive attitude.

'We mean you no harm, Brother,' Fidelma was saying. She had been repeating it several times.

Eadulf retched again and Gáeth helped him to his feet.

'Are you all right, Eadulf?' Fidelma demanded, glancing at him.

He massaged his throat ruefully.

'If surviving death by a fraction is being all right, then I am,' he muttered as he turned to examine his attacker. The man stood arms and legs akimbo as if waiting for someone to attack him.

'I presume that you are one of those who have escaped from Seanach's Island?' Fidelma asked.

'You'll not take me back there alive,' returned the man in a curious accent.

'We do not mean to,' replied Fidelma. 'We are here to rescue you.'

The man stepped back in surprise. 'You do not mean to kill me?'

Fidelma's voice was pacifying. 'We heard of your escape and came in search of you. We are no more friends of those who held you as prisoner than you are. What happened to your companion? Are you the only survivor?'

From behind another of the stones a dark shadow slowly emerged. It was that of a woman.

'I am Sister Easdan,' she said. 'Who are you?'

'I am Fidelma of Cashel. I came here in search of the killers of the Abbess Faife and to trace her companions.'

'Fidelma of Cashel?' The woman spoke slowly. 'I have heard the name. Aren't you a *dálaigh*?'

Fidelma nodded in the lamplight.

'These are my companions, Brother Eadulf and Gáeth the smith. We have other friends further down by the shore.'

'How did you trace us here?' demanded Sister Easdan.

Fidelma made a dismissive gesture with her hand.

'It is a long story, Sister Easdan. I presume that you are one of Abbess Faife's companions from Ard Fhearta?'

'I am.'

'And this is Brother . . . ?'

The burly man was hesitant.

'You can trust me,' Fidelma said encouragingly.

'My name is Esumaro,' the man replied haltingly. 'I am . . . I was skipper of the *Sumerli*, a merchantman out of An Naoned.'

'An Naoned?' Eadulf frowned. 'That is in Gaul.'

'Was your ship wrecked near where you were taken prisoner?' asked Fidelma.

'It was – and that, too, is a long story,' replied the Gaulish sailor grimly. 'The men who held me prisoner destroyed my ship and killed my men. It was only by the quick thinking of Sister Easdan and her colleagues, who disguised me as one of them, that my life has been saved so far.'

'We found him some way from the shore.' Sister Easdan joined in. 'And then the raiders rode down on us, killed Abbess Faife, and took us away as prisoners.'

'We heard that you had seized a canoe and escaped,' said Fidelma. 'You were seen making for this island. It was thought your boat was leaking and that you might not make it here. But your captors plan to come at first light to make certain.'

Esumaro made an angry hissing sound between his teeth.

'We nearly didn't make it because the boat was damaged. It was thanks to Sister Easdan here that we managed.'

'There was nothing else to do,' the girl said simply. 'Water was coming into the stern through a hole. I was wearing a leather apron and I used a knife to puncture the leather then tied it to the hide with little strips cut into thongs. My father was a fisherman and I have seen it done before on a *naomhóg*. It was simple and kept us afloat for long enough to reach here.'

'It was impressive,' the Gaulish sailor corrected with vehemence. 'The leak would have sunk us within a short time. Sister Easdan worked with frozen fingers and waves cascading over her, struggling to tie a piece of leather over the hole. It was bravely done.'

Gáeth nodded appreciatively at their story.

'How did you know where to land? Have you have sailed these waters before?'

'I have sailed through these waters,' affirmed Esumaro. 'I have traded with the abbey of Ard Fhearta and know this coastline.'

'So you knew where best to land on this island?'

Esumaro gave a bark of laughter.

'Had I done so, my friend, I would not have lost the canoe that was our only hope of reaching the mainland. In trying to land on the island, I misjudged in the dark and the canoe broke up in the surf.'

'You were lucky to come ashore then,' observed Gáeth.

'It was not without difficulty,' agreed Sister Easdan with quiet humour.

There was a shout in the distance and a flicker of light. Esumaro started nervously.

'What's that?'

Fidelma calmed him. 'That is the rest of our party, anxious for us. They probably heard the sounds of our struggle. I think it is best to get back to the mainland before light and you can tell us the main part of your story. Then we must form a plan to rescue the others.'

They rejoined Conrí, Gaimredán and the others. Some corma was drunk to put warmth into them and they ate some wheaten cakes, which Gáeth had kept dry in his leather bag. Then they clambered into the *naomhóg* and the oarsmen began to pull away from the island, heading out into the darkness back towards the mainland.

Eadulf tried to concentrate on analysing what this adventure meant. It was one way of trying to prevent the seasickness returning, although he did not hold out much hope of it. He only prayed that he would not make an idiot of himself and vomit in front of everyone. Concentrate!

After Ganicca had described what had happened at his village, he suspected that Fidelma and Conrí were now presuming that Uaman the Leper was still alive. That could not be. Eadulf was sure. He tried to recall the memory of how the leper had been sinking into the quicksand when the great wave had come sweeping in and Uaman was there no more. He would stake his life that Uaman had perished in spite of what everyone now thought.

Who was Olcán? Why would a group of men on a warship abduct a group of religious and imprison them on an island of hermits? Why would they kill them when they tried to escape? Why kill the Abbess Faife? Why would they also wreck a merchant ship from Gaul? They were questions that he realised could not be answered with the knowledge he had. He knew what Fidelma would say. Never try to make a deduction until you have sufficient knowledge. And how did this matter connect with the murder of the Venerable Cináed? Indeed, did it have any connection at all? Was it simply a coincidence?

On reflection, he believed that the young girl – what was her name? Sister Sinnchéne – had killed Cináed. It was a classic tale of jealousy and rejection. Then he considered further. There was the Venerable Mac Faosma to consider. He hated Cináed. That much was obvious. But would a scholar resort to killing a fellow scholar? Then there was the physician Sister Uallann and . . . Uallann? He had heard that name recently from someone. Who?

He realised with abruptness that his mind was racing. There were too many possibilities. Fidelma was right. You could not make any deductions without sufficient knowledge. He was merely guessing.

The increasing noise of seabirds make him glance up. To his left he saw a headland and his heart leapt. Had they already reached the mainland? The plaintive call of gulls was growing stronger, mingling with the crash of the surf, and he could see, by the pale light spreading in the eastern sky, a long low belt of sandy shore stretching away in a curve to the south.

They were back in Bréanainn's bay.

He had heard much about the Blessed Bréanainn and his fabulous seven-year voyage out on the high seas. Well, the saintly man was welcome to such wanderings. Eadulf vowed he would never step on board ship again – not if he could help it. He had done enough sea travelling in his life. It was reassuring to see the mainland again. His spirits lifted and he sat back more comfortably.

It was not long before the *naomhóg* turned and went racing ashore with Gáeth and Gaimredán bringing it almost to the very spot they had set out from. And looking at the eastern sky Eadulf realised that they had set out when the sun had gone down in the west and now there was a light in the east. He was exhausted and wondered how Gáeth, his companion and the warriors who had taken the oars were able to stand.

With quiet instruction, Gáeth hid the oars at the top of the shore by some trees. Then the men lifted the *naomhóg* on their shoulders, balancing bottom upwards, and set off down the path to Loch Gile. Fidelma, Sister Easdan and Esumaro came behind while Eadulf was given the task of carrying Gáeth's leather bag.

They walked in silence and kept that silence even after they had deposited the boat by the loch shore and moved to the forge.

As if by common consent, the first task was banking the fires at Gáeth's dwelling house and then, without more ado, still in their sodden clothing, they spread themselves around it and were all asleep within moments.

CHAPTER FIFTEEN

It was a little after midday when Eadulf awoke and found the others also stirring from their exhausted slumber. Gáeth and Gaimredán were already preparing food that smelled appetising over the fire while Fidelma was also up and washed. Eadulf excused himself and went to the cold stream outside and splashed his face in a perfunctory manner before rejoining them.

The winter's day was bright and sunny, yet the cloudless sky meant that it would be cold again. Snow lay on the mountains and there were still traces of a frost in the shadowy parts of the buildings around Gáeth's forge. In the paddock at the back of the forge it seemed that the horses had been fed already.

To Eadulf the previous night seemed like some kind of nightmare. He mentally repeated his oath never to take to the sea again. Apart from a few greetings no one among the company spoke until after the meal was eaten and the fire was stoked and burning brightly again. Then they sat round the central hearth in a circle and finally Fidelma invited Esumaro and Sister Easdan to tell their story.

It was Esumaro who told his tale first. Of the storm that had driven his ship into the long inlet that would have led him to the safe anchorage outside the abbey of Colmán. But he described how he had been lured on to the rocky shores of the islet by a false signal and his ship dashed to pieces. He went on to graphically recount how the survivors of the *Sumerli* had been killed on the shore and how he had hidden himself before making it across a sandy strait to the mainland in the darkness and then had fallen into an exhausted sleep. He ended with being woken by a group of religieuse.

It was then that Sister Easdan took up the story of how they were on their way to the pilgrimage shrine on Bréanainn's mount when they came upon Esumaro. A short while later, they were taken prisoner by a band of warriors who killed the Abbess Faife.

'Tell us who led these warriors,' instructed Fidelma, wanting to get down to detail.

'There was a man whom the men called Olcán,' replied Sister Easdan immediately.

'While my men were being killed on the shore where we were wrecked, I heard the killers speak this name – Olcán,' added Esumaro. 'The warriors were the wreckers and they became our captors. I owe my life to the good sisters who disguised me, pretending that I was also one of their religious brothers on the same pilgrimage. I called myself Brother Maros lest they found out the name of the captain of the ship they had wrecked.'

Sister Easdan was looking troubled.

'While Olcán clearly led the warriors, I don't think he was really in charge.'

'What makes you say that?' asked Fidelma encouragingly.

'There was a small person among them from whom Olcán appeared to take his orders.'

'Describe this person,' Fidelma invited, not revealing that she had already had a good description from Ganicca.

'We never saw his features,' the girl replied. 'He was on horseback but clad from head to foot in grey robes, rather like a religious, but he wore no crucifix round his neck.'

'Can you describe him further?'

'A slight, bent figure, speaking in a high-pitched, almost whining voice.'

'But you never caught sight of his face once?' pressed Eadulf.

Esumaro shook his head.

'But I can tell you his name,' he said suddenly, making them all turn to look at him. 'When we stopped at a village among the mountains after we had been captured, one of the villagers – an old man – pointed to him and called, in my hearing, the name Uaman.'

Eadulf sat back shaking his head.

Conrí let out a long, deep breath.

'It makes sense if Uaman the Leper still lives,' he observed. 'Now we know with whom we are dealing.'

Fidelma did not seem perturbed.

'Esumaro, did any of the company, the warriors, ever address the man as Uaman?'

It was Sister Easdan who replied.

'It was just as Esumaro said. The old man in the village seemed to recognise him. But Olcán was the only person who was allowed to address him. Olcán simply called him "master".'

'Master?' echoed Fidelma. It was an odd form of address

in the five kingdoms of Éireann for it meant more of a teacher, a spiritual guide and leader, than one of rank.

Sister Easdan nodded.

'I think that he was an evil man for, at the village where we stopped in the mountains, he ordered the warriors to fall on it and sack it. They killed many people.'

'Do you know why?'

'There seemed no reason that I could see,' Esumaro replied. 'It was done out of sheer ill-will.'

'Where were you taken after that?'

'We were marched north through the mountains until we came to the sea again,' Esumaro continued. 'I knew we had crossed the peninsula and had come to the broad bay with the port that lies not far from Ard Fhearta on the northern side. I had sailed several times into that bay.'

Sister Easdan reached forward and laid a hand on the Gaulish sailor's arm.

'But don't forget that before we came to the bay, our party met that other ugly-looking warrior.'

Fidelma raised her head in interest.

'What warrior was this?'

'I don't know,' Sister Easdan replied. 'But it was obvious that this man had been expecting us for he was waiting at a spot where there was a memorial stone, a large stone with a cross inscribed on it, not far from a river which we had forded.'

'So you believe that the meeting had been arranged between your captors and this man?'

Sister Easdan nodded thoughtfully.

'He was certainly waiting for us. He greeted Olcán like an old friend. We were halted and told to rest awhile. I saw Olcán draw the man aside to bring him to this man they

called the "master". They engaged in some conversation and
then the master took a small bag from his saddlebag and
handed it to the warrior. He seemed to be thanking them
and then he turned, mounted his horse and rode away. He
took the western road.'

'You seem to have a sharp eye, Sister Easdan,' Eadulf
commented. 'Are you sure he went westwards?'

'Indeed, he did.'

Fidelma pursed her lips thoughtfully for a moment.

'Can you describe anything further about this man? You
called him ugly.'

'Ugly is the word I think of,' replied Sister Easdan. 'He
was a tall, burly-looking man. He had a mass of red curly
hair and a beard. He also wore something I have never seen
before. It was a . . . like a picture, painted on his arm. His
right arm, I think.'

Fidelma leant forward quickly with a gasp of interest.

'Do you know what sort of picture?'

'I can't be sure. Only that it was something wrapped
round a sword. Creatures, I think.'

Fidelma sat back and glanced at Eadulf.

'That is a description of Slébéne's *trén-fher*, his personal
champion,' he replied in answer to her unasked question.

'This small bag that you say the "master" gave to this
warrior . . . what did it look like to you?'

Sister Easdan paused and thought carefully.

'Just a small bag, although the contents seemed heavy.'

'Slébéne is involved in this matter,' Eadulf said. 'This
confirms it. Perhaps he is being paid by this man . . . the
master.'

'I think we can agree that Slébéne has some involvement,' Fidelma concurred. 'His champion, whatever his

name is, would not be acting on his own. He would do nothing without his chief's permission. However, in law we cannot find a person guilty on such evidence. But the law will accept that there are grounds for suspicion.'

'But if Slébéne is involved in this matter, it would explain a lot,' Eadulf pointed out.

'That is true. But first we have to find out what this matter, as you call it, is. What is involved here?' She turned back to Sister Easdan and Esumaro. 'What happened next? What happened after this warrior rode off?'

Esumaro glanced at his companion as if seeking permission to continue with the story.

'It was then that this person called the master also left us.'

'He rode off in an easterly direction along the shore and we saw no more of him after that,' added the girl.

'He rode away alone? None of the warriors went with him?' asked Eadulf.

'None.'

'And what did Olcán do then?' queried Fidelma.

'He and his men took us to a sandy shore. A short way out we saw a large warship at anchor,' replied Esumaro. 'The women and myself were rowed out to the warship. We were brought to an island, the Island of Seanach, as I later learnt, and taken ashore. There we found a dozen or so hermits who used to live on the island. They, too, were prisoners of these men.'

'Was nothing said to you during this time about why you had been made captive? No reason was given for your capture?'

'Our captors spoke not a word to us except to say "do this", "do that" or to hit us if we moved too slowly. They told us nothing of who they were or what they wanted,' explained Sister Easdan. 'We learnt that when we reached the island.'

'I see. Go on, then.'

'With the hermits, there was not enough shelter for everyone and our captors set up tents for us behind the chapel. They gave us hardly any warmth or shelter. Nights were spent in freezing conditions and it was almost joy to be given work during the day. However, it could have been worse. The hermits had built a wall around their settlement and this enclosing wall had been made exceptionally strong – it was seven metres thick in places. That, at least, stopped the harsh winds from blowing us away.'

'There were two small oratories in which the warriors used to sleep themselves. Some of their number remained on the ship,' Esumaro added. 'But there was always someone on guard over us to raise the alarm if we disobeyed. Olcán slept in a *clochán*, one of the small round stone huts near where the old hermits had their souterrain for storing food. There was always someone ensuring that we worked and did not slack.'

Eadulf was puzzled.

'What work was there to do on that small island?' he asked.

'It was the reason why these men, these swine, were there,' Esumaro replied bitterly. 'We were brought there as slave labour to cut and polish stone.'

'Cut and polish stone?' Fidelma's eyebrows arched.

Sister Easdan was apparently unaware of the surprise the announcement had caused.

'That was the interesting point,' she said. 'How did these men know about us?'

Fidelma looked frankly bewildered.

'I don't understand.'

Sister Easdan realised that she had been assuming knowledge.

'Did you not know that our task at Ard Fhearta was to cut and polish stones that were brought in to the abbey from other parts of the country? Abbess Faife had chosen us to go on the pilgrimage this year because we all worked in the jewellery workshop making necklaces and brooches for the abbey to trade.'

'Ah.' Fidelma suddenly realised what was meant by the word stone. 'You mean that these stones were *lec-lógmar*, precious stones that are cut to shape and engraved for personal ornaments . . .'

'. . . or used by artists in their ornamental works. Red jasper, rose-coloured quartz, jet, amber, diorite . . .'

Fidelma's eyes widened slowly in understanding.

'So are you saying that all the religieuse who accompanied Abbess Faife had worked on cutting and polishing these stones in the abbey?'

'Of course,' Sister Easdan said. 'Each year Abbess Faife chose certain groups to go on the pilgrimage. This year she had chosen us workers in stone.'

Fidelma peered accusingly at Conrí.

'No one told me that those abducted held any special position at the abbey,' she commented in irritation.

'I did not know this either,' Conrí protested. 'I did not know they were stone polishers. The abbot never told me.'

Eadulf had turned to the girl. 'And this was what you were made to do on the island?'

'Even worse, we were made to use, as tables, three of the rectangular burial platforms, quartz-covered *leachts*,

under which the old leaders of the community were buried.'
Sister Easdan shivered and crossed herself. 'They made us
work on their graves as if they had been nothing but slabs
of wood.'

'Why not deny that you were workers in precious stones?'
asked Eadulf.

'They had obviously found out who we were and what
we did,' Sister Easdan responded. 'That's why they seized
us and took us to the island – so that we could work for
them.'

Esumaro leant towards Fidelma.

'I have been captain of a merchant vessel for many
years. I know the trade between here and Gaul. I can tell
you that the stones I saw on the island – what do you call
them, *lec-lógmar*? – were valuable beyond anything I have
seen elsewhere. Amethyst, topaz, emerald and sapphire . . .
never have I seen such riches before.'

Eadulf looked doubtful.

'Where would such precious stones come from?' he
demanded.

Gáeth the smith, who had been listening intently to the
questioning, smiled gently.

'Do not be surprised, Brother Saxon. Such stones as these
are to be found, often in abundance, in these mountains and
the coastal areas. They are extracted from clefts between
the great rock surfaces, tiny shining crystals in the sand-
stone cliffs. They are difficult to find but now and again a
rich seam of them comes to light. They are very expensive
for artisans to use. I know that Ard Fhearta has its own
craftsmen who use the stones that these sisters cut and polish
to embellish crucifixes and chalices and other icons for your
Christian church.'

'But emeralds, sapphires . . .' began Eadulf sceptically.

'Believe me, Brother,' Esumaro said earnestly, 'I tell you I have seen several boxes of those glittering gems. The unworked crystal was brought to the sisters and when they had done with it the stones were stored in boxes in the chapel. The man, Olcán, and his master are amassing a fortune.'

'So these stones are local? Do you know where exactly they came from?' asked Fidelma in curiosity.

'They would not tell us,' Sister Easdan said, 'but we found out that some of the hermits had been made to work on the far side of the island. We believe that there was a seam there where the crystal was plentiful. It was clear purple stone, amethyst. I am not sure where they brought the other in from. But as Esumaro says, there were some sapphires and emeralds and a few topazes.'

Eadulf glanced at Esumaro.

'You did not possess the cutting and polishing skill of the sisters, so what did you do?'

'I simply acted as a general handyman,' the sailor replied. 'I lifted and carried. Towards the end, though, I think they suspected that I was not really a religious.'

'Why was that?' Fidelma asked.

'Well, when I was first taken captive Sister Easdan intervened after they recognised me as a Gaul. She explained that I was a noted scholar, and I gave them the name of Brother Maros. When our captors pointed out that I wore no tonsure, Sister Easdan' – he smiled quickly at her – 'claimed that I was a follower of the Blessed Budoc of Laurea, and his followers did not wear tonsures. She said I had been with them some time at the abbey of Ard Fhearta.'

He paused.

'Very well, go on,' Eadulf said encouragingly.

'At first they seemed content enough with that explanation. Truly, I had never heard of Budoc of Laurea. Sister Easdan quickly instructed me on the march through the mountains. Budoc had apparently become Bishop of Dol over a hundred years ago. That is in Armorica – which we are now calling Little Britain because of the countless refugees from Britain who have come to live in there since they were driven out by you Saxons.'

A colour sprang to Eadulf's cheeks.

'I am not responsible for what my ancestors did,' he protested.

Esumaro chuckled. 'Is there not a saying about the sins of the fathers?'

Fidelma laid a hand on Eadulf's arm.

'We are in Muman, not Britain, Esumaro. Let us concentrate our minds on the immediate matter. You said that your captors were initially content with the explanation that you were a member of the religieux. This implies that they were not content later. What happened?'

'I had the feeling that this strange person, the one called the master, was watching me for some time after we were captured. It is hard to explain. Several times I glanced in his direction but it was difficult to see anything with the hood of the robe drawn down. There was nothing to show which way his eyes were turned. But I had this feeling . . .' He paused and shuddered. Then he continued: 'I saw this Olcán talking to him and soon after, when we had paused on our march, Olcán came over to me and started asking me questions.'

'Such as?' prompted Fidelma.

'Such as how long did I claim I had been at Ard Fhearta.

318

Whom did I know there and so on. I presumed that one of the sisters had slipped up and told them that I had not been at Ard Fhearta. I said that there must have been a mistake about what had been claimed. I said that I had been at the abbey of Colmán and after the pilgrimage I would be going to Ard Fhearta.'

'And did that satisfy this Olcán?'

Esumaro shook his head.

'He questioned me further on where I had come from, what sort of scholar I was. Who Budoc was and so on. I did my best. But the only scholarship that I knew anything about was how to navigate the oceans by the stars. So I pretended that I was an astronomer and talked of this star and that. Of course, Olcán knew a little but not as much as I did. Do you not have a saying that the blind of one eye is a king among the blind of both eyes?'

'So they accepted you?'

'Not entirely. I think they continued to be suspicious. However, they did not bother me any more, although I was aware, all the time, that I was being watched.'

'So when you reached the island, Seanach's Island, the religieuse were put to work cleaning the stones and you did fetching and carrying while the original inhabitants of the community were actually cutting the crystals from the rocks on the far side of the island,' Fidelma summed up. 'What prompted you to escape?'

Esumaro continued their story.

'It was an old man who inspired us. I do not know his name, but I think he was the head of the community there. He was a sprightly man in spite of his age. I was taking a box of the polished rocks to the chapel when I heard shouting. I turned and saw that he had evaded his captors and was pushing out one of those canoes into the surf from the beach on the east side.

'The guards had seen him, of course, but the old man could handle that canoe. I admired him. He paddled with the tide so that he had slipped past their advantage points and was heading away out to the sea in the direction of the mainland before they spotted him. Olcán was on the warship when it happened and I heard him shouting in his fury. Then – I think it was at his order – his men began shooting at the old man who was now rowing for all he was worth. Arrows fell on his craft but never seemed to touch him. I thought for a few moments that he might make it. I was rooted to the spot, box still in my hand, and wanting to shout and cheer. But an arrow must have struck him in the back and he gave a scream. I could hear it over the waves. He slumped on to his side.

'Then I was knocked to the ground by one of the guards. I saw no more of the old man and could hear nothing except the guard rebuking me for my idleness because I had stopped to watch. I had to pick up the polished stones that had spilt from the box. When I had done that, I was given to understand, by the coarse laughter and jesting of the guards, that the old man was dead.'

'Which was not true,' intervened Conrí. 'Somehow that old man, whose name we discovered was Brother Martan, managed to struggle with the *naomhóg* and reach the shore on the mainland where, by coincidence, we were. Alas, he died in our arms, having warned us about the island.'

Esumaro looked impressed.

'So how did you make your escape?' prompted Eadulf.

'That same evening, I realised from the way the old man had been shot that we could expect no mercy. As soon as they had finished with our labour, they would kill us. I had noticed that there was a second canoe – a *naomhóg* you call it? Well, there was a second canoe alongside the one that the old man took. If I attempted to run in daylight, I would not get far so I decided to make the attempt at night.'

'The sea had no perils for you?' interrupted Eadulf, slightly enviously.

Esumaro laughed.

'I am a son of the sea,' he said confidently. 'The sea is my friend and I respect its moods. I have often rowed small boats and know how to handle the canoes that you use. I also knew these islands, having sailed them, and I realised that the only chance was to go south to the mainland where the old man had been going. I also felt that I could not leave Sister Easdan behind. She had been instrumental in saving my life and so I suggested to her that we should make the attempt together and then try to raise the alarm so that the local chieftain could rescue the others.'

Conrí's expression was cynical.

'Slébéne would not have been much help to you,' he muttered.

'Continue, Esumaro,' Fidelma said, with a glance of annoyance at Conrí.

'Well, it was towards dusk that Sister Easdan and I managed to sneak away. The guards were lax then, eating their meal. Sure enough there was the canoe still where it had been with the paddles and it was light enough for the two of us to be able to launch it. We started to head south-west towards the mainland but there was a high sea running against us and then Sister Easdan called out that we had a leak. Water was coming through the side of the craft.'

'We had forgotten in our haste to depart that the rim of

the western sky was still light and we could be seen against it,' continued Sister Easdan. 'We heard shouting from the shore for the wind carried it to us. We knew then that we had been spotted. God looked down on us, for at least we were beyond arrow reach.'

'We could not pull back to shore,' chimed in Esumaro. 'Anyway, I don't think we would have reached it alive, after what they did to the old man. Sister Easdan, as we told you before, was busy with the leather apron and thongs in the half-light, but by then I realised that we had no hope of reaching the mainland with the tide running up from the south-east against us.'

Gáeth made one of his infrequent interpolations.

'That was the same tide which helped us run swiftly to the islands.'

'I was sailor enough to know that I would have to run with the tide,' continued Esumaro. 'But I knew that there was another large island to the north-west of Seanach's Island and hoped that, with luck, the tide would help me and we could be carried there before the leak was so bad that we sank.'

Gáeth clapped his hand on his thigh in approval.

'Your captors did not give much for your chances, according to what we overheard. They had seen what direction you were going but thought you'd sink long before you reached the island.'

'We nearly did,' Esumaro admitted. 'But thanks to Sister Easdan, we came within reach of it. It was while I was trying to estimate the best place to land that I saw the cave entrance and took a chance. We were within a hand's reach when the canoe cracked against the rocks and began to break up. I grabbed Sister Easdan and we jumped for our lives. We fought the tide for a few moments and managed to scramble up the rocks on to the island.'

'Precious the foot on shore,' muttered Eadulf reverently, uttering an old landsman's prayer.

'We were cold and tired and had no means of making a fire on that bare rock. Indeed, I couldn't see anything, although I knew there were birds about which I could have caught in the daylight, and made something to eat.'

'We simply huddled together from the cold,' Sister Easdan added. 'There was nothing else to do.'

'We had dropped off to sleep when I was woken by the sounds of voices and oars,' went on Esumaro. 'It could only be Olcán and his men. I knew that if they had knowledge of the island they would come down to the cave where we were sheltering. So we decided to get further on to the island and see if there was anywhere else we could hide. There was the small hill and the ancient stones set up there. We hid there. Then we saw a light and heard people going down to the cave. A few moments later the light returned and the next moment someone came charging up the hill. There was only one thing I could do . . . I threw myself upon the man . . .'

'And nearly killed me,' Eadulf said ruefully.

'You cannot blame Esumaro for trying to protect himself,' Sister Easdan admonished. 'Anyway, that is our story.'

There was a silence until Gáeth rose and put more turf upon the fire.

'Doubtless when our friends went there this morning and did not find you they would think that you had indeed gone down beneath the waves and drowned,' he said.

Fidelma agreed.

'I do not think we need concern ourselves with any

immediate pursuit from the people on Seanach's Island,' she said thoughtfully.

'At least we have solved the mystery,' Conrí observed in satisfaction.

They looked at him curiously.

'How do you come to that conclusion?' There was a dangerous softness in Fidelma's voice.

Conrí looked surprised at the question.

'Why, is it not clear? Uaman and his followers are to blame for all this. He is back to his old ways of trying to gain riches and build up a power base again.'

'As simple as that?' said Fidelma.

'It is hardly a simple matter,' protested Conrí.

'In that I can agree with Conrí,' Eadulf observed.

'You might have to admit that Uaman is still alive,' Fidelma suggested. 'Are you certain that you saw him die?'

Eadulf shrugged. 'I was. But I cannot go against so many people who claim to have seen him.' His voice was not emphatic.

'Believe me, this mystery is far from solved,' she said. 'We have learned only a few more details to add to our fund of knowledge, that is all. There is much to discover yet.'

'But we know that the religieuse from Ard Fhearta were abducted because they were experts at cutting and polishing precious stones . . .' Conrí began.

'And why were we not informed of their expertise at the abbey?' Fidelma demanded.

'That is a question I cannot answer,' replied Conrí. 'Anyway, we know who killed Abbess Faife and abducted them. This man Olcán.'

'But who is Olcán and whom does he work for?'

'We must accept that Uaman the Leper is alive. He is

this mysterious "master". Also Slébéne is in his pay.'

'Uaman has miraculously returned from the dead?' smiled Fidelma. 'Remember that no one has yet positively identified the man except Ganicca. I have enough trust in Eadulf to accept that when he claims to have seen something, he has seen it. No one has gazed upon the man's face clearly enough to identify him. They have seen a shadow and that is all.'

She looked from one to another.

'Certainly, whoever is behind all this, they have found rich seams of the *lec-lógmar*, and have abducted those who know how to work the stone to make it saleable to merchants. We know this man Olcán is ruthless. So is the person he works for – whoever he is. I agree that they probably pay a bribe to Slébéne in order that he will not interfere in what they are doing. But there is another question that preoccupies me. Why did Sister Sinnchéne want to accompany Abbess Faife and the others when she was not a stone cutter and polisher? And was that why Abbess Faife refused to take her?'

They waited in uncomfortable silence for her to continue.

'What can we do now, lady?' muttered Conrí.

Fidelma glanced towards the sky. The short winter day was darkening yet again.

'Little enough today.' She sighed. 'We will have to impose on Gáeth and Gaimredán for another night of hospitality. But at first light, we must set out for Ard Fhearta again. I believe that it is there that these strands will intertwine.'

Conrí could not control his expression of surprise.

'Why at Ard Fhearta?' he demanded.

She shook her head sorrowfully at him.

'Have you forgotten about the murder of the Venerable Cináed?'

There was a soft gasp of horror from Sister Easdan who had not, of course, heard the news.

Fidelma turned to her with a quick look of apology.

'Ah, I had forgotten that you did not know of his death. Did you know him well?'

The girl shook her head.

'Not well. He was a friend of our mentor, Abbess Faife. Some time ago he spent a little while in our workshop talking about what we did. He was writing some tract about it.'

'About the working of stones?'

'About the *lec-lógmar*,' confirmed the girl. 'He was a nice old man. A wise old man. He was not arrogant, like the Venerable Mac Faosma. He would speak to anyone on equal terms no matter what rank they were. How was he murdered, Sister?'

Briefly, Fidelma told her the facts.

'Who could have done such a thing?'

'I cannot tell you yet. But I think, finally, I might see a light on the path ahead.'

Conrí gave her a curious look.

'So we start back to the abbey tomorrow?' he asked after a moment or two.

'Indeed we do,' she replied. 'But you, Conrí, do not. Eadulf and I will go to the abbey with Sister Easdan and our friend Esumaro here. You, Conrí, will have to raise a band of warriors and warships to go back to Seanach's Island and rescue the others there. Try to take the man called Olcán captive; take him alive. We need him to unravel the thread that will lead us to this man "the master".'

'And then? If we succeed?'

'You will succeed,' she said with emphasis. 'You will bring all the prisoners back to the abbey. By which time I hope I shall have sorted out this conundrum.'

'What about Uaman?' demanded Conrí. 'If it is Uaman he will have gone back to his fortress on the south side of the peninsula. Even if he has not, then he will be in hiding somewhere. We need to search for him.'

Fidelma smiled with calm assurance.

'You will be wasting your time, Conrí. All the strands of this mystery will entwine with one another at the abbey of Ard Fhearta.'

CHAPTER SIXTEEN

The journey back to Ard Fhearta took the best part of a day but seemed very rapid. The day was still cold and the pale sun hung in a limpid blue sky but the winds had apparently died away. Fidelma, Eadulf and their companions took the coast road. Sister Easdan and Esumaro were mounted behind Socht and the other warrior as Gáeth was unable to supply them with extra horses. They came to the end of the Corco Duibhne peninsula in hardly any time at all before turning north to take the ford across the River Lithe. Then it was a short ride north-west towards Ard Fhearta. Within sight of the abbey buildings, with the sun resting on the western horizon far out to sea, Conrí and one of his warriors parted company from the rest. It had been agreed that Fidelma and Eadulf would take Esumaro and Sister Easdan back to Ard Fhearta and Conrí insisted that they be accompanied by his warrior Socht.

'I shall go on to Tadcán's fortress at the north end of the bay,' Conrí said. 'Tadcán is loyal to me, one of our best chieftains, and he has three good warships. We could sail tonight and be able to raid Seanach's Island at dawn tomorrow. You can expect word of the outcome by tomorrow evening at the earliest. We could sail directly back to An Bhearbha.'

'May God go with you, Conrí,' Fidelma replied softly. 'Remember, we need Olcán to be captured alive.'

'If I fail it will not be for want of trying,' returned the warlord of the Uí Fidgente with a grim smile.

He raised his hand in farewell and disappeared swiftly, with his companion, along the road that led northwards. Fidelma led the rest of the party towards the abbey on the hilltop.

Someone must have seen their approach long before they arrived for the young *rechtaire*, Brother Cú Mara, was at the open gates and waiting impatiently to greet them.

He immediately recognised Sister Easdan, staring at her in amazement before his eyes swept round the rest of the company.

'What has happened?' he demanded excitedly. 'Where is the lord Conrí? Is he dead? How did you find Sister Easdan? Are the others dead?'

His questions came out in a nervous tumble.

Fidelma slid from her horse and bade him calm himself.

'There will be plenty of time for explanations later.'

Undeterred, Brother Cú Mara turned to Sister Easdan.

'You must tell me what happened, Sister,' he demanded. 'The abbot will want to know at once. Come, I shall take you to him.'

Fidelma frowned at his attempt to override her instructions.

'You have not listened to me. The abbot will know everything in good time. Sister Easdan and Esumaro are here as witnesses and will not be questioned until I say so. They are now under a prohibition forbidding them to speak about what has happened these past few weeks. I will give them such permission when I am ready to do so.'

Fidelma used the old word of *urgarad* to explain the importance of the prohibition, which meant they were forbidden under ancient law to disobey her on pain of dire misfortune. They knew it was very dangerous to break such a prohibition. The High King Conarí, who reigned in the first century of the Christian era, had broken such a prohibition and his peaceful reign descended into violence, plunder and rapine before culminating in his assassination.

Brother Cú Mara grew angry. His face reddened.

'This is a very high-handed way of going about things,' he said stiffly. 'I am steward of this abbey and it is my right to know what has happened to the members of its community.'

He paused, finding himself staring into the narrowed, glinting eyes of Fidelma.

'You know who I am, *rechtaire*?' Her voice was soft but sharp as a needlepoint. 'I do not have to remind you. Therefore, do not speak to me again of your office and its rights. I know them well enough. Just as you know mine.'

Brother Cú Mara's face was bright scarlet. He hesitated and then gave a sour grimace.

'Abbot Erc will want to see you immediately,' he persisted stubbornly.

Fidelma glanced at the darkening sky.

'We will see him later. I want hot baths to be prepared

for all of us. Then we shall eat. After that Brother Eadulf and I will attend the abbot. Do I make myself clear, *rechtaire*?'

Brother Cú Mara was about to say something more when he appeared to have second thoughts. He seemed to realise that he had come up against an immovable object.

'Abbot Erc will be displeased,' he muttered audibly as he turned away.

'And his displeasure will be matched and made insignificant by my own annoyance if we are kept arguing at the gate in this fashion,' Fidelma snapped after him.

Brother Cú Mara turned back.

'It shall be done as you say, Fidelma of Cashel.' He placed heavy emphasis on her title. 'I will order Sister Sinnchéne to prepare baths for you and Brother Eadulf and . . . and this man.' He nodded towards Esumaro. 'Sister Easdan can join her sisters at their evening ablutions and—'

'Sister Easdan will remain with us for the time being in the guests' hostel,' Fidelma replied firmly. 'That goes for Conrí's man as well.'

The steward's jaw dropped a little in his astonishment. He seemed about to protest again and then he swallowed.

'So be it,' he said tightly.

'Good.' Fidelma suddenly smiled in satisfaction. 'Get someone to see to our horses. We have ridden long and hard today. Make sure that they are well looked after and fed. They belong to Mugrón the trader.'

They paused only to remove their saddle bags before Fidelma led the way to the *hospitium*.

Brother Cú Mara had already set matters in motion and members of the community appeared to be running here and there at his orders.

When they reached the guests' hostel, Eadulf looked censoriously at Fidelma.

'You were rather hard on the steward,' he said.

'No more than he deserved. There is much to be done and a killer to be caught.'

She turned to the rest of them, to Sister Easdan, Esumaro and the warrior Socht, an old name which suited the man's temperament well for it meant 'silence'.

'You heard me tell the steward that you were all under an *urgarad*, that is a prohibition forbidding you to say anything until I tell you to. You realise that is a solemn undertaking?'

Sister Easdan and Socht nodded immediately, but she had to explain to Esumaro, who as a Gaul was unaware of what this prohibition meant.

'You see, I want no word of what you have experienced reaching anyone until I hear that Conrí and his men have been successful in rescuing the other prisoners on Seanach's Island and capturing Olcán and his men.'

That they could all understand.

'Then we are agreed?' When they confirmed it, she turned to the impassive warrior. 'One thing, Socht. Although we are within the walls of the abbey, it does not mean we are safe here. I believe that there is an evil here as great as any we faced on Seanach's Island. So keep your arms ready at all times and do not sleep too deeply.'

'I understand, lady,' grunted the warrior.

'That goes for all of you,' she added, glancing at them. 'Be watchful.'

As she finished speaking Sister Sinnchéne entered the hostel. She seemed sullen and a faint look of disapproval crossed her features as her eyes fell on Sister Easdan. It was obvious that she had already received orders from the steward.

'The baths are already prepared for you and Sister Easdan, lady,' she announced. 'The Saxon brother, the stranger and the warrior will have to wait their turn.'

Fidelma returned her sour look with a smile.

'I know, Sister Sinnchéne. The facilities of this *hospitium* are primitive and you have no separate arrangements for men and women to bathe at the same time.'

Only Eadulf noticed that she was being humorous.

The custodian of the *hospitium* stood stiffly, doubtless recalling the nature of their last meeting.

'Very well,' Fidelma said, rising to follow. 'Sister Easdan and I will bathe first.'

'I will take the opportunity to nap,' Eadulf said, sinking on to one of the beds with a groan. 'I have promised myself two things on this trip – one, never to get on a small boat ever again, certainly not at sea, and two, to avoid getting on a horse when I can use my two legs to walk.'

Socht regarded him with astonishment but diplomatically made no comment.

Some time later, when everyone had bathed and eaten and was feeling relaxed, Fidelma and Eadulf made their way through the abbey complex to Abbot Erc's chambers. They had left the others in the *hospitium* and Fidelma had warned them once again not to say anything if anyone seized the opportunity to try to get information from them.

Abbot Erc was sitting staring moodily into the fire crackling in the hearth in his chamber. Behind his chair stood Brother Cú Mara, a study in peevishness.

PETER TREMAYNE

The abbot raised a stern face and bade them enter and seat themselves.

'My steward has reported your arrival with that of one of our missing sisters and a stranger. Yet the lord Conrí has not returned with you. Why is that?'

'All will become clear soon,' Fidelma replied easily.

The abbot's frown deepened.

'My steward also tells me that you refused to answer any of his questions and seemed to be making a secret of your journey and its results. Is that so? For I would look upon that as an insult to this holy establishment.'

Fidelma returned his angry look with a diplomatic smile.

'No insult is intended to you or your house, Abbot Erc. Let me explain, if I may, for I am sure you will understand my reasoning on this matter.'

The abbot gestured impatiently and she interpreted it as a sign to continue.

'Sometimes the rule of an abbey must give way to the rule of law,' she began.

Brother Cú Mara started to sneer from behind the abbot's chair.

'The rule of God comes above all things,' he interrupted.

'There is no rule of God that is contravened here,' replied Fidelma evenly. 'Tell me where it is written in scripture that I must answer the questions of a young *rechtaire*?'

Abbot Erc raised a hand as if to dissipate their exchange.

'You were invited to this abbey to resolve a murder and the abduction of some of our members,' he pointed out. 'Obviously you have news of this and so we would expect you to inform us what that news is.'

'There can be no restrictions placed on a *dálaigh* quali-

334

fied to the level of *anruth*, as I am, other than by the Chief Brehon of the kingdom.' Fidelma kept her voice even. 'However, I expect to be able to tell you everything within the next day or two at the most. My intention is to expose the guilty and not allow them time to escape. Therefore, no word of what has happened must be known within this abbey.'

Abbot Erc looked shocked.

'Are you implying that the guilty are here in this abbey?'

'I told the Venerable Mac Faosma once that I never imply things. You may take it as a fair interpretation,' returned Fidelma calmly.

'Then I demand that you tell me what you know,' snapped the abbot.

Fidelma's brows came together.

'Demand?' Her voice was cold. 'You demand of a *dálaigh*?'

Abbot Erc blinked at her tone. But Brother Cú Mara, young and now a little headstrong, replied somewhat sarcastically.

'You had best remember that times are changing, Fidelma of Cashel. Your laws are becoming outdated. The new Penitentials of Rome are replacing them and the law and its administration will soon be in the hands of abbots and bishops.'

Fidelma regarded him with a piercing stare.

'God save us from that catastrophe,' she said reverently, as if in prayer. 'When, in ancient times, the High King Ollamh Fodhla ordered the laws of the Brehons to be gathered so that they could be applied evenly over the five kingdoms, it was guaranteed that no king nor priest stood above the law and every judge had to justify his judgements. All were equal before the law. Abbots as well as kings. When that system is overthrown then our people will truly be in bondage, whether it be to your Roman Penitentials or to some other power.'

Brother Cú Mara flushed angrily.

'Bondage?' he snapped. 'That is something you Eoghanacht of Cashel need give us no lessons in. You keep the Uí Fidgente in bondage!'

Fidelma had to control her own growing anger.

'Indeed? So you would disagree with the policy of your chieftain, Donennach, that peace with Cashel is better than constant rebellion against the king?'

Brother Cú Mara seemed to forget himself and took a threatening step forward.

'Cú Mara! Enough!' cried Abbot Erc sharply. 'Your fidelity is to this abbey and to the welfare of its people. Remember that and leave us.'

Brother Cú Mara paused for a moment. His expression seemed to show that he was struggling.

'Leave us!' repeated the abbot harshly.

Exhaling with a hissing sound, Brother Cú Mara left the chamber.

'There is an enemy in that one,' Eadulf whispered softly to Fidelma.

Abbot Erc grimaced as if trying to make an apology.

'Cú Mara is a young and headstrong man,' he sighed. 'Diplomacy is not a gift of youth. Yet he does have a point. The Uí Fidgente were defeated by your brother at Cnoc Áine and our ruling family were killed. Many now feel we are in bondage to Cashel.'

'That's not exactly accurate, for your new chieftain Donennach traces his lineage back to Fidgennid after whom the Uí Fidgente take their name. Peace for the clan is better than the centuries of continued warfare that have taken place.'

Abbot Erc bowed his head. 'Let us not talk of politics, Fidelma. I know that you are gifted with eloquence in such matters.'

Fidelma was serious. 'We may have to speak of such matters before long.'

The abbot looked puzzled. 'Are you suggesting that politics enter into this matter of murder and abduction? Most of our community here are loyal Uí Fidgente. Most were supporters of our old leadership.'

'Most,' agreed Fidelma. 'But the Venerable Cináed was not. I think you disapproved of him, didn't you?'

The abbot was trying to fathom the meaning behind her words.

'I will not attempt to deny it. I disapproved of Cináed's ideas. But that does not mean I killed him. I knew him for many years and we worked together. Yet I simply had no liking for Cináed's ambition to seek out controversy.'

'You call it an ambition?' said Fidelma. 'That is an interesting choice of word.'

'Everything he wrote was designed to contradict orthodoxy. What else is that but courting controversy? He was resolute in his pursuit of controversial arguments so that it can be truly said that he had a strong desire to achieve notoriety in these matters.'

'It might also be called adhering to one's principles in search of the truth,' interposed Eadulf, having kept quiet so far during the conversation.

'Perhaps,' agreed the abbot absently. 'Cináed was a cross to bear in the running of this abbey, for many found him and his views objectionable.'

'Like young Brother Cú Mara?' Eadulf queried in an innocent tone.

'And others,' Abbot Erc replied with quick emphasis. 'But do not misinterpret what I say. As an individual, Cináed was stimulating in conversation and likeable. I took an opposite view to his. I admit that I disliked his arrogance in contradicting what others knew to be truth – and then there was the matter of him and the woman Sister Buan. I disapproved of that liaison and refused to bless their marriage.'

'That was rather extreme, wasn't it?' Fidelma reproved. 'Why would you disapprove?'

'I believe in the call for celibacy among the clerics.'

'Yet Ard Fhearta is a mixed house, a *conhospitae*, in which you have men and women raising their children to Christ's service.'

Abbot Erc was dismissive.

'One cannot move a mountain in a day. *Vincit qui patitur* – he prevails who is patient. You are right that this is a *conhospitae* and Abbess Faife and I shared its governance. Now that Abbess Faife is dead, I am sole governor of the abbey and it will be my rule that prevails. Abbess Faife will not be replaced. Within the year, Ard Fhearta will become a male domain ruled by the new laws. I agree with young Brother Cú Mara. More and more of our abbeys are adopting the Penitentials. We shall change our church laws to the rules we receive from Rome.' He glanced at Eadulf. 'That should be pleasing to you, Brother Saxon, for you wear your tonsure in the manner of Rome and therefore, I presume, you believe in its rule.'

For a moment Eadulf looked uncomfortable.

'Perhaps I have spent too long in your country – and I

seem to recall the writings of the Blessed Ambrose, the bishop of Milan – *si fueris Romae, Romano vivito more; si fueris alibi, vivito sicut ibi.*'

Abbot Erc regarded him with an expression of reproof.

'Well done, Brother Saxon. "If you are at Rome, live in the Roman style; if you are elsewhere, live as they live elsewhere,"' he translated. 'It is a good philosophy, perhaps. But since you have raised the subject of the teachings of Ambrose let us remember that when the Emperor Theodosius massacred the Greeks in Thessalonika because they killed a Roman governor, Ambrose condemned it as a crime that needed to be expiated by public penance. "The emperor is within the church," he wrote, "he is not above it." Thus he made Theodosius make that public penance. You, Sister Fidelma, might do well to remember that fact when you say the church comes within the law. Rome teachers that the church is the law.'

Fidelma smiled thinly.

'Your scholarship is admitted, Abbot Erc. However, we are, as Eadulf has pointed out, not in Rome. I still need time before I complete my investigations. Until I am ready, I want no one to attempt to question the witnesses I have brought back with me.'

'You are a stubborn woman.' The abbot was disapproving.

'I am a *dálaigh*,' she replied simply.

Abbot Erc was dismissive. 'I presume that the lord Conrí will be returning here?'

'That I can assure you is his intention.'

'Very well. I hope that by the end of two days you will come before me and present me with the information that you are currently withholding. I will instruct Brother Cú Mara that he must accept this ruling.'

Sister Fidelma rose. 'Then I am sure that we will have a good outcome to this mystery.'

With a quick nod of her head in acknowledgement of his office, she left the abbot's chamber, followed by Eadulf.

Outside, they paused for a moment.

'Not the most supportive of persons,' observed Eadulf. 'He seems to have profited in his ambitions for himself and the abbey by the death of Abbess Faife.'

'That is so,' agreed Fidelma. 'One wonders whether he profited by design or accident. That must be borne in mind.'

'Either way, I think that he and Brother Cú Mara need watching.'

'There are many who have secrets here, Eadulf,' Fidelma agreed. 'The question is, are those secrets connected with the activities of Seanach's Island?'

'Hopefully, we will know when Conrí returns.'

'Perhaps,' she replied in a non-committal fashion. 'I hope we will be able to find out more even before that time. Let us get back to the *hospitium*.'

They were leaving the main building when Eadulf suddenly halted and apologised to Fidelma, saying he would catch up with her in a moment. Fidelma saw that he was heading towards the male *defaecatorium*. She paused under a hanging lantern to wait for him.

'Sister Fidelma!'

Fidelma swung round at the sound of her name.

It was Sister Buan, emerging out of the shadows.

'I am glad to see your return.' The sharp-faced woman smiled. 'I have been worrying a little about the matter we spoke of.'

'The matter we spoke of?' frowned Fidelma, trying to stir her memory.

A look of dismay crossed the other's face. She raised a hand to her cheek.

'Oh, you have forgotten! I was hoping that you would resolve the legal problem for me. I know that you have other things . . . more important things . . . on your mind. But . . .'

Memory came back to Fidelma in a flash. So much had happened in the meantime. She had given the matter thought before she had left Ard Fhearta to join Mugrón's ship. She smiled apologetically, and held out a hand to catch the sleeve of the apparently embarrassed Sister Buan as she was about to turn away.

'You must forgive me, Sister. You are right. There is much on my mind. But I have been checking on your situation. I can tell you the position now, if you like. It is not complicated.'

'Come inside my chamber and let us be comfortable while you tell me. My chamber, as you may recall, is just here.' The woman indicated a doorway. She seemed almost fawning now in her eagerness. Fidelma felt sorry for her. She was about to explain her hesitation when Eadulf came hurrying up through the darkness.

'Ah, there you are . . .' He paused when he realised that Fidelma was not alone. 'Sorry,' he muttered. 'I did not see that you were with Sister Buan.'

Fidelma gestured towards the door that Sister Buan had just opened.

'I am just going to explain some law to Sister Buan. It will not take a moment, so you can come in and wait for me.'

Sister Buan was immediately deprecating.

'It does not matter, Sister. Come and see me when you

are not so pressed. I do not want to keep you from your companion.'

Fidelma shook her head with a smile.

'There is no time like the present. It will not take long. And you are right, I have kept you waiting long enough for the information.'

Sister Buan was almost reluctant as Fidelma and Eadulf entered her chamber and seated themselves. Afterwards, Fidelma realised that Buan might have been embarrassed to discuss her marriage contract before Eadulf, but by then it was too late.

'When we were last here, Buan, you told me that Abbot Erc had been against your marriage to the Venerable Cináed but you had legally been married by an ordained priest from the abbey of Colmán. Can that be proved?'

The woman nodded quickly. 'It can.'

'Therefore, under the law, you are legally a *cétmuintir*.'

'That was my understanding.'

'You asked me for a legal opinion as to whether in these circumstances you could keep the possessions of the Venerable Cináed, your late husband, and seek some compensation for the manner in which he met his death.'

'I did so.'

'I examined the law texts in the abbey library. As I see it, the *Díre* text puts limitations on your ability to make a contract without the authorisation of your father, a foster father, or, as a member of the religieuse, the abbess or abbot of your community. But even with those limitations, and even in a marriage, such as apparently yours was, where a wife has brought no goods or property into the marriage, the wife can still impugn contracts relating to personal goods.'

'What does that mean, Sister?' asked the woman, looking bewildered.

'I am sorry.' Fidelma smiled. 'I should say that the *Bretha Crólige*, one of our central law texts, says that you can go before a Brehon and be assessed by that judge in proportion to your *míad*, that is a legal term meaning your "dignity" or worth, rather like an honour-price. In other words, you can claim compensation. In fact, as a religieuse you are better off than a lay person. Your rank as a lay person, from what you say, would be a lesser rank than that of the Venerable Cináed. But here, in the abbey, as a religieuse you are recognised as being part of a marriage of equals. Therefore the division of inheritable assets, the *díbad*, means that you inherit two-thirds of the assets of Cináed while one-third has to go to the abbey.'

Sister Buan smiled broadly.

'It is so kind of you to have taken this trouble for me, Sister. I have been really worried. The law can be very frightening.'

'*Dura lex sed lex,*' intoned Eadulf solemnly.

'Exactly so,' agreed Sister Buan with a smile of relief. 'It is good to know that I have a legal right to retain something.'

Fidelma rose and Eadulf with her.

'I am only too glad to be of some help.'

'Are you any the closer to finding out who killed Cináed?' asked Sister Buan as they were crossing the threshold. 'It is frightening to think that someone in this abbey is his killer and not yet discovered.'

'You need have no fear,' Fidelma replied with assurance. 'I am progressing very well in the investigation and soon we shall be able to put your mind at rest.'

They left Sister Buan and made their way back to the *hospitium* as the abbey bell began tolling the hour of the final prayers of the evening.

ChAPTER SEVENTEEN

After they had eaten the next morning, Fidelma asked Sister Easdan to show her and Eadulf to the workroom where she and her companions plied their art. Sister Sinnchéne, who seemed in a slightly more agreeable mood, came to tidy the *hospitium* and asked if there was anything else that was required of her that morning, as she had to distribute the robes that she had washed the previous day to members of the community. Fidelma had not forgotten that one of Sister Sinnchéne's chores at present was running the *tech-nigid* or washing room of the abbey.

'I think not,' Fidelma replied. 'If anyone wants us we shall be at the workshop where Sister Easdan and her companions worked.'

It was an isolated two-storey building with a flat roof, situated on the southern side of the abbey complex, sticking out at right angles to the main dormitory building but separated from it by a narrow passageway. It had been built on the south side, Sister Easdan explained, so that it caught the maximum amount of sun. Light was precious to the task of cutting and polishing the stones. The workroom contained a long central table or workbench, access to water and, along one side, a series of cupboards and other benches with all manner of implements and tools.

Fidelma stood still on the threshold, casting her eye about the place.

'What is it that you wish to see, lady?' asked Sister Easdan. 'The place looks exactly as we left it.'

'You and your companions were all known as experts in this art, that of stone polishing?'

'Known only within the abbey,' the girl corrected pedantically. 'We were, indeed.'

'But surely your names and reputation were known outside the abbey?'

'The abbey was well known for our work but Abbot Erc insisted that we should not be known by name outside the abbey.'

'Why was that?'

'Because he wanted the reputation for the abbey, I suppose, and not for individuals. He wanted to avoid personal vanity.'

'You and your companions have all done this work for some time?'

'I started my training as soon as I came to the abbey, which was just after I reached the age of choice. Most of the others have worked about ten years or so at the art.'

Eadulf pointed to some implements on a bench.

'Are those bows?' he asked curiously. 'In what manner would you use those?'

Sister Easdan smiled easily.

'They are what we call bow lathes, Brother. We work the stone with them and drill holes in the stones with them so that we may string necklaces. It takes a long time to prepare a single necklace, including the cutting and polishing of the stones. Sometimes we have to use special liquids to lubricate the crystals for the grinding and polishing.'

Fidelma was silent for a while, looking at the range of work tools.

'If the expertise of you and your companions was not known outside the abbey, how do you think it came to the ears of those who abducted you?' asked Fidelma.

Sister Easdan considered the matter silently for a while and then she said: 'I suppose the only answer is that the information came from inside the abbey. Or, of course, the merchant Mugrón would have known.'

'But the information would have had to be specific,' Fidelma said thoughtfully. 'Your abductors would have had to know that you were all travelling with Abbess Faife on your way to Bréanainn's mount, and to know exactly by what road and the day on which you would be passing the spot where you were attacked.'

'Only a few people would have known that.'

'Did Sister Sinnchéne know it?'

'There is no reason why she should.'

'Did you know that she asked Abbess Faife if she could join you?'

As the girl was shaking her head, something caught Fidelma's eye, flickering in the rays of the sun, something that sparkled and flashed in a thousand little points of light on the workbench.

She moved to it and ran a finger over it and then, with a pinching movement, held up a few of the hard grains she had encountered and turned to Sister Easdan.

'What exactly is this?' she asked.

Sister Easdan peered at the granular crystals and then grimaced.

'It is only powdered stone.'

'Corundum?' Eadulf intervened.

'Exactly so,' Sister Easdan replied. 'We use it in the grinding process of the precious stones. We choose a particular crystallised rock, crystal we know is especially hard. The crystals are almost opaque and we have to smash them until they fragment into little pieces, just as you see there. We sort them until we find splinters that we can use with the bow lathe to drill holes into those stones we wish to string together. Other particles, the finer ones, we use to grind against the stones to produce the shapes which are required. The process is called *lec-géraigid*.'

Fidelma's eyes suddenly widened. A look of triumph began to spread across her features but she swiftly controlled it.

'You said once that the Venerable Cináed visited here?'

Sister Easdan made an affirmative gesture.

'When was this?'

'Some time ago.'

'Months?'

'About two months, only a short time before we left. Why?'

'He came to this workshop and talked to you and your companions, you said. Remind me, about what?'

Sister Easdan shrugged.

'Just generally about our work, the techniques. Although, now I think of it, he was especially interested in where the stones were found, their type and value . . . I think he was especially interested in their value.'

Fidelma smiled at Eadulf.

'I think I am beginning to see the connection,' she said with some relief in her tone. 'I think I finally see where the Venerable Cináed may be involved in all this.'

'I don't understand,' replied Eadulf in bewilderment.

'We were concerned with a book that the Venerable Cináed had written. We were concentrating on his political work. Don't you remember? We should have been thinking about his new work – *De ars sordida gemmae*, a critical tract on the local trade in these gemstones.'

'Do you mean that he was murdered because of a book he wrote on our work?' gasped Sister Easdan.

'We must find out some more,' Fidelma replied. 'It is a pity that book was destroyed but I believe we can guess the reason now.' She gave a last glance around the workshop and sighed. 'I have seen all that I need to see.'

They moved through the door and paused while Sister Easdan turned to lock it.

It was a slight sound, a movement of air, which caused Eadulf to turn with a cry of alarm and throw himself at Fidelma, knocking her sideways from the step.

As they both fell sprawling, a heavy stone block smashed into the spot where Fidelma had been standing a moment before.

Sister Easdan turned with a scream, staring at the shattered stone. Eadulf was already on his feet, hauling Fidelma up but scanning the upper storey of the stone building. He saw at once the gap in the parapet from which the stone had fallen.

'How do you get to the upper floor?' he shouted to the still shocked Sister Easdan. 'Quickly now!'

Unable to speak, she simply pointed to a side door.

It was unlocked. Eadulf was through it and racing up a

narrow enclosed stone stairway that led along the side of the building, passing the second floor and up to the flat roof. There was no one there. He looked around. He made his way to the parapet where the stone block was missing. He bent to examine the markings where the block had stood.

There was a noise behind him.

He swung round in a defensive position and found Fidelma had arrived.

'A loose block?' she asked.

He pulled a face.

'A loose block that was helped,' he replied sharply, pointing to the scratch marks. 'Someone has deliberately prised it loose. They meant to kill you, I think.'

Fidelma took the news in her stride.

'That means that we are fairly close to a resolution,' she said calmly. 'But how did they get off this roof so quickly?' she added, looking about.

The answer was obvious. The end of the building was close to the main dormitory block of the abbey. A leap of a metre would take one on to a flat narrow walkway designed for the maintenance of that building's roof, and the walkway led to a small door.

'Shall I follow?' Eadulf asked.

Fidelma made a negative gesture.

'They are long gone, I think. You will never be able to identify the culprit.'

There came the sound of footsteps below from the narrow passage that led between the two buildings at ground level. Sister Sinnchéne was walking along with a basket of clothing in her arms, obviously carrying out the task of delivering the washing. Fidelma turned back to the stairway.

'We should see that Sister Easdan is all right,' she said. 'She had a shock.'

As they rejoined Sister Easdan in the workshop, Brother Cú Mara entered.

'There is some debris on the ground outside, a stone seems to have fallen,' he announced worriedly.

'We know,' Fidelma smiled thinly. 'A loose stone has fallen by accident but no harm has been done.'

The steward hesitated a moment and cleared his throat.

'I came to offer my apologies for my rudeness yesterday,' he said stiffly. 'As steward of this abbey, I should not give way to personal emotion. I am sorry.'

Eadulf examined the steward with narrowed eyes. 'How did you know we were here?' he asked abruptly.

Brother Cú Mara frowned. 'Sister Sinnchéne passed as I was speaking to Sister Uallann and Sister Buan and I asked her if she knew where you were.'

'Ah, I see,' Fidelma said solemnly. 'Your apology is accepted, Brother Cú Mara, these are stressful days for us all. It might have helped if I had been told earlier that the missing members of the community were all stone cutters and polishers, though.'

'I don't see how.' At once the young steward was defensive again.

Sister Fidelma answered with a smile.

'That is my job,' she pointed out softly. 'But I can only make deductions from information when it is provided. At least I have that information now.'

She left the workshop with Eadulf and the young Sister Easdan trailing in their wake, leaving the steward of the abbey looking thoughtfully after them.

* * *

Late in the afternoon they heard a commotion at the main gates of the abbey. It was Socht who came to report to them, quiet and unemotional as ever. A member of the community had arrived in a breathless condition from the port of An Bhearbha with news that two warships were entering the harbour. They belonged to Tadcán, lord of Baile Tadc, and Conrí had been spotted on board. News swiftly spread that he was coming to Ard Fhearta with prisoners and the other missing members of the community. There was an excited movement to the main gates to await the arrival of the Uí Fidgente warlord. Fidelma and Eadulf, accompanied by Socht, joined the others and saw that most of the major figures of the abbey were already assembled there.

Fidelma noticed that only the Venerable Mac Faosma and Abbot Erc were absent. Sister Uallann, the physician, stood with folded arms next to Sister Buan. Nearby was Brother Cillín. Even Brother Eolas had been enticed from his library with the nervous young Brother Faolchair.

When Conrí and half a dozen warriors arrived they were escorting only one prisoner but behind them came the five missing young women of the community. Sister Easdan raced forward to greet them. They all threw their arms about each other, laughing, crying and making a considerable noise, much to the disapproval of some of the senior members of the abbey,

The prisoner was a dark, brooding man whose coarse features maintained an impassive expression. His hands were bound before him with rope.

Conrí grinned as he saw Fidelma and Eadulf, raising his hand in salute.

'It was easy,' he reported immediately. 'Our two warships came upon Seanach's Island at first light and when they saw

our overwhelming force they laid down their arms immediately . . . all except this man.' He prodded the man with
his sword tip. 'Allow me to present our friend Olcán. He
wanted his band to fight to the death but was finally
persuaded not to do so himself.'

Fidelma regarded him with a keen scrutiny. Olcán tried
to meet her gaze arrogantly. She turned to Conrí.

'Where are the other prisoners?'

'Have no fear, lady. I have left them in the capable hands
of Tadcán at the harbour. They are still shackled on one of
his warships and await your word as to what should be done
with them. A curious bunch. Most of them are northerners,
men from the Uí Maine and some of the Uí Briúin Aí. They
claim to follow Olcán purely for payment. The hermits
refused to leave Seanach's Island and are now trying to
rebuild their community. I have returned the missing
members of the community to the abbey, as you can see.
The boxes of' – he lowered his voice – 'of stones we found
are under guard on the ships.'

'You have done well, Conrí,' Fidelma said approvingly.
'Very well.' She looked for Sister Sinnchéne and waved her
forward. 'The young religieuse can bathe and be fed before
I examine them.' She glanced at Eadulf and confessed
quietly, 'I do not think they will add anything to what our
friend Sister Easdan has already told us.'

Sister Sinnchéne came forward. Suddenly she stopped
dead, staring at Conrí, and then she stumbled and collapsed
on the ground.

Eadulf was at her side immediately. A moment later she
was stirring.

'She seems to have passed out,' Eadulf said. Two of the
community came forward and volunteered to help the girl

back to her quarters while someone else was found to take the young women under her charge.

Abbot Erc had now arrived, glaring at the gathering.

'What happened?' he demanded, looking at the disappearing women.

'Sister Sinnchéne seems to have fainted, that's all,' Fidelma replied. 'Since you are here you may tell me whether you have a secure chamber in the abbey where we can hold this man?' She gestured towards Olcán.

'There is such a chamber below the *tech-screptra*,' replied the abbot stiffly. 'There is a good lock upon the door.' He glanced at Olcán. 'Who is he?'

Fidelma's features were grim.

'This is the man who slew Abbess Faife and imprisoned her companions. Let us make sure he is locked up safely and treated well, so that he may have no complaints when he comes before the Brehon.'

Abbot Erc motioned Brother Cú Mara forward. The steward had been hanging back but now the abbot repeated Fidelma's instructions.

The man, Olcán, did not speak or even glance at his captors. He remained gazing woodenly before him, head unbowed.

Brother Cú Mara led the way through the buildings to the stone edifice of the library. They passed through groups of curious bystanders. The physician, Sister Uallann, whose apothecary stood near the library building, was staring at Olcán with narrowed eyes. The songmaster, Brother Cillín, had retreated to the library door with Brother Eolas the librarian and his young assistant, Brother Faolchair. They appeared interested in the proceedings. Fidelma noticed that Sister Buan had disappeared among the crowd. Nearby was an intent-looking Brother Benen, the Venerable Mac Faosma's student. Brother Cú Mara took them into the building and down a stone stairway to a series of chambers that were so dark they had to be lit with torches and lanterns. There was a musty smell in the gloomy passageways.

The steward unlocked one of the thick wooden doors with an iron key and pushed the still bound Olcán into a cell.

Fidelma glanced in by the light of a lantern. There was a wooden cot, a table and a chair but, being below ground, no window, and no entrance or exit except by the single door.

'I think he can have the freedom of his hands and arms,' she decided, speaking to Conrí. 'He can have food and drink later and I shall question him then.'

Conrí was indifferent.

'I doubt if you will get anything out of him, lady. I tried to question him and he has remained as silent as if he were mute.'

Nevertheless, the warlord severed the dark man's bonds in accordance with her instructions. They left him alone in the cell and Brother Cú Mara locked the door and hung the key on a nearby hook.

Fidelma was looking around at the musty smelling cellars.

'To what use are such rooms put?' she asked with curiosity.

The steward seemed to have overcome his animosity of the previous evening. He was polite, even helpful.

'Originally, they were storage rooms,' he explained. 'When it became the custom for a visiting Brehon to hold court in the abbey, we used a couple of these chambers to detain those who were due to face serious charges before the Brehon.'

Fidelma made no comment but led the way back up into the light and the fresher air. She noticed that the onlookers had dispersed.

She glanced at Eadulf with a satisfied smile.

'And now our course is set,' she said mysteriously. 'We will soon have our prey in the snare.'

It was after the main meal when Fidelma, Eadulf, Conrí and Brother Cú Mara returned to the subterranean cell of Olcán. The steward had brought a tray of food. He handed this to Eadulf while he took down the key and opened the door. He did it warily but the lamp beyond showed the big warrior sitting immobile on the bed staring as if at some distant object before him.

The steward put down the tray of food and, at Fidelma's signal, withdrew, while Fidelma sat in the only chair and Eadulf and Conrí took up positions just inside the door.

Fidelma examined the man carefully. She summed him up as a man without feeling. A killer who obeyed orders without question. His cruel features were not possessed of sensitivity or much intelligence.

'Do you know who I am?'

Olcán made a slight movement with one shoulder which expressed either affirmation or disinterest.

'That your name is Olcán I know. Of what clan are you?'

The man continued in silence.

'You have a choice of two paths before you, Olcán. You may make things hard on yourself or easy. It is up to you.'

Olcán glanced quickly at her.

'I have nothing to say.'

'Then things will go hard with you. You are already facing

charges of heinous crimes. There are witnesses to them. The wrecking of a Gaulish ship. The murder of Abbess Faife. The raids and destruction of settlements among the Corco Duibhne. The imprisonment of six young religieuse from this abbey as well as the hermit community on Seanach's Island, one of whom you slew or had slain.'

Her voice was remorseless as she recited the litany.

Olcán eyed her with hate simmering in his eyes.

'And do you expect me to admit to all this, sister of Colgú the usurper?' he sneered.

Fidelma smiled faintly.

'At least you admit that you know who I am.'

He was silent again.

'And since you describe my brother as a usurper I presume that you felt you owed allegiance to Eoganán of the Uí Fidgente?'

Once more only silence met her.

'Let me put it this way, Olcán. You may well be responsible for all these evil deeds. You may well have been in command of the war band that carried them out. Yet I do not believe that it was your own design. The command was given by another – your so-called "master"? Is that not so?'

Olcán laughed harshly.

'Then you will have to capture this "master" and ask him. That you will never do.'

Fidelma forced herself to remain relaxed.

'What I am trying to tell you, Olcán, is that if you tell me who gave you those orders, then things may not go as harshly with you.'

'The chief of the wolf tribe does not betray his lord,' snapped Olcán.

Fidelma frowned as a chord of memory suddenly struck.

She was about to say something when Conrí exclaimed: 'Olcán! Olcán the wolf! I have heard of you.' In spite of Fidelma's warning glance, he turned to her excitedly.

'This man was head of a band of raiders when Eoganán ruled the Uí Fidgente. They called themselves the wolf tribe.'

He paused when he saw Fidelma's angry look at the interruption to her interrogation.

Olcán had missed the silent warning and was smiling viciously. He seemed proud of his reputation.

'Is that why you continue to take your orders from Uaman the Leper?' Fidelma asked quietly.

Olcán turned to her with a brief look of puzzlement that was gone before she had time to register it. Then he burst out with a short laugh.

'You must have heard, woman of Cashel, that Uaman is dead. He died in the month of *Cet Gaimred*.'

'And so we must assume that it is his troubled wraith that rides through the Sliabh Mis valleys with you?'

'It would be hard to take orders from a shade from the Otherworld, woman. Oh, but have no fear. The seed of Eoganán will lead the Uí Fidgente against Cashel once more and that very soon.'

'That will be difficult,' interjected Conrí with a sneer. 'The true Uí Fidgente do not follow ghosts or voices from the Otherworld.'

Olcán smiled knowingly for a moment.

'They will hear a voice shortly. A voice crying vengeance for our people. And, indeed, it will not be a voice from the Otherworld.'

'You are in no position to be truculent, Olcán,' Fidelma warned him.

The man, however, relapsed into a pugnacious silence.

Fidelma uttered a deep sigh of disgust and rose to her feet.

'Very well, Olcán, chief of the wolf tribe. We can be patient also but not too patient. You have much to answer for. Your crimes are many in the counting. As I have said, the path you choose may be hard or easy and that is your choice. Your future is black—'

Olcán glanced up belligerently. 'And your future, the future of all the spawn of the Eoghanacht of Cashel, does not even exist. The Uí Fidgente will find their backbone again and come against you – even in spite of your lapdog' – he gestured to Conrí – 'or a thousand treacherous Uí Fidgente like him. They will not alter the course of the river we have set in flood. That river will lead the Uí Fidgente not only to recover their lost lands but to claim Cashel, and beyond Cashel they will claim Tara, the seat of the High Kings. The master has prophesied it and so it will come to pass.'

He suddenly seemed to realise that he might have said too much and returned his sullen gaze to some distant point before him.

There was a silence after his outburst.

'Very well, Olcán,' Fidelma finally replied. 'We will leave you to think on this during the forthcoming night. If you continue to take the hard path, then I can assure you that it will be harder than you can ever imagine. I will come to speak to you in the morning when you have contemplated your future more carefully because, whatever your prognostication about my future, and the future of Cashel, your future is a certainty and you will never live to see your master's prediction come to fruition.'

They left the man still staring into space.

Outside, when they had relocked the cell door and hung the key back on the hook, Conrí was apologetic.

'I suddenly remembered hearing tales about this man,' he explained. 'I never knew him personally and he was not at the battle of Cnoc Áine, but I think he was with Torcán, the son of Eoganán, in the south-west.'

'Well, your comment at least provoked the man to speech.'

'I fear that he is a die-hard, lady,' Conrí replied. 'If, as we have been told, Uaman still lives, then it seems that some of this activity must be concerned with an attempt to place Uaman in control of the Uí Fidgente . . .'

'But that would never happen because the law is specific. No one with a physical blemish can be king. Even one of the greatest of High Kings, Cormac Mac Art, had to abdicate when he was blinded by a spear cast. Even Olcán seemed to discredit the idea that he took his orders from Uaman.'

Conrí did not agree.

'We have had Uaman identified. If it is not Uaman, then I can think of no descendant of the Uí Choirpre Áedba who can claim the chieftainship of our people.'

Eadulf looked blankly at him.

'I thought that the Uí Fidgente were the descendants of Fiachu Fidgennid? That Donennach is just as much a descendant as was Eoganán?'

Conrí was patient.

'It is easily explained. Our current ruler, Donennach, is descended from the line of the family we call Uí Chonaill Gabra, from Fidgennid's grandson Dáire. Eoganán was descended from Fidgennid's grandson Choirpre, hence that line is now called the Uí Choirpre Áedba.'

It didn't clear Eadulf's understanding at all. He knew

that the Éireannach placed much store by their ancient genealogies, delineating cousins and distant relatives; more store, he felt, than the Saxon kings set by their own simple direct father to son genealogies. He shrugged but did not pursue the matter.

Fidelma, however, seemed to follow the argument.

'You have never heard of any other legitimate successor to Eoganán who might be persuaded to attempt a coup against Donennach?'

Conrí shook his head at once.

'Uaman was certainly the only male descendant of Eoganán who survived after Cnoc Áine.'

They had emerged by the closed doors of the *tech-screptra* and saw Brother Eolas standing before them, talking to Sister Buan and Sister Uallann.

'Brother Eolas,' Conrí called, before Fidelma could stop him. 'Do you have a genealogy of the princes of the Uí Fidgente?'

The librarian turned curiously in their direction.

'We do have such a manuscript,' he confirmed.

'Is it up to date? I am interested in the children of Eoganán.'

Brother Eolas shook his head.

'It is as up to date as time allows. My assistant and I have much to do in maintaining the records of the library and there was the fire . . .'

'Can we see it now?' interrupted Conrí.

Brother Eolas sniffed in irritation at Conrí's demanding manner.

'The library is closed. You will have to return tomorrow.' He inclined his head in farewell to his companions and turned on his heel.

Sister Buan and Sister Uallann seemed to decide their presence was no longer required, muttered an excuse, and also left, leaving Conrí looking a little crestfallen.

'I thought that it might have given us some further information,' he explained. 'There might have been some line of descendants that I've forgotten about. Anyway, it doesn't alter the fact that it was the figure of Uaman that the old man Ganicca identified as riding with Olcán.'

Eadulf was shaking his head in disagreement but he said: 'There must be a means of getting Olcán to talk further about this master.'

Fidelma was not optimistic.

'I doubt it.' She found that the steward, who had waited outside so that he could ensure the cell was locked, was still standing with them. 'We will not detain you further, Brother Cú Mara,' she said, bidding him good night before leading the way back to the *hospitium*. Once out of earshot of the steward she lowered her voice.

'I'll wait until tomorrow, but I now realise that I may have something up my sleeve that might induce our friend Olcán to talk. He has a close relation in the abbey and that fact may induce him to speak.'

Conrí and Eadulf stared at her in surprise but her expression forbade any further questioning.

CHAPTER EIGHTEEN

Brother Cú Mara reached for the key and unlocked the cell door.

It was dark inside. The lamp had been allowed to go out, so the steward held up the candle he had brought with him.

The first thing that Fidelma, who was standing at his shoulder, noticed was that Olcán was sitting on his bed with his back to the wall. He was slightly slumped forward. Then she saw a dark stain on his tunic just below his heart.

She called to the steward to stand aside, took the candle from his hand, and went forward. She knew what she would find even before she touched the cold body.

'He's dead,' she announced.

The steward let out a long gasp of breath.

'A single stab to the heart,' she continued, holding the candle nearer to the wound.

'But he had no knife,' protested Brother Cú Mara. 'I made sure of that. Even when his food was brought to him, it was already cut.'

Fidelma turned with a grim face.

'This was no self-inflicted wound. Olcán was murdered.'

The steward stared at her with wide, frightened eyes.

Fidelma was annoyed with herself for not pressing Olcán harder the evening before with her questions. She had thought of an idea which might have led the man to start talking, but she had kept it to herself, thinking to use it this morning if he was still uncooperative. Now it was too late. One thing she now knew for certain was that the Uí Fidgente warrior was a mere pawn in this strange mystery and not its chief architect. But her suspicion that whoever was behind the mystery was connected with the abbey itself seemed confirmed.

She gazed down a moment on the corpse and then turned to Brother Cú Mara.

'You had better inform the abbot and also the physician, Sister Uallann.' She glanced quickly round the cell before returning her gaze back to the dead body. 'There is nothing more in here for me.'

Brother Cú Mara relocked the cell after they exited. As he was about to leave to find the physician Fidelma halted him.

'One question for you, Brother Cú Mara – do you remember when I questioned you and Sister Sinnchéne together?'

Reluctantly, the steward nodded.

'Do you have cause to visit the workroom where the members of the community polish and prepare gemstones?'

Brother Cú Mara was clearly puzzled by the question, but acknowledged that he did. 'I am the steward. It is my task to see that everything is in order. I visit all the work-shops regularly.'

'Very well. You can find Sister Uallann now.'

She knew what she had to do first as she watched him

hurry off in search of the physician. Her expression hardened a little as she walked towards the *hospitium* buildings.

She found Sister Sinnchéne engaged in the task of sweeping the floor.

'I have some bad news for you,' she announced without preamble.

Sister Sinnchéne straightened and returned her gaze uncertainly, perhaps with a little hostility. She waited in silence.

'It is about your father,' Fidelma said.

At that the young woman blinked but fought to control her features. She still made no reply.

'It is about Olcán.'

Sister Sinnchéne's chin came up defiantly.

'What makes you think Olcán is my father?' she demanded belligerently.

Sister Fidelma was unrelenting.

'You fainted when you saw Conrí's prisoner being brought into the abbey yesterday afternoon.'

The girl replied sourly, 'There can be any number of reasons for fainting . . .'

'But the one which caused you to pass out,' Fidelma replied, 'was the shock you had when you beheld your father in manacles.'

'That is a weak reason to accuse me of being Olcán's daughter.'

'Then let me give you the other reasons. Olcán's name means "wolf" and his warriors were known as the "wolf clan". Your mother, I understand, died a few years ago of the pestilence. Didn't she tell the merchant, Mugrón, that your father was named "wolf" and he was known as "chief of the wolf clan" and that is why you were named "little vixen"?'

Sister Sinnchéne stared at her for a moment or two and then it seemed she let her shoulders relax.

'My father walked out on my mother when I was twelve years old. I had not seen him from that day until I saw him walk through the gates of the abbey as Conrí's prisoner.' She spoke slowly and clearly. 'Even when my mother was dying of the Yellow Plague, he did not return, and that was well before the battle of Cnoc Áine when he could have easily come to us. He never came to her funeral. So what misdeeds he has done are nothing to me.'

Fidelma saw the bitterness in her eyes.

'So for nearly ten years you have had no contact with him?'

'I have said as much.'

'But you could still recognise him?'

Sister Sinnchéne shrugged.

'His image was burned in my memory all these years; years when I needed a father and prayed each day for his return. He had aged a little but I recognised him.'

'Do you know why he deserted your mother and you?'

She shook her head. 'The word was that he had led his warriors in raids to the north, against the Uí Fiachrach Aidne, the Uí Briúin Seóla and the northern clans. Then, after Eoganán fell at Cnoc Áine and the Uí Fidgente surrendered to Cashel, there was word that my father refused to swear allegiance to the new chief Donennach. I heard he was raiding in the south and in the war band of Uaman . . .'

'Uaman the Leper?'

The girl nodded. 'Uaman was not a leper then but simply Lord of the Passes on the southern Uí Fidgente borders.'

'How did you come by this knowledge?'

'I heard talk from travellers.'

'Mugrón the merchant knew about your father,' Fidelma pointed out.

'He knew of my father because my mother told him. But I do not believe he could identify him. He knew only that my father had deserted my mother and me.'

'How did your mother know Mugrón?'

'Because, after my father left, my mother went to live near An Bhearbha, near the port where Mugrón has his base.' She suddenly turned wide pleading eyes upon Fidelma. 'Olcán has not recognised me, has he?'

Fidelma frowned at the question.

'He has not mentioned you,' she said truthfully. 'Why do you ask?'

Sister Sinnchéne ignored the question. 'Then I would ask you a favour. Do not reveal that I am his daughter.'

'Why?'

'Because if he did not want to acknowledge me, there is no reason for me to acknowledge him now.'

Fidelma gazed thoughtfully at her. 'And are you telling me that during all these years you never told anyone here, in the abbey, that Olcán was your father?'

The girl raised her head a little but a colour sprang to her cheeks.

Fidelma smiled grimly. 'There was someone, wasn't there?'

Sister Sinnchéne hesitated and then nodded.

'Was it Brother Cú Mara?'

To Fidelma's surprise the girl shook her head. 'The only person that I ever told was Cináed.'

Fidelma was silent and then she said slowly, 'You told the Venerable Cináed?'

'I did.'

'In what context did this arise? When did you tell him?'

The girl spoke nervously.

'I have told you about my relationship with Cináed. We were talking about the changing situation in the lands of the Uí Fidgente and he was speaking of the stories that were being spread about Uaman. It was said that Uaman, in spite of his blemish in that he was a leper, was plotting to return the Uí Choirpre Áedba to the throne of the Uí Fidgente. The Uí Choirpre are—'

Fidelma raised her hand.

'I know all about the two divisions of your chiefs,' she said.

'Very well. There were stories that Uaman was amassing wealth on the borders of the lands of the Corco Duibhne so that he could buy an army to lead the assault on Caola's fortress which is Donennach's capital.'

'But how did your father's name come into this?'

'Cináed told me that he was just completing a book – this was just before we celebrated the Nativity. In this book he said he would reveal how Uaman was raising his wealth and his army. He mentioned that he had heard that a warrior named Olcán was Uaman's commander in this enterprise. I showed my horror and Cináed pressed me on the point. I told him my story.'

'What was his reaction?'

'I told you that Cináed and I felt for each other. He told me to put Olcán out of my mind. I did so until . . .' She paused.

'Until?' pressed Fidelma quickly.

'It was a few weeks before Cináed's murder. There had been some travellers from the Corco Duibhne and they were talking of the rumours that Uaman the Leper had perished.

Cináed was preoccupied with the news and kept asking me if I had heard any recent rumours about my father. I told him that I had heard nothing.'

'Did he say anything further?'

'He seemed fascinated by the stories that had spread about Uaman's death and then stories of Uaman being alive again. He kept muttering something about "the old story might be true".'

'The old story might be true?' Fidelma repeated. 'Do you know what he meant by that?'

The girl shook her head. 'I asked him and he simply smiled and said he had to look up something about trees in the library.'

'Something about trees?'

'Then he told me that Abbess Faife was taking her band of pilgrims to Bréanainn's mount soon and they would be passing Uaman's Island. He wanted me to go with them to see if I could identify Olcán if he dwelt there. Faife refused to take me. Although a friend of Cináed, she did not believe my . . . my relationship with him was right. That was the last time my father was mentioned by Cináed. Then I saw Olcán coming into the abbey as a prisoner. It is true, as you say, that I recognised him and fainted.'

'This book that you said Cináed had prepared . . . ?'

'I think he had finished it and it was given to young Brother Faolchair to copy. I suppose . . .' She paused and her mouth formed an 'o'. Then she said: 'Was it one of those that were destroyed in the library?'

'It might well have been,' countered Fidelma evasively. 'Can you recall what it was called?'

She shook her head. 'Only that it had a Latin title.'

'*Scripta quae ad rempublicum . . .* ?' began Fidelma.

'I would not recognise the title,' replied Sister Sinnchéne firmly. 'All I know is it was something about gemstones.'

Fidelma smiled quickly. She had only been seeking confirmation of the title she had suspected it would be.

'*De ars sordida gemmae*,' she said softly.

'I told you that I would not recognise the title,' protested the girl.

'No matter,' Fidelma said. Absently she began to move away. Then she turned abruptly back to the girl.

'Did you kill your father last night?'

It was a brutal way to get to the truth but it produced an immediate result. The look on Sister Sinnchéne's face told her that the news came as a shock. Fidelma found herself watching curiously as the emotions played across the girl's face and finally resolved themselves into a grim mask.

'Are you saying that he is dead?' she asked coldly.

'This morning Olcán was found in his cell. He was dead.'

The girl's face was now without animation.

'He killed himself? Perhaps he felt that he had to do so rather than face the disgrace of being a prisoner of the Eoghanacht.'

She now spoke quietly, almost in a matter-of-fact way.

Fidelma reached out a hand and touched the girl's shoulder and shook her head.

'I said that he was murdered.'

The girl's expression still did not change but Fidelma felt her muscles harden under her hand.

'That's impossible.'

'I am afraid it is not only possible, Sinnchéne, but it is a fact. That is why I cannot promise you that I can keep your secret now. I will keep it if possible but it may be that it will come out as a means of tracking down the person or persons responsible.'

Sister Sinnchéne still stood immobile.

Fidelma hesitated.

'Do you want me to send for anyone to help you?' she asked.

Sister Sinnchéne sighed and stirred. Her eyes were fathomless.

'Help me? I need no one's help. The time I needed help was when I was a young child and needed a father's support, a father's help. In reality, my father has been dead these last ten years if only in my mind . . . now he is dead in reality.'

She spoke without feeling.

Yet Fidelma felt a passing sorrow for the poor, lonely young girl whose father had deserted her and who was still hurting in spite of her outward coldness.

Outside, crossing the frosty courtyard, she saw Eadulf. She left Sister Sinnchéne and went quickly to tell him the news. Eadulf was shocked.

'Does that mean Esumaro and the six religieuse are in danger also?'

'I think not,' Fidelma replied. 'Our killer was only afraid of the one person who could probably identify him. I think the others are safe.'

'Are you talking of this master?'

She nodded.

'The one thing I cannot understand about Sinnchéne's story is why trees made the Venerable Cináed so excited.' She reflected. 'Something to do with the sacred tree of the clans? Sinnchéne said that he muttered "the old story might be true" and then hurried to the library to consult a book on trees. What old story? What trees?'

'The trouble is,' complained Eadulf, 'when you speak of trees in your language, it can mean so many things. Why, even the mast of a ship is called by the same word. Cináed might have been speaking of ships or even a family tree . . .'

Fidelma gave a little shout of laughter.

'Eadulf, what would I do without you? Sometimes one cannot see the wood for the trees!'

Eadulf looked bewildered, knowing that she had made a clever joke but unable to see the meaning of it.

'What do you mean?'

'Family tree! That is what the Venerable Cináed was after. Exactly that.'

'But whose family tree?'

Fidelma was smiling happily now and was turning towards the library.

'Uaman's family, of course. The family tree of the Uí Fidgente rulers. The very book that Conrí asked Brother Eolas for last night.'

In the library they found Brother Faolchair, looking as bothered as usual, continually glancing over his shoulder to see whether Brother Eolas was nearby. But there was no sign of the librarian.

'I am still being blamed for the burning of the Venerable Cináed's books,' he told them with a sigh, when he realised that Fidelma and Eadulf had spotted his nervousness. 'I am afraid that Brother Eolas is of an unforgiving nature.'

'Well, we might soon be able to resolve that matter,' Fidelma encouraged him. 'But now we need your help. Do you have a work on the genealogy of the Uí Fidgente?'

The young assistant librarian answered at once.

'Of course. As one of the best libraries in the kingdom,

we keep all the records of our great chiefs and nobles.'

'May we look at the genealogy?'

'Oh, we don't have it at the moment. It has been borrowed.'

Their faces fell. Fidelma asked: 'By whom has it been borrowed?'

Brother Faolchair smiled. 'That's another easy one – Brother Benen came this morning and asked for it on behalf of the Venerable Mac Faosma. He has it.'

Eadulf exchanged a quick glance with Fidelma but she did not appear to have been surprised or to have seen any significance in the fact.

'There was another thing I wanted to make sure of, Brother Faolchair,' she went on. 'The last book that Cináed appeared to have finished and gave you to copy was . . . ?'

'De ars sordida gemmae.'

'Exactly so. Do you remember it?'

'I remember it very well. It was one of the books that were destroyed in this very library.'

'When had he given it to you to copy?'

'A few days before his death.'

'I think you said that you had not finished the copy?'

'I had not. Those pages that I had copied were destroyed along with the original.'

'Do you remember anything at all about the book? What were its arguments, its conclusions?'

Brother Faolchair shrugged. 'I did not read it.'

Fidelma was astonished. 'But you had started to copy it? You must have read it through first?'

The assistant librarian shook his head. 'When you are a copyist, Sister, you learn that the first rule is never to read the manuscript that you are copying. You follow line by line, copying what you see, otherwise you will find yourself making mistakes.'

'I don't understand.'

'If you think that you know what is written, you will find yourself racing ahead; putting down what you think is coming next instead of what is actually on the page before you. Best not to know and then you are more accurate in the copy.'

'So you have no knowledge of the text?'

The young man shrugged. 'I recall that it started with the idea that wealth is needed to create and sustain wars, justly or unjustly. It went on about the wealth of this land being used to sustain the Uí Fidgente chieftains in their wars against Cashel and then argued that it became a never-ending cycle. That wealth was needed to create wars and the more wars that were fought, the more wealth was needed. Wealth created wars and wars created wealth. So the more land one had to conquer to extract the wealth to pay for the wars that needed that wealth, the more wars had to be fought. He called it the unending circle.'

Eadulf raised his head quickly.

'The Unending Circle,' he repeated softly, with a meaningful look at Fidelma.

'What else?' prompted Fidelma, ignoring him.

'The Venerable Cináed went on to develop a theme about the extracting of gemstones to raise money . . . no, to say this was being done to finance a war . . .'

'And?'

'That is as far as I remember. I was still working on copying the thesis.'

A nervous look entered his eyes. Fidelma turned and saw Brother Eolas entering the library.

'Thanks, that is all we need. You have been helpful as always, Brother Faolchair.'

Outside the library, Eadulf was almost beside himself with excitement.

'The Unending Circle. Do you see the connection? It is the songmaster who must be behind this. That is the name of his organisation. Remember what the chorister told me at Daingean?'

'You have frequently remarked on it,' Fidelma observed drily.

'Then we should go to see Brother Cillín?'

He was disappointed when she shook her head.

'We will go and see the Venerable Mac Faosma and ask to see this genealogy. I think that will answer my question.'

Eadulf sniffed in disapproval. 'I fail to see how.'

Fidelma exhaled softly. 'Well, it does not need the two of us to do this. While I am talking to the Venerable Mac Faosma, why not go and find out what you can about Brother Cillín and any other information about this organisation of his. Make sure that you do it surreptitiously so that he is unaware of your inquiries.'

Eadulf drew himself up with injured pride. 'My inquiries are always done carefully. You know that.'

Fidelma patted his arm. 'Of course I know it. But we must be careful now, though, being so close to our prey.'

Slightly irritated, Eadulf left Fidelma and made his way through the covered walkway from the library towards the *hospitium*, wondering how best to approach the subject. Conrí suddenly appeared before him, hurrying along with a preoccupied look. He nearly collided with Eadulf, stopped and then recognised him.

'Where is the lady Fidelma?' he asked quickly.

'You look apprehensive, Conrí.'

'I need to speak to her at once,' the warlord of the Uí Fidgente said. 'We have had some unexpected visitors at the abbey gates.'

Eadulf raised an eyebrow in query.

'Slébéne and a warrior escort have just arrived,' Conrí explained. 'We know that he was mixed up in this matter. His arrival means trouble. Where is Fidelma?'

Eadulf was startled at the news.

'She has gone to see the Venerable Mac Faosma,' he replied. Before he could question Conrí further, the warrior was moving at a swift trot in the direction of the scholar's chambers.

Eadulf stood looking after him in indecision. He was wondering whether he ought to join Conrí when a voice called to him.

'Brother Saxon! So you are here as well?'

He swung round and it was a few moments before he recognised the chorister who had been at Slébéne's fortress of An Daingean. The very chorister who had spoken to him of the Unending Circle. A coincidence indeed!

The chorister was smiling at him.

'Remember me? I have just arrived in the company of lord Slébéne. A fortunate chance as you must know.'

'I am sorry?' muttered Eadulf, not understanding.

'Why, surely you are at Ard Fhearta for the same reason as I am? The meeting of the Unending Circle?'

CHAPTER NINETEEN

After she left Eadulf, Fidelma found her way to the chambers of the Venerable Mac Faosma. This time there was no muscular Brother Benen between her and the oak door and she knocked boldly.

The Venerable Mac Faosma greeted her with a hostile eye as he opened the door and recognised her.

'Have you come to bother me yet again?' he demanded irritably before she had time to say anything. 'I would have thought that you had better things to do.'

Fidelma smiled sweetly at the old scholar.

'I am engaged in those things that I should be engaged in,' she replied, her icy tongue not matching the sweetness of her smile.

'Indeed?'

'I am told that you borrowed a genealogy from the library.'

Mac Faosma's forehead furrowed.

'You take a curious interest in the books that I borrow from the library?' he said, inflecting the words to form a question.

'I do, don't I?' she responded innocently. 'Perhaps that it is because you borrow some very interesting books. However, I would like to see this one, if I may . . . that is, if it has not perished in the same way as did the book of Cináed?'

Mac Faosma stared at her and if looks had the ability to kill, her life was worthless. Then he shrugged and stood aside, motioning her to enter.

'I do not want you to be sitting *troscud* outside my door to impel me to show it you,' he sniffed. 'Time is too precious without wasting it on melodramatic gestures.'

She entered his chamber and he closed the door behind her, before leading her to a corner of the room.

'I cannot think why you want to see the genealogy of the Uí Fidgente,' he said, drawing the manuscript across the table.

'Indulge me,' Fidelma replied quietly, peering at the rectangular vellum book which had several bound pages. It was, indeed, what she was looking for. She started turning the pages of the various generations.

'Is there anything in particular that you want from it?' Mac Faosma queried with interest.

'I want to check the descendants of Choirpre, the grandson of Fidgennid.'

Mac Faosma shrugged.

'I have not come so far as yet. I am working on the generations showing the descent of the Uí Fidgente from Eoghan Mór to support the rightful claim that the Uí Fidgente are Eoghanacht and should not be excluded from the councils of Cashel.'

Fidelma smiled thinly.

'Then your work is going to be long and hard, Venerable

Mac Faosma,' she replied, still bent to her task. Suddenly she halted on a page, tracing the inscribed names with her finger.

'Here it is. Oengus Lappae, son of Ailill Cendfota, and his son Áed, and Áed's son Crunmael to his son Eoganán who perished at Cnoc Áine. There are Eoganán's sons Torcán and Uaman and—'

She stopped short. It was so neat that she had not noticed before. A tiny rectangle had been cut out of the page. Its size and position showed that it had been cut to obliterate a name . . . a third name after Uaman.

She turned and glanced accusingly at the old scholar, but he was staring at it with a bemused expression that could not have been feigned.

'I presume that you knew nothing of this mutilation?' she asked, knowing full well what the answer would be.

He shook his head.

'So Eoganán did have a third child,' she said softly. 'But the name has recently been cut out of this book.'

'Recently? How do you know?'

'See where the cut has been made with a sharp pointed instrument, probably a knife point? The edges of the vellum are whiter than the page itself. How old is this book?'

'Ard Fhearta has had it in the library for fifty years. The scribes who wrote it are long since dead.'

'But the name of Eoganán's third child must be known to many. You yourself must know it.'

Mac Faosma shook his head.

'I recall there was talk of a third child at the time when Eoganán's second wife fled from his fortress with her lover, leaving a child behind. There was talk of its being sent away to fosterage to some local chieftain but I don't remember the details.'

'Is there anyone who would know the name of this child?'

'If the child was of the same generation as its siblings, Torcán and Uaman, it would be more than a child now,' the old man pointed out.

Fidelma was thoughtful.

'That is true,' she said. 'I understand that Brother Benen collected this book for you this morning?'

'That's right.' Mac Faosma pointed to his writing table where he was working on sheets of vellum. 'You see, I am preparing a book which lists the generations of Uí Fidgente and needed this for reference. I merely went to the pages that concerned me and did not look at the page about Eoganán.'

'So we may safely assume that this was done before the book came into your possession.'

'I am a scholar,' protested Mac Faosma. 'Books are sacred things to me. I would not destroy a book no matter how bad or ill formed.'

'Of course,' conceded Fidelma. 'My main concern now is to find out who this third child was . . . or is.'

'Why are you so interested? I doubt that any progeny of Eoganán is likely to claim the title now that Donennach is chief.'

Fidelma ignored his question.

'You have been most helpful in this matter, Venerable Mac Faosma. Keep that book safe. It may be wanted as evidence.'

In the courtyard Eadulf was staring at the chorister from An Daingean.

'The meeting of the Unending Circle?' He was trying to hide his astonishment. Then he attempted to look enthusiastic. 'Of course. The meeting.'

'And just in time.'

'In time?'

'Indeed, I was told by one of our number at the gates that the meeting was about to start in the small chapel. Brother Cillín is already there. I presume that you are on your way there now?'

Eadulf hesitated only a moment. There was only one thing to do and that was brazen it out.

'Oh, of course.'

The chorister seized his arm in a display of comradeship.

'Come, then. We mustn't miss what Brother Cillín has to tell us.'

Eadulf found himself almost reluctantly pushed towards the chapel. There were several others hurrying towards the building and Eadulf noticed that all of them had their cowls pulled over their heads. His companion now did likewise. It was with relief that he did the same.

Inside the small chapel, Eadulf found at least thirty or forty male members of the community assembled in rows, all hooded. He entered uneasily and stood with his new-found companion at the back of the chapel by one of the pillars.

There was a hush and then Brother Cillín, the song-master, came from a side door with two companions and stood before the assembly. Although he, too, was cowled, Eadulf recognised him easily.

'My brethren, it gladdens me to see so many of you gathered here,' he began in a resonant baritone. 'Soon the great day is coming and what we have been working for will finally be achieved. That day when we gather in the great abbey before the high altar, the company will fall astounded before us.'

Eadulf eased nervously backwards as if this action would somehow hide him from Brother Cillín's piercing glances as the songmaster surveyed the brethren before him. Eadulf tugged nervously at his hood to make sure it hid as much of his face as possible. Brother Cillín was continuing: 'You have all been chosen to join the Unending Circle. It is a unique honour and in the future we will be spoken of in hushed tones throughout the five kingdoms. In the old days the unending circle symbolised life: no beginning and no end. The circle encompasses the cross and the unending knot symbolises life. We chosen few have taken as our motto the Latin phrase *sic itur ad astra* – thus one goes to the stars! For it is our work and destiny that will take us to the stars, my brethren. We will fly there as singing birds.'

Eadulf was beginning to think that Brother Cillín must be quite mad. The rhetoric was overwhelming in its imagery to the point where no sane person would employ it.

Suddenly, Brother Cillín had bent down and picked up a small square-shaped stringed instrument. Eadulf had seen it before and knew that it was called a *ceis* – it was far smaller than a harp but of the same stringed family.

The songmaster passed his hands over the strings, striking a chord.

'We shall start with the *súan traige* – the lullaby. Are you all prepared?'

A chorus of assent greeted him.

The chord was struck again.

To Eadulf's surprise, the entire assembly burst into a chanting song.

Fidelma met Conrí outside Mac Faosma's chambers. The warlord had a worried expression on his face.

'Slébéne has just arrived at the abbey,' he said without preamble. 'I came to warn you, lady.'

'Now that is interesting,' she said grimly but she showed no surprise.

'How so?' demanded the warlord.

'Doubtless he has heard of your attack on Seanach's Island and the freeing of the prisoners. He will now hear of Olcán's murder. He has come here for orders from the "master". The strands are coming together. How many warriors does he bring?'

'He arrived in a single warship, which is anchored in the harbour, but has brought only two men to the abbey with him. One of them is his champion.'

'Where is he now?'

'He is with the abbot.'

'And his men?'

'In the stables, I imagine. They seem to have acquired horses in An Bhearbha.'

'Has he given an excuse for his visit?'

Conrí shook his head. 'None that I know.'

'I suggest that you send your man Socht down to your warships in the harbour and tell your captain, Tadcán, to keep a careful watch on Slébéne's men. In fact, lookouts should be posted just in case Slébéne has some other surprises in store for us ...'

'You mean that he might have other warships lurking off the coast?'

'With the discovery of what was taking place on Seanach's Island, I think the so-called "master" will be pretty desperate now.'

'You suspect that Slébéne might be so involved that he will launch an attack on the abbey? To achieve what?' demanded Conrí.

'Slébéne is part of a plan to overthrow Donennach. That will have repercussions for all Muman. I still need a little more time before I can demonstrate it. Tell Socht to return as soon as he has delivered your orders.'

Conrí started to turn away.

'Wait!' called Fidelma. 'How many warriors do you have in the abbey?'

'Just Socht. The ones who escorted Olcán here with me have returned to the ship. Abbot Erc tolerates no more than a personal guard for visiting chiefs in the abbey.'

Fidelma compressed her lips for a moment.

'Then tell Socht to return as quickly and unobtrusively as he possibly can and bring a couple of your men with him.'

Conrí was hesitant. 'Do you expect something to happen, lady?'

Fidelma actually smiled. 'I do, my friend. Something very soon. I just hope that before it does, I can work out the final details of this mystery so that we may prepare ourselves. When you have given your instructions to Socht, find Eadulf and come and join me. I am going to the *tech-screptra*.'

Eadulf had many abilities including a strong voice. But it was not a singing voice. It was true that he liked to sing but his idea of singing was certainly not shared by anyone with a trained musical ear.

Brother Cillín, waving his hands to indicate the rhythm, strode among the lines of cowled brethren, sometimes plucking notes from his *ceis* to keep them in time.

Eadulf's head was bent as he tried his best to cope with the chant so that he would not appear out of place in the company.

As Brother Cillín reached the row in which he stood, the songmaster paused, head to one side.

'Silence!' he suddenly roared.

The singing of the brethren came to a ragged halt.

Eadulf thought that he could feel the steely eyes of the songmaster staring directly at him.

'There is an ear here that is tone deaf!' thundered the songmaster. 'The voice obeys the ear and has no concept of melody.'

There was a murmur of surprise and horror from the brethren as they turned round to try to catch a glimpse of the culprit.

'Surely not someone among the Unending Circle?' cried a young man at the end of the row.

'Surely not,' repeated Brother Cillín with sarcastic emphasis. 'I have hand-picked you all, every one, each for the beauty of his voice, to join in what will be the greatest choir in the five kingdoms of Éireann. A choir that this year will win every prize at the Assembly of East Muman and go on to dominate every festival and gathering throughout the land.'

A horror was coming over Eadulf as he began to understand the mystery he had been pursuing. The Unending Circle – it was simply the name of Brother Cillín's choristers.

Brother Cillín was continuing: 'I have chosen you from many communities, and although it is not often we are all together to practise I was assured that within a few months we would be ready to enter our first singing competition. Now, what do I hear? A voice that has no tone in it, no understanding of music. How could I have chosen such a voice? Or did I?'

Eadulf had been aware that the *stiúirtheóir canaid* had now halted before him.

Reluctantly Eadulf raised his head to meet the steely eyes of the songmaster. He smiled weakly.

Brother Cillín gazed at him with distaste.

'Ah, Brother Saxon. So it is you. And were you over-come with such a desire to become a chorister that you felt you did not need to be able to sing?'

A sniggering broke out among the lines of the brethren. His erstwhile companion from An Daingean had been staring at him in horror and had moved as far away from him as possible in an attempt to disassociate himself.

'I did not think I was that bad,' muttered Eadulf, his face red.

Brother Cillín actually laughed, but with ill-humour.

'We have an old saying, Brother Saxon – better be silent than sing a song badly. I would remember that if I had your voice. Now I wish to continue with this rehearsal, so if you have tasks more fitting to your talent, you may leave us.'

He stood aside and Eadulf, head down, moved down the row to the chapel door.

Behind him he heard the waspish tone of the *stiúirtheóir canaid*.

'We of the Unending Circle must seek purity in our voices. Each voice must contribute to the whole. That is why we call ourselves the Unending Circle. There is another old saying that we'd best remember. One scabby ewe will spoil the flock.'

There was a burst of laughter among the choristers.

Outside the chapel, Eadulf closed the door none too gently and threw back his hood. He was still mortified.

'Unending Circle!' he snorted. 'A stupid name, indeed! A bunch of baying mules.'

From inside the voices rose in song. Eadulf grimaced and sighed. He had to admit the sound was sweet and melodious.

Fidelma made her way quickly to the *tech-screptra* and sought out Brother Eolas.

'I have just been to see the Venerable Mac Faosma about the genealogy that Conrí spoke of last night.'

The librarian pursed his lips in a sceptical smile.

'And the old man refused to let you see it?'

'On the contrary, I saw it,' she replied grimly. 'However, it came to our notice that the book has been defaced.'

Brother Eolas' features dissolved into horror.

'Defaced?' he whispered.

'A section of one page has been cut out. It was obvious that it happened recently.'

'That cannot be!' he replied, aghast.

'I can assure you that it is so,' said Fidelma calmly.

'I take a pride in my library, Sister.' He turned swiftly and beckoned to the reluctant young Brother Faolchair. 'I tell you that until you came here we have had no trouble. Then the burning of Cináed's books . . . I do not understand it.'

Brother Faolchair came hurrying over, pale-faced and nervous.

'Do you know of the Uí Fidgente genealogy?' the librarian demanded angrily. 'When did the Venerable Mac Faosma borrow it?'

'Brother Benen came here this morning and borrowed it on behalf of the Venerable Mac Faosma. I told Sister Fidelma of this a short time ago.'

'You were most helpful, Brother Faolchair,' Fidelma said gently. 'The Venerable Mac Faosma did have the book, which I saw. However, the book had been defaced and I think that we can be sure that this was done before Brother Benen took it to the Venerable Mac Faosma.'

The young man gasped in horror.

'I noticed no such thing when I handed the book to Brother Benen, Sister.'

'Do you check through the books before and after they have been borrowed from the library?' she asked.

The young man shook his head, puzzled.

'Why would one do that?'

'To ensure that those who borrow them do not damage them but treat them well. You said that you had not noticed the damage. I admit, it would take a sharp eye to spot it for it was only a small piece of the parchment cut from a page by means of the point of a sharp knife. I do not blame you for not noticing it.'

Brother Eolas intervened with a disapproving look.

'Sister, when religious come to a library to look at the books one does not expect them to be vandals. Most are scholars, scribes and students. Why would we not trust them to behave in a manner befitting their calling?'

'Someone obviously did not behave in that manner.'

'I have never heard the like. You say that this damage must have been done recently?'

'I do.'

'The book has not been borrowed for some time,' Brother Faolchair said. 'No one has asked me to take it from the shelves. Not since . . .'

He paused, trying to remember.

'Well,' intervened Brother Eolas irritably, 'are we to ask Brother Benen if he defaced it?'

'And would you expect him to answer if he had?' said Fidelma sarcastically.

'I remember the last borrowing.' Brother Faolchair was suddenly triumphant. 'It was borrowed by the Venerable Cináed.'

'So the Venerable Cináed also borrowed this book?' Fidelma spoke quietly.

'He did. It was shortly before his . . . his death. I remember because Sister Buan returned it to the library with some other books that he had borrowed. It was after his funeral.'

'Did anyone borrow it before the Venerable Cináed?'

Brother Faolchair nodded.

'As I am in charge of any borrowing that leaves this library, I try to keep a record in my mind. Before the Venerable Cináed, Sister Uallann and before her, Brother Cillín. You see, very few people are allowed to take books away from the library. Most of the community has to come in here to read them. But Brother Eolas has made . . .'

'I make certain exceptions,' interrupted the librarian. 'Our great scholars, of course, are the exceptions – our physician and songmaster are recognised as scholars in their own right.'

'And all four of these exceptions had borrowed the book . . . when? Within a few weeks of one another?'

'That is so,' affirmed Brother Faolchair.

Fidelma turned from them with a quick word of thanks and left the library.

Outside she found Conrí and Eadulf looking for her.

She smiled at each of them.

'I think the mystery is about to be unravelled. Let us go to see Abbot Erc and make plans to put this grim tale into the public domain.'

CHAPTER TWENTY

Fidelma had suggested that Abbot Erc request the attendance of certain members of the community to assemble in the *aireagal*, the oratory. As congregations usually stood in the oratory during the services, benches had been brought in and the lanterns were lit. Opposite these benches another bench had been arranged so that Abbot Erc, along with his steward, Brother Cú Mara, were seated facing the congregation. Next to them were Fidelma and Eadulf.

The small oratory was crowded. Conrí sat to one side with Sister Easdan and her companions as well as the Gaulish seaman, Esumaro. On the other side sat the physician, Sister Uallann, alongside Brothers Eolas and Faolchair. Sister Sinnchéne sat behind them. Sister Buan sat further back with Brother Cillín. Fidelma had asked Abbot Erc to insist upon the attendance of Slébéne, who was seated behind them. His champion was nowhere to be seen and, rather than reassure Fidelma, his absence worried her. There was some surprise among the company when the Venerable Mac Faosma entered, escorted by the watchful Brother Benen. The Venerable Mac

Faosma attended hardly any gathering unless he was giving one of his lectures or debates. But, again, Fidelma had asked Abbot Erc to especially request his presence.

The last person to enter was Socht, with two of his fellow warriors. They stood near the oratory door, which Socht closed. He signalled to Conrí that all was secure and Conrí then nodded towards Fidelma.

Abbot Erc found Fidelma looking at him. He realised that he had to govern the proceedings. He gave a nervous cough and began, speaking quickly.

'We are gathered here at the request of Sister Fidelma, who is here in her capacity as a *dálaigh*, as you all doubtless know.' The abbot sounded in a bad temper. 'There is no need for me to remind you of the tragedies that have struck our abbey, although, thanks to Sister Fidelma, we have been blessed with the safe return of the six members of our community who were abducted and who we thought had vanished for ever. Sister Fidelma now intends to explain the reasons behind these tragedies.'

He sat back with mouth closed firmly, glancing at Fidelma, who, perceiving that he had said all he was going to say, rose and looked around at the upturned, expectant faces that greeted her.

'This is not a court of law,' she began. 'No one here is on trial but from what occurs here a trial will doubtless result, for we are dealing with murder; not merely the murder of Abbess Faife and the Venerable Cináed but of many unfortunate Gaulish seamen, of villagers who dwelt among the Sliabh Mis mountains, and of an ill-fated religious member of the community of Seanach's Island named Brother Martan. In addition, we now must deal with the murder of the prisoner Olcán.'

Abbot Erc seemed irritated by her self-assurance.

'And you are claiming that all these events are connected?' he demanded.

Fidelma smiled.

'I would not say so were it otherwise,' she replied softly, but Eadulf heard the waspish rebuke in her tone.

She turned back to the still quiet assembly.

'This has been a frustrating mystery, involving several strands. Each strand had to be followed and unravelled before one could be sure that they all led back to one central point. It makes a long story.'

The harsh voice of the Venerable Mac Faosma came from the assembly: 'Then the sooner the story is started, the faster it will end and we can return to the comfort of our chambers.'

Fidelma was not perturbed by the old man's rudeness. She merely glanced in his direction.

'Are we not in the Lord's house, Venerable Mac Faosma?' Her voice was acrid. 'Where else is more comfortable in his sight than in the place sacred to him?' She delighted in the disconcerted expression on the old scholar's face. Eadulf realised that she was pricking at the bubble of his piety with her irony. She continued before he could think of a suitable riposte: 'Remember that it is not just the sister of the king of Muman who stands here. It is a representative of the laws which govern all this kingdom, all the territories, petty king-doms and provinces of this land. When insult is delivered to the representative then it is delivered to the law itself. I should not have to remind a scholar such as yourself of the offence and the punishments that are entailed when one insults the law.'

The Venerable Mac Faosma made a spluttering sound. But Fidelma was now ignoring him.

'I will not keep you all longer than I have to. Yet I have to peel away the strands that envelop this mystery. I will begin by showing you the prime cause behind what has happened here. The prime motivation behind the deaths and abductions. I regret to say that we have to return to the ages-old conflict between the Uí Fidgente and the Eoghanacht of Cashel.'

An immediate murmur of outrage came from several quarters. Conrí looked about him unhappily.

Fidelma was slowly shaking a finger at them.

'Noise does not drown out truth,' she remonstrated.

'Nor words without evidence will make it the truth,' snapped the Venerable Mac Faosma.

'Then listen and you will soon hear the evidence that supports the words,' replied Fidelma, unperturbed. 'Or is that demanding too much courtesy from this gathering?'

There were still some angry protests from the predominantly Uí Fidgente gathering. Conrí rose, facing them, and held up his hands to motion them to quiet.

'There is a saying – do not bring your reaping hook into a field without being asked.' It was a reminder to the assembly to behave properly. 'We will hear what Fidelma of Cashel has to say and we will hear her without insult, jest or clamour. Remember that truth can come like bad weather, uninvited. But denial of bad weather does not make the day fine nor make the truth less than the truth. If I, as warlord of the Uí Fidgente, can bear to listen, then you can also.'

He sat down again, folded his arms, and stared woodenly ahead of him.

The murmurs of dissent subsided.

'I shall not trouble you with history,' Fidelma continued.

'Nor with arguments of who is right and who is wrong in that conflict. We all know the conflict has lasted many generations between Uí Fidgente and Eoghanacht. A short time ago, both peoples thought that the conflict was at an end. A new ruler of the Uí Fidgente came to the belief that peace was a better way of life than conflict. We hoped that we had all moved on.

'However, there were still members of the Uí Fidgente who refused to accept the rule of Donennach of the Uí Chonaill Gabra. They wanted to see the return of the rule of the old dynasty of the Uí Choirpre Áedba. Yet both families traced their descent to Fiachu Fidgennid. One sought to rule in peace while the other in war. With the death of Eoganán at Cnoc Áine it was believed that the Uí Choirpre Áedba dynasty was no more. But Eoganán's seed had survived, plotting and planning for the day when Donennach could be overthrown and the young men of the Uí Fidgente flung once more on to the hardened steel of their enemies . . . for the glory of the Uí Choirpre Áedba dynasty and for no other cause,' she added with emphasis.

This time there was an uncomfortable silence in the oratory. Finally the Abbot Erc spoke with a querulous note.

'You forget, Sister Fidelma, that Eoganán's son Torcán was slaughtered as well.'

'I have not forgotten. Eoganán had more than one male offspring.'

'She means Uaman!' called Sister Uallann, and her tone showed that it was meant as a jeer.

'As a *dálaigh*, you should know that Uaman could not become chief of the Uí Fidgente,' the librarian Brother Eolas intervened. 'Even I know enough law to realise that. It was well known that he was a leper and therefore ineligible to claim the office. He would not be recognised as legitimate even if he arrived at Loch Derg with a thousand warriors behind him to place him on the seat of his ancestors.'

Slébéne, the chief of the Corco Duibhne, was nodding slowly.

'What if Uaman still lives?' he demanded, causing some surprise among them. 'We have heard many rumours that it is so.'

Sister Uallann turned to him, exhaling sharply.

'The stories cannot be true,' she snapped. 'Wasn't it said that before the last Nativity he perished in the quicksand of his own island? Several travellers brought the story to the abbey.'

Eadulf was about to stir when he caught Fidelma's eye and saw the slight shake of her head.

It was Conrí who replied.

'It was so reported. There was an eyewitness.' He cast a quick look at Eadulf. 'But we saw that there are burnt-out villages among the passes of Sliabh Mis, there are mothers who weep for the loss of their sons, wives for their husbands, children for their fathers. We met with people who reported seeing Uaman leading a band of warriors through these passes. It was that band of warriors that I and the lord Tadcán captured on Seanach's Island and brought hither with Olcán their leader.'

'And Uaman as well?' called Brother Eolas. 'Where is he, then, who would be "master of souls"?'

Sister Easdan now rose in her place.

'While we did not know who the man was, Olcán took orders from a man clad from head to feet in robes and whom he called "the master". Esumaro will bear me out. Others identified him as the one they call Uaman the Leper.'

The Gaulish seaman nodded in support.

Brother Cillín called out from his seat.

'You mean that man you imprisoned here, Olcán, was one of Uaman's men?'

'Even if it were so,' smiled the Venerable Mac Faosma sceptically, 'you have heard that Uaman would have no chance at all of being regarded as ruler. He might force himself upon the Uí Fidgente as their chief by force of arms but then he would split his people – there would be warfare. The Uí Chonaill Gabra would appeal to the Brehons. They would appeal to Cashel. Cashel would intervene with the support of the High King because the law is clear. Blood feuds would rip the Uí Fidgente asunder . . . parties of avengers would rule the country by fear. We could not have someone unqualified by law force his rule upon us. I freely confess that I was a supporter of Eoganán and all he stood for. I believe that the rule of the Eoghanacht of Cashel is unjust. But I believe in the rule of the law and not of the sword. I would condemn Uaman, if he usurped the power of the Uí Fidgente. Only a ruler qualified by law can take Donennach's power from him.'

Slébéne was smiling cynically.

'As you all well know, I am chief of the Corco Duibhne and it is against my eastern borders, the valley passes, where Uaman the Leper has been seen. Many times have I sought to confront him and he has outwitted me. Now, there sits Conrí, warlord of the Uí Fidgente. I give him this invitation. Bring those men that are loyal to him and his lord, Donennach, and come into the passes of Sliabh Mis and together we will hunt this leper down.'

He sat down and there was a murmur of applause.

Conrí was about to rise to accept the challenge when

Fidelma motioned him to remain seated. She had been standing with a whimsical smile on her features at Slébéne's suggestion.

'Well said, Slébéne, well said,' she applauded, but they could hear the cynicism in her voice. 'But I think you know as well as I do that Uaman the Leper will not be found in the passes of Sliabh Mis. Chasing shadows in the passes of Sliabh Mis would merely take Conrí and his men away from the area where the rebellion against Donennach would occur, wouldn't it?'

Her quiet tone held their attention and for a moment there was total silence.

'What do you mean, Sister Fidelma?' Abbot Erc finally demanded.

'The stories that you heard in the month before the Nativity were true. Uaman, son of Eoganán, was dragged into the quicksand surrounding his own island fortress. Eadulf here was a witness to his death.'

The silence continued as Abbot Erc remained staring at her with a puzzled frown.

'Then what are we discussing? With Uaman dead as well as his elder brother Torcán, there is no one else of the Uí Choirpre Áedba to claim the chieftainship.'

'If Uaman is dead,' called Esumaro, 'who is this "master" who gave orders to Olcán?'

Fidelma glanced towards the Venerable Mac Faosma.

'Perhaps you could enlighten us?' she invited.

As they all turned towards him, the Venerable Mac Faosma leant back and stared at her with growing astonishment.

'Of course! That is why you were examining the genealogy. Eoganán had three children. But surely that doesn't help us because the third name was removed from the genealogy?'

The librarian had picked up the train of the argument.

'You told us so yourself,' Brother Eolas said. 'Something had been cut from the page of the genealogy. Was it the name of the third son of Eoganán?'

'It was the name of Eoganán's third child. The one who now means to overthrow Donennach and claim the rulership of the Uí Fidgente.'

A whisper of surprise spread like a tide around the oratory with people looking at one another in surprise.

'I said,' Fidelma told them, 'that there were many strands that had to be unravelled. I have given you the motive for the events that have happened here. I have told you who was behind it but have not yet identified that person. So let us now turn to this strand of identity, bearing in mind what I have said about the ambitions of the sons of Eoganán and the fact that he had three offspring and not two . . .'

'One thing, lady,' Esumaro called out. 'Was my ship wrecked by accident or design?'

'It was wrecked by opportunity. Olcán and his men seized the chance to wreck your ship when they saw it trying to weather the island. They were there awaiting the arrival of Abbess Faife and her companions. They saw a rich merchantman and decided, on the spur of the moment, to gather some extra booty. Olcán, as many of you may know . . .' she let her glance linger slightly on the white immobile features of Sister Sinnchéne, 'was one of Uaman's commanders when he was alive. Now Olcán changed his allegiance to Eoganán's other child. He had received instructions to go to the island and wait by the ruins of Uaman's fortress. He knew that his new master badly needed money to pay mercenaries to help them overthrow Donennach. He had been told that Abbess Faife and her companions would be passing by on a certain day at a certain time. Olcán's orders were to capture the sisters unharmed. However, it did not matter about the abbess. It was her companions who were needed for they had important skills.'

Sister Easdan was animated.

'The precious stones. Olcán and his people were mining the crystals but needed experts to cut and polish them so they could sell them to raise money for their cause. That is why they were not bothered about killing poor Abbess Faife. That's why they took us to Seanach's Island where the hermits were forced to dig the crystal and we were forced to polish it.'

'Exactly so,' confirmed Fidelma approvingly.

'But what of my crew, my ship?' demanded Esumaro angrily. 'What had they to do with anything?'

'As I have said, you happened to be in the wrong place at the wrong time,' Fidelma assured him. 'Olcán must have seen your ship being driven into the bay in the bad weather. He thought it was a godsend to his master. Who knows what goods might be aboard? Olcán was a perverse and evil man. He strung up the light to misdirect you on to the rocks and . . .' She shrugged. 'He stored the goods in the ruined fortress to await a more suitable time to bring his warship around the coast from Seanach's Island to pick it up. But you survived, Esumaro. You were the only survivor. You brought us a particular piece of important information that helped me reconstruct the story.'

'What was that?' the seaman asked.

'You heard Olcán telling his men about the rendezvous with the abbess and her companions, showing that he had been informed precisely when they would be passing along that road. In trying to escape from Olcán and his robbers in the early hours after the wreck, you fell in with Abbess Faife and nearly shared her fate. Thanks to Sister Easdan there, and more than a little luck, you survived.'

She had their complete attention now. They were leaning forward in their seats, hanging on her every word. Even the Venerable Mac Faosma was sitting attentive and quiet.

'The precious stones were going to be the real key for raising money to pay an army of mercenaries, warriors from the north, the Uí Maine and Uí Briúin Aí, the sort of scum that Olcán was leading, to help overthrow Donennach.'

She paused and looked towards Sister Easdan.

'Now, one thing especially interested me. This abbey was certainly known for producing polished stones and jewellery. For having expert *lec-garaid* or stone polishers. But Abbot Erc did not like individuals to be named. He wanted the abbey to have the reputation but did not want to encourage individuals to share it because of vanity. So who identified the six workers who went off with Abbess Faife on the annual pilgrimage to Bréanainn's? I found that the pilgrims comprised different groups each year. So who told the so-called "master", and thereby Olcán, who they were and that they would be passing along that road on that particular day?'

She paused as she studied their upturned expectant faces.

'Only someone from inside the abbey could have had such information.'

It was the steward Brother Cú Mara who articulated the conclusion.

'Are you saying that someone here connived in the murder of their own abbess and the abduction of six of our members?' he demanded.

'Who?' demanded Abbot Erc. His features had grown less aggressive.

'Who else but Eoganán's third child, the so-called "master" who, having been fostered by Slébéne of the Corco Duibhne, then came to dwell in this abbey. When Uaman was killed they realised they might legitimately claim the chiefship of the Uí Fidgente but it needed an army, and an army needed money.'

Slébéne had turned pale, his eyes flashing with anger.

Conrí was on his feet, slowly moving towards him.

'Name the man, Fidelma,' he instructed, hand on the hilt of his sword.

'Did I say that this "master" was a man?' Fidelma let her eyes roam the upturned faces before her. Then she said: 'Stand forth, Uallach, daughter of Eoganán.'

'Uallach!' Conrí suddenly swung his gaze on Sister Uallann, the abbey physician. He thought that the name was familiar. She was fiercely supportive of the deposed Uí Fidgente chieftain, against the peace with Cashel, and admitted that she had been raised among the Corco Duibhne. Of course, it made sense. The physician did not move, her pale eyes fixed on Fidelma.

'Not Uallann,' Fidelma said softly. 'Someone trying to hide their true name would not choose another so close to it.'

It was then that Conrí realised that Fidelma was looking directly at Sister Buan.

'Stand up, Uallach. You do not have to deny it,' she instructed quietly.

Sister Buan rose slowly to her feet. Her face was contorted with a mixture of emotions.

'You consider that you are very clever, Fidelma of Cashel.

My regret is that I failed in both my attempts to kill you. That was remiss of me.'

There was a gasp from the assembly.

'For my part, Uallach, I am grateful that you did not succeed,' Fidelma replied calmly.

Abbot Erc was regarding them both with utter bewilderment on his features.

'I think we deserve some explanation, Sister Fidelma. I have no idea of how you can make this accusation. We have known Sister Buan for many years. She has been trusted with trading for this abbey. She was . . . she was the Venerable Cináed's companion and he would hardly support the aspirations of a child of Eoganán!'

'I shall show that the person you knew as Sister Buan was, in reality, Uallach, daughter of the late ruler of the Uí Fidgente, sister to Uaman the Leper. It was Buan who arranged for the abduction of the six gem polishers from this abbey. Buan was one of the few people in the abbey who had the freedom to move about the country in her position of trader. Olcán and his men worked for her. Because she was in many ways like Uaman, her brother, she donned a robe and people thought she was Uaman still alive. She was responsible for the death of the Abbess Faife and what followed on Seanach's Island. She also killed her husband, the Venerable Cináed, when he began to suspect her, and she was the person who killed Olcán when she thought he would betray her.

'Only Olcán knew that Uaman was not the "master". He told me so on the night before Buan, whom he trusted, murdered him . . .'

The murmur erupted into a chorus of angry voices.

Abbot Erc had to raise his voice to make himself heard.

'You will have to prove these accusations,' he said, still filled with doubt.

'Oh, indeed, I shall. I shall take you through it with each piece of evidence.'

Conrí had nearly reached Slébéne but the chief of the Corco Duibhne was on his feet.

He drew a short sword, which he had hidden under his cloak.

'Time for a strategic withdrawal, Uallach,' he called.

'Don't be stupid, Slébéne!' Conrí cried, his own sword drawn. 'You have no chance of leaving here.'

'Do I not?' sneered Slébéne. 'Then look to the windows, my friend. There are arrows aimed at Fidelma of Cashel and at the abbot. If anyone moves against us to prevent us leaving here, then they will be the first to die. Conrí, put down your sword now and tell your warriors to stand aside from the door and do the same. Do it now or Fidelma dies!'

Eyes had flitted to the windows on either side of the oratory. Through the slits two of Slébéne's warriors with drawn bows, arrows steadily pointed at their targets, could be seen. One of them was the red-haired champion. The chief of the Corco Duibhne had not told lies. The arrows were well aimed.

Conrí, with a hiss of anger, dropped his weapon and stood back.

'Now tell your man to move away from the door!'

Conrí did so and Socht and his companions reluctantly discarded their weapons and stood aside.

Sister Buan, the woman Fidelma had identified as Uallach, was staring at her with features contorted with hate. She did not seem in a hurry to leave.

'Come, Uallach!' cried Slébéne. 'There is no time—'

'Kill them!' the woman suddenly screamed. 'Kill them all!'

The abbot flinched and closed his eyes, waiting for the impact of the arrow, but Fidelma stood firmly returning Sister Buan's malignant gaze.

Luckily it was Slébéne who was in command of his warriors and they waited for his orders. He realised that if his men loosed their arrows, Fidelma and Abbot Erc might die but he would have no chance of escape from the oratory. The threat that his own death would almost certainly result prevented him from giving the order.

The chief came forward and gripped Sister Buan's arm tightly.

'Think, Uallach! Think! If we kill them, we will never get out of this abbey. We must leave, get to An Daingean and raise our army. It is the only way. Come quickly while my archers can cover us. These others can be dealt with later.'

Reluctantly, Sister Buan, or Uallach, allowed herself to be drawn back along the aisle to the door of the oratory.

'Tell your man to open the door,' yelled Slébéne as they backed towards it.

Conrí signalled to Socht to do so.

The warrior turned in disgust and opened the door. While he was still bending to swing the door back, Slébéne brought the pommel of his short sword down on the man's unprotected head and he fell with hardly a sound.

Slébéne and Uallach were gone through the door. Outside, Slébéne drew it shut behind them. Those inside heard the door slam shut and something placed against it. Then the two archers at the windows withdrew without releasing their arrows. With the threat that confined his actions now gone, Conrí sprang forward, grabbing his fallen sword, and shouting to someone to attend to Socht who was trying to staunch the blood on his head. Conrí tried the door. Socht's two companions joined him but their assault on the door was useless. It had been well jammed from the outside.

There was a general hubbub in the oratory and Fidelma called in a loud and clear tone for order and quiet. They heard the sound of horses from outside. She and Eadulf hastened to Conrí's side.

'They'll be heading for their warship,' she told Conrí. 'Will Tadcán be able to deal with them? Is there a way to warn him?'

Conrí grinned and took from his belt a small horn, which had been hanging by its thongs. He went to the window and raised it to his lips. The blast was long and shrill and he sounded it three times. By this time, other members of the community had come to the oratory to see what the commotion was and removed the obstacle, which turned out to be a couple of poles, that had held the door fast.

Conrí seized a red-faced and bewildered brother. The warlord demanded to know where Slébéne and his companions had gone.

'Lord, they left by the main gate. They all went on horseback and seem to be taking the road to the coast.'

'Then it is up to Tadcán,' muttered Fidelma.

Conrí once more raised his horn and blew the three sharp notes into the still winter air. He paused and then, faintly in the distance, they heard three answering blasts.

The warlord turned to Fidelma and Eadulf with a smile of triumph.

'Tadcán has heard, lady. He will be waiting for them.'

Fidelma peered round and caught sight of Brother Cú Mara.

'Get our horses, quickly!' she called.

The steward was looking confused. However, Socht, having partially recovered from the blow, was coming out of the oratory with his two fellow warriors helping him. Hearing Fidelma's order, they ran towards the stables. While Fidelma and Conrí fretted impatiently, moments passed, and then the warriors returned leading their horses.

A short time later, Conrí, followed by Fidelma and Eadulf, swept out of the gates of the abbey at a canter. Eadulf was hanging on for dear life, unused to the pace. Socht and his companions were left behind trying to organise horses for themselves.

Fidelma, keeping pace alongside the warlord, shouted across as they rode along the path to the coastal port.

'What if they stand and fight before we reach the coast?'

'That is not Slébéne's style, by all accounts,' cried Conrí. 'He'll make for the protection of his ship and his men.'

'But he must realise that Tadcán has been forewarned.'

Conrí did not bother to reply. They rode on in silence. It was soon evident that Tadcán and Slébéne were in conflict. As they neared the port of An Bhearbha they saw smoke rising. A moment or two later they swung over the hill and down into the bay.

A warship was burning in the harbour. It was tied close to the quayside. A few other merchant ships were being towed away from the quays by small craft, apparently drawing them out of harm's way. Two more warships were stationary some way off near the entrance of the bay but they could see warriors milling about the quay. Some bodies lay nearby.

Conrí called to Fidelma to hold back while he investigated. She halted her mount reluctantly and allowed Eadulf to catch up with her, reining his horse to a stand at her side. Together they watched Conrí trot down towards the quayside, his sword unsheathed.

A warrior came running up on foot towards him, sword in hand. But Conrí halted and seemed to greet the man. The warlord turned and waved them forward.

'This is Tadcán, lord of Baile Tadc,' he grinned. 'Good news, lady. Tell her, Tadcán.'

The warrior, a broad-shouldered, well-built young man, with a shock of fair hair and a pleasant grin, saluted her.

'It is a story that is easy in the telling, lady,' he said. 'We heard lord Conrí's signal which had been arranged with Socht. We knew something was up. And we decided to pre-empt the danger by seizing Slébéne's warship. His captain decided to fight, so we had to set fire to it. I know Slébéne of old. He doesn't believe in fighting fair, so I decided not to give him the benefit of the doubt. I wasn't wrong, as it turned out. There were many armed warriors waiting below decks but we bested them.

'While we were thus engaged, along comes Slébéne with two of his warriors and a religieuse. They fell on us and so we fell on them.'

He laughed a little harshly.

'In truth, lady, the lord of the Corco Duibhne was no great warrior, and when we had dispatched his men, especially the red-haired warrior, he seemed to go berserk in fear. He leapt for his ship's rail from the quayside rather than surrender. He did not make it. He slipped into the harbour waters and when the tide caused the ship to nudge against the quay he was crushed between them. We hauled his body out of the waters and his men, realising their chief is dead, are even now surrendering to us.'

He jerked his thumb to the burning warship.

'His ship is well alight and it is beyond our abilities to douse the flames.'

Conrí was smiling approvingly.

'You have done well, Tadcán.'

Fidelma, however, was looking about with a frown as if not interested in the warrior's report.

'Where is Uallach?' she demanded.

Tadcán looked bewildered.

'Who, lady?'

'The woman who was with Slébéne. The religieuse.'

A look of understanding crossed Tadcán's features.

'When we attacked her companions, she ran into one of the buildings there.' He pointed to one of the stone buildings that stood back from the harbour.

'That is Mugrón's house,' muttered Conrí.

Already Fidelma and Eadulf had dismounted and were heading in its direction. Crying to them to be careful, Conrí also jumped from his horse and followed them. He called to Tadcán to follow him.

'We must capture her or she will remain a rallying symbol for the Uí Fidgente dissidents,' Fidelma told Conrí as he caught her up.

They came to the house and halted before the door.

'Tadcán, you and Brother Eadulf go round the back,' hissed Conrí.

Then, waiting for a few moments until he judged they had taken up their position, Conrí ran swiftly at the door and thrust against it with his foot. The door went flying from its hinges and he was inside with Fidelma at his shoulder.

The first thing they saw was Mugrón lying on the floor, his upper body propped up against a wall. Blood was spreading over one shoulder. His eyes were wide open with pain. His features were greying.

There was a crash as Tadcán and Eadulf entered through the back door.

Conrí looked swiftly round in the shadows of the room. Apart from Mugrón's body there was no sign of any other occupant.

Eadulf bent to the merchant and quickly examined the wound.

'Painful, but he will survive. The blade has penetrated the shoulder muscle.'

The merchant licked his lips and then indicated with his head towards a closed door that led to an adjoining room. He frowned and indicated again.

Conrí raised a finger to his lips before motioning Tadcán forward. The fair-haired warrior took two swift steps and then kicked the door in.

Sister Buan, or rather Uallach, was seated in a chair, facing them. Her face had a wild-eyed, angry expression that was not pleasant to look upon. She saw Fidelma at Conrí's elbow. Her face was screwed into a picture of hatred, the eyes flashing darkly.

'Eoghanacht bitch!' she spat. 'You will never take me to be a slave at Cashel! *Fidgennid go Buadh!*'

Before they realised what she was doing, she had jerked in the chair, given a gasp and fallen sideways.

Eadulf pushed forward and knelt beside her.

He removed something from her lower chest. It was a tiny white bone-handled dagger.

'Dead?' asked Fidelma.

Eadulf felt for a heartbeat and looked up in surprise.

'Not dead,' he said. He turned quickly and eased the unconscious form into a more comfortable position.

'Can you save her?' Fidelma peered over his shoulder.

'I can try. It looks like a clean wound. She did not make a good job of it. I don't think the blade dug deeply enough to be mortal. I'll do my best.'

Fidelma glanced at Conrí. 'I didn't understand what she shouted before she dug the knife in.'

The warlord grimaced.

'It was the *barrán-glaed*, the old Uí Fidgente war cry – Fidgente to victory. If nothing else, she believed in the Uí Fidgente.'

CHAPTER TWENTY-ONE

Abbot Erc was looking grim as Fidelma and Eadulf filed into his chambers early the next morning. Conrí was with them. Brother Cú Mara and Sister Uallann, the physician, were already seated there. The elderly abbot waved them to the remaining seats that had been arranged before his table.

'I have been told by Sister Uallann that Sister Buan is dead. Her death has to be accounted for, Sister Fidelma, as also the deaths of Slébéne and his men at An Bhearbha.'

There was sadness in Fidelma's features.

'We had hoped that Uallach, or Sister Buan, as you knew her, would have survived. We had brought her to the abbey so that she might have better attention than could be provided at An Bhearbha. Has Sister Uallann informed you of exactly what happened?'

The physician sniffed.

'I have not explained in detail. I was about to say that when she was brought to me, I found that the initial wound was clean and had penetrated only the muscle. The woman could have survived. She did not want to.'

Abbot Erc leant forward in his seat.

'Explain what you mean,' he instructed with a puzzled expression.

'I had applied medicaments, the healing poultices,' continued the physician. 'Buan, whatever her name was, recovered consciousness. She was in truculent mood. She was angry that she had been cheated of her death. Fidelma of Cashel, the Saxon brother and lord Conrí came to question her but that was against my advice. I remained in the room during this time and can testify to what she told them. Afterwards . . . well, we left the room and when I returned a moment later I found that Sister Buan had finished the job she began. She had taken one of my surgical knives and thrust it into her heart. It would have been an instant death.'

Abbot Erc regarded her with a shocked expression.

'When you left the room where she was confined, there were surgical knives left within her reach? Surely that was negligent when we are told that the woman had attempted to kill herself?'

Sister Uallann looked unhappy at the reprimand but Fidelma intervened quickly.

'Sister Uallann did not realise that the woman was still intent on taking her life,' she explained. 'In fact, none of us realised how strong her will was.'

Abbot Erc sat back with pursed lips, thinking for a moment or two.

'You claim that she was really Uallach, daughter of Eoganán, and was intent on becoming his *banchomarbae* – his rightful heir? You accuse her of being responsible for the death of Abbess Faife, for the abduction of the stone polishers of our community, for the murder of her own husband Cináed, as well as all else that has followed. It is now time that we had some explanations. Are you saying that she was solely to blame for all this evil?'

'Solely to blame?' Fidelma paused reflectively. 'Not solely to blame. I believe it could be argued that it was Eoganán, son of Crunmáel, one time ruler of the Uí Fidgente who was the true architect of the evil that has come upon his people. His actions have conditioned the lives of his offspring and that includes Uallach. In a way, you have to feel some compassion for Uallach. Eoganán was the true "master of souls". Despising the value of his own life in pursuit of his ambitions, he despised the value of other people's lives, particularly those of his own offspring. He became the master of other's lives and thereby the master of their souls. So that, even after his death, he was governing what paths in life they have taken.'

Abbot Erc grimaced in irritation.

'Leave compassion to priests who are best able to bestow it. Your task is the law. While I will accept that Sister Buan was this woman Uallach – indeed, her actions now seem to have confirmed your accusations – I am at a total loss to understand how you came to suspect it.'

Sister Fidelma smiled sadly.

'Before I answer that, I have to say that without compassion there can be no administration of law. I do not think you will be able to share my philosophy, Abbot Erc, therefore I will not pursue this. As to the practicalities of the case, I think this was one of the most difficult investigations that I have ever undertaken. As I began to explain yesterday, there were various layers. But once we had discovered the prime motive then all else followed swiftly. The motive, as I told you, was to reinstate the dynasty of the Uí Choirpre Áedba. So far as we knew, Eoganán and his son Torcán had been killed during the rebellion against Cashel. His other son Uaman was dead. Eadulf had seen his death. But then we found that he appeared to have returned from the Otherworld.'

'Even I began to question my own memory,' confided Eadulf easily. 'Especially when Ganicca was so sure that it was Uaman who rode with Olcán and his men.'

Fidelma glanced at him with a smile.

'Eadulf does not imagine things. I trust when he reports that he has seen something that he has indeed seen it. So who was this wraith who rode about in Uaman's robes? When questioned closely, none had seen the features of the wraith and that fact made me suspect that this was someone passing themselves off as Uaman.'

She paused and looked round. Seeing that she held their attention, she continued: 'We had a lot of information, many strands, and I knew that all the strands wound their way back to this abbey. That was not only because of the death of Cináed but because someone here had to give instructions to Olcán about the six stone polishers leaving the abbey for the pilgrimage.'

Abbot Erc interrupted with an impatient wave of his hand.

'I followed your argument on that yesterday.'

Brother Cú Mara added: 'I think the abbot means – how did you come to suspect Sister Buan? She had been in this abbey for years and no one suspected that she was Eoganán's daughter.'

'I will come to that. I was looking for the motive. When I accepted that Uaman was dead there were two possibilities. Either the person imitating Uaman was doing so because of the fear that his reputation instilled or because they were preparing the way for the reinstatement of the dynasty. Olcán made a remark in his cell which implied that Uaman was dead and that Eoganán had more than two sons. There was another who could claim to be his heir. Conrí pointed out the answer lay in the genealogy of the Uí Fidgente. And after we saw Olcán, Conrí asked the librarian for a copy . . .'

'Buan was standing next to him when I asked,' Conrí recalled excitedly. 'So that is what alerted her and she went off to eradicate the name of Uallach from it?'

To his surprise Fidelma shook her head.

'She had already eliminated it some time before. It was when Cináed was beginning to suspect her that he had borrowed the genealogy. She had cut her name Uallach from the book. But what she did fear was that Conrí's question meant that Olcán was boastful and could not be trusted. So she returned that night and stabbed him in his cell.'

There was a silence. Then Brother Cú Mara asked: 'If the name in the genealogy was deleted how could you tell the identity of the heir?'

'Buan had told some truth about her background. Her mother ran off with a young man, and her father sent her away to be fostered by a chieftain of the Corco Duibhne. Who would that be but Slébéne? Cáeth, the smith, who had been fostered by Slébéne, told us that Slébéne had fostered a daughter of a noble from the east. Her name was Uallach.'

Conrí smiled apologetically to Sister Uallann.

'I mistakenly thought that Uallach was you. The similarity of the name.'

The physician cast a glance of dislike at him but made no comment.

'I pointed out that anyone disguising his or her name would not simply change a syllable,' Fidelma explained. 'Anyway, although we heard that Uallach was arrogant, any ambition was killed by Eoganán's rejection of her. So she came to Ard Fhearta and entered the abbey. After her father was killed and her brothers also, she realised that she could now claim to be a *banchomarbae* – a female heir – and strike out to claim the leadership of the Uí Fidgente. She sought and gained support from her brother's right-hand man, Olcán, and from her foster father Slébéne.'

'What I don't understand is that if she was a princess of the Uí Fidgente,' broke in the abbot, 'why was she not acknowledged as such? Why did she enter this abbey under an assumed name?'

'Uallach herself gave the answer. Her father rejected her when her mother left him, and sent her to fosterage with Slébéne. She had little to do with her father nor her half-brothers. Buan admitted the bitterness she felt when I first spoke to her. That bitterness now made her ambition the greater.'

'But why did she marry the Venerable Cináed?' demanded Brother Cú Mara. 'He was surely everything she detested both as a man and for his views about the Uí Fidgente.'

Fidelma assumed a wry expression.

'In that matter, we must accept she spoke the truth. She needed Cináed's authority and protection within the abbey. It was Cináed, of course, who helped her. And remember this was a few years before she began to develop her ambition. But it was Cináed who eventually began to suspect his wife. She did not love him and he found romance with Sister Sinnchéne.'

'He had not realised her connection—' Eadulf suddenly saw the warning glance that Fidelma gave him. He had been going to mention that Olcán was her father, and he compressed his lips firmly.

'Eadulf was going to say that Cináed gave her a necklet.'

Eadulf drew out the necklet that he had borrowed from Sister Sinnchéne and laid it on the table.

'Cináed gave her this and told her to keep it safe, to let no one see it. It is evidence, he said. In fact, it was symbolic evidence because Buan had been travelling on behalf of the abbey selling the precious stones that were produced here. She had realised that this was the great source of wealth through which she could purchase, through Olcán and Slébéne, armed mercenaries to place her in power. The freedom to travel and to trade allowed her to maintain contact with Olcán.

'Cináed had already begun to suspect that Uallach, or Buan as we know her, was involved in the precious stone business but for her own ends. I am not sure the exact evidence the necklet was to be but I am sure he found it among Buan's things. That should have made me think about the book he had written on the sordid trade in local precious stones. He had handed that to Brother Faolchair to be copied.'

'Ah, Cináed's books,' muttered Abbot Erc. 'All his books were destroyed. What have you to say about that?'

'Cináed had already written a book arguing against Eoganán's reasons for making war on Cashel. It was destroyed in the Venerable Mac Faosma's rooms. It was Buan who destroyed it because she realised that her husband had seen the genealogy and mentioned Eoganán's third child. She found the genealogy in his rooms and so she cut her name from it.

'But Buan was unsure later whether Cináed had made references in other books. That concern grew as I began to take an interest in his writings. I was talking to Buan when I realised that I had been concentrating on clues in the wrong book. I had thought the secrets lay in Cináed's denounce-ment of Eoganán's regime, the book she had destroyed in Mac Faosma's chamber. It was much later that I came to realise that the book on the gem trade was more important. Eadulf and I had mentioned the title in front of Buan. A short time later we found that all Cináed's books in the library had been burnt. That was to prevent our search. Buan was cunning enough to realise that if she burnt the book on the gems only, suspicion would have fallen on her. She burnt them all.

'I believe that not everything had come together in the Venerable Cináed's mind until Abbess Faife was murdered and the six gem polishers had been abducted. Then he knew Buan must have been involved. Buan also realised that he had made the connection. So he had to be killed. She lured him to the oratory with a false message from Sister Sinnchéne. She hoped that this would be evidence against Sinnchéne but Cináed was astute enough to try to burn it. She handed the remains over to the abbot hoping for suspicion to fall on Sinnchéne. She went out of her way to incriminate Sinnchéne to Eadulf and me. Buan waited in the chapel and bludgeoned her husband to death.'

Eadulf was nodding in agreement.

'We did suspect Sister Sinnchéne for a while,' he admitted. 'Only she knew that we were going to be in the workroom where they polished the stones at the time the attempt on Fidelma's life was made.'

Abbot Erc was astonished.

'How was this?'

Fidelma quickly explained the circumstances.

'I think that Buan was becoming increasingly fearful and knew that I suspected her. The previous evening she had asked me to come to her chamber on the pretext of discussing her rights, which she knew anyway. I think that she was going to arrange my death there. However, Eadulf arrived and she had to abandon her plan. So the next day she attempted to push a stone on my head as we were leaving the workroom.'

'But if only Sister Sinnchéne knew you were going to be there, at the stone polishers' workshop, how did Sister Buan find out?' demanded Brother Cú Mara.

'You told her,' Fidelma smiled.

The young steward's eyes widened.

'I told no one,' he denied hotly.

'Not directly,' agreed Fidelma in a mild voice.

'I remember that morning,' interrupted Sister Uallann. 'Sister Sinnchéne was delivering washing. I was standing with Brother Cú Mara and Sister Buan. Brother Cú Mara felt he had been too abrasive to you and felt he should apologise. He asked Sister Sinnchéne if she knew where you were. She told him. That's how Sister Buan learnt the information and I remember that she left us immediately.'

'So Buan was able to get through the dormitories to the roof of the workshop in a matter of moments, pry loose the block and make her second attempt on my life.'

'Thankfully it failed,' Eadulf added. 'Ever since I first met Buan I kept thinking that I had met her before. Her features seemed so familiar to me. I mentioned it to Fidelma. But it was not until Buan made her final mistake that it all came together.'

'A final mistake?' Abbot Erc was shaking his head, perplexed.

Fidelma looked appreciatively to Eadulf.

'She was trapped into making that mistake by Eadulf.'

All eyes turned to him and he shrugged modestly.

'All along, Sister Buan had been pretending a lack of education. She claimed not to know a word of Latin, thus trying to assure us that she would not have had any knowledge of Cináed's work. Had this been so, we would have had to accept that she must have been innocent of the book destruction and that would have been a fatal flaw in our argument. However, as the daughter of a chieftain, raised by a chieftain, she would naturally have learnt Latin.'

Abbot Erc was still puzzled.

'But I can vouch that she was no scholar. She had neither Latin nor Greek.'

'No, she pretended not to, but made a fatal slip,' contradicted Eadulf. 'We were talking and I commented *dura lex sed lex* – the law is hard, but it is the law. And she turned and agreed with me without my needing to translate. And I knew then that she had been lying about her knowledge. Everything fell into place and I finally understood the significance of her resemblance to Uaman.'

Sister Fidelma nodded appreciatively.

'Thanks to Eadulf, that was the point when the evidence tied into the knot that sealed Buan's fate.'

'She was ambitious to the point of blind evil,' Abbot Erc sighed deeply. 'What profit a person, if they gain the whole world, and lose their own soul?'

Fidelma nodded agreement at his quotation from scripture.

'Publilius Syrus said . . .' She paused, glanced to where Eadulf was waiting with a stoic expression for yet another of her many quotations from the moral sayings of her favourite Latin philosopher. Then she gave him one of her rare mischievous grins: 'But that's another story. Let's make a start on the road for Cashel and little Alchú.'

PRONUNCIATION GUIDE

As the Fidelma series has become increasingly popular, many English-speaking fans have written wanting assurance about the way to pronounce the Irish names and words.

Irish belongs to the Celtic branch of the Indo-European family of languages. It is closely related to Manx and Scottish Gaelic and a cousin of Welsh, Cornish and Breton. It is a very old European literary language. Professor Calvert Watkins of Harvard maintained it contains Europe's oldest *vernacular* literature, Greek and Latin being a *lingua franca*. Surviving texts date from the seventh century AD.

The Irish of Fidelma's period is classed as Old Irish; after AD 950 the language entered a period known as Middle Irish. Therefore, in the Fidelma books, Old Irish forms are generally adhered to, whenever possible, in both names and words. This is like using Chaucer's English compared to modern English. For example, a word such as *aidche* ('night') in Old Irish is now rendered *oiche* in modern Irish.

There are only eighteen letters in the Irish alphabet. From earliest times there has been a literary standard but today four distinct spoken dialects are recognised. For our purposes, we will keep to Fidelma's dialect of Munster.

It is a general rule that stress is placed on the first syllable but, as in all languages, there are exceptions. In Munster the exceptions to the rule of initial stress are a) if the second syllable is long then it bears the stress; b) if the first two syllables are short and the third is long then the third syllable is stressed – such as in the word for fool, *amadán*, pronounced amad-awn; and c) where the second syllable contains ach and there is no long syllable, the second syllable bears the stress.

There are five short vowels – a, e, i, o, u – and five long vowels – á, é, í, ó, ú. On the long vowels note the accent, like the French acute, which is called a *fada* (literally, 'long'), and this is the only accent in Irish. It occurs on capitals as well as lower case.

The accent is important for, depending on where it is placed, it changes the entire word. *Seán* (Shawn) = John. But *sean* (shan) = old and *séan* (she-an) = an omen. By leaving out the accent on his name, the actor Sean Connery has become 'Old' Connery!

These short and long vowels are either 'broad' or 'slender'. The six broad vowels are:

a pronounced 'o' as in cot á pronounced 'aw' as in law
o pronounced 'u' as in cut ó pronounced 'o' as in low
u pronounced 'u' as in run ú pronounced 'u' as in rule

The four slender vowels are:

i pronounced 'i' as in hit í pronounced 'ee' as in see
e pronounced 'e' as in let é pronounced 'ay' as in say

There are double vowels, some of which are fairly easy because they compare to English pronunciation – such as 'ae' as *say* or 'ui' as in *quit*. However, some double and even triple vowels in Irish need to be learnt.

ái pronounced like 'aw' in law (*dálaigh* = daw-lee)
ia pronounced like 'ea' in near
io pronounced like 'o' in come
éa prounced like 'ea' in bear
ei pronounced like 'e' in let
aoi pronounced like the 'ea' in mean
uai pronounced like the 'ue' in blue
eoi pronounced like the 'eo' in yeoman
iai pronounced like the 'ee' in see

hiDDEN VOWELS

Most people will have noticed that many Irish people pronounce the word film as fil-um. This is actually a transference of Irish pronunciation rules. When l, n or r is followed by b, bh, ch, g (not after n), m or mh, and is preceded by a short stressed vowel, an additional vowel is heard between them. So *bolg* (stomach) is pronounced bol-ag; *garbh* (rough) is gar-ev; *dorcha* (dark) is dor-ach-a; *gorm* (blue) is gor-um and *ainm* (name) is an-im.

the CONSONANTS

b, d, f, h, l, m, n, p, r and **t** are said more or less as in English
  g is always hard like the 'g' in gate
  c is always hard like the 'c' in cat

s is pronounced like the 's' in said except before a slender vowel when it is pronounced 'sh' as in shin

In Irish the letters **j, k, q, w, x, y** or **z** do not exist and v is formed by the combination of bh.

Consonants can change their sound by aspiration or eclipse. Aspiration is caused by using the letter h after them.

bh is like the 'v' in voice
ch is a soft breath as in loch (not pronounced as lock!) or as in Ba*ch*
dh before a broad vowel is like the 'g' in gap
dh before a slender vowel is like the 'y' in year
fh is totally silent
gh before a slender vowel can sound like 'y' as in yet
mh is pronounced like the 'w' in wall
ph is like the 'f' in fall
th is like the 'h' in ham
sh is also like the 'h' in ham

Consonants can also change their sound by being eclipsed, or silenced, by another consonant placed before it. For example *na mBan* (of women) is pronounced nah *m*'on; *i bpaipéar* (in the paper) i *b*'ap'er and *i gcathair* (in the city) i *g*'a'har.

p can be eclipsed by **b, t**
t can be eclipsed by **d**
c can be eclipsed by **g**
f can be eclipsed by **bh**
b can be eclipsed by **m**
d and g can be eclipsed by **n**

For those interested in learning more about the language, it is worth remembering that, after centuries of suppression during the colonial period, Irish became the first official language of the Irish state on independence in 1922. The last published census of 1991 showed one third of the population returning themselves as Irish-speaking. In Northern Ireland, where the language continued to be openly discouraged after Partition in 1922, only 10.5 per cent of the population were able to speak the language in 1991, the first time an enumeration of speakers was allowed since Partition.

Language courses are now available on video and audiocassette from a range of producers from Linguaphone to RTÉ and BBC. There are some sixty summer schools and special intensive courses available. Teilifis na Gaeilge is a television station broadcasting entirely in Irish and there are several Irish language radio stations and newspapers. Information can be obtained from Comhdháil Náisiúnta na Gaeilge, 46 Sráid Chill Dara, Baile Atha Cliath 2, Éire.

Readers might also like to know that *Valley of the Shadow*, in the Fidelma series, was produced on audiocassette, read by Marie McCarthy, from Magna Story Sound (SS391 – ISBN 1-85903-313-X).

The Leper's Bell

Peter Tremayne

In a cold dark wood, a woman is attacked and brutally murdered. The baby she was carrying is abducted, seemingly never to be seen or heard of again.

However it is no ordinary child that has disappeared, but the son of Fidelma, the famous Irish advocate of the ancient Brehon Courts of Ireland, and her husband Eadulf. A huge search is undertaken for the missing child but as time passes even Fidelma's legendary investigative skills and insight can gain no clues into his possible whereabouts.

What is the motive for the kidnapping? Could someone seeking vengeance on Fidelma and Eadulf have done the deed? They have made enemies in their pursuit of justice . . .

As Fidelma's anger at the kidnappers grows, so does her own guilt for leaving her son in the care of others, until she is taking steps that put her in mortal danger herself.

Praise for the Sister Fidelma series:

'This is masterly storytelling from an author who breathes fascinating life into the world he is writing about' *Belfast Telegraph*

0 7553 0226 5

headline

Whispers of the Dead

Peter Tremayne

'The dead always whisper to us. It is our task to listen to the whispers of the dead.'

Whispers of the Dead is a sumptuously rich feast of fifteen short mystery tales, never before published in book form, featuring the brilliant and beguiling Sister Fidelma, the seventh-century sleuth of the Celtic Church.

Sister Fidelma has become one of the most fascinating and compelling figures in contemporary fiction. A red-haired, quick-witted and extraordinarily wise religieuse, Fidelma is hugely popular in many countries as she successfully tackles the most bewildering of crimes.

This collection contains an astonishing range of crimes and misdemeanours and seamlessly blends historical detail, character and story into mysteries that will confound and surprise. *Whispers of the Dead* is Sister Fidelma at her very best.

Praise for the widely acclaimed Sister Fidelma mysteries:

'The background detail is brilliantly defined ... Wonderfully evocative' *The Times*

'Definitely an Ellis Peters competitor' *Evening Standard*

0 7553 0230 3

headline

The Haunted Abbot

Peter Tremayne

Their business with the Archbishop of Canterbury now complete, Sister Fidelma and Brother Eadulf are preparing to return to Ireland when they receive a mysterious message. Eadulf's childhood friend, Brother Botulf, has requested their presence at Aldred's Abbey at midnight on the old pagan feast of Yule. Puzzled and intrigued by their summons, Fidelma and Eadulf battle against the harsh winter storms to make their appointment, only to find they are too late. Botulf is dead – killed by an unknown hand.

And as they struggle to comprehend this staggering news, it soon becomes clear that the murder of this young monk is not the only trouble facing the abbey. Another, less tangible danger threatens – the ghost of a young woman haunts the cloister shadows – a woman some say bears a startling likeness to the Abbot Cild's dead wife. But can Fidelma and Eadulf discover the truth before they themselves fall victim to the danger which pervades the abbey walls?

Peter Tremayne's eleven previous Sister Fidelma books are also available from Headline.

'The background detail is brilliantly defined ... Wonderfully evocative' *The Times*

'This is masterly storytelling from an author who breathes fascinating life into the world he is writing about' *Belfast Telegraph*

0 7472 6435 X

headline

Smoke in the Wind

Peter Tremayne

En route from Ireland to visit the new Archbishop of Canterbury, Sister Fidelma and her faithful Saxon companion, Brother Eadulf, find themselves on the coast of the Welsh kingdom of Dyfed when their ship is blown off course by a storm. The elderly King Gwlyddien is quick to offer hospitality, not least because the famous Irish *dálaigh* may be the only person capable of solving the mystery which has baffled the wisest of men – the entire monastic community of nearby Llanpadern, to which Gwlyddien's eldest son belongs, has vanished into thin air.

Who, or what, is behind the disappearance of the monks? Is it sorcery or some sinister plot – and what does the perpetrator hope to achieve? But before Fidelma and Eadulf can begin to answer these questions, they must contend with the shocking and seemingly unrelated murder of a local girl – a death whose consequences will be more tragic and more far-reaching than anyone can imagine.

Peter Tremayne's ten previous Sister Fidelma books are also available from Headline.

'The background detail is brilliantly defined... Wonderfully evocative' *The Times*

'Sister Fidelma is fast becoming a world ambassador for ancient Irish culture' *Irish Post*

0 7472 6434 1

headline

Our Lady of Darkness

Peter Tremayne

Arriving home from a pilgrim voyage, Sister Fidelma is told that her faithful Saxon companion, Brother Eadulf, has been found guilty of murdering a young girl. She hastens to the capital of the neighbouring kingdom of Laigin, where he is being held, determined to prove his innocence.

Her quest begins at the abbey of Fearna, where the murder took place, and where Fidelma clashes with the sinister Abbess Fainder, who is in no doubt of Eadulf's guilt. Fidelma can't deny that the evidence against her friend is overwhelming. Is it conceivable that Eadulf is actually involved in this sordid case of sex, shame and murder? She has little time to discover the truth for the King of Laigin has given in to Abbess Fainder's demand that the ecclesiastical Penitentials from Rome be used. The ecclesiastical law demands 'an eye for an eye'; Eadulf is due to be hanged . . .

All of Peter Tremayne's previous Sister Fidelma books are available from Headline:

'The background detail is brilliantly defined . . . Wonderfully evocative' *The Times*

'Sister Fidelma is fast becoming a world ambassador for ancient Irish culture' *Irish Post*

0 7472 6433 3

headline

Act of Mercy

Peter Tremayne

'The Sister Fidelma stories take us into a world that only an author steeped in Celtic history could recreate so vividly' Peter Haining

Sister Fidelma sets out on a pilgrimage to the Holy Shrine of St James in the late autumn of AD 666, her main goal being to reflect on her commitment to the religious life and her relationship with the Saxon monk, Eadulf, whom she has left behind. But during the first night out, with the ship tossed about by a tempestuous sea, one of the pilgrims disappears, apparently washed overboard. The discovery of a blood-stained robe raises questions: was the pilgrim murdered and thrown into the sea? If so, why?

With the blessing of the captain, Fidelma has to focus all her abilities on solving the mystery. But death dogs the tiny hand of pilgrims in the close confines of the ship, and Fidelma finds herself not only battling against the antagonism of her fellow pilgrims but struggling to survive the turbulent elements of the storm-tossed sea. It is not until the Holy Shrine is almost reached – and time is running out – that the amazing truth is uncovered . . .

'The background detail is brilliantly defined . . . Wonderfully evocative' *The Times*

'A brilliant and beguiling heroine. Immensely appealing . . . difficult to put down . . .' *Publishers Weekly*

0 7472 5782 5

headline